THE CURE FOR STARS

THE CURE FOR STARS

The Sphere Trilogy
Book two

Nassim Odin

2021

Copyright © 2021 by Naseem Uddin
The following is a work of fiction or fantasy or wonder literature. Any names, characters, and incidents are the product of the author's imagination. Any resemblance or closeness to individuals, living or dead, is absolutely coincidental.

ISBN ebook: 978-1-954313-02-6
ISBN Paperback: 978-1-954313-07-1
ISBN Hardcover: 978-1-954313-12-5

Cover Design: Grigorii Gorshechnikov
Map: Chaim Holtjer
Cover and map are protected under copyright 2021.

Publisher: Odin Fantasy World
All Rights Reserved. No part of this publications may be reproduced, scanned, photocopied, or transmitted in any other form, digital or printed without the written consent and permission of the author Nassim Odin.
writer.odin@gmail.com
https://www.nassimodin.com

Reviews

WINNER OF LITERARY TITAN SILVER AWARD

The hero of Odin's trilogy is immensely likable in this outing...An exhilarating cliffhanger sets the stage for the series conclusion.
— The Kirkus Review

The imaginative juxtaposition of historical setting and futuristic detail keeps the readers intrigued.
— The Prairies Book Review

The Cure for Stars is entertaining and interesting on a more intellectual level as Al-Khidr uses religion and politics to achieve his aims.
—John Derek

The story continues to shape the characters and to show us more and more of their deep emotions, fears and hopes.
— Alice Branch

This is still a refreshing mixture of Arabic culture/history and science fiction unlike any other book I have read.
— Literary Reviewer

Dedication
To all the people interested in the pyramids

Al-Eard Soundtrack Musical Score

Odin Fantasy World - You Tube Channel

The Arrival on Al-Eard
Music Artist: Mecheri Kheireddine (khairsound)

The Misery of Space Traveler
Music Artist: Armen Voskanian

The Revenge of Hatathor
Music Artist: Arkady Akhidzhanov

(As above so below)

Prologue

Here is book two of the Sphere Trilogy. The book is still science fiction but set in an environment of historical fiction that readers can enjoy. A number of books were used in the development of this part of the series. The alien Lyrian language is constructed with words taken from the ancient Egyptian language. The trustworthy dictionary, An Egyptian Hieroglyphic Dictionary by Sir E. A. Wallis Budge, is used for this purpose. Also, the milieu of eighteenth-century Egypt under French occupation is depicted using the elements from the following three books:

- Egyptology: The missing Millennium by Okasha El-Daly, UCL Press, 2005.

- Mirage: Napoleon's Scientists and the Unveiling of Egypt by Nina Burleigh, Harper Perennial, 2008.

- Napoleon in Egypt: Al-Jabarti's Chronicle of the French Occupation, 1798, by Abd Al-Rahman Al-Jabarti (Author), Shmuel Moreh (Translator), Makus Wiener Publishers, Princeton, 2003.

I hope that the readers find Al-Khidr's journey interesting.

Odin
2021

Contents

Prologue		i
1	The Cosmic Tunnel	1
2	The Nile	15
3	The Souq of Al-Qahirah	25
4	The French	41
5	The Sea of Salt	63
6	The Blinking	73
7	The Requiem on Doom	93
8	The Visit	111
9	In Damanhur	129
10	The Boraqis	163
11	The Encounter	195
12	The Embalming	211
13	The Lure of Zodiaque	225

14	The Martyr	245
15	The Antique Collectors	261
16	The Mayhem	281
17	The Mirage	301
18	The Twist of Fate	321
19	The Opening	339
20	In the South	355
21	The Pyramid	375

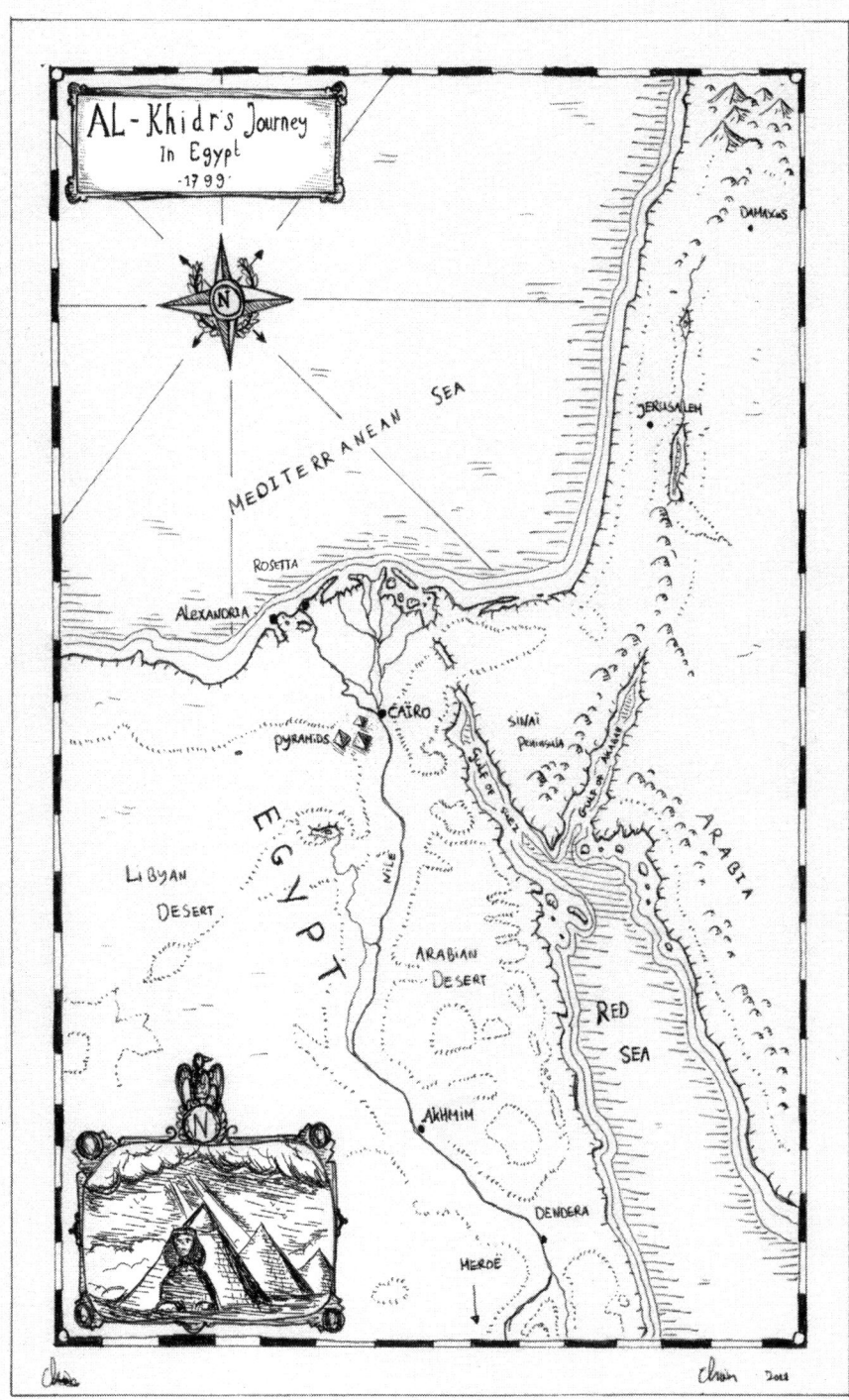

Chapter 1

The Cosmic Tunnel

AL-KHIDR was moving towards his home, the planet Earth. A few minutes earlier, he was inside the Usekht Sehetch, the Hall of Stars but now he was in an energy cocoon, which was traveling inside the wormhole — a cosmic tunnel. The cosmic tunnel that had opened right above the Hall of Stars was spiraling down through galaxies like a coiled serpent, stretching from Lyra towards Earth. The whole tunnel was crackling in a blitz of light and plasma. The energy around Al-Khidr was issuing from Maft-Shespt, the metalic jump-sphere. This space-travel device designed by

Chapter 1. The Cosmic Tunnel

aliens was now stuck to Al-Khidrs hands. Kam-t Nenui — the black matter, was persistently boiling, but Al-Khidr didn't feel the heat. It was generating the the tiny particles which were illuminating the Ar-t Heru seal on his wrist. The Maft-Shespt, although it was only partially charged, but still it was generating a cocoon of energy, protection for the intergalactic jump. When activated, it was designed to catapult the possessor between galaxies. The orrery in the Hall of Stars had given Al-Khidr an idea about just how vast the galaxies were and how far the Earth was from the planet Lyra.

The sphere sometimes glitched, but it was currently working. Al-Khidr's lips were constantly moving. He was thanking God for saving him from the attack by Hatathor but was also worried whether the sphere was working correctly. The jump-sphere was not fully charged, and Hatathor had interfered during the charging process, throwing his weapon at Al-Khidr.

Nervousness engulfed Al-Khidr. He could feel a tingle in his hands, which held the Maft-Shespt. His forehead was sweating profusely.

The sphere is not charged. If the sphere does not work correctly, I could end up landing on some other planet with no breathable air. Even if I reach Earth, will my people believe me? He thought.

He beseeched aloud in earnest, "Oh, Almighty God of the hidden and the vivid, control this path and send me back to Al-Eard. I keep the promise that I gave to them in your name, and certainly most exalted is your name."

Many thoughts ran through his mind. His mind was full of thoughts, not only on what was ahead but also on what had happened to Nefertiti and Ehsis. "Oh, God, save Nefertiti and Ehsis from the evilness of Hatathor. Only you can protect them," he said aloud.

The tunnel between stars was endless; it seemed to go on forever. His whole body was shaking now. The blue aura was interacting with magnetic fields and giving different colors to the wormhole path. His acceleration was so fast that he sometimes felt like he was looking back at his own body. The entire experience was surreal. Suddenly, the energy sphere emerged from the wormhole, appearing right above a planet. It was familiar to Al-Khidr, something he'd seen before, a moment he was waiting for. Earth was right in front of him. His body swelled with joy, and he erupted into tears.

The sun was illuminating one side of Earth, but he was on the dark side, only partially lit by the moon. The sphere then descended like a meteor toward Earth, and a detached shockwave formed around the energy sphere.

The Kam-t Nenui in the Maft-Shespt was still boiling and releasing energy. The boiling intensified while the drag on the energy sphere pushed Al-Khidr toward the wall, which itself was only an energy field emanating from the jump-sphere. His cheek was touching the energy shield, and he could see the intense shockwave

Chapter 1. The Cosmic Tunnel

around the cocoon.

He prayed under his breath. The entire experience was terrifying, even though this was not the first time he experienced such a thing. With blitz-like speed, the energy cocoon was still moving toward Earth. When it neared the clouds, it started descending straight down, and though it was night, Al-Khidr could see the topography of the structures below because of the brightness of the energy cocoon. It was towards the Great Pyramid of Giza, on which the energy sphere was descending.

The Lyrian have set the course exactly to the spot where they had left the Earth before!

He peeked once again through the energy sphere, and sure enough, he could make out the Great Pyramid's silhouette and the other pyramids nearby. He was shocked to see that the pyramids in Giza were all exposed; the great male pyramid and nearby young female and colored pyramids had no outer casing stones. The images and paintings on the pyramids were all gone!

"The pyramids are naked. What destroyed the casing stones? An earthquake?" he said in surprise.

The brightness of the energy sphere revealed the eight facets of the Great Pyramid of Giza. He took a deep breath of relief; he was, at least, on his home planet. The sphere slowed as it reached the Great Pyramid and hovered above. The sphere rerouted its course to circle the pyramid. It felt to Al-Khidr as if the sphere was looking for something on it to latch on to or land on, but Al-Khidr couldn't see anything like that. Then the energy sphere began to do something weird; it started circling the Great Pyramid in accelerating motions.

Al-Khidr stood inside the sphere, irritated by all of it. He exclaimed, "What the hell is it trying to do? Just stop. I can't take this much longer." His head hurt, and the circles were making him sick. The sphere then hit the pyramid with full force, spiraling downward, then bouncing over it.

Thump. Thump. Thump. Thump.

None of this was pleasant for Al-Khidr.

Suddenly, the taste of acid came into his mouth as he tried to keep it together. A few more times, he felt the urge to vomit inside the sphere. On the fourth bounce, Al-Khidr was unprepared and spat out vomit inside of the energy sphere. The energy sphere burst and Al-Khidr fell on the sand right in front of the megalithic Great Pyramid.

The galactic jump and bouncing had left him exhausted; his body was aching, and his insides vibrated. He was losing consciousness as he looked toward the stars of Orion's belt and Sirius shining over him. His body could not take the intense exertion of the journey, and he lay motionless on the sand. Nefertiti and Ehsis were far, far away in a distant galaxy now. He had to find the cure on Al-Eard and save the dying breed of aliens on their planet. It was late at night, and the sky was dark, though the sunrise was about to occur when Al-Khidr landed on Earth. He was back on the

Chapter 1. The Cosmic Tunnel

familiar hot sand, still hot even though it was night. He looked at the sky again, thinking about Nefertiti.

The weariness of the long, intergalactic travel had started to wear on his muscles. The fatigue took over his mind and body as he lay on the sand, falling fast asleep. In his dreams, he had a vision that he was standing in front of Queen Hathor's chambers where Nefertiti was ordered to bring him in. He then saw himself in the vast chambers with Queen Hathor in front. The three looked at each other, thinking about what to do or say. Without warning, the Queen took out a laser gun and shot Al-Khidr with it, sending him flying across the room. He fell on his back, hot fumes coming off of his chest. Al-Khidr looked to see Queen Hathor and Nefertiti glaring at him with murderous looks on their faces. Nefertiti aimed her weapon at him. He had barely stood up when another shot sent him crashing to the gate. The door's lock had hit him hard in hand. Al-Khidr fell on his face, and his nose was bleeding.

The sudden surge of pain in his wrist woke him up. He was holding his left hand in pain, but the pain dissipated quickly. He looked around.

What was that? he asked himself. It had to have been some sort of nightmare. He was still all alone in the desert, surrounded by an eerie stillness. The sound of crickets chirping and dogs howling could be heard in the distance.

A light breeze touched his face, making him smile. Surely things could wait until tomorrow, he reasoned.

He crashed into the warm sand again. In a minute, he was fast asleep, this time with no nightmares.

He woke up an hour before the sunset, feeling tired and lazy. His muscles ached from the intergalactic travel, and his whole body and face were covered in sand. Luckily, it had been a cloudy day; he had slept through the entire day! The sun was leaving the orange sky, and it was getting darker and darker. He could see the sun approaching the west, but it was not sunset yet. He had to move.

Lazily, Al-Khidr sat up and rubbed the sand off of his clothes. Looking around him, he noticed he was still alone in the big desert. Feeling rested after a long sleep; he felt more energetic than yesterday. After standing there briefly, he suddenly remembered the sphere. Where was it? It was in his hands while passing through the cosmic tunnel.

A jolt of realization went through Al-Khidr like lightning as he frantically kicked and moved his hands through the sand. "Holy God! Have I lost it? Where did it go?" Al-Khidr said, still tense. *It was with me; I remember that much!* he said to himself.

Another thought came to his mind, which troubled him even more. The desert was vast; it stretched for miles and miles in either direction. If he had, by chance, dropped the sphere during the landing, it could be lost forever. His stomach clenched tightly when the thought came to his mind. After moving his hands through the sand, he gave up and sat on the sand with his head sunken low. His hope was setting

CHAPTER 1. THE COSMIC TUNNEL

with the sun. He thought to himself, *Nefertiti would be waiting for me on Lyra in the stars, and I am stranded on my planet. I have to go back.*

Sitting on the sand, he remembered the kind and scared face of Queen Hathor. How she narrated the tragedy on Earth was still in his mind; it had left Al-Khidr sad. The Queen saw her husband and people die on Earth right in front of her eyes, and she had left Earth with a heavy heart. She said that her heart and soul were still on this strange planet.

"With the name of Allah, my promise will be fulfilled!" he said and gave another look at the sky, pushing his hands back into the sand. His hand touched something hard. His heart flipped as he turned back and dug up more sand. By the looks of it, he was getting closer and closer. Finally, he felt the sphere in his hand. "Thanks to Allah. My heart was about to burst," he said, relaxing a little more now.

He took the sphere out and put it in front of his eyes to examine it a bit. It was the same sphere as before, with a strange, cryptic engraving on it and looking as beautiful as ever. He lifted it and flipped it over to clean it of sand. The sphere and he were inseparable like there was a magnetic force that bound them together. Looking at it now, he felt there was something different about the sphere. Where was the blue light that it was giving off before? Did this lack of light mean that it was no longer working? What would he do without it? How else would he travel to Lyra without the sphere? It was also glitching during the jump from Lyra to Earth. Will it work again? Only Allah knows.

More and more questions came and troubled him more than he was just a few moments before. The sphere was his only ticket off of Earth. He brought it closer to his eyes for inspection, but he could not tell what was wrong with the sphere or if it would work again. Tears welled in his eyes, and he kneeled on the ground, looking at the sun that was about to set ahead of him.

What if Nefertiti waited for him forever? Would Ehsis save the dying breed of aliens? She seemed troubled herself from his presence on their planet. He remembered the parting words of Nefertiti. "You have to come back. We need you," she said when he was preparing for launch, standing inside the Hept Sehetch Sheta facility with Nefertiti. The thought warmed his heart, and he smiled to himself. Her words were still echoing in his mind as the sandy wind blew in his face. He looked at the sky once more, his resolve stronger than before. "I am coming for you, Nefertiti. By Allah's will, I will return to your planet Lyra," he said, looking at the sky. With the sphere clenched tightly in his fist, he walked through the desert. Hopefully, the path would take him to the River Nile.

Born and bred in North Africa, walking in deserts was not very tiring for Al-Khidr. As he moved uphill on a dune, his foot would sink into the sand, each step he took on a shaky foundation. It would take some time before he reached the summit of the dune.

Chapter 1. The Cosmic Tunnel

Looking back, he could see the pyramids at a leveled height. It pleased him to see the summit of the pyramids, a remnant of Queen Hathor and her crew. Had the epidemic not spread in their colony, they would still be here collecting data for fuel and information. Descending the dune was much easier, and he felt as if an unknown force kept pushing him down to the base of the dune. He continued walking; his path was very clear to him.

While walking through the desert, he was reminded of Nefertiti's kind face. He thought of when he told her the story of Alladin and the Magic Lamp. The tale had woven some sort of magic on her, bringing out her truest self.

Her look brought a warm smile to his face. It was something he could never forget. This was just one story that Al-Khidr had told to her. He had so many stories to tell her that would leave her enchanted and wanting for more. Now, which story could he tell her when he returned? He stood on the sand for a while, racking his brain for an answer. Perhaps he would start with The Thousand and One Nights. It featured ferocious beasts, shipwrecks, and so much more. It would surely leave Nefertiti breathless. He smiled at the thought; there were so many stories to tell.

Thinking about Thousand and One Nights diverted his attention to the seal on his hand, looking at the number on his wrist. He brought the sphere closer to his left wrist, and it suddenly emitted light, and his seal was visible, but only for a fraction of a second.

Was it caused by the twilight merged with light from the sphere?

***

Birds were flying above, probably scavenging for evening snacks. The sight of those birds filled him with happiness. For a while, he was glad to be back on his planet Al-Eard. In a way, everything was back to normal, like he had wanted. The sound of the birds revived him from his weariness. *Oh. The birds*, he thought. *I hope they are going toward the Nile River.* With the sphere still in his hand, he continued walking, following the birds. He then saw that the sun was going towards the horizon. He started walking briskly to follow the birds. The terrain changed, and the sand touching his feet was now quite damp.

Sure enough, the sound of the gushing flow of the Nile could be heard from a distance. The sounds of animals, grasshoppers, and crickets were clear to him. His throat was parched, and as soon as he saw water, he ran towards the river to quench his thirst. He bent down and cupped his hand to take a sip. The rushing water refreshed him immediately. He drank his heart out, and his insides felt alive again.

He threw some rushing water on his face and cleaned the sand away. As he stood up, he noticed that the water flowed in the north as far as his eyes could see. He recalled that the Nile flowed out of Egypt into the White sea ahead.

Chapter 1. The Cosmic Tunnel

"Glory be to Allah for this great river," he exclaimed in gratitude. The water had instilled a new life in him. Revived and energized, he started his walk along the River Nile.

***

Mosquitoes were buzzing over reeds along the Nile. Strangely enough, as he passed one swarm of mosquitoes, the swarm fell at his feet, all dead. Surprised, he knelt to look at them. *It is strange! The mosquitoes had died suddenly? What was that all about?* he thought. He stood up and continued to walk again. Maybe it was an epidemic or something like that. A bug flew near him and dropped to the ground, and he picked the insect and looked at it.

"What is happening here? Why are insects falling all around me?" he exclaimed but did not hear an answer in return. Was he given protection by Allah or something? He just shrugged at the thought. It was almost sunset, and the call of Al-Maghrib prayers could be heard.

***

The riverbank brought him closer to a village with fields and houses. The birds had flown away in the distance, leaving him stranded. Cattle were slowly grazing in the fields. He reached a house and knocked on its door, waiting patiently. *Maybe I can get some food!* He thought. The door opened after a while, and an old man came out and looked at him from head to toe. His face reddened. "Shame on you, dress up, boy!" he shouted in his ears.

Al-Khidr looked at himself and nearly screamed; his clothes were falling off! It was just like last time when his clothes had worn out after he had landed on the alien planet. It took him a few moments to realize that it was the energy released from the sphere during the galactic jump that had ruined his dress again. "Ya 'iilhi' ana earia!(Oh God, I am naked!)." he exclaimed.

He stood at the old man's door, confused about what to do. The old man closed his door without another word to Al-Khidr. He decided to ask for food from the next house. As soon as he turned, the door reopened, and the old man came running after him with a sandal. His intentions were not friendly. Covering his genitals with his hands and jump-sphere, Al-Khidr made a run for it, heading into the nearby fields. "Don'tdo these pranks with me, boy. Do you understand?" The old man shouted from behind Al-Khidr. "It is not a prank. I promise you!" Al-Khidr said while running.

But the old man was not listening, and he continued to sprint after Al-Khidr. Some of the local children stood by, laughing and pointing at him. He was, after all, running naked through their village. Strangely, they all started vomiting as he ran past them. It must be due to the jump-sphere effect, but he could not stop to help them now.

Chapter 2

The Nile

SOME young men at a distance saw Al-Khidr running while the pedestrians he crossed vomited. They thought that Al-Khidr was a thief and did some harm to them, and they shouted at him.

"*Qif, Ya Harami! (Stop o bastard thief!)*" they yelled at him.

Al-Khidr continued to run out of the village with five young men following him. Al-Khidr saw that there were fields ahead, but he stumbled and fell on the ground, and the sphere rolled into the grass. By the

Chapter 2. The Nile

time he stood up, the men had reached him, and as one moved forward to punch him, intense radiation emitted by Al-Khidr's body overtook him, and he fell to the ground. Al-Khidr was now vary nervous and didn't know what to do. He needed to get the jump-sphere as well, and there was no time to negotiate with these men, so he turned towards men and said, "*Anna Ibn Ibleess! (I am a son of the devil)!*" Then he screamed with full force.

The remaining men saw the misery of their friend, so they ran off and left their friend on the ground, who was lying in a state of nausea, panting, moaning in pain, and sweating. Al-Khidr saw the shiny sphere in the moonlight. He picked it up and ran into fields. The sphere was still intact. The man on the ground was stunned by the entire experience. While his head still on the ground, he saw Al-Khidr vanishing into cotton fields. The man thought, *Who was he? Where had he come from? Was he a vagabond or a djinn? What was in his hand?*

***

Al-Khidr had entered the fields, running madly without looking behind. A little while later, he realized that he did not hear the following sound of footsteps. He stole a glance behind him to look for the young men. There was no one there. He breathed a sigh of relief and stopped to catch his breath, tired from the running in the rough village terrain.

He looked back and was surprised to see the narrow lane of the field where he was running had turned ashen black. He took one long strand of grass to inspect it closely. The grass strand withered more in his hand, seeming to have burned as it lay lifeless in his hand.

What has this sphere done to me? Everything I touch turns to dust and death, he thought to himself, horrified at what he saw. Maybe heat has accumulated over me due to intergalactic travel? The thought of the young man lying in an agitated state on the ground troubled Al-Khidr even more.

***

Al-Khidr was standing buck-naked in the fields and he looked around for a solution to cover himself.

With the sphere clenched tightly in his hands, he walked carefully out of the fields. His throat was dry and running had made him hungry.

"I have not eaten since yesterday. Let's see what the village has in store for me," he said to himself. He started evaluating his options. The thought of going back into the village to ask for food seemed scary to him. More people would run after him, thinking him a thief, a vagabond passing by, or a djinn. He was puzzled by their reaction, as the people in this village used to come to him for cures to their ailments. He personally knew some of villagers, as well.

He went away from the settlements, but stuck close to the Nile. It was all darkness around, and even he

Chapter 2. The Nile

thought that he was beginning to look like a djinn.

He headed towards the reeds. Maybe he could find something over there to eat and be able rest for a bit. The ducks along the River Nile would be his best bet for a quick dinner. The River Nile had a particular breed of ducks that lived near the river. They sometimes nested in dry spots near the flowing water, but their preference would be grassy spots or somewhere near the reeds to protect their eggs and new ducklings.

It was not fully dark yet and he tiptoed carefully near the river bank. A duck was sipping water along the edge of the river. He looked at the duck with a satisfied grin. Some minutes of inspecting the field led him to the ducks nest, where he found six white eggs. "Oh, boy. I have never felt this hungry," he said to himself. He stooped low to pick up the eggs and he noticed the duck was staring at him. Al-Khidr looked at the eggs and then at the duck. He ran at the duck to scare it off. It took off faster than he had expected, quacking loudly.

The eggs looked delicious and fresh. He broke the shell carefully, making sure that the egg yolk was still inside. The taste was very salty, but his hunger pangs were too much to take. He broke the shells of the other five eggs and gobbled down the egg yolks.

After finishing the eggs, he noticed the duck was not approaching him. It must be the heat from my body, he thought to himself. He patted his stomach and burped loudly. Walking back, he came across a gigantic tree. The sight brought a smile to his face.

Under the tree was a sleeping grey duck sitting on its eggs. Its nest was all too obvious with the patchwork of grass in the otherwise empty tree hole.

Al-Khidr did not have the heart to eat the eggs of another duck. He patted its head and walked towards the river bank. A warm breeze touched his face, causing him to smile.

Something in his stomach quickly began to bother him. The pain spread, and he crumpled to the ground, clutching his stomach and sphere in his hands. "Was it the eggs?" he said in pain. The pain grew and grew and Al-Khidr had tears in his eyes. His stomach growled. He went into the bushes to vomit to clear his stomach. Coming back, he felt much better and lay down near the river.

"Ah, it is so peaceful out there. No crocodile or other animal can harm me," he said. The thought brought him some comfort. The chilly air and roaring water beside him were more than enough for a good night's sleep.

***

He looked at the night sky above, which was a beautiful sight, the stars cluttered in the dark sky. He gave a few fleeting moments of thought to Ehsis and Nefertiti. Lyra's beautiful landscape came to his mind. The pleasant climate, pristine hills, and scenic beauty had his heart. He missed the place dearly. He dozed off, thinking about the new friends he had made

Chapter 2. The Nile

on the other planet. Friends who were eagerly awaiting hid return. "IIIIIII caaan not see anything," he yelled to Nefertiti.

"Yesssss. I knowwww. Justtttt don't talk that much until we areeee throughhhhh with this," Nefertiti said to him. "Alllll righttttt, Nefertiti," he screamed to be heard.

She just nodded and looked ahead. The sphere was vibrating violently. As they left Lyra, they were surrounded by something black. It was huge and never-ending. Little, tiny twinkles flashed all around them, and shooting stars could be seen at a distance.

A terrifying blackness surrounded them. Eons and galaxies hurtled by. Nefertiti and Al-Khidr sped up helplessly through the black hole, going into the unknown. "Caaaaannnn yoooouuu at leastttt telllll me whereee areee we goinggggg?" he screamed again. She looked back and said. "We call it a blackkkkkkk holeeeee. Aaaa blacckkkkk holeeeee," she shouted at him.

Al-Khidr nodded his head. It was troublesome to speak while they entered the massive black hole. Darkness had surrounded them from all angles. They then came into open skies. Al-Khidr felt so much better now, the feeling of nausea and tightening of his body had gone. He felt lighter and clear-headed. For a moment, the sight in front of Al-Khidr terrified him. A loud explosion threw him in the corner. Nefertiti was still holding on. Somehow, he guessed she knew what was going on.

"Relax. Just stay there," she shouted.

Some more shock waves threw him against the wall. His head felt dizzy, as he was still glued to the wall.

"Close your eyes. It's going to be intense. You could go blind," she warned and shut her eyes.

Al-Khidr was a bit late to follow her lead. He saw a blinding blue light stretch all over the galaxy, which kept going farther and farther. The blue light entered the sphere.

"Nefertiti, what is that?" he asked with his eyes closed.

"A star has exploded. These things can explode, giving us a spectacle now and then," she explained.

He looked at her blankly; the things he had heard about stars were very different.

Nefertiti looked at him and shrugged. "I told you that you would not understand this. Maybe someday," she said dismissively.

They had passed the supernova after an hour and entered another black hole. It was pitch dark again.

"AAAAAAAAAAAHHHHHH!" he shouted.

There was another Al-Khidr standing right beside him, screaming at him. They were both screaming at each other. He put his hands on his head. He looked to his side to see two Nefertiti's. They were both laughing at him, with their hands on their stomachs. Al-Khidr walked over to Nefertiti, who was still laughing. He noticed his own self walking behind him. When he stopped, the figure also stopped.

"It'ssss aaaa shadowwwww. Do not worry about

Chapter 2. The Nile

it. It will keeppppp doingggg what you are doing," she shouted.

It was then that Al-Khidr understood. Nefertiti's figure was imitating her actions and all of its movements were like the real Nefertiti.

He relaxed and waited for the end of the harsh ride through the black hole. It was making him nauseous; he spat inside the sphere, his stomach turning and twisting. Nefertiti rolled her eyes. Things were complicated with the alien, for sure. Any gravitational pull or forced jerks inside the sphere caused him to thrown up everywhere. Then, she had an idea.

Al-Khidr watched her coming towards him. She had something in her hands. Nefertiti took his wrists and injected something. He felt freezing inside as if he had drunk icy cold water. He couldn't feel his hands or legs. Nefertiti slapped him in the face, and then punched his arms and legs, and gave a hard one to his gut. Al-Khidr was still just standing there, looking at her.

He tried to speak, but only jumbled words came out. What had she done to him? Her figure looked at him, smiling. He fell to the ground, his eyes still fixed on Nefertiti. She had an evil smile on her face. His eyes slowly closed. This was when Nefertiti kicked on his face. BAM!

***

He awoke from his slumber to the sound of morning prayers. The sky was still dark, but he could hear a few birds chirping at this early hour. He sat up and looked for the source of the Adhan, the morning prayers. The prayers sounded distant because they were near the bazaar.

He took a bath in the Nile and now had to find some clothing, as the time for the morning prayers was running out. He went to the cotton and cornfields to do something about this condition. The cornfields looked parched, like a famine had recently hit the place. After some meddling around, he had an idea. He tore some pieces of cotton from the fields and some long leaves from the corn plants. He weaved them around to make a makeshift dress and put the cotton underneath. He thought that he must have looked hilarious.

He did his morning prayer and thanked God for a safe return to Earth and he also prayed to receive a cure for the disease, Mutmut. He drank some fresh water from the river and poured it on his face again. The chilly water revived him immediately.

After he was done, he had another task in mind. He took a bunch of leaves from the cornfields and wove them together into a basket. He walked over to the tree hole he had seen the day before. The duck was not inside, and Al-Khidr took this opportunity to steal the eggs from inside the tree trunk and carefully placed them on the leaves in the basket. He then placed the jump-sphere beside the eggs. He was tired of holding it in his hand. The eggs looked tempting. Feeling hungry, he grabbed one egg from the basket and ate

Chapter 2. The Nile

it. Yesterday's incident was still fresh in his mind, so he are only one egg. It was then time to head over to the local bazaar.

***

A boat was passing, driven by a teenager, and it was early in the day so the boat was not crowded. He asked the boy to give him ride: "Salamalaikum, I am a beggar and want to go to Fustat," he said.

The boat-driver chuckled and said, "Al-Qahirah (Cairo). The boats only go to souq (the bazaar) in the morning."

"Al-Qahirah!" Al-Khidr uttered, as if he was learning how to pronounce it.

"Really an odd name! The city name could have an element of mercy. Isn't it?... or is it related to a planet Mars," he had no clue.

The teenager gave him a boat ride, and he shouted with full voice, "Souq Khan Khalili... Souq Khan Khalili."

Al-Khidr sat in the boat as he was not sure about the exact location of the bazaar. The boat docked on the city side of the Nile. I will visit Fustat and Al-Askar in evening and then go to my home, he thought to himself as he made a plan.

Chapter 3

The Souq of Al-Qahirah

After thirty minutes of walking on the well-constructed stone pathway, Al-Khidr saw many buildings which he had not seen before. Everything looked so different. He had a hunch that the bazaar was nearby, as many people were walking in that direction. From a distance, some towers were visible. Al-Khidr had no clue what these towers were, as he had not seen them before.

He could see many people and the place was bustling with movement. He noticed that the souq of Al-Qahirah

Chapter 3. The Souq of Al-Qahirah

differed from Fustat's souq. I like Fustat more. This place is too crowded, he said to himself.

The sellers had started erecting their stalls. He saw a kid carrying a waterskin and selling water to everyone as he went along. He almost asked the kid for some water but then remembered that he had no dirhams.

The kid noticed that Al-Khidr needed water. He gave him water and said, "Pray for my mother."

Al-Khidr drank water with grateful eyes and prayers on his lips. Al-Khidr pointed towards towers and asked, "What are they?"

"Minarets of Mosque!" the child responded.

The kid vanished into the crowd, and Al-Khidr followed as well. He was surprised to see many stone buildings. Soon, he was right in front of a huge door, which people were calling *Bawabbat al-Mitwali*. He continued and entered in the door.

Al-Khidr passed by a massive animal market. He could see slaves, cows, goats, camels, oxen, lambs, and chickens on display by the vendors. He guessed it was a viable source of income for the local traders.

He notices one chicken that seemed to be quite popular among the local buyers. This was something new to him; he could not recall this kind of chicken. "This chicken is the best in the market. Take it away for two dirhams!" one seller screamed in his ear.

Al-Khidr was rattled to the bone by his loud voice. He shook his head and moved along. Maybe the market was having a slow day, the hawkers were screaming at the top of their voices, jarring him. The animals' cries and the smell of the sheep were all too familiar to him. He patted a black goat as he moved along. When this city was founded, Fustat and Al-Aksar were the only two major cities in this area, as far as he remembered. Al-Khidr noticed that Al-Qahirah was more organized than those two. The market layout seemed clearer now, with distinct sections separating them. Animals, jewelers, food, and everything were sold in various sections of the bazaar.

"*Ya, Ilahi (O God)*. This place has changed so much only in few days? I can see unfamiliar faces all around me," he said to himself. The morning sun was burning his skin. The market stretched for hundreds of Zara' (cubits). Al-Khidr could not find a spot where people were not present. He eventually reached a better part of the market that seemed cleaner and less noisy. The people greeted him with a friendly smile, and he returned it passionately. *Maybe they are smiling because they found my leaves and cotton dress funny,* He thought, and felt nervous. The architecture of this new city was completely different. The shop roofs were made up of wood and metal.

The change was greatly visible in several areas. There were bridges, huge mosques, madrassas, and the such. But he still saw caravans of camels bringing stuff from other places. The Arabic tone and dialect had also changed invariably. He could sense a hint of Berber and Amazigh dialects, among others. Also, there were many Turkish words were spoken in the

CHAPTER 3. THE SOUQ OF AL-QAHIRAH

market.

As he stepped deeper into the bazaar, a cacophony of buyers and sellers yells, cries, and other sounds greeted him. Straight ahead were snake charmers, and boys his age with trickster monkeys were beckoning him to watch the show. It was fascinating, coming back to his people after such a long time. He was not sure how long. This was his kind of place; relaxing and less burdensome on his mind. The area was bursting with pricey stuff. Some of the things enticed him immensely, thus stopping him in his tracks. The aroma of spices drew him toward the hawkers. The last time he ate a full meal was back on Lyra, and it was excruciating to digest. He stood in awe in front of the spice sellers.

"*Yal-la!, Yal-la!, ataa masaha (Go, go, give space),*" Al-Khidr looked behind him as some hawkers screamed, knocking some sense into him. "Do not stand there. You are blocking the view for others!"

"Okay, okay!" he replied.

He smiled thoughtfully and moved further. As he moved further into the market, he eyed statues, silver jewelry, souvenirs, gold, and clothes sold by the hawkers. They have dressed for the occasion. Fusat changed completely, he noticed.

"*Akhi Al-Kareem* (dear friend), come watch the show for one dirham. This monkey is a cut above the rest. I promise you," a performer said to him with a smirk. Al-Khidr returned the smile and shook his head. There was no way a trickster monkey could surprise him. He was all too familiar with the dreaded tricks of a monkey. Only a few years ago, he trained a monkey in those tricks. Al-Khidr continued to walk, unfazed by the market, but still in awe.

He felt something in his basket and saw the monkey running off into the distance. A shiny thing was in his hand.

"Oh, no! That is my sphere! Come here, you stupid monkey! Give it back!" he shouted.

He looked for the monkey's owner. The boy had also disappeared among the swarm of people. It completely slipped his mind that it was common for monkeys to steal unique stuff at the whim of their owners. They would sell it in the same bazaar hours later. The monkeys were just the partners in crime for these owners, as it was so easy to blend in with the crowd. He had seen monkeys steal stuff all his life; it just slipped his mind. He was inching closer to the monkey, who surprised him with the next move. It stopped and went straight for his face. Al-Khidr saw the pouncing monkey and caught him in mid-air by the tail.

"Oh, boy. Where do you think you were going?" he asked, laughing roughly. The monkey looked at him with blank eyes. "Do not steal stuff you have no idea about, understand?" he said nicely.

He forcefully opened the grip of the monkey and snatched the sphere. The monkey made another move and went for his eyes. Al-Khidr was too quick for him. He dodged him and hung the monkey further from his face. The monkey still stared at him.

Chapter 3. The Souq of Al-Qahirah

"Hey! Give me my monkey back! Give it back!" a man shouted from behind. Al-Khidr gazed at the owner he had passed by some moments ago. "Why did you send him after me?" Al-Khidr said. The owner looked at him for a moment. "I did not send him after you. The object sent a blue light when you passed by us. My monkey ran after it," he explained.

Al-Khidr shook his head as he understood that a monkey would have less reason than a man to steal this object. The owner took the monkey without a word and went back to his place. Someone shouted in his ear. He turned around to see a man on a donkey cart. The man was selling vegetables and seasonal fruits. "Look where you are going, boy!" he shouted, passing him by. He passed through some beggars who looked at him amusingly. Al-Khidr could see the joke that amused them. They were still clothed compared to his clothes of leaves, and the sun's heat was drying them up more.

Eventually, he arrived at the spot he had been trying to get to after experiencing the entire market. He sat beside the beggars who ignored him and continued to solicit the passersby. Even though these beggars had spread out their hands, Al-Khidr put the duck eggs out in the open for the people to see. "Fresh eggs, fresh eggs. Come on. Buy them right here. Four eggs for one dirham!" he chanted loudly. The beggars looked at him and burst out laughing. One beggar said after laughing, "Who gave you the bright idea that people would buy duck eggs. You stole them?"

Al-Khidr passed them a smirk. It was enough to tell them to mind their own business. They turned back to their begging, trying to attract people with sob stories about feeding their hungry children.

The day was getting hotter and hotter. It was only a matter of time before the shade Al-Khidr was sitting in would disappear. He privately started praying that his eggs would sell before that. Some women moved past him wearing *niqaab*, the veil which covers half of their face. He could still see their eyes since the veil did not hide the eyes. The woman looked at the eggs and excitedly whispered to the other lady, "Feed your husband with these eggs!"

Al-Khidr had an idea where they were going with this. The whispering one seemed younger, while the older one was probably her mother.

"What are you selling over there? Are those duck eggs?" the older lady asked.

He looked up and smiled the best smile he could muster, while nodding his head. The ladies felt satisfied by the answer. The younger lady asked suspiciously, "Are these your eggs, or did you steal them from somewhere?"

"The duck belongs to my father. We are raising a bunch of them. Want to come and see?" Al-Khidr replied. The beggars looked at him in disbelief; he was a good liar. "No, no. That will not be necessary. We will take the eggs," the older lady said. Al-Khidr smiled. The ploy had worked. "That will be six dirhams. Come again, I will have more eggs," he said,

CHAPTER 3. THE SOUQ OF AL-QAHIRAH

smiling brightly.

Al-Khidr was near a mosque. He went close to see it. He was impressed. The name was Mosque of Al-Azhar.

Who is this man? he thought to himself, *He could be a rich person who donated money to Caliph Al-Mamun, and that is why the mosque is named after him?* He could see the skyrise round structures reaching toward the sky over the mosque. He was surprised to see the obelisks protruding out from a mosque, so he asked the ladies what these structures were.

One woman laughed and said, "Are you a foreigner? These are minarets of a mosque. Now most of the big mosques have these structures to help the caller climb and give the call of the prayer."

Before Al-Khidr went to Lyra, he had not seen this invention. The two ladies then walked away, talking about his odd lack of knowledge.

He showed his dirhams to the beggars, who winced in return. The dirhams handed over by the ladies were also very different from what he could remember. The coins had the face of some beardless person from beni-Asfar (Yellow European race), and the inscription said Bey Al-Kabir.

What happened to Caliph Al-Mamun? he thought to himself. More importantly, the first thing he had to do was buy a dress to look somewhat decent. *I need better clothes to enter Fustat. Otherwise, my friends would make fun of me,* he thought. They won't believe me if I tell them everything. Nay, I could not spill the beans of my whereabouts. Not that anyone would understand me here.

He made his way to the hawker selling clothes. His eyes were set on a shiny white jalabiya. Without much haggling, he purchased it and proudly put it on and then removed the leaves.

"You look handsome," the hawker said, clapping his hands.

"*Shukran* (Thanks). I wanted to wear something like this. This cloth is so good." Al-Khidr remarked while stopping himself immediately. How come so much had changed? He wanted to ask the question but remembered to tread with caution. The safe way was to stay quiet and observe. Some white people passed him by. They spoke a different language, but amazingly, he could understand them quite well. They were dressed differently from the rest of the people in the market. It was as if they were outsiders.

He could understand their language. Well, there were some things the sphere had given him. The sphere had given him the knowledge of words and languages. He could comprehend many languages. He felt thankful for that.

Who are these people? He thought. He asked a local seller in Arabic, who informed that they were French. Al-Khidr tiptoed behind them, hoping to get some information on them and their whereabouts. Keeping some distance from the white men, he listened in on their conversation.

The white men talked to the local vendors without

Chapter 3. The Souq of Al-Qahirah

noticing that Al-Khidr was listening to them. He was glad to eavesdrop and felt grateful to the sphere for the knowledge of languages.

Their conversation shook him to the core. As things stood, Egypt was no longer under the Caliph Al-Mamun. Egypt had just recovered from a failed rebellion.

***

"What year is this?" Al-Khidr inquired of one shopkeeper.

"Are you lost? Today is 23 *Jumada Al-Thani,* 1213 *Al-Hijra* (December 2, 1798)," he answered in irritation.

An electric shock went through Al-Khidr's body. He was standing in the 13th Hijra already. Ten centuries had passed since his own time, a thousand years since he left Egypt. No wonder it changed so much.

He stood there, looking at the ground, lost between two worlds. He saw a book shop nearby, he entered and asked with parched throat, "What year is it?" The shopkeeper gave the same answer and looked at him with bewilderment.

"What happened to Fustat?" he asked an old man who was most likely a buyer and was sitting inside the bookshop and reading a book. "This is Fustat, child. Ancient name of this city." The old man replied.

Al-Khidr said nothing. His head was shaking. He was about to fall, the bookseller and the old man held him and offered him a chair. "What has happened to you? Are you alright?" They asked.

Al-Khidr said nothing. Why did the time shift? Is it because of crazy Hatathor, who disturbed the sphere charging? He did not know. He left the shop and everything suddenly looked different. Then, he remembered his friends and relatives. They all had passed away a long time ago, nearly a thousand years ago. The thought made him cry; he looked at the heavens and cried.

"Why, Allah, why me, of all people?" Al-Khidr said pleadingly. He was sobbing; his friends and all the people he knew had already died thousand of years ago. "Oh Allah, why me," he cried and cried.

He stood there, still thinking about how much he had lost. Suddenly, several French soldiers arrived in a procession with drummers preceding them. The procession included prisoners and also had several Bedouin children as well, both boys and girls. Behind the entourage were three carts loaded with the prisoner's merchandise and some camels which had been confiscated by French soldiers from the merchants when they were returning from the Hajj.

"We are traders. They took our merchandise and imprisoned us!" the poor traders were shouting for help. Al-Khidr realized that world had completely changed. Egypt currently was no longer the Egypt that he knew of. Pain erupted in his left wrist, causing him to fall to the ground.

***

Later, Al-Khidr talked to a hawker who told him

Chapter 3. The Souq of Al-Qahirah

that Egypt was under the rule of the Ottoman Empire. It used to be a colossal empire that spread over the Asian, African, and even Middle Eastern regions. Because of superior weaponry, France had taken over Egypt. Al-Khidr found this all difficult to absorb. The hawker said that infidels had entered into the holy land, too. It was only because of the sins of the Ottomans that they fell to the French force. Many Egyptians revolted but unfortunately were killed.

Al-Khidr listened intently and thought about it. He heard the white men talk about the battle plan in its entirety. Napoleon Bonaparte had attacked Egypt at night-time with his full force of soldiers and artillery. He is one who is now called Bey Al-Kabir.

The Beni-Asfar (European people) called themselves the Arme d'Orient and came with 33,000 men on 400 ships. They looted *Al-Iskandriyah* (Alexandria) first and then attacked Al-Qahirah (Cairo). The city gates were thrown open, with the soldiers covering the city completely. The Ottomans had roughly only 500 men to defend the large business center, so it was only a matter of time before the imperial forces captured the city and Ottoman bey ran off. Later, Ottoman beys came back with an army of 21,000 men but lost in the battle of Embabeh. After that in revolt, 6000 inhabitants of Cairo were killed. The declaration by Napoleon was that he was seeking revenge for the abuse perpetrated by the Ottomans over the French traders.

The sound of the afternoon prayers filled Al-Khidr

with hope. He headed toward the direction of the mosque, hoping to find some solace in the house of Allah. He offered his prayers and sat in the corner, thinking through things. A lot of thoughts came to his mind and a plan of action formulated in his head. He stood up and left the mosque.

The first thing he had to do was find the cure for Mutmut, to save the plants for the people of Lyra. The planet was now far, far away, but it never left his thoughts. He had to find it now because life on Earth was something he did not want. He must get back to the people who are still waiting for him. He still had a dirham in his pocket; he rechecked to make sure. After all, the afternoon had set in, and he was feeling hungrier by the minute. He bought a delicious meal from the local bazaar and savored it. The taste was heaven on Earth. He missed the soul and spice, which was so absent back in Lyra's prison. Al-Khidr decided to fast the next day. He fell asleep inside the mosque after hiding the sphere inside his clothes. He woke up at the call of Asr prayer from the Mosque. After offering the evening prayers, he asked Allah for help in his noble mission.

***

Walking out of the mosque, he saw his fellow Egyptians going somewhere in a line. Curiosity set in, and he walked with them. He emerged on a large pavement road lined with Al-Qahva (coffee) shops.

Chapter 3. The Souq of Al-Qahirah

The evening sun was setting and the noise of the men and women increased. Cairo became a lively hub of discussion, talk, and laughter. Al-Khidr broke his fast and started his stroll. He saw poets reciting poetry spontaneously to an audience, laughing their heads off. On the other side of the street, he saw hawkers selling honeyed hash and Persian opium.

Al-Khidr sat inside a Qahva shop to enjoy the nightlife of the city. Coming from Lyra, it was not all that bad. Maybe he could enjoy some things here. The people were cursing the French around the clock and loving it.

A barrage of verbal abuses flew over him as people talked about the French. Some people compared them to animals, while others called them the devil incarnate. Al-Khidr laughed at the banter. Other people were in favor of the French occupation, calling their leader the Sultan Al-Kabir.

Al-Khidr was undecided himself. He was a fish out of water, and the politics of the region were unknown to him.

After sipping his qahva and eating a few dates, he headed out for a nap. He found a wooden bench long enough for him to stretch his legs and he decided to sleep on it. His basket was near him with jump-sphere tied up in an extended cloth, one piece of which he tied to his wrist. "Now God take cares of it." He said as he was calming himself down and struggling to sleep. "Dammit! My aura is gone. I cannot believe this living hell," Al-Khidr exclaimed disappointingly.

But soon enough, he was sound asleep, snoring loudly.

This time it was different. The mosquitos kept buzzing and biting him constantly as he slept under the starry sky.

Chapter 4

The French

Cairo, Egypt, December 1798

"Hey, wake up, mister. We need to attend the royal wedding today. What is with you?" Nefertiti said. Al-Khidr lazily woke up, noticing her getting dressed for the occasion. As things stood, he could not recall a wedding, let alone a royal wedding. He sat up on the bed, still groggy.

"I think I was on Earth if I recall correctly. The one where I came from. Ugh," he stated, getting up.

Chapter 4. The French

"Dear, I think you have not gotten over that Earth hangover. Every now and then, you have this dream and wake up only to receive clarification. We are no longer on your planet!" she exclaimed while throwing a pillow at him.

"Hey, I get it. I have left my planet for good," Al-Khidr replied in annoyance. He looked at himself in the mirror. His hair was messed up from last night. He turned around, and Nefertiti kicked him in the stomach. Al-Khidr dropped to the ground like a ragdoll.

Then came another kick.

Al-Khidr woke up to see a white soldier dressed in a blue uniform; he was preparing for a third kick. The soldier's partner was laughing his head off. Al-Khidr caught the soldier's third kick and pushed it away, throwing the soldier off-balance.

"Baïonnette!" he shouted and the other soldier, clearly not ready for this, he pointed his rifle and bayonet at him. Al-Khidr stood up to inspect the scene. One soldier had his rifle pointed at him and the fallen soldier had now stood up and was running toward him, infuriated by the fall.

"Guess it was only two kicks," Al-Khidr exclaimed boastfully.

The French soldiers were wearing frock coats. Al-Khidr was a little slow in taking in his immediate environment. The soldier threw a punch at him and it hit him on the jaw. He crashed on the ground, dazed from the blow.

One of the soldiers grabbed Al-Khidr by his neck

and pulled him up. He gave Al-Khidr a look from his head to his feet. The soldier's eyes then went over to the basket made of corn leaves; something shiny caught his eye.

He muttered something in French and Al-Khidr knew that the soldier was going to inspect the basket. His heart leapt into his mouth. "What the hell! Do not go over there!" Al-Khidr said, not wanting to give away his fear.

The other soldier holding the rifle also got distracted by the sphere. He lowered his rifle and walked over to the first soldier. The two began to inspect the shiny object, the jump-sphere, exchanging surprised looks with one another. They flipped the sphere and threw it high into the air. Al-Khidr wanted to punch the soldier in the gut so badly. The two soldiers thought it was only a piece of useless metal and decided to throw it.

A voice stopped the soldiers. The two soldiers looked behind to see the source of the voice.

"*Ne faites pas cela s'il vous plait!* (Please don't do this!)," Al-Khidr shouted, red in the face. Their hands went to their rifles, careful with their next move. One of them asked, "How can you speak French so fluently? Where did you come from?" the soldier asked.

"A spy. He must be a spy for the Ottoman Empire. Point your bayonet at him, quick," the other soldier muttered. Al-Khidr looked at the soldiers who both had their rifles pointed at him. "*Je ne suis pas un espion* (I am not a spy)," he said.

Chapter 4. The French

"Raise your hands in the air slowly," one soldier exclaimed.

"I am an alchemist. I am here to collect a plant for medicine," Al-Khidr stated with his hands in the air.

The two soldiers told him to walk with them. He agreed, although had no idea where he was going. The sphere was back in the basket, which was a tremendous relief. He was about to explain the mission to these French soldiers. But then, he decided against it.

A lot depended on him, as far as Lyra was concerned. Divulging information regarding the mission would jeopardize the people of Lyra and his chances of leaving here quietly. He walked silently ahead of the soldiers, who were constantly watching all his steps closely from behind.

As they walked, one soldier laughed at the word *alchimiste*.

"What is this concept, alchemy? I don't believe a word of what he says. Who the hell studies alchemy? No one studies it; maybe in earlier times," they were talking each other.

"Maybe he is a lunatic. That is a pity," the other soldier exclaimed. They both burst out laughing.

"No. They are eons behind everyone. Look at their military technology. If that is not old, then I don't know what is," one soldier exclaimed sarcastically. They both laughed profusely. Defeating Egypt was a piece of cake, after all. Napoleon had the wits to attack this country in the dead of the night when its ruler and army slept under the moonlight. The attack took them by surprise, and by the time they woke up, Napoleon had surrounded Alexandria's port. The forces invaded the port city, taking control of the high castle and plundering the Ottomans.

Al-Khidr interrupted his thoughts to ask the soldiers a question. "Hey, guys. Where is France, by the way? I have never heard of this country. Maybe I can live there someday," he asked hopefully.

The soldiers answered the question, "It is in western Europe. That sounds about right. You have not heard of the place? A lowly alchemist like yourself can rarely go so far," the soldier remarked with a smirk. "It is on the opposite side of the Mediterranean Sea. The sea divides the two continents: the modern world and the Dark world. Your lot is behind," the other soldier exclaimed plainly.

Al-Khidr understood the gist of the message; the world was changing beyond the borders of Egypt. The power structures were changing as well. He was thinking about it all when the soldiers changed the direction of the conversation.

"My *Amis*. I have heard from the battalion heads that the Mighty Napoleon may present us with six acres of land. That land is in Toulon. What are your thoughts on that? Will he follow through on the promise?" one soldier asked, hopefully.

"I don't know yet. But Toulon sure is a good idea. A way better idea than other cities. I think he will fulfill his promise," the other soldier stated excitedly. This gave Al-Khidr an idea about their supreme

Chapter 4. The French

leader. Napoleon Bonaparte held the same reverence in the eyes of his people as the locals viewed Sultan Al-Kabir. From the conversation, he gathered that Egypt was under this man's control. As a result, the future of the country was also in his hands right now.

The three passed by the flea market. The hawkers stood, as usual, shouting over the top of their voices. Some semblance of silence prevailed as the two French soldiers and Al-Khidr made their way through the market. Women and children looked at him with curiosity. *Where are the soldiers taking me?* Al-Khidr thought to himself.

Al-Khidr had a feeling that the entire flea market was gazing at him as he passed by, wondering where the soldiers were taking him. His clothes gave him some special attention, too.

They continued to walk until the flea market was way behind them. The passed along narrow streets, yet they were still walking. After some time, Al-Khidr could see a large mansion in Cairo; a massive brick structure. Al-Khidr was surprised by its sheer size and magnitude.

It seemed like the soldiers knew the guards standing at the entrance. They exchanged some pleasantries and turned to business, conversing in hushed voices. The guard nodded and opened the huge doors of the mansion. As they went inside, Al-Khidr read Institut d'Egypte on the main entrance. The interior was something unexpected for Al-Khidr. He saw a lot of French people in weird clothes, talking to one another.

He arrived on the second level, a room laden with drawings and paintings of animal sketches, *Khat-el-Faruni* (Egyptian Hieroglyphs), and temples.

Al-Khidr was definitely not going to prison. He could understand that; it definitely looked like a place of learning. The soldiers went to a middle-aged man whose back was toward Al-Khidr. They whispered something in his ears and the man turned around to see Al-Khidr and smiled a bit.

He spoke in a loud voice: "Ask Nicolas-Jacques Cont to come here. I wish I could speak Arabic. We need an interpreter here. Let's see what he has to say." He seemed to be in a good mood. The soldiers left and returned his basket with the jump-sphere inside. Al-Khidr seemed to know what he was doing. "There is no need for an interpreter. I can speak French perfectly fine," he remarked. The man looked at him in astonishment.

"That is something. Come on over here then. Let's talk," the man raised his hands in delight. "My name is Vivant Denon. Good to see you. What is your name, lad?" he asked.

Al-Khidr cleared his throat. "My name is Al-Khidr Al-Nasir Al-Din Al-Berberi ibn Al-Tahir," he exclaimed a bit loudly.

"You Arabs live up to your reputation. Such long names," Vivant replied, making a silly face.

Al-Khidr could see that Vivant was different and exciting. "People outside have shorter names? My father and his grandfather had names of this tremendous

Chapter 4. The French

length as well. It is a cultural thing among the native Egyptians," Al-Khidr explained, finding the conversation interesting.

Vivant found this very amusing. He sipped his wine, stifling his laughter at the same time. "No, my dear child. We have two names. My name followed by my father's name. Two names it is," he exclaimed, still laughing at the silly conversation.

Al-Khidr decided to talk more about himself, even though he did not know why he was there. The soldiers had taken him to this place of learning and leisure without saying much and then had left him there. The noise of glasses clanging, people chattering, and laughing out loud put him at ease.

Al-Khidr said, "I am an Amazigh speaker (Berber) from North Africa, from one of the tribes of Amazigh people but moved to Baghdad to gain knowledge. After my education was completed there, I came to Egypt to help my people."

Vivant nodded in acknowledgment. "Oh, that is nice. What are you studying in Baghdad and where you were in Egypt?" he asked, staring at him with interest. These were a lot of questions for Al-Khidr "It is a small piece of land you have probably never heard before. It a small village is near River Nile. My father raised and sold cattle. He sent me to learn alchemy in Baghdad. People from faraway places come to Egypt to learn the art of alchemy," Al-Khidr said.

He was making it up as he went along. Vivant seemed to trust his account, even though Al-Khidr had yet to visit Baghdad.

Vivant spoke up, saying, "Ahhh. The art of alchemy is popular in my land, too. Some people wanted to make gold by mixing two metals. Others wanted to transform water into wine. I still know some men who wish to create medicine with alchemy. You should go to Europe if learning alchemy is your purpose in life. We are definitively ahead of Egypt and this Baghdad you speak of; that I can say for sure," he stated with a smile.

A wave of laughter came from downstairs. It caught Al-Khidr's attention pretty quickly, and he and Vivant exchanged looks. Vivant could sense his confusion. "Oh, there is a poetry battle going on there. You will see a soldier taking on a famous Egyptian boy. It is a routine thing over here. If you visit daily, you will see new faces going at it every day," Vivant explained, sipping more of his wine.

Al-Khidr had taken a liking to Vivant. He stretched forward, extending his hand to shake hands with Vivant. He looked like a harmless French man who had more interest in Al-Khidr than the war. "Pleased to meet you, Vivant. You are a nice French man. I wish more people were like you," Al-Khidr claimed. He meant the compliment. Vivant was surprised by the compliment and firmly shook his hand. The boy doesn't look like a spy! Vivant shrugged off this thought from his mind, despite the soldiers suggestion otherwise. "And it is a pleasure to meet you, my child. We have taken control of the country and its innocent

Chapter 4. The French

people. Ottomans are power-hungry and the usurpers of freedom. It is a despicable monarchy. Be gone these imbeciles. The French will bring new light to the country," he said. Al-Khidr did not comment on that. He had barely arrived on the planet a few days ago and didn't want to say much about anything. Vivant looked at him. "You know, you don't really look like an Egyptian-born by face. Are you an Egyptian?" he asked, turning a bit serious.

"Well, I am from several places. I cannot say one place for sure," Al-Khidr replied, throwing clouds of uncertainty over his past.

Vivant let that pass. Maybe he was the son of a vagabond. "Are you with Ottomans or us? I hope not the Ottomans. They have no regard for their people. Just a glimpse of their long-standing history shows the expansion of their lands and overstretched territory," Vivant went on a bit of a tirade. Al-Khidr nodded his head in agreement. "Yes. I feel the same way. The Ottomans are a curse on our country. We are glad that a foreign force has defeated it," he exclaimed, feeling that this was the correct answer at the moment.

He had no idea about the Ottomans, but he could guess that they were the ruling powers of Egypt at the time. To be honest, he found Vivant a fair and rational man. Maybe he was speaking the truth!? Al-Khidr snapped out of his thoughts due to Vivant's interest in the ensuing conversation. He made a face showing his utter disgust for the Ottomans.

"These Ottomans are a sad bunch. So many rebels

were killed around three months back. They did not hesitate to kill us as well. We came in peace, not all of us were soldiers," he exclaimed annoyingly. "Yeah, someone tried to slash my throat," he quipped. Vivant finished his glass of local wine, and a thought struck him. "Where were you at the time when the rebellion in Cairo took place? It was one all-out war, I can tell you that. The citizens of Cairo took arms against us, vowing revenge against the infidels. It was a rebellion of the citizens. Napoleon had to take action to bring peace to the city. So much bloodshed; so much violence," Vivant exclaimed, looking sad for a moment.

Al-Khidr's heart was pounding hard now. He looked at Vivant, who was looking at him, waiting for the answer. "I was not in Cairo at the time. I was in Meroe, Nubia, on a trading mission. I was selling Egyptian spices over there to merchants. We could not settle on a price," Al-Khidr started explaining his mission. Vivant looked at him with a blank face. It seemed that he hadn't heard of Nubia or Meroe. "It is a place outside Egypt in south. You probably never heard of it. People inside Africa move around for trade and exchanged things," he told Vivant. He seemed relieved by the explanation.

"I did hear about the rebellion after I returned to the city. It looked visibly changed by the effects of the in-fighting. A sad and extremely unfortunate sight," Al-Khidr mourned. A servant was passing through, holding a tray with wine and qahva. The sight tempted Al-Khidr. Vivant noticed the sparkle in his eyes and

Chapter 4. The French

hissed at the man. He stopped and bent low to greet Monsieur Vivant. The kind French man took another wine and passed a qahva to Al-Khidr, who accepted it gleefully. "Tell me something, Al-Khidr. You can speak French very fluently. How did you learn the language? I have been with an interpreter nearly every day to work," he said, shrugging. Vivant had unknowingly thrown another trap at Al-Khidr. He could not reveal how every language could be translated with alien technology nor the details of his true mission. Perhaps he would pose a difficulty for him somehow.

Al-Khidr smiled at the question. "My father once travelled to a distant land. He claimed that it is very far away from Egypt. He met a French slave woman on this journey. and he thought she was so beautiful. My father fell in love with her. He bought her, freed her, and married her," Al-Khidr said, drawing Vivant into the story. Vivant sat up straight, forgetting his wine for a moment.

"She had golden hair and blue eyes. Men would stop in their tracks when she would step into the Cairo bazaar. The hawkers would forget their chants and chickens. When she walked the streets, a silence would ensue. I felt so proud of my mom. The talk of her beauty spread far and wide," Al-Khidr exclaimed fondly. "She taught me French every day. When I was born, she could speak Arabic, too. In a way, my father and mother taught me two languages," he remarked, smiling ear to ear. "Boy. What happened then? Is your mom still alive? I would like to meet the sweet lady.

Let's go meet her!" Vivant exclaimed excitedly. Forgetting the wine, he stood up as if to begin a journey to meet Al-Khidr's mother.

Al-Khidr was trapped; he had to do something fast to protect the web of lies he was spinning. The answer had to come quick. A look of sorrow crossed Al-Khidr's face. He looked at the ground, pretending to be sad. Vivant was quick to notice the sadness on his face.

"Monsieur Al-Khidr, did I upset you? I apologize for the intrusion. I just got a little excited," he said, coming closer to pat his arm. Al-Khidr let him pat his arm. "No, no, no. It is not anything you did. The thought of my mother's death always upsets me. Something strange happened," Al-Khidr enticed Vivant again. "Tell me what happened. Perhaps it was something that we could have cured. Maybe, our medicine is very much ahead of yours," Vivant stated, still worried. "Well, in her last month, she was in bed. My father worked hard all day and night to find the cure for her illness. She had a high fever. When I touched her face, it was like it was on fire. The heat was something devilish; maybe it was hell calling her," Al-Khidr exclaimed, lost in thought.

"What kind of fever was it? Did she present other symptoms? Fever is a diseases itself," Vivant remarked, trying to figure out the mysterious illness. Al-Khidr nodded in agreement. "That is what my father said as well. He said fever could mean several diseases, but we could not figure out what it was. He brewed herbal

Chapter 4. The French

medicines and went into alchemy to find out the disease. Nothing worked on my mother," he said, still in sorrow. "She took her last breath on the bed. Her hand was in my hands. Sometimes, God tests us with love and loss. Not a day passes when I do not think about her," Al-Khidr stated.

Vivant regretted asking the question. The sadness ruined the flow of conversation. Al-Khidr began again. "After her unfortunate demise, I decided to study alchemy and learn about diseases in Egypt. Medicinal alchemy is my specialty. Maybe I could save more lives and the loved ones of others. It had become my life's mission," he continued.

Vivant found an opening here. "Well, if it makes you feel any better, I can send you on a study trip to France. You can find people who study medicinal alchemy. Maybe it can help in your journey," Vivant said.

Al-Khidr brightened at the idea. "I have never been to France. How far is it?" he asked excitedly.

"Well, it is far away, but a month of travel at sea will take you to France. The people are very kind there, even though you are actually a foreigner to them," Vivant said, equally excited.

Al-Khidr considered the idea for a moment. "Well, I could learned a lot of alchemy in Egypt as well," Al-Khidr said, thinking.

Vivant nodded. "I am glad that you did. Now, you can gain the knowledge of western alchemy. More knowledge to help people in Egypt," Vivant proposed.

A slightly older French man was passing by them. He did not pay much attention to them until Vivant called to him. The man turned around, —he was wearing an eye patch. That was odd, Al-Khidr thought. "Did you call me? I am in the middle of something, Vivant," the man stated, slightly irritated. Vivant ignored him. "Meet this fine young man. He can speak fluent French and specializes in Egyptian alchemy. He is a very learned man," Vivant introduced Al-Khidr to him.

Al-Khidr could see the light in the Frenchman's eye, his attention turned towards the two of them.

The man was a bit younger than Vivant and way more energetic. He moved with a surprising speed, scaring Al-Khidr a little bit.

Vivant began again. "Yes. He has French blood flowing through him. Come and meet this sweet child, Al-Khidr, meet Mr. Nicolas-Jacques Cont. He shares your passion for alchemy and is an accomplished scientist himself. He can talk about alchemy all day," Vivant explained while rolling his eyes. Vivant hoped that the two would hit it off nicely. He would then join the fiery poetry session down below and laugh his insides out. Maybe the two could share knowledge of different worlds and do great things.

Nicolas-Jacques shook hands with Al-Khidr and Vivant. "I am honored to meet a fellow scientist like myself. I would gladly show you my work and developing projects. Some are great, some are just acceptable, you know," he said, chuckling. He sat quietly

Chapter 4. The French

for a while, waiting for either Vivant or Al-Khidr to start the conversation and take it from there. Al-Khidr looked at Nicolas, a man with his rakish eye patch, and then back to Vivant.

"Don't look at me. Talk to him, my child. You do not need my permission to get things started," Vivant exclaimed while laughing half-heartedly. Al-Khidr looked at Nicolas-Jacques, who smiled warmly.

"I am from Normandy, which is in France. You should check it out sometime, or, perhaps, you can join us for a trip to France whenever possible. You can live in my house and move around the city. I am sure you will make friends easily in the city," Nicolas-Jacques exclaimed kindly.

Al-Khidr was quite amazed. Here was a person he barely met, but he was willing to take him to France just for the heck of it. Maybe the French people had a big heart? "Sure, I would love to do that. Thanks for the invitation. I like the French people; they seem very, very hospitable," Al-Khidr exclaimed in amazement. "Just for a select few. A select few only," Vivant remarked, smiling broadly. They sat silently for a while. Laughter could be heard from downstairs. Nicolas turned to Al-Khidr with curiosity. "So, tell me about your expertise in alchemy. Which branch of alchemy piqued your interest? I know fellow alchemists who have tried to make gold, fly like birds, and even make water into wine," he stated, letting out a little laugh.

Vivant spoke with great interest at the mention of

wine, "I would like to see the day when water becomes wine. I will make that alchemist a very wealthy man. He won't need another dime for the rest of his life," he remarked with great enthusiasm.

Nicolas looked at Vivant with immense disdain, as Vivant had said something totally rubbish. To him, Vivant was a rich drunkard and useless socialite, who was good enough to only write erotic novels. Vivant had come to Egypt to explore the country and talk to the local people. After returning to France, he would publish a book about his travels in Egypt.

Al-Khidr looked around to confirm whether it was his turn to speak. The two nodded their heads, so he began, "Well, when I was young, I did try many things you mentioned just now. Unfortunately, they did not work. Perhaps I did not have the right apparatus or the ingredients required to get me going. My interest has moved and transformed over the years. At one point, I wanted to cure leprosy. These days, I am making a vinegar that can slash stones in two pieces. Cutting stones in pieces is very important for us Egyptians," he explained.

Nicolas did not seem much impressed by a liquid that could cut stones. He was more interested in some breakthrough for his fellow alchemists in France. "Is there something else you are doing within the ambit of alchemy? I would like to know," he pressed Al-Khidr.

Al-Khidr was taken aback. There was no appreciation in his gestures or his tone for the work he was doing. This showed that Nicolas was a specialist in a

Chapter 4. The French

different branch of alchemy.

Vivant could guess that Al-Khidr did not like this question. He broke the tense air, saying, "I have an idea: why don't we, the three of us, go to dinner and meet the other scientists? It would be so much fun. Nicolas has met all of them. Perhaps the other scientists would take more interest in your work. Some people are so full of themselves that it is nauseating," Vivant remarked, glaring at Nicolas-Jacques.

Nicolas-Jacques nodded in agreement with Vivant. He understood his point, but no remorse was visible on his face. "While we are at it, you should take a bath and dress nicely to meet our colleagues. I don't want you to go looking like this," Nicolas remarked, stifling a burst of laughter. Vivant also found this hilarious and burst out laughing.

"Come to think of it. What are you carrying here? A basket made of leaves? Really? Shall I arrange new French clothes? You can speak French fluently and have sound knowledge of alchemy. I guess the right clothes are the only missing thing you need," Vivant said.

Nicolas had an idea. "I have a few spares items of clothing down the hallway. Come with me. I will show you. You may look a bit French; I must say," Nicolas interjected. He wanted to clear the air of discomfort he created a while ago.

Al-Khidr nodded and started to leave. Vivant relaxed a bit, waiting for them to return. "I cannot wait to see the real you; must be something," he exclaimed while chuckling.

As Al-Khidr started walking towards Nicolas' room, he also took the basket in his hands. Nicolas and Vivant did not notice it, but he could not take any chances with these imperialists. The mission couldn't be compromised in any way.

"Boy, you need a bath, that I can say for sure. Where were you living, and what did you eat?" Nicolas asked as they walked down the hallway. This would be a very embarrassing story and Al-Khidr had no interest in talking about it. The less he told the better. "Well, I am not really in a mood to talk about it. Things have not been good lately. I wish for peace to prevail so that we can live a normal life," Al-Khidr stated, taunting the French invasion.

"Well, it is not all our fault. The Ottoman Empire did some bad things, and I cannot blame Napoleon for his actions. Who do they think they are? We do not care. Injustice should not be tolerated anywhere, not even in Egypt. We will offer Egypt a lot more. The Ottomans are just a bunch of power-hungry freaks," he remarked with a smirk.

Al-Khidr decided not to comment on this. He had little to no knowledge about the actions of the Ottomans. He could neither defend them nor justify them. "Those power-hungry Ottomans think that they could take over Marseilles to expand their empire. The French not only took the island back, but also launched a surprise invasion of Egypt. A taste of their own medicine. Huh, that will show them!" he

Chapter 4. The French

boasted.

Al-Khidr listened to him silently, making a mental note about the Ottoman Empire. Nicolas opened the door and beckoned Al-Khidr to enter. "Well, I suggest you first take a bath. You smell like someone who has recently died. I do not know how Vivant survived for so long," Nicolas said, putting his hand on his nose. Al-Khidr gave him a scowling look, but Nicolas was not impressed. "Go inside. Do not come outside until the smell is gone," Nicolas stated and broke into laughter.

"Yeah, thanks a lot for your kindness," Al-Khidr exclaimed sarcastically and slammed the bathroom door. "Don't mention it. I am doing you a huge favor here. Vivant is kind enough not to mention these things; I am not that nice of a person," Nicolas stated sternly. Having taken the basket into the bathroom with him, Al-Khidr was taking precaution to avoid attention on the jump-sphere, which was laying in the basket along with some duck eggs. He took a bath, feeling quite refreshed at the end. When he came out, Nicolas has already left a dress on the bed.

Hmm, the disgruntled Nicolas eventually decided the dress for the evening, Al-Khidr thought. It was a flowing black robe, and his newly slick hair immediately added more class to his personality.

"This looks great," Al-Khidr said, impressed.

"Yes. Yes. I know. Let's get moving, shall we?" Nicloas remarked, beckoning him to leave the room. Al-Khidr looked at himself again in the mirror and laughed. It was unbelievable that he could look so nice. They left the room without exchanging a word. Al-Khidr was happy that he was not considered a spy for the Ottomans. These people embraced him with open arms and he seemed to be making new friends.

At the back of his mind, he remembered to collect the plants for his mission. After all, Lyra was still calling. He thanked Allah for his many blessings and bounty. Things could have taken a sour turn here.

After half an hour away, Al-Khidr returned with his new set of clothes. Vivant saw, and his eyes went wide. "Dear, dear. You look like the French nobility that we are fighting against back home. Well, I know you are not one of them. Come here. I will show you some table etiquette as well," he exclaimed kindly. "Why, thank you, Vivant. Nicolas here has the best collection of clothes you could find. I am glad that I slipped into something comfortable and exotic," Al-Khidr boasted to Vivant.

"Shall we go, dear boy?" Vivant asked Al-Khidr.

"Yes, yes. Let's go," he exclaimed brightly. They set off together towards the entrance, both lost in a world of their own. *Silly boy,* thought Vivant, *Nicolas and a sense of fashion were two very different things*, if only Al-Khidr knew. Back in France, Nicolas was the source of jokes due to his archaic fashion sense. He would pick something so odd and weird that he would stand out from the crowd.

Seeing his antics and dressing, Vivant preferred to call him a distant friend from his college days. Over

Chapter 4. The French

time, Nicolas became interested in alchemy and began hotly experimenting in his favorite area; the creation of gold. The dream of chasing gold had him traveling far and wide in his attempt to mix different metals in order to create gold in excess amounts.

Egypt was one of the places which caught his attention. He hopped aboard the first ship he could leaving for the country. Vivant was pretty angry when Nicolas told him that he would accompany him on his tour throughout Egypt. He booked a room on the lower deck while Nicolas was on the upper deck. The two did not meet each other until the ship docked at Alexandria. Vivant enjoyed his journey without Nicolas adding his weirdness to journey.

Chapter 5

The Sea of Salt

A few days ago

A spherical field of energy was all around Hatathor. He was rolled up in an energy ball, ascending up towards the sky at an incredible speed. His hairs were all raised up as an electro-static charge was building up around him, generating intermittent sparks. The sphere entered an already opened up cosmic tunnel

Chapter 5. The Sea of Salt

and he stood up straight and in utter confusion and panic, looking all around himself.

His mind raced, and the last thing he could remember was that he was in the *Usekh-t Sehetch* where he saw Al-Khidr, the earthling he despised so much. He thought to himself, *I threw the bident at the human to kill him and then something happened, a black viscous fluid spilled out of the charging unit and then... The spilled black matter engulfed me in a fraction of second. But why? It should have burned the human alive. But why did it take me? Is it some sort of trick by Ehsis?*

He had many questions, but no answers.

The human was sucked up towards the sky, and I as well. But where is he now?

Hatathor was anxious. He did not know what went wrong and when. He realized that the energy field around him was actually generated from the sphere he had casually put in his pocket. The blue particles were seeping out of his trousers and merging together to form the energy field. The thing was now stuck to his leg, and he felt uncomfortable about it.

"The weapon is stuck to me!" He shouted in shock and disbelief. "Ehsis threw me in space to blast me out here!"

He punched the sphere pretty hard to try to remove it, but it didn't even make a dent. *Weird*, he thought. Ah.

Many things were sweeping into his mind. *This ball-like device from Hept Sehetch Sheta facility, can-*

not be a weapon! But is it so powerful? This device has sucked up some of the spilled-over stuff... but, what was that? What ritual was the witch Ehsis doing there? She and Hathor had hidden so much technology from military. What was that matter that spilled over Al-Khidr?

Hatathor rested for a few seconds, then he suddenly recalled: *Is this the Maft-Shespt which Hathor mentioned in the meeting?* The voice of Queen Hathor was echoing in his head: The Maft-Shespt is a device made by us to jump from one plane of stars to another... made during the reign of King Ptah... Maft-Shespt ... from one plane of stars to another... made during a time of King Ptah... Maft-Shespt ...

He was looking into the stars with total disbelief. Hatathor's mind started moving and he was having a psychedelic, trance like view of Queen Hathor all around him. He had visions of Hathor; she was smiling and kissing him when he was a child and then he saw her with hands on her belly, pressing hard, holding her wound with blood oozing out. She was screaming incessantly at him, shouting "Traitor...traitor...traitor!"

"No, no, no!!" Hatathor shouted and in his hysteria with all his force, he again tried to push the jumpsphere away. However, as much as he tried, nothing could move it.

"*Abaqer* (Bitch) Ehsis, she tricked me," he exclaimed angrily in Lyrian language. His hairs were no longer electrostatic but were now fluttering back as if he was

Chapter 5. The Sea of Salt

sailing on a sea. The sea of stars was all around him. The Iteru of sky, *Anart Sehetch* (Milky Way), was all laughing at his misery. The vastness of space made him like a man without blood. Like a thunderbolt, he was moving through space. There were miles of blackness that transcended stars and galaxies. A cosmic tunnel was warping space and opening up in front of him, creating a path towards the unknown.

"*Tepta Ankh* (The stars tunnel)," he uttered in lyrian language. It was a grand gallery through space; a shortcut.

"It must be something that Ehsis did to get me out of Lyra. I will never forgive her. Once I return to Lyra, she is dead, DEAD!" Hatathor vowed. The events before the journey were coming back to him as clear as daylight.

"I will save Lyra from diseases, from doom, from curses. Not you two bitches; you failed us all. Ankhamon was right!" he exclaimed angrily towards Hathor and Ehsis.

The thought of the murderous Ehsis further infuriated him. Why was she protecting that defenseless human? That action was the last straw; no one crosses Hatathor. His mind shifted towards Al-Khidr for a moment.

"Where is that mischievous and cunning human that had fooled the gullible bitches? Offering services to bring a cure from the cursed planet. My foot!" He shouted.

"Where are you, bloody human?" Hatathor was

pushing himself to the front of curved energy field to try to get a glimpse of the human. But he saw no human around.

What he did not know was that his jump sphere was also connected to Al-Khidr's jump sphere, though it was also not fully charged. The two jump-spheres were connected by *Kam-t Nenui* (black primeval matter) like an infinity symbol (∞), stretched over incredible distances. The distance between them was increasing as the sphere was descending in space towards the planet Earth.

Hatathor could not see Al-Khidr because of the warping of space in front of him. The cosmic tunnel was passing like a needle through the folded cloth of space. But there was a problem; Hatathor had committed a grave mistake. The disruption in the charging sequence had altered the quantum state of the black matter and now the targeted time had been altered. The disruptions could lead to the incorrect trajectory, wrong planet, or even the wrong time. All these were possible, and the possessor of the jump-sphere could lose his sense of time. Only God knows where in space and when in time the cosmic tunnel would be closed. It would close by itself as soon as the main jump sphere completes its trajectory, whatever that may be. As soon as it was over, Hatathor's jump-sphere would be disconnected and he could end up dying out in space.

Oblivious to all of this, Hatathor was watching the stars, the planets, and the galaxies which were passing by him at incredible speeds. *Wow, am I going back?*

Chapter 5. The Sea of Salt

He thought, as he saw Lyra another time. Or was it my hallucination again?

An idea came to him. He had no bident, but he still had the sleeve-device on his left hand, which had multiple functions. He pressed a few buttons on his sleeve device and in Lyrian script, the display panel read: Electromagnetic field disruptions detected. Device in saver-mode. The sleeve-device then shut itself down automatically.

"Lousy device!" Hatathor cursed.

***

Suddenly, the warping of the space-time continuum started modulating in waves. But before Hatathor could make sense of the situation, the energy cocoon momentarily halted, as if it was confirming the location. He could see the burning bright star right in front of him. The star surrounding area was pretty clear, signifying that it was a young star. He was unaffected by the sun's intense radiation and he could clearly see everything. Lyrian bodily shells were capable of withstanding the intense radiation. Still, the star seemed awfully small. "Weird," he exclaimed. The white light of the star took him by surprise, as he was accustomed to a different color of light on Lyra. Vega is much better! He thought. This wasn't the star Vega; there was no debris surrounding it. "That bitch sent me on another star's level, meaning she does not want me on Lyra again!" He was fuming at the thought.

The energy sphere sped up and descended towards a planet like a meteor. Hatathor was a moment late in realizing what was happening before he was thrown backward, and a detached shock wave formed. He thought to himself, just get this over with already, man. I am tired of this.

As the energy-sphere descended towards the planet, Hatathor noticed that it appeared like a gloomy and dark place. The planet did not show any signs of technological development and there were no massive structures that were visible from outer space. He had no clue about just how the people on the planet would see him. What he could see was that the planet had a lot of water; more than half of the planet was covered in water with gigantic waves flowing across its vast oceans.

He tried to recall any planet with such a volume of water, but his memory failed him. The course he took on Interplanetary Science did not help him since this seemed to be such a distant planet and far removed from the immediate surroundings of Lyra.

More pressing questions came to his mind. *Does the planet have breathable gases? Was the water drinkable? Does it have a hospitable temperature? Would I survive the atmosphere of the planet, and for how long? Did Ehsis send me deliberately or was it my mistake?*

The sphere descended towards the planet and started cruising roughly a hundred meters over the sea. The water was lurking towards the sphere, and Hatathor

Chapter 5. The Sea of Salt

felt as if the sphere was attracting the water. The sphere moved over the sea and was heading towards the desert.

It is going somewhere...., Hatathor thought.

He looked underneath him and behind. A wall of sea water formed in the path of the sphere as it moved over the sea water's surface. The wall of water collapsed as the sphere moved forward towards the desert. But before the sphere reached land, some sea water touched the spherical energy field, causing it to burst like a bubble and Hatathor fell into the vast sea.

He was swimming for his life. The water had foulness in it. It smelled bad, and there was sand in it, almost everywhere. The water had a fishy taste, and he spat it out.

God! This water was terrible to drink. Feels like something had rotted in it, he thought.

Luckily, his training with the army had taught him well and he started swimming. He could see the fish below, minding their business. The first thing he had to do was find land.

The jump-sphere that was the origin of the energy field and was emitting blue light, was rolling out of his pocket while he was swimming. He saw the sphere was sinking deep towards the ocean floor and he tried to catch it, but it went further and further down, sinking into the depths. His ticket back to Lyra was slipping away. Fear took over Hatathor as he realized that he would be stranded on this planet without the sphere. He chased the sphere down into the sea, but it was falling deeper at a breakneck speed. Hatathor could not keep up with the it's pace. He realized he could not go much further; his lungs were burning and desperate for air. Hatathor swam out of the sea of salt. Struggling for air, he barely managed to get topside. He gasped and thought to himself, The sphere is gone forever. Where am I? What planet is this? Where is that cunning human who made the most learned of us a bunch of fools?

Unbeknownst to Hatathor, he had fallen into the Mediterranean sea far away from Giza, but nearby Alexandria, Egypt. He had reached the shore and his voice mixed with the crashing of the waves as he yelled, "I will slaughter you for this, human! Where are you!?" He was looking at the vast sea and reactivated his sleeve-device. He pressed some buttons and an spatial grid map appeared in front of him.

Where are you, prisoner? You cannot run away from me! he said to himself and pressed a few buttons on the tracking unit attached to Menkht Sekhem, the sleeve weapon, and commanded: "*Agem khaku asti, Khena!* (Locate the despicable liar, the prisoner!)" The sleeve beeped and a voice sounded aloud: "Senth Khena, Shaa Res 6,657.623 Supris Ahau Khetem (Prisoner found, in south, 6,657.623 Supris, location sealed)"

"What the heck? What planet is this?" he shouted at his device and pressed few more buttons. "Agem Peta? (Find my location?)" he said. The sleeve-device beeped and displayed the following data: *Ahau Seqetiu Aitenn, Ahau Seqetiu Keb, Ahau Ta Mera ...*

Chapter 5. The Sea of Salt

(Location: planet Keb; location: Egypt... Lyra is located on top. You are 25.05 light years away from Misraim city, kingdom of Akhom).

"Noooo!" Hatathor shouted while looking at sky and landed on his knees. His worst nightmare had come true: he was on Keb (Earth), the cursed planet.

Chapter 6

The Blinking

AL-KHIDR was looking at his clothes, proud of how they looked on him. However, Vivant was focused on their meeting outside. He was staring into the distance, clearly lost in a world of his own. As they stood up to leave, Al-Khidr felt a burning pin on his wrist. He looked at his wrist and there were three small holes like the vertices of an upward triangle; the mark of Lyra on his body!

It was at the police station on Lyra when he received this mark, and there was a tracker inside. A

Chapter 6. The Blinking

day after the installation of this unit, a prison guard told him, "Prison escapes happen all the time. Some silly ones still try to do it anyway, but they do not go that far. Most of them are bounty hunters and pirates looking to steal some stuff and sell it on the intergalactic black market."

He stared at his wrist, where the three holes repeatedly blinked, causing a burning sensation in his arm with each blink. This hadn't happened since he arrived back on Earth. Why now? He was not sure. Al-Khidr was getting nervous, but he had to keep his composure and avoid the attention of the French savants who were engaged in their dinner table chatter.

The last few days were a whirlwind for Al-Khidr. Everything had happened so fast and he did not have time to think. He took his place at the dining table between Vivant and Nicolas. The implant did not hurt that much after the initial shock, it only caused a slight burning sensation, indicating abnormal activity. His hand also felt quite heavy. It was like he was holding some unseen weight.

Vivant introduced him to many savants, but most noticeable was a young lady with light green eyes and curly brown hair. Vivant kissed her hand, and she nodded with a grace that impressed Al-Khidr.

"Meet Al-Khidr," Vivant said, "We discovered him today. An alchemist and fascinating gentleman."

Then Vivant looked at Al-Khidr and said, "Meet Mademoiselle Estelle, daughter of late Lieutenant-colonel Jacquous Molire. Madam Estelle Molire is a an avid naturalist — she likes plants very much." She shook Al-Khidr's hand firmly and motioned him to sit. "It is so nice to meet you. Please, have a seat, I am sure you have a lot to say to an outsider like me," she said with a smile.

Al-Khidr had forgotten that he was standing to meet her. Mesmerized by her beauty, he had also forgotten to speak. He briefly nodded at her and turned his attention to Vivant and Nicolas. His words had left him momentarily, and he was silent for most of the ensuing conversation. During the conversation, he stole a few glances at her. Their eyes met a few times. *Maybe she knows the plants I am looking for*, he thought to himself.

Vivant and Nicolas were busy talking to other people. Al-Khidr looked at his wrist a bit more closely and he pressed the three points gently as he did several times before, but nothing happened. Al-Khidr discreetly blew some air into the holes. Still, nothing happened, so he then sucked the three holes, hoping the tracker would enter his mouth. Out of the corner of his eye, Vivant noticed Al-Khidr engaging in this strange activity. This is not good, Al-Khidr realized. To avoid further suspicion, Al-Khidr wrapped a serviette on this wrist. Luckily, no one noticed the oddity of his actions.

The blinking was a sign of abnormality, and Al-Khidr had not expected it to happen on Earth. Al-Khidr remembered that that he requested Nefertiti to remove the implant. However, the situation at Lyra

Chapter 6. The Blinking

had developed quite fast and its removal got delayed. Now he was stuck with the tracker. *God knew why it activated now.*

He decided to let it go. Allah will protect him as always. So far, Allah had not left his side, his protection was greater than anyone. Al-Khidr's mind relaxed at this thought.

He sat with the fellow alchemists, and a warm discussion started. The people from France were full of questions for Al-Khidr. He told them about his story, the death of his mother, and his interest in alchemy; he had them hooked on his information. Vivant laughed at the scene and prided himself on bringing such company with him. Al-Khidr was enjoying himself a lot; after a long time, he could relax and talk with people who knew nothing about him.

It felt like a friendly atmosphere. He noticed Mademoiselle Estelle passing a sweet to him and staring at him with some interest. Al-Khidr started to look around. They were sitting in a dining room with wide windows on the upper floor of the building near Institut d'Egypte.

The evening air had everyone in a good mood. Al-Khidr stared back at Estelle to see her looking at him intently. He wondered what was wrong with her "Can I help you?" Al-Khidr asked timidly. Estelle smiled and put a hand on her mouth. "Hahhahaha. Help me with what?" she asked, confusing Al-Khidr a bit more. Al-Khidr was stumped. This girl was playing games with him; what could he do here? Vivant had caught some of the conversations. He was smiling ear to ear, thinking that this was vintage Estelle: confusion and chaos were her game.

Estelle smiled at Al-Khidr's confusion and decided to let the moment pass. She could gauge Al-Khidr as somewhat not-so-intelligent and indeed a product of a different culture. She moved her hair back to reveal her face. *God, she is so beautiful. More beautiful than Nefertiti*, Al-Khidr thought.

"I was just teasing you, do not worry. I am Estelle. Like Vivant told you, I am a naturalist. I was over here in Egypt to study the plants and their families. It helps with collecting data for the plant species of every region. I have mostly explored plant life in France thus far. The species in Egypt are very different and exciting. I am surprised, makes me realize that I should go out more," she said to him.

"You are here with these French alchemists? Or someone you know is here," Al-Khidr asked, straying away from the subject of plants. She looked at him and replied in a sad tone, "No, no. I am here with Vivant, of course. My father, Lieutenant-colonel Jacquous Molire, has passed away two months ago. He was a soldier in the French Army but caught Nile malaria, a local virus. He had a high fever ... unfortunately, he didn't make it." "Oh. I am sorry to hear that," Al-Khidr said. "And your mother?" he pressed further.

"I lost her when I was ten years old. I have no siblings either. Daddy received the orders, and he did

Chapter 6. The Blinking

not want to leave me in France alone, so I accompanied him on this supposedly short mission. Oh, life becomes unbearable sometimes. But such is life." She wiped away newly forming tears.

"I have requested a return to Paris. But war broke out in Syria and it is not safe at the moment to take a sea journey," she said further.

This girl has strong nerves, and Al-Khidr admired her. He nodded his head, "Oh, leaving Egypt next week then?" he said.

Estelle turned slightly angry at that and replied, "Well, we cannot leave without the approval of our Emperor Napoleon Bonaparte. The leader. Supreme of the supreme. After the invasion, some more regional in-fighting started. He had to take care of some stuff and the rebel forces. I just hope that he comes back soon to Cairo. At least that is what I am told," she said worriedly.

Her hair fell on her back. She looked so beautiful with her wavy hair. The perfume she was wearing only added to her allure. She raised her hand, taking Al-Khidr by surprise a bit. "Tell me more about yourself. You seem very different than the French guys I know. You know, they look at me in a certain way," her voice trailed off. "In what way?" he asked. Estelle broke into loud laughter. "No. Just tell me about yourself. You would not understand it," she said, motioning for him to speak. "Well, I am an alchemist. There is not much to talk about myself. My mother was French, so I can speak French fluently. She passed away, unfortunately, leaving dad and me behind," he repeated his concocted story. She nodded. "And your dad is in Cairo then?" she asked. Al-Khidr pretended to feel sad.

"No. He also passed away when I was on a mission outside Egypt. By the time I returned, he had died of some unknown disease. I could not find out which one it was," he said, shrugging. Al-Khidr felt terrible for making up so many lies. In fact, his father died before he left for Baghdad centuries ago. Estelle looked very sad. "Oh. God. I am so sorry to hear that, that's so sad. Living as an orphan must be so hard for you," she said. Her beautiful face was sad, but the moonlight falling on her made her even more beautiful.

"Living alone has its ups and downs. But I love my work here," he said, relaxing in his chair. Then something strange happened. She took Al-Khidr's right hand in her hand and stood up. "Can you come with me for a moment? This is going to be interesting," she said excitedly.

"Of course. Of course," he said, standing up.

She took Al-Khidr to the roof of the institute. Vivant, Nicolas, and the rest were left sitting at the table. Vivant passed a smile to Nicolas, who smiled back. "Where are you taking me, Estelle?" he asked, running after her.

"Just wait and watch. I do not want to ruin the surprise," she said, running. They eventually made it to the roof, deserted at this time of the night. The sight of the full moon was beautiful.

Chapter 6. The Blinking

"I like the starry nights with the full moon. Sometimes I wish I go to stars," Estelle said.

Al-Khidr was looking at the sky, too. Estelle started looking at him. The stars were shinning his eyes.

"Not everything shinning is beautiful. You know them more when you go closer. These are the burning stars. Multitude of them... they are like a person. You know them more when you go closer to them," Al-Khidr said.

"You say that as if you have been to stars," she laughed.

"Yes!" he uttered, but then quickly said, "I mean... I went there in my dreams".

"You are so adorable!" she said and looked into his eyes.

"You have beautiful eyes and a beautiful mind," she said further.

She took his hands in hers and kissed him.

"Did you like it?" she said, smiling. Al-Khidr was still surprised by the shock of the kiss. Before he could do anything, she kissed him again. The thought of Nefertiti came to his mind. He pushed her away from him and turned around. The kiss made him regretful.

"What's wrong?" she asked, patting his arm. Al-Khidr was thinking a bit.

"I am sorry. I cannot do this. I am sorry," he said, looking at the moon. She came face to face with Al-Khidr. He looked to face her.

"I have someone in my life. It would be wrong to her. You are a beautiful girl and I am sure you will find someone else," he said. Poor Nefertiti was still in Lyra, waiting for him.

"Oh. Right. I heard that Muslim man can marry four wives. I am single, if you are interested," she said with a sly smile. That made him smile, despite her persistence.

"My fiancée — She is a fascinating girl. I know she is anxiously waiting for me. When I am finished here, I will leave Cairo and return to her," he said. Estelle laughed at this hopeless romance. "Where does she live? I want to meet this lucky girl," she said naughtily.

Al-Khidr looked at her with a smirk. "Well, she does not live here. Quite far away, actually. She would faint at the sight of you," he said dismissively. "Hey. Why? What is wrong with me?" she said. Al-Khidr did not answer that question. "Let us head downstairs. I am glad we have had this talk today," he said. He began walking downstairs. They came back downstairs to see Vivant and Nicolas staring at both of them. "Anything you want to tell us?" Vivant asked pressed Estelle. Estelle smiled at the question. "Tell you what? Nothing happened, Vivant. Just shut it," she said. And that was that as Al-Khidr and Estelle sat down and began chatting with others on the table.

They enjoyed the night for a few more hours. Al-Khidr had an idea. He came near Vivant's ear and smiling ear to ear, whispered, "Thank you so much, Vivant. I appreciate you bringing me here. At first, when the soldiers apprehended me, I was decidedly scared that they would imprison me. But now I realize

Chapter 6. The Blinking

that their heart was in a good place."

"Don't mention it, my boy. What were you doing with your left hand when we were walking here and during dinner?" Vivant threw the question at him. Al-Khidr was not expecting this at all. "Ummm. It is nothing. No need to worry about it," he exclaimed while shrugging. Vivant had a vague feeling that the boy was hiding something. He decided to let it go since they had met only a few hours ago. People did not get terribly cozy with each other in only a matter of a few hours. They time to unwind and get things off their chest.

He stole a glance at Estelle and Al-Khidr. The two were deeply immersed in a world of their own, oblivious to the people around them. The alchemists kept to themselves, exchanging notes on herbal medicine and side projects they were working on at the moment. It was exciting, except for the fact that Vivant felt a bit lonely. He was a man of art, literature, and culture; these things defined him and life in general.

Even Nicolas had found an interested listener, talking to him avidly about his latest pursuits in alchemy. The man was testing the waters with a new medicine that could cure leprosy, perhaps permanently. Naturally, this caught the tables attention, even from Estelle and Al-Khidr, who snapped back to reality and listened to the heated debate around leprosy.

Al-Khidr thought it was an interesting conversation. Curing this disease seemed imperative to these foreigners; it's no wonder Estelle had also forgotten him temporarily. The talk ended when Nicolas said he was working on a permanent cure to wipe out the disease in Europe. Then, maybe, he would not charge a dime for this medicine, as the extent of human suffering just upset him on the inside.

"Aww. That is so nice of you, Nicolas. Let me hug you," Estelle exclaimed and leaned forward. She hugged him tightly, and a smile curled on Al-Khidr's face; she was so full of life and love. He was almost reconsidering her over Nefertiti. But things were different here. Nefertiti was a police officer first and a human-loving alien second. However, she had lifted her veil and revealed her softer side. But Al-Khidr could see himself falling for Estelle, the enchanting beauty from France had his heart when she first sat at the table and spoke to him. Estelle suddenly looked at Al-Khidr, who was caught feeling mixed emotions.

"You all right there, bud? Something tells me you are jealous," she said, quite amused with herself. Al-Khidr was looking at her dumbfounded. He had no idea what to say at this moment. Instead, he was caught watching her affectionately. "Having second thoughts right now?" she exclaimed, confusing him even more.

"No second thoughts here. I am pleased to see that everyone here is so nice and cozy. I am rethinking delaying my other mission to outside of Cairo. Perhaps I can stay here for a while. The French are not bad people, to be honest. But some ruffians on the streets will

Chapter 6. The Blinking

murder you for some extra coins," he stated thoughtfully.

"Well, don't change the subject, man. That look on your face said something. It spoke volumes. That one look told me so much more about you than up on the roof," she said staunchly. Al-Khidr wished a giant hole would swallow him into the ground. He was trapped by his own doing. Estelle raised her eyebrow, waiting for an answer from him. He looked at his feet and thought curse you, Estelle. Curse you. Vivant, who was about to leave, suddenly took a new found interest in the conversation. He waited with bated breath just to see how this would unfold. Al-Khidr noticed Vivant leaning in to listen.

"Come with me, Estelle. I need to say something privately. Too many people here." Al-Khidr exclaimed sheepishly. Estelle stood right away. It was as if she was waiting for this moment to come. She had barely known him for an hour, but there was something about this primitive man from Cairo. He was hiding something. They briskly walked under the moonlight, both thinking very different things. He turned to her and took her hand in his.

"I swear to God, what I am telling you is the truth. Nothing but the truth. Maybe you can understand someday," he remarked solemnly. Estelle smiled sweetly, thinking that is was nice that he was honest about his intentions. However, she had a wild thought: what if he was ready to live with her in France? "I like this girl a lot even though she lives very far from here.

But the thing is, you are as extraordinary just like her. I wish I could pick from one of you. It is difficult for me to decide," he exclaimed timidly.

Estelle smiled and patted his arm. Then, she looked at the moon and said, "I like you a lot. I wish there was another way. Perhaps if I met you earlier, we could have been together, you and me. I am still amazed that you can speak French so effortlessly," she exclaimed, smiling coyly. Al-Khidr was still racking his brain for a response that he could use to avail an open invitation like this. He was, however, left speechless. Thankfully, Estelle came to his rescue. "No worries. Maybe I can tag along as a friend and live with your people. I don't know where you are going right now, but maybe something can work out," she stated cleverly.

Al-Khidr thought that Estelle was not a bad person. He could take her to Lyra and she could have a life there, a better one and a more sophisticated one at that. This was something he could do, probably, and Nefertiti would not bat an eye. A decision was becoming evident on Al-Khidr's face, and Estelle could see that. "We could be friends if not anything else," she exclaimed optimistically, holding his hands.

This time, Al-Khidr also held hands with the young and beautiful woman. She bent forward to kiss him. It happened so fast and Al-Khidr was not ready for it. He longed for the French girl but... he could not do it. He thought about Nefertiti.

They separated from each other, still looking into

Chapter 6. The Blinking

each other's eyes. "In our culture, a kiss is a sign of love and affection. So you should not feel bad or anything," she explained her gesture to him. Al-Khidr nodded in agreement, feeling unfaithful to Nefertiti. Vivant was watching, sitting down. He had nothing much to do as the evening wind blew in his face. Nevertheless, he predicted something like this would happen. It was Estelle; the young woman would fall for any and every foreigner she would see. After her divorce from André, she became a loose cannon.

Vivant could recall and felt frightened by the previous events as they had unfolded. As a friend of her father, Jacquous Molière, Vivant took a special interest in her love life. Unfortunately, poor Jacquous Molière was no longer alive, so Vivant felt obliged to intervene. Estelle could not judge people as he could, which is why elder supervision was of paramount importance. Her previous fling did not seem like a monster in the beginning. She met a princely young man in Marseilles who promised her a child and a blissful ride into the sunset. However, Jacquous could see the warning signs in him way before Estelle could.

Vivant took Estelle aside to explain the possible damage she was causing to herself. Estelle looked like a different person to him at the time. He remembered that her father had beat up a boy once for rude behavior with Estelle. Unfortunately, it only resulted in Estelle straying away from her father, who was her only known relative at the time.

André was a charming lad; Vivant would give him

that. Vivant, a chatty person himself, found a lot to talk about with André. The way he talked, walked, and his mannerisms made him quite likable. Even the local bartenders liked him. Drinks were on the house most of the time, and André would talk people into doing the things he wanted. The world was convinced that he was a harmless, well-intentioned guy.

Estelle, much younger than André, fell head over heels for him. They had met at a tavern on a lazy Friday evening; Estelle was crying after a guy who had stood her up on their first date. André saw her and felt terrible for the young girl, so he moved in to make her feel better. The two got to talking, and before Andr knew it, Estelle invited him to his house.

André became a very private person after he moved in with her. She was not allowed to see her friends nor talk with them. If she wanted to talk to someone, André would be standing nearby with a spatula in his hands. Estelle was taught lessons by him in the manner of informing him of her whereabouts. Estelle could not see that André was choosing to keep people at some distance. Her life was her life, after all.

To her, the definition of abuse was not clear. When you are in love blindly, things always become clear when it is too late. Vivant would often come around to visit and Estelle would refuse to open the door and hid her face behind the curtains. Jacquous did not like the secrecy and red flags. Jacquous asked Vivant's advice, and this is how Vivant become a guardian of sorts for Estelle, in absentia of her father. Vivant's face

Chapter 6. The Blinking

darkened at the thought of André and their relationship. He could recall that he and Jacquous dragged him by the collar and beat him outside of his house. The neighbors looked from their windows as Vivant and Jacquous beat Andr to an inch of his death.

"Never ever see this girl again, or I will kill you! Is that understood?" Vivant said through gritted teeth.

André slowly nodded his head, half-conscious after the beating. Blood gushed from his mouth, but Jacquous threw him on the sidewalk nevertheless; maybe someone would take him to the hospital. Jacquous fought an urge to crush his windpipe as André lay on the sidewalk, gushing blood and gasping for air. However, he looked at Estelle and felt bad; he was not a monster. He left André, took Estelle, and walked away from the neighborhood.

Vivant snapped back to reality. Estelle was still talking to Al-Khidr in the distance. Never again would Vivant let Estelle out of his sight.

The two were laughing while talking. Vivant stood up as it was time to leave. "Hey, where are you going? We have a few hours to go before leaving, so have some more of this qahva," Nicolas exclaimed. Vivant looked disdainfully towards Nicolas. The sight of his face repulsed him. He pretended not to hear him and decided to leave. Walking past Al-Khidr and Estelle, he grabbed her hand, forcing her to come with him. "Hey. What's gotten into you, man? We are talking here for a reason. What is wrong with you? Let go of my hand. Let go!" she protested.

He took her to a corner, out of earshot from Al-Khidr, and said, "What do you think you're doing with him?" Estelle looked at him with scorn. What was this question? Who was he to ask this anyway? "Excuse me. Who are you? I am returning to France after Napoleon signs my approval. I thought we had established that already," she stated sternly. Vivant knew the first line of defense. "And you wish to take him with you? You don't know this kid, just like Andr. I am worried about you, Estelle. I promised Jacquous that I take care of you," his tone turned serious.

Estelle's face turned white like a sheet. How dare he bring that up? He still remembered the disaster after so many years.

"That was an honest mistake, Vivant. It will never happen again. Al-Khidr does not seem that type. He is sweet and nice," she exclaimed with her voice shaking. Vivant raised his eyebrows. How was that different from the last time? "And was André neither of those? Need I remind you that everyone likes André to this day? I am the bad guy in the city after beating him to an inch of his life," he exclaimed, the anger rising in his voice. Estelle could recall the events of that day. Back then, with her legs shaking, she walked down the stairs out of the house, leaving André. The French police came on their horses later in the day. They were wondering who had left the boy there on the sidewalk. Upon asking the neighbors and with affirmation from André, Vivant was thrown into jail for assault.

Chapter 6. The Blinking

***

Vivant left, still muttering things under his breath. *That conversation did not go well*, Al-Khidr thought. He stared at the moonlight to appreciate its beauty. What were they talking about? Was it something about him or an issue that he did not need to know about? He was scratching his head when Estelle came up to him. "Are you all right? You seem worried," she asked, patting his arm.

Al-Khidr was taken aback with this gesture. "You are asking this question? Weren't you and Vivant arguing about something back there? Can I ask what it was about? Maybe it was something private. You can keep it to yourself," he offered, sounding nosy. Estelle smiled at this. The boy wanted to know if they were talking about him. "I have always been a caring person. I could see your curiosity when Vivant and I were arguing; the concern on your face was apparent. But yes, we were talking about you. Vivant was cautioning me; he did not want me to get romantically involved with you, or consequences could be severe like last time. I thought he was a bit scared. That is all," she explained, revealing everything.

Al-Khidr considered what she said for a moment. This was fair advice as far as he was concerned. Al-Khidr was, after all, not entirely honest with Estelle about his real mission on this planet. He was also not ready to talk about Nefertiti; not right now. He thought that Estelle was ready to leave if he could persuade her. "I think he is right about that. You have known me for a few hours or so. How can you think of getting romantically involved with me? Also, that is another matter. You need to know me and how I live. My life is very different from the people in France, even though my mother was French," he remarked, not disclosing the intricate details. Estelle raised an eyebrow, although she understood what he meant by that.

"Yes. I know. The clash of cultures and ideologies is something she had to understand. I feel you are a sweet girl and your culture is much more open than mine. But please do keep some distance," Al-Khidr stated. Estelle started to laugh and stopped the conversation. "Well, I have to sleep, it's getting late. Walk me back to the institute?" she asked.

"Wait. You have no idea where the institute is?" he asked in surprise.

"Well, perhaps we can talk for a while. I don't like walking alone in the middle of the night," she became a little defensive. Al-Khidr started to laugh, indicating that it was a joke. Estelle smiled at that. "God. You scared me there," she said while chuckling.

"I know I did. Yes, I will walk you to the institute," he exclaimed laughingly.

They proceeded towards the institute, holding hands. Estelle told him that he shouldn't worry about finding a place as Vivant made arrangements for Al-Khidr to spend the night in a comfortable bed. To Vivant, he was a guest, and he had everything under control; the

Chapter 6. The Blinking

food, the bed, and everything else was taken care of. Estelle said that all Al-Khidr had to do was not make Vivant angry. Al-Khidr laughed at this. "Why else would I not be romantically involved with you?" he exclaimed snidely.

Chapter 7

The Requiem on Doom

HATATHOR sat on the sandy floor looking towards the Mediterranean Sea. His eyes were sobbing, and he was still not sure what on Earth he was doing on this planet? The destiny has catapulted him from Lyra to this planet of doom.

"I am on Earth, father! You are lying here in this sand". He took sand in his fist and viewed it slipping down from his hand—like a hope!

Chapter 7. The Requiem on Doom

"Hathor has already paid for her sins and now it's Ehsis's turn. It's God's wish, father. He wants me to breach Ehsis belly as I did with her friend." Hatathor was burning in a rage and talking to himself like as if he was talking to his father's ghost.

He stood up and started walking along the shore. The waves of sea, the chirping birds were all creating a musical cacophony like a requiem on his doom. He was silent, lost between the worlds. Just walking towards unknown.

A swarm of insects fell to the ground. Hatathor realized, but he continued walking.

He walked for half an hour when his device beeped. 'Nekhen (Hostile enemy),' the device announced in Lyrian tone.

A couple of hounds stumbled on his route. They stared and howled at him at a distance of 10 meters. Hatathor didn't grasp that he going towards the four-legged animals. "Sekhi Khaku abaqer! (Repel despicable dogs!)," he shouted.

"Go away or I make a garland of your intestines around my neck!" Hatathor growled like a dog.

Suddenly, he realized his clothes were falling off like dried leaves from the dead dilapidated tree.

He braced for an attack. A single punch was enough to knock them out. However, he didn't want to touch them. The dogs approached him with gritted teeth. He raised his fists to strike when the biggest among of them neared. His teeth were wide open.

The dogs started wheezing heavily as they neared

Hatathor. They dropped to the ground while coughing for a few seconds. It appeared as if they forgot Hatathor was there. Finally, the dogs strolled to a distance, where they felt slightly better. Hatathor examined the developing scene. The dogs were getting sick when they approached him.

As he watched with mixed amusement, the dogs disappeared into the distance. *'Something made them sick,'* he wondered.

He activated the sleeve-device again.

"Give me measure of radiation levels!"

"Radiation levels around 56.77.90 dgt detected, but not hazardous for Lyrians," the device announced in Lyrians units.

Hatathor guessed right. The creatures of this planet cannot sustain certain radiation levels. Their threshold is low.

"Ha, ha, ha," his laugh mixed with sea waves.

Hatathor walked further down the side of seashore when he saw three men talking to each other. They were French military surveyors and were measuring something using theodolite. One of them nudged the rest to observe the naked man walking aimlessly.

"He does not look Egyptian to me. Should we ask him where he is going? He could be a spy for the Ottoman forces," the soldier remarked anxiously. Hatathor noticed the three men looking at him, busy with their discussion. He saw them come near him at a reasonable pace. However, they too dropped on the ground like the dogs before.

Chapter 7. The Requiem on Doom

One soldier held his stomach, trying to control his vomit. He spilled his insides, staring at Hatathor with horror and confusion. Another soldier fainted when he neared him. The third soldier raised his baïonnette, but he didn't dare to come near to Hatathor. He had seen enough already. Hatathor did not recognize this weapon. But if a soldier carried it, it didn't bode well for Hatathor.

Hatathor ordered to sleeve weapon:

"*Kheper qenu Bennt!* (Create fiery sphere!)"

The sleeve weapon responded: "*Qenu kamtcharna, khebt aati* (Armor field activated, destroy your enemies)!" Menkht Sekhem—the sleeve weapon directed.

The soldier took time to prepare his Baïonnette for approaching Hatathor. He fired shots while moving backward, but nothing happened. He fired again, emptying his chamber on Hatathor, who was standing right in front of some hemisphere of energy—a protective shield made from his sleeve weapon.

He stared at the bullets lying on the ground—a puff of smoke emerged from them. He picked up the bullets for analysis, but got distracted by the soldiers running away from him.

After abandoning the fainted soldier, he sped across the sand to grab the other two. The super strength and speed of Hatathor were too much for them. The French were hardly accustomed to the scorching weather of Egypt. Breathless, they aimed to reach the city limits to call for backup. As things stood, Hatathor leisurely grabbed them by their collars.

Snap.

He broke the neck of one soldier, who dropped to the ground like a rag-doll. The second soldier was moving away in horror from Hatathor. Hatathor stood there laughing. One thing was clear, the humans of this planet were feeble. The Lyrians were a far stronger race. The second soldier was still running. Hatathor laughed at the sight—poor bloke. It was pointless escaping him. He ran a few steps and caught the fleeing soldier. Grabbing him, he threw him several feet away. The soldier hit the sand with a thud. He tried to stand up but was a bit shaken up. Hatathor grabbed him by the collar and threw him again.

Splat!

Hatathor was caught by surprise. The soldier's head smashed against a big rock in the distance. His body was lying separated from his head. A mixture of meat and bones greeted the sight.

This happened, he thought. He looked at the other soldier lying lifelessly on the sand and headed towards the east. However, after a while, he stopped and thought for a moment. He could not barge into the city walking like that.

He checked the uniform of the French soldiers. The half-fainted one was his height. The man sleepily opened his eyes, trying to comprehend the situation. "*Suh!* (Utter what you wanted to say)," Hatathor shouted in his language.

"Please don't kill me. I have children and a wife

Chapter 7. The Requiem on Doom

back in France. Please. Please. I am begging you," he pleaded with Hatathor. "*Mett* (foreign speech)," Menkht Sekhem announced.

Hatathor pressed some buttons on the sleeve-device and it sent necessary signals to his brain. He now could comprehend the language of these stupid creatures, thanks to the Lyrian technology.

"Haven't you figured it out already? Your friends are no longer alive. Look over there," he exclaimed, annoyingly. The soldier looked to his left, where his friend's head was smashed against the rock.

"Now look there," he ordered again.

The other soldier was lying with his neck twisted.

"I am solider of France. Napoleon will not spare...," Hatathor smashed his head meticulously.

"Hmm soldier! pity. I am a real solider and I need a uniform," Hatathor said to the dead French soldier.

The element of surprise was necessary if he were to complete his mission successfully. He reasoned that the sight of a soldier would easily ward off the attention from him and make things easier.

After feeling satisfied with his work, he moved towards the city. The rage taking a backseat; he thought about the challenges and tribulations ahead. "Curse Al-Khidr, the vermin. Curse his existence; I cannot believe I am in this mess," he seethed at no one in particular.

He thought a bit about Al-Khidr. *One feeble human changed everything on his planet. Thanks to him, he was on an alien planet, facing a tumultuous situ-*

ation. Ehsis and Queen Hathor took a liking to him. The human, a convict, was liked by these two. He wondered why there was love for him? Was he any less of a Lyra citizen than others? His mind wandered to the peaceful life he was living before Al-Khidr arrived.

The uniform that he put on stank of human body sweat, he thought. God, the soldiers didn't take a bath. He made a mental note to have the clothes washed someway. The shoes were hurting him. After the killing, he stole the shoes to prevent the scorching sand from hurting his feet. The weather of this planet was unrelenting and completely different from Lyra.

The human arrived before me on Keb, that means he must have another sphere with him, as he might go back to Lyra using the same sphere. I should stop him or snatch sphere from him, he thought.

"Wait till I get my hands on that sphere. Then, I will hightail out of here. Al-Khidr can stay here for all I care. Ugh, cursed planet," he muttered again. "I still have my military-grade sleeve-weapon, equipped with a superfood compartment," he stated with a bit of relief. "I just need the tracking device to grab that sphere from him. Then I am ready," he reiterated.

***

After walking some time, he sat for a while at coast and then lay down on the sand. Unintentionally, he drifted into sleep. He was tired because of inter-galactic jump and combat he had.

CHAPTER 7. THE REQUIEM ON DOOM

When he woke up, he found flies buzzing over him. He quickly sat and found a circle around him. The dead bodies of insects were piled up around him. *These bugs must have died because of radiation, but why so many? Have I overslept?* he thought further.

He realized he was sleeping for almost a length of Lyrian day; oblivious to what was happening in his surroundings. It was now second day since he had arrived on the planet Keb.

He pressed few buttons and started the counter to count the day-length.

"I need to energize myself," he said to himself.

He checked the superfoods to see if he had one. Luckily, he had the military grade food inside his sleeve. He took out the Akh Seshkhat superfood bottle from a hidden compartment in the sleeve-weapon. It contained a green viscous paste, much like earthly Mumio. He inspected the amount. "With this much superfood I can stay here 470 days," he roughly estimated.

He took a chickpea size from it and threw the ball into his mouth.

Akh Seshkhat (Green superfood), enough for the entire day, hopefully, he thought.

He measured and found that his radiation levels were also diminished in two days.

He stood up and turned the tracking device on. Tracking was an add-on feature in his sleeve-weapon, the Menkht Sekhem. The two were brought together solely because of ergonomics, however they both have a different power arrangement. The tracking equipment charging was actually designed for Vega-lights, and it was running great in Lyra. However, he noticed that tracking unit's display panel had become dim whenever clouds come over sun.

"What the heck is wrong with it?" he asked himself. The thing looked dead.

Either it could be because of electromagnetic surges during the inter-galactic jump that the battery storage capacity is affected, or it's that the direct radiation from the sun is much lower than that of Vega. He thought about potential issues.

He continued to walk, thinking about his now-defunct tracking device. It beeped.

When he walked under the open sun, the panel of tracking-device kick-started immediately. Hatathor waited for a while until the device resumed its default setting. 'User: General Hatathor,' the device announced.

There you go; everything is back to normal. The tracking device charged itself. However, he noticed that the charging process was way slower on Keb than on Lyra. He continued walking along the shore until he could see the boats in sea. The human men here were mostly fishers searching for their daily catch. They talked with each other as Hatathor walked past the shore.

I need a boat; now, but how will I pass through this? He thought. His time at the military academy made him learn how to swim. However, he recalled that water was salty and fouled on this planet.

Chapter 7. The Requiem on Doom

He discarded the idea of swimming and continued waking along the coast. He stared at tracking-unit and said: "*Agem Khena!* (Locate the prisoner!)"

It pointed at Al-Khidr in the east, still moving in a linear direction.

"*Khena gi en reg!* (Prisoner is moving!)" device announced.

"Damn it; I need to move fast."

He looked at three boats lined up along the coast. All belong to one family. One teenager came running at him. "Do you want to go somewhere?" he asked, smiling widely. "*Mett* (foreign speech)," the Lyrian device announced. Hatathor looked at the teenager, who was surprised to see a non-white solider in French uniform. He looked like a giant compared to the Arab and French people. The boy was wondering as though he was wearing an oddly fitted French uniform; he looked nothing like a French soldier though. They were white, while his skin tone was more reddish in comparison. Hatathor couldn't understand as device took time to translate from Arabic. But he jumped into the boat.

"Where you wanted to go, French solider?" the human asked.

"Towards east to the nearest city?" Hatathor said.

"Three Dirhams. Only new ones, issued by French. You must pay first," the father of teenager said.

Hatathor could not understand the word dirham. He looked at Menkht Sekhem's panel for help, but the device has no information on word dirham. The human took out a coin from his pockets and showed it to Hatathor.

Strange way of transactions! He thought.

Hatathor said to felucca boat-owner: "I will pay you when I reach the land. I don't have dirham now."

The man pointed at the sea. "Just jump now. I don't want non-paying customers on my felucca," he said, annoyingly.

"Who will make me?" Hatathor stated with a grim smile.

The old-man took out his knife and said: "Disgusting French army. Wallah! (by God), you took our land but you cannot take my boat!" the old Egyptian man become too furious.

Seriously? A piece of metal that small?

The old-man tried to stab Hatathor with the knife, but lost his balance. Hatathor lazily snatched the blade from the old man and put it at his throat. His son came forward and said: "Spare my father, please!"

Hatathor looked at him, and his intentions changed.

"I lost my father when I was of your age," Hatathor said to the teenager and released his old father, who was powerless in front of Hatathor, and fell on the boat floor.

The boy and his father are now slaves of Hatathor.

Hatathor sat on the edge of the boat, waiting for land to arrive. The boat gave him a clear assessment of how weak these humans were. The old-man and his son were using a boat-paddle to propel the boat forward. Hatathor cannot help, as he was not trained for

Chapter 7. The Requiem on Doom

propelling boat in this way. "How primitive!" he said in Lyrian, recalling the technology he was accustomed to.

Hatathor regretted his decision about boat-travel. He could have covered much longer distance by simply walking along the shore. It took him several hours to reach the port of Al-Iskandriyah (Alexandria). It was close to sunset. Hatathor threw the knife at the frightened old-man, who caught it. Hatathor left them, as it was time to find Al-Khidr. His Maft-Shespt (jump-sphere) was gone, but Al-Khidr's could still have one, and he had to stop the prisoner. The twilight appeared on the horizon. The boats were returning to the shore.

He looked at the tracking-unit which showed that Al-Khidr was still moving around somewhere in east. Now, he was 6,157 Supris away from the prisoner. This distance is long but nevertheless I will reach you, prisoner!

***

Leaving the boat, Hatathor continued to walk inside the city, which humans were calling as Al-Iskandriyah (Alexandria). He was wearing the French uniform. Arab men and the women gave him weird, scornful looks as he passed them in the bazaar.

Wow, I am not very well-liked here. Is it me or the uniform? he thought to himself.

Some women were in veils, and some were having no veils. It was also a puzzle for him.

Hatathor continued to look around and observe the culture of this new planet. It was an utterly dull way of life. The people had yet to see the spaceships, power plants, hovering vehicles, flying vehicles, cosmic-tunnels, and transportation-docks. The functional strength of these people was less—remarkably less. It would only take a quarter of the Lyrian army to take all the human beings as hostage.

Nutiuo! (Primitive natives!)

He looked into his tracking unit. Damn, it is down again!

The sun was already setting. He had to wait till morning in this city, but where he can hide? He was in a spoiled mood.

The night was vibrant in Alexandria. The streets were lit up with flame torches and large glass chandeliers holding candles. People were enjoying their Shisha time, throwing fumes into air, and it was mixing with the smoke which was rising from the hot coal whenever the meaty kababs juice dripped over them.

There were many people on the streets with different skin tones, a variety of dialects, and languages. There was an indistinct chatter all around him.

Some of the drunkard French soldiers called him greetings, some called him to hang around with them to chat about European politics. However, Hatathor moved on without looking at them. It was possible that the soldiers didn't recognize him and asked him any further questions. It would lead to more challenges in finding Al-Khidr.

Chapter 7. The Requiem on Doom

"Weird guy. His skin tone is not white," one drunkard French soldier muttered.

"I did not see this soldier on the ship. But man, he is tall!" the other said, who was wearing a uniform drenched in wine.

Hatathor could understand these conversations and he has to think fast. He needed to get rid of the military uniform fast and blend in with the crowd. Most people wore a flowing dress that extended to their feet. With his reddish skin color, he should wear something that people could easily forget. He passed by a coffee shop—the enticing aroma of the Al-Qahva (Coffee) beans almost made him enter the shop. However, he stopped himself, as the plants from this planet could be poisonous to him. I can't do that!

***

While he was standing there, he was thinking about where to spend the night; he saw a man with moustache approaching him.

The man thought that Hatathor was a French guy because of his uniform. He came near and whispered into his ear: "Salute *Bonghjornu,* my French friend. I have virgins for your entertainment. Only 10 dirhams for each!"

Suddenly, it started raining hard. It was a thunderstorm. They ran for a shelter. Within a few minutes, it was rain water everywhere. The streets were all converted into channels.

Hatathor was not expecting such a situation. He wanted to stay inside for a few hours, as most likely thunderstorm would have been over by then. The man asked Hatathor to follow him and led him to a dark small alley. He advised him to climb up the stairs, and Hatathor followed him. When Hatathor entered the room, the man introduced him to the brothel manager. She was a chubby-fat woman with revealing cleavage, lying on lectus at the end of the room. She was enjoying her evening *shisha* and puffing off intermittent vortex rings of smoke. The curtains on the windows were fluttering because of thunderstorm winds and the smoke from shisa and incense was whirling inside.

The manger glanced at two ladies and with a frown of her eyebrow directed one of them to call others. One of them stood up, smiled, and looked at Hatathor. She called others and a bunch of ladies came out from the rooms and stared at the tall and sturdy Hatathor, who's clothes were now all wet. Smiles and sounds began oozing from their mouths.

Hatathor said: "I only need few hours to stay..."

But before he could complete his sentence, the man said something while opening his arms. Three ladies obliged and took him inside a room. "What is happening?" Hatathor was confused.

The ladies were immersed in a fragrant perfume, sufficient to bewitch the olfactory senses of the newly arrived Lyrian warrior. They locked the room and removed their dresses. Then they took off his uniform and his sleeve-weapon as well and pushed him onto the

Chapter 7. The Requiem on Doom

bed. The sleeve-weapon beeped and issued warnings, but Hatathor ignored all. The ladies giggled as they found Lyrian language funny.

They want to have *setcherit* (pleasure) with me! He assessed the condition in Lyrian manner.

When he was done with three of them and his climax waned, he realized that two ladies were unconscious and the last one was dead. Hmm, was it exhaustive for them? he was confused.

He pushed the dead off the bed, took his sleeve-weapon, and hurriedly got out of the chamber. He saw the man and other women looking at him with a puzzled face. Hatathor pointed at the room. The men entered the chamber, and then screamingly came after Hatathor, who was about to leave the house. Hatathor felt something sharp had penetrated his back. He turned around to see the man staring at him with a dagger. The Lyrian kind of blood was dripping down from the dagger. Hatathor got furious, and he killed the man with one punch, who flew in air and crashed into the wall.

The wave of screams and ululations filled the brothel. Because of thunderstorm no one outside noticed the shrieks of the women, but, unfortunately, the situation was getting worse. The women in the lobby fled in horror into the rooms inside to save themselves. They were now really afraid and silent.

Hatathor was naked. He found it the right opportunity to take off the dead man's clothes for himself. He quickly put on the jalabiya and left the brothel with his sleeve-weapon.

Hatathor fled the scene, fearing more unnecessary attention.

"Never, ever, remove the Menkht Sekhem," Hatathor said to himself. He had learned the lesson. Not only would the soldiers find out about his true origin, but also about the people. He had to find Al-Khidr quickly.

Chapter 8

The Visit

Al-Khidr slept peacefully throughout the night. He had weird dreams about the French soldiers fighting tooth and nail with the Egyptian rebels. More weirdness followed as he stabbed an arrow into Vivant's heart. He crumbled to the ground, holding his chest to stop the bleeding.

He saw Estelle from up on the balcony. She was wailing and cursing Al-Khidr for killing the only family friend she had.

Chapter 8. The Visit

"How could you, Al-Khidr? He was like a friend and father to me? You killed my family— you killed my family. Where will I go? What will I do?" she screamed at him.

Al-Khidr just shrugged and began fighting more French soldiers. There was no way in hell that the French troops were invading. He punched a soldier pretty hard. "Ouch," remarked a familiar voice. He heard this voice somewhere.

Vivant was standing right beside him with Estelle. They looked worried to see him. However, the most interesting part was that his hand was caught in mid-air by Vivant.

"Are you all right, Monsieur?" He asked.

Al-Khidr was too confused to answer the question. He was looking at his hand when Estelle broke the silence.

"It seems you had a bad dream. So, Vivant and I came to wake you up. He touched you, and your clenched fist came right up. I was scared that perhaps you planned this after last night," she exclaimed. Al-Khidr was still looking at the two people, dumbfounded.

"I had a weird dream." He hesitated.

"I want you to join us at the breakfast table. This is a special menu I have lined up today. I am sure you will like it. Get ready!" He exclaimed and turned around to leave his room.

Estelle sat beside him, patting his shoulder.

"It is okay. You are going through a lot. Vivant does not mind. Clearly, coming to the city amid chaos, making new friends, and dealing with your own trauma is a lot to deal with," she exclaimed in an understanding manner.

She bent closer to Al-Khidr. Her hair was falling on him—she was eerily closer to him. Al-Khidr held her head, but she leaned closer—their lips were about to caress.

It happened! He pulled away from her.

"No. This doesn't seem right. I am with another woman. I'm afraid that's not right and dishonest." He said.

Estelle was looking at him and burst out laughing.

"Come on. Kissing does not mean you are cheating on someone else. I guess in France, that is not the case," she lied.

The weird explanation disgruntled Al-Khidr.

She smiled inside; he would not know.

"Say, your mom was French, right? She did not tell you that? We, French, are very open-minded people." She exclaimed cheekily.

"Hey, don't be so mad at me!" Al-Khidr said.

Estelle looked at him and smiled.

"You are fine. You are just a product of your culture; that is all. I thought you would be different," she exclaimed dismissively. Al-Khidr leaped out of his bed to stand up.

"What are you talking about?" he asked her, still feeling sleepy.

She shrugged and left his room, leaving him stand-

Chapter 8. The Visit

ing there wondering about her change in attitude. He came out half an hour later wearing clothes and smelling nice. The table was all set with a wonderful breakfast. However, most items on the menu were new to him. He looked at it in shock, failing to differentiate one thing from the other.

This was a weird breakfast table. It was more like the food he saw on planet Lyra.

He sat down and enjoyed the breakfast.

"Say, Al-Khidr, what is your plan for today? I have practically nothing to do. I have seen the bazaars and the hawkers selling animals and milk. Can you show me some interesting places inside Egypt? I would just love to explore the natural landscape here," she stated, putting her hand on her heart. Al-Khidr was quick to respond without looking at Vivant.

"Yes, you can join me. I am looking for some unique plants to cure a disease. The disease was once an epidemic in Egypt, so I need to find a cure," he exclaimed lazily.

Vivant was staring at both of them.

"Well, this is really not my area of interest. I would rather have you show me local beers and wines. One can always try them and save them for France," he offered his idea.

Al-Khidr was dismayed by that.

"Unfortunately, I am against drinking. My religion forbids me from any intoxicants. I can take you to the Greek Christian shops where they sell it. I saw many Greek Christian grocers who opened several taverns for selling alcoholic beverages, such as wine, arrack as well as coffee. But I will not take any part in drinking alcohol," he fabricated some ideas, as he was not well aware of all these places.

Estelle shook her head; this person was very unexciting.

Vivant was not impressed by that answer, although he was always diplomatic.

"Well I will come along for beer hopping. I am looking for something local and strong!" He exclaimed laughingly.

By now, Al-Khidr began enjoying himself with Estelle. She slid her hand in his hand, pressing it firmly. Finally, Estelle stood up and announced her plans for the day. "Okay, everyone. Al-Khidr and I have to leave to search for something. It could take an entire day or half, depending on how much I can survive in this heat," she remarked.

She grabbed his hand, and the two went out of the dining hall back to his room. "I will be back soon. Just wait in your room," she stated confidently and slammed the door in his face.

Al-Khidr did as he was told.

How long is she going to take? Al-Khidr was less aware of the needs of a new woman on Earth, so naturally, he thought Estelle would be out in a jiffy. Al-Khidr stood there like a patient boy waiting for her. It would be half an hour before Estelle was out. He looked at her. She looked adorable today.

She was wearing a new dress that Al-Khidr had

Chapter 8. The Visit

not seen. She wore a tight dress around her chest, but it went down like a fountain from her waist. It was so elegant, with all the white frills around the collar and sleeves. She looked ethereal as the light peach dress complimented her skin. The sight was so mesmerizing that Al-Khidr stared at her with his mouth wide open. Estelle noticed the impression she had created and burst out laughing. "Wait, a minute. I will be right back," she said sweetly.

She briskly walked back to her room and admired her own beauty. Well, here was a guy who had fallen head over heels for her. She laughed at the thought. Only if she could take the place of this mysterious girl he kept talking about. God! She dismissed the thoughts and came out of the room.

"Thank you, Al-Khidr. Your stunned look said more than you could on your own. Although in all honesty, you can find many beautiful girls like me in France—I wish I could take you to France. But why can't you and that girl come with me to France? You can always return to Egypt or wherever she comes from," she suggested, smiling. Al-Khidr found the offer too tempting to resist. But he had things to do and places to be. Maybe he could talk to people on Lyra and make it happen. But his success depended on his bringing back the herbal medicine from Keb to Lyra. They could surely grant a favor of this sort. Estelle saw the changing colors on his face. He was considering the idea. She picked up her stick.

"Let's go. The afternoon will be boiling. We have

to return before that," she said seriously this time.

"Right. I totally forgot about that trip we have to take," he said, laughing.

Estelle shook her head. The man was still lost in her beauty. She had infatuated him. They walked outside Institut d'gypte with Estelle.

"Where are we going, Estelle? I do not know where to look. The landscape of Egypt has changed since I last came here. It seems the soil and riverbed have also changed directions. I cannot remember the river flowing in this direction," he said without thinking.

He realized his mistake. Maybe he had spoken a bit much in front of Estelle, who would suspect there was more to his story than he let on. Fortunately, Estelle had stuff on her mind as she had missed out on the brief monologue by Al-Khidr. She was staring ahead.

"Estelle!" he said a bit loudly, forcing her to come out of her absent-mindedness.

"Sorry. I was lost in a world of my own. You were asking me something?" she said.

Al-Khidr reiterated the previous question. She smiled at that.

"Oh. I am taking you to my friend Luca's place. He also likes herbs and plants. In the past few months, we have collected some variations of the plant life over here. Lucas studies these plants and the potential qualities they have. I envy him, as he can speak and write a little Arabic too and has collected many manuscripts," she said flatly.

He nodded at that. That was an excellent suggestion—

Chapter 8. The Visit

he had lost track of the plant life in Egypt. Some species were new to him when he returned to Keb. It was a gap of roughly ten centuries, after all.

"That is a good idea. I will brush up on my plant knowledge," he said.

"Good boy. And I will draw these plants to create a collection of plant life in Egypt for my research work in France," she said, smiling. Estelle and Al-Khidr reached the garden of her friend. His eyes opened wide. It was huge with birds flying. He could vaguely remember the last time he lived in Egypt. Some of the local farm-bred animals were roaming as well.

"What kind of garden is that, Estelle?" he asked her.

She laughed at the question, but she could tell that he was taking in all of this right now.

"Oh. I am sorry. I did not tell you this before. This garden is not your average garden with vegetables and fruits. Lucas collected many plant species here. Maybe you can find the plant here that you were looking for," she suggested.

He nodded and looked around the plant section of the garden. Without saying much, he went there and examined the plant life. Estelle followed him with the pen and notepad, ready to take notes. *This would be interesting*, she thought.

"Let me check on Lucas. I guess he is still sleeping!" she said and went to the door of the house in front of which this garden was. Al-Khidr was busy inspecting the plants. But he had problems with plants identifications. As an alchemist, he worked mostly with extracted tinctures, essential oils, salts, acids, etc. He knew the extractions and distillation processes, but he had never worked in herbs identifications. However, he was sure that once he gets the book 'Dying Animals' he will figure out the right herbs.

Estelle was back.

"Lucas is not opening the door. Either he is not at home, or he took alcohol last night."

Al-Khidr examined some of the plants, walking past the new flowers and leaves that were quite longish.

"Wow. This is strange. New plants that I cannot recall when I used to live here," he remarked.

Estelle raised her eyebrow. "What do you mean when you lived here? How long were you gone from Egypt? Was it a hundred or two hundred years? Don't tell me you are immortal, man. You are scaring me," she said, laughing.

Al-Khidr realized he had made another blunder. Too much information about his background would lead to his capture into prison and no way out. The French soldiers would say that the boy was full of made-up shit. At that point, Vivant or Estelle could not save him from capture and torture. They were intellectuals and wielded less influence on Napoleon for releasing alleged spies. Though Vivant was less inclined to help him, he thought. Estelle saw the darkened expression on his face and came to his rescue.

"Don't worry, man. Your secret is safe with me. You can tell me when you are ready. Right now, trust

Chapter 8. The Visit

me and let's do this thing we were doing," she said, patting his shoulder.

That comforted him a bit. He would reveal his intention and reason for the visit to Keb once everything was okay. It was too early to say anything. "Estelle. I have a problem over here. The plants I see here are not suitable for medicines. I will head to the rugged areas of Egypt to find those plants. This is a waste of time for me," he said in irritation.

Estelle turned somber.

"Relax. Relax. Relax. Why, in a sudden hurry? No one is going to arrest you as long as you are with me. I came here just to explore the garden and enjoy the scenery with you. Is that too much to ask?" she asked sadly.

He nodded, but relaxed as well.

"Maybe we go out in the bazaar and look for some old bookseller and search for the manuscripts on herbs?" she suggested, "as now you want a book instead of plants. But that is another good idea," Estelle brightened at that, "And it would be wonderful. I will finally see where you live and keeping this place secret? Is it on this planet?" she tested the waters.

Al-Khidr thought about what to say when the door of the house opened, and a young man appeared.

He looked smart and cultured enough. He was a French guy and looked great.

"Bonjour! Finally, you woke up!" Estelle said to Lucas.

"I thought you were not at home. We were about

to leave," she snapped. "Sorry, Estelle," Lucas said as if he was tired and yawned a bit.

"I didn't expect you at this hour. I thought the gardener arrived, and he was unnecessarily banging the door. So how is it going? How is Monsieur Denon?" he asked lazily.

"All fine. I just want to bring Al-Khidr here. He is an alchemist looking for some particular herbs. Sometimes he says herbs, sometimes books. I guess you can help him out,"

She turned to Al-Khidr.

"Meet Lucas. He is the guy who did this all. You two can talk. I will just check some fruits. I'll be right back," she said and went towards the trees. Al-Khidr and Lucas shook hands and smiled at each other.

"You are an alchemist?" Lucas excitedly asked.

"Yes, I am," Al-Khidr said.

"Wonderful. You are an alchemist and an Arab. I guess you are God-sent. I was looking for some translations. You are looking for a plant of a specific variety. Tell me more about it," he said.

Al-Khidr nodded at this.

"Yes, God is forgiving and most merciful. It is in the darkest of times when he comes to us. It is in the moments of most desperation when we have no one to look for but God," Al-Khidr said and paused.

"Yes. I also believe that God has sent me for a purpose and spread goodness along the way. Maybe we met for a reason, and I will make sure to help you as much as I can," he said, further confidently.

Chapter 8. The Visit

The two shook hands again, having established some faith and understanding.

Al-Khidr nodded, and Lucas offered him a chair. They both sat and started talking.

At the far-end corner, they could see Estelle checking the fruits in the garden. She was examining a greenish mushroom and decided to pluck it. Lucas stood up in fright and shouted.

"Don't eat that. That is a poisonous mushroom. Do you want to die right here? I am working on something with this thing. I picked it from some bushes near the river. Leave that alone," he said loudly.

Estelle raised her hands, apologizing, and walked forward.

"I ain't touching anything here," she roared back. Lucas nodded.

"These girls are inquisitive. What would I say to Vivant if she had tasted it? It is the best natural poison I have found. A little of it is lethal for humans. It stops heartbeat and other vital organs in the body," he said, surprised himself.

Al-Khidr nodded, feeling scared at the thought of Estelle lying dead on the floor. The foamy, white liquid coming from her mouth would have reduced him to tears. "And here we go," he said, opening his journal on ancient plants and their families.

"This is my journal that I have compiled, though not that extensively, but just some parts of it. It was valuable in my research to map the plant life of the region. There are other sections that I have no expertise in, so that is beyond my scope. What are you looking for exactly?" he asked Al-Khidr. Al-Khidr thought for a bit before explaining.

"Well, it is a plant that I suspect could be extinct by now. It was prevalent maybe a thousand years back when the climate was different," he said, not convinced himself entirely.

The name escaped him at this point because so much had happened.

"Give me the book. I will see what I can find," Al-Khidr said. He did not wish to give his prime motive away to Lucas.

Al-Khidr saw that the first page of the manuscript was missing—he turned pages and pages to see the title but couldn't find it. He could see many plant types and their herbal properties as well.

"Dear God. Do help me find the herbs—the antidote to disease Mutmut. With your power, we will cure the diseased population," he prayed silently. He gave the book to Lucas, who was surprised that Al-Khidr had found what he was looking for so early.

"That was fast. You just needed the right book to help you out. I am glad I could help," Lucas said. "No, this is not the book I am looking for—besides that, the title is also missing. The one I am looking for is titled 'The Dying Animals' by some anonymous author. Some thought that it was Apocrypha. I believed that too, but now I want to recheck it," Al-Khidr said.

Lucas thought for a while and then said: "I have a manuscript which is in archaic Arabic script. I cannot

Chapter 8. The Visit

fathom it. Perhaps you can read it. Let me dig that up for you," Lucas said.

He went to a trunk and took out some manuscripts from it. He dusted it off.

"Well, I got these books after paying much money from the old bookseller in the bazaar. It was before the revolt. His shop was burned down. Unfortunately, he died too in a sniper attack," Lucas said with a sad face.

"See these books. The book's title is Book of Stones by Geber. You can read the name since it is your area of expertise," he said candidly. Al-Khidr read the author's name as Abu Musa Jabir Ibn Hayyan Al-Azdi. Al-Khidr could not recall the author Jabir since Jabirs date of birth and date of death were a few centuries after he had accidentally left Egypt and went to Lyra.

"No problem. I will help you out," Al-Khidr said, smiling.

Lucas was happy to learn that Al-Khidr knew the different writing scripts of Arabic.

"You know he is a famous alchemist. We are translating many of his works into European languages to read and understand. This book is kind of weird. I hope you can do something. We call him the father of modern alchemy. He has laid the foundation of many faculties all on his own," Lucas boasted proudly. Al-Khidr looked and nodded. He was on Lyra.

"Oh, yes. He is famous all right. I have not gotten around to reading his works. I should, though," he said without thinking. Lucas did not like the comment. "Come on, brother. We are studying his body of works. This is one of the many books currently translated by many westerners. But I am not thrilled with their translations," Lucas said.

And thus began Al-Khidr translating the voluminous book by the famous Muslim scientist who had died but left an indelible mark on the civilizations. "It's not that straightforward!" Al-Khidr said.

"You are an alchemist. I thought you could work this out easily," Lucas said, sounding dismayed. Al-Khidr regretted saying that. God! He wishes he had a foot in his mouth sometimes. He decided to ignore the comment and talk about the book more. "This is utmost odd. This book here seems to be written in a code of some sort. I cannot understand anything about it. It is Arabic, but none of it makes any sense. Are rest of the books like this as well?" he asked Lucas.

Lucas shook his head. "None of his other books are difficult to translate. They are rather easy to read since I can also read Arabic and have read his other books that are detailed treatises on Al-Chemia or chemistry. I have learned a lot. If you need to read any of his works and stuff like that, I can help you with that. Maybe you can work out something in your research," he said, smiling and nodded.

Lucas was a good guy. He could learn a lot about the advances made in modern alchemy. But unfortunately, he had a mission at hand and could not wait to leave Keb "That would not be necessary, but thanks.

Chapter 8. The Visit

I really like you and Estelle. You, Vivant, and she are talented people. I would certainly invite you later on. But I do not have the time or the luxury to read his works. I am doing something very important that I cannot wait. Maybe we can meet up later and talk about his works. I would like to see how we have progressed. I left the field temporarily because of some engagements. But a project has drawn me back into the field," he explained. Lucas nodded. Al-Khidr seemed like a friendly lad as well.

"I wish you the best of luck with the project. I hope I can get some help with the book here, Kitab Al Ahjar. Things are weirdly written in it," he said, changing the subject to his agenda.

Al-Khidr nodded and continued.

"This book is actually written in codes. I do not know how to crack this. Our famous scientist and chemist wanted things inside to remain a secret—a jealously guarded secret. I think we cannot go anywhere with this book," he said, handing it over to him. As he was about to hand the book to Lucas, something caught his attention. There was some inscription written in the book in small Arabic. He read the smallish inscription and was left surprised. "Look at this. Look at this. I am surprised that you have not read this before. It literally says that only the chosen few can unlock the mysteries. He says that a particular school is exalted in the highest knowledge can receive this information. Those men are sworn to secrecy by the Order of the School. The truth shall never get out," Al-Khidr finished reading.

They both looked at each other in silence. The boys were thinking the same thing. There was a school that taught this book in its entirety. As things stood, Lucas had to find this school that taught the coded book to students unknown.

"Wow. I did not bother to read the back of this book, like ever. Thanks a lot," he said, shaking his hand. Al-Khidr was secretly intrigued.

His life's work in alchemy and other fields left a lot to be desired. He wished that he could join forces with Lucas and join him in this hunt. What was this secret school, and what did they learn from the famed alchemist? He was thinking the same thing Lucas was at the moment. Intriguing, is it not?

Al-Khidr nodded. "Oh, here is another book here. You try to read what is written here. It has no Ashkaal (dots) on the words. I cannot read Arabic without the dots on alphabets," Lucas said.

Al-Khidr took the manuscript, and he couldn't believe his eyes.

"That's the book I am looking for all over!" he shouted with joy.

"Oh, you can read it!" Lucas was surprised that AL-Khidr can read the ancient Arabic script.

"The Dying Animals! This is the book that I need," he said.

Estelle had returned by now to see the boys lost in a world of their own.

Al-Khidr showed Estelle the ancient manuscript of

Chapter 8. The Visit

Dying Animals.

"Lucas had the book that I was looking for—it is a lucky day today!" Al-Khidr said. "Oh, really," Estelle laughingly said.

"Lucas has a treasure chest!" she said further. "Al-Khidr has given me a significant lead, too. I am thankful to him. It will help a lot. I know what to do," he beamed at him.

She laughed at that.

"I told you. He is full of surprises. I need to know more about him. He is not letting on how much he knows," she snapped. Lucas and Al-Khidr looked at each other, lost for words.

"I am just kidding. Al-Khidr is kind of shy and stuff. He will open up once you get to know more. He has promised to take me to these plants he was talking about," she said, smiling.

"Soon, we will set off for the plants," she assured Al-Khidr.

Al-Khidr thanked Lucas and went back to the institute.

Chapter 9

In Damanhur

Hатathor was running far from the brothel. The howling and ululation of the ladies was mixed with the loud thunderstorm. He did not want to become the talk of the town. He wanted to execute his plan with as little trouble as possible. Since his arrival on Keb, it had been a short time, yet somehow unintentional events surrounding him were making more noise than necessary.

Chapter 9. In Damanhur

Dear lord! What have I fallen into? He asked himself while running. He looked up at the sky. The night was still stormy and thunderous as he ran. He had to find a way to get out of sight as fast as possible. The brothel was lost in some far corner of the city as he jumped over wet carts and hawkers to flee the scene.

"I cannot jeopardize finding the prisoner," he told himself. Finding Al-Khidr was the key to return to Lyra. Whether dead or alive, he had to recover the time-space folding device from the human. The sphere was of paramount importance to Hatathor, who had lost his own sphere in the depths of the sea before coming here. That thing was his only get out card from this planet. Frankly, his military training came in handy this time around. His stealth and speed on the move proved helpful, but sometimes he felt like as if the mob of humans was chasing him. One after the other, he could hear the footsteps fading away in the background. He looked behind, but there was no one following, as thunder had created the darkness in small alleyways.

"This is the protection from God!" Hatathor whispered and thanked eternal God.

He stopped by a roadside corner to catch some breath. He thought about Lyra and how quickly he would have been surrounded and thrown in prison. The armed guards of the police force would chase him in their lightning-fast vehicles. Not just that, the heat sensor systems would track him from afar. Eluding these primitives was a bit too easy, although few people had seen him running around.

It was raining, and the streets were pretty sparse with people. The torrential rain had blown off the lamps and torches lined neatly in the alleyways and roads at night. Hatathor understood the gist of the city after spending a few hours running around in it. It seemed these people had centuries to go before they could compete with Lyra on any level.

He looked around himself. The brick houses, a lack of skyscrapers and aerial vehicles. These people still had to discover a lot. Their lifestyle was a far cry from what he had on Lyra.

While running, he saw one hawker selling herbs, citing it as a cure for some disease he had never heard.

"Disgusting planet—full of many diseases!" Hatathor uttered his curses. He looked around. The clothes he was wearing did not fit him fully. The dress of the dead broker only reached his calves, leaving legs bare naked. He saw a wet cloak hanging on the house's balcony, probably for drying under the sun. The heavy rain did not do any favors because the piece of cloth was still wet. Hatathor made one swift jump to yank the clothes on the clothesline and took it.

I have to lie low for a while, he thought to himself, covering his face with the cloth.

He felt this was not enough. He had to put more clothes on his body to hide from the common people. Hatathor sat down under the shade of a tree, waiting for the rain to stop. It would take another hour for the rain to dry up. He activated his sleeve device and ate

Chapter 9. In Damanhur

some green paste from inside. So tasty as he relished the taste, sitting alone.

The military developed this superfood for the soldiers to eat and enjoy during their missions. The snack gave him some strength to walk and look around for Al-Khidr. As the rain subsided, the sunshine came into full view. Hatathor looked around to realize he was sitting in a cul-de-sac. He eyed a house with a balcony. Climbing over the fence, he entered the lush, green courtyard. The place looked deserted, mostly. He found some bushes in the far end of the courtyard and crashed behind them. Before he knew it, he was asleep.

The birds were chirping loudly. Something gooey fell on his face as he was sleeping. He licked it and swallowed the taste.

"It was delicious! What was that?" he was at the horizon of his sleep and wakefulness.

Hathathor slightly opened his eyes and saw a bird cage right over him. No way! No way!

He had swallowed bird poop.

"Curse you, stupid birds," he shouted at the birds.

The sun was shining right in his face. "God! This sun will kill me!" he muttered loudly, trying to hide his face.

He sighed. Nothing had helped him from the day he had arrived on Keb—the cursed planet. He was attacked by dogs, killed army personnel and women at the brothel. It was like he was leaving a trail of bodies behind him. Soon enough, someone would add the pieces of the puzzle and go after him.

This was not a comforting thought for Hatathor. He looked at the birds inside the cage again, sitting there idly.

He spat in disgust. God! That bird poop was tasty but... yuck!

The loud cursing brought a kindly lady into the garden.

"Who the hell is shouting at this hour of the morning?" he said to herself.

"Who's there?" she asked. But no answer came.

Hatathor had heard the woman's voice but lied low in anticipation. It could be a trap or something. He was not sure. But his skills to eliminate opponents gave him some confidence.

He understood his booming and guttural voice was loud enough to wake several neighborhoods. A middle-aged woman noticed the tall Hatathor behind the bushes. She had longish, curly white hair and a petite figure.

I could just blow her away from here, he thought.

"Hey. What are you doing over here?" she shouted in weird Victorian English.

Hatathor just shrugged. He could not understand what she was saying. Quickly, he activated the sleeve device to turn on the translation. The lady was speaking in a typical Victorian accent. The device's artificial intelligence system took some time to decode while various symbols appeared and merged into letters to give the language spoken by a woman some sense. Hatathor pressed the button, and the connec-

Chapter 9. In Damanhur

tor with the skin beneath his sleeve device sent data to his brain. "Stop shouting or I will drop my water closet on you," she stammered.

"Say what?" Hatathor weakly said.

What is a closet, he thought?

He stared at the woman for a bit. She resembled her teacher back in school in Lyra, almost a picture-perfect resemblance. Was she the same person on a different planet? He thought, but dismissed it quickly. "Can you control the birds up there? They just spit in my mouth while I was sleeping," he complained to the woman. The woman raised her eyebrows.

"And who are you?" She asked him, talking in English, throwing him off his game.

Hatathor realized he was squatting in someone's house.

"Look! I was sleeping peacefully and minding my own business when they pooped in my mouth," he complained even then. "It is not every day when someone squats in my house behind the bushes. You speak English very well. Now tell me, who are you and where are you from?" she asked sternly.

Hatathor thought about this for a moment.

The woman was looking at him, trying to figure out. The man did not look like anything French, nor British, let alone an Arab. He seemed like a different person. Hatathor had not answered yet.

"Are you some local Egyptian?" she asked him. He did not answer. Hatathor was not sure where he was right now.

"Are you a French guy then?" she asked again.

He said nothing this time around, too.

The woman could not know his identity and the specifics of the mission.

Hatathor was silent mostly. Any answer would cause more cross-questioning, and he could not accommodate that. The woman was no closer to finding his identity than he knew the whereabouts of Al-Khidr and the sphere.

The woman softened up.

"Come on in. You need coffee. Coming?" she asked.

He nodded and followed her on the flight of stairs. God! They use the stairs. Someone is really behind the times here, he thought. Suddenly, he recalled the events of yesterday and became cautious. He had to play carefully after the fiasco yesterday.

The woman raised an eyebrow but continued walking. She was in no mood for small talk. *But I need some answers*, thought Hatathor. Only then can I reach the destination if by a stroke of luck. The woman looked like someone who knew the area, living here for a long time. The house was not perfect though but was well kept. "You can sit here on the couch," she said.

Hatathor did as he was told.

The lady had many cats roaming around the house, which took him by surprise. "I see you have cats of all shapes and sizes," he pointed out. The lady nodded and sat.

It was a beautiful house laden with interior decor.

CHAPTER 9.   IN DAMANHUR

The lady knows how to make things attractive, he thought. His attention was taken over by the seven to eight cats, which licked him and examined him like he was some artifact.

"Please keep these creatures away from me," he said in irritation.

"Cats—you mean?" the lady said.

"Yes! I don't want any diseases," Hatathor said.

He could not be rude to the lady because she could be a goldmine of information. If he could play his cards right, things would turn right for him.

"What is the next big city in here, the East, I mean to say?" he said, regretting the way he put the question.

The woman sounded suspicious.

"Hey, why are you asking this? Also, who are you and why were you sleeping in my garden? You are running from someone?" she said flatly.   Hatathor thought for a moment. He had to throw her off. She crossed her arms and stared at him from across the table. Hatathor looked at the ground for a moment and spoke up.

"Well, my dad died in an accident. They took my place, and in a few moments, I was homeless. I have no place to go and no relatives," he explained with some remorse.   The woman heard his improvisation and started to giggle.

"You are lying to me. A man as strong as you cannot be poor. You can do well for yourself. I mean, look at you. I bet you are a spy for some country. I am not sure yet. But something is off about you. And if you are a spy, then I have nothing to say to you. I am a researcher, and the work I do is very important. No one should interfere in my work. Not some other scientist or some spy. I am a British woman who arrived here long before the French were here. I was the only woman on the ship, too," she said plainly.

Hatathor smiled a little inside. This woman was not as naïve as she looks. The lady had told everything about her he had not asked. *God! She would crack in an interrogation.* He laughed at the thought. She was a good woman. He was not ashamed to admit that he low-key liked her. The woman continued further.

"Who are you? I am still unsure where you came from? The skin color is different. Were you a Mummy inside one of those tombs?" she said but lost herself in giggles. "I am sorry for that. That was not right," she said in an apologetic tone.

Hatathor warmly smiled at her. It was a long time when he genuinely liked someone. Some of the cats sat beside Hatathor, while others leaped in her lap. The lady saw all this but ignored it.

"Now, will you tell what you were doing in the garden? Spying at me?" she posed the question again. Hatathor shook his head.

"I am actually a traveler. I have no home. But I can tell you this. I am heading towards East in search of my friend. I lost him by mistake. He has something that I need. It would be helpful if you can tell me the areas in the East. I think he might be there. Although

Chapter 9. In Damanhur

it is a pain finding him, I will do it. What are the cities in the East?" he explained to her.

He had taken a liking to this lady. She nodded suspiciously.

"Was this friend of yours a thief? A treasure hunter? A bounty hunter?" she asked flatly.

Hatathor smiled and played along. "You are right. He is a thief and took something I own. I trusted him, but look where I am now. It is an ancient artifact that holds great value. I am looking for it," he explained yet again.

The lady liked the explanations. Maybe he could help her. "I see. I am an archeologist. Maybe you can help me with the history of objects and things like that. I am doing research work independently. Later on, I plan to publish them for the world to read," she said excitedly.

Hatathor was contemplating the idea when she broke his train of thoughts.

"I suggest you visit Cairo quickly, before someone buys that artifact from the market. You have little time. The French and Italians are the biggest buyers in the market. Once they purchase it, you can bid the item goodbye," she said.

Hatathor considered this for a moment. She was buying the story hook, line, and sinker. God! She was naïve but also a good woman to have around. The two sat in silence for a while.

"What is your name, may I ask?" she asked.

"Hatathor," he said, lost in thought.

"My name is Laura. Pleased to meet you, Hatathor. Nice name. I bet it is Egyptian in origin," she tempted him.

He nodded in agreement.

"My mom is my superhero. She would tell me that the more things change, the more they stay the same. People look at mummies and statues and start to take their faces. If you see something many times, your face would resemble that after some time. She was right. After four decades of marriage, the faces of the husband and wife become the same as well. It is strange how nature works. But it is what it is," she said, staring into the distance. She looked at him for whatever reason. Hatathor could not decipher what she was on about. But this conversation was strangely pleasant and enjoyable—only if he could live here for some time.

"Yes. I believe my face resembles these mummies and statues. I guess I should find something else to do," he lied.

She smiled and nodded at him. The air was very comfortable in the room. Hatathor and Laura liked each other.

"Can you tell me about the artifact a bit? Maybe I can also help or come with you. The British Museum in London has sent me to collect some relics in Egypt. British empire do this for regions they invade," she said proudly.

Hatathor did not understand what she was on about but just nodded.

Chapter 9. In Damanhur

"Well, I found this weird artifact by the sea. It was buried deep underground. The thing is that my friend stole something else. He was supposed to take something else. That is just inexperience speaking," he explained to her. Hatathor explained a bit more to put up a convincing show.

"This thing is like a ball with a hole in the middle. This sphere is different from others. It is an adventure finding the object and exploring Egypt," he said cheerily.

Hatathor did not want to talk more about the sphere then she needs to know.

"Would you like some coffee?" she asked suddenly, standing up.

She opened the jar of coffee beans—the aroma filled the room, enticing Hatathor all the same. He was worried that she would mix something in the drink and pass it on to him. It was a scary proposition, but he was not concerned right now. He was willing to spend some time with her. Laura did not wait for an answer.

"I was waiting for someone to translate the script on the relics. I have made many discoveries in the last two years. Life was very peaceful here until Napoleon came here one day barging in, ugh," she said, brewing the coffee.

Hatathor found the aroma of coffee very enticing.

"Napoleon came from France to avenge something recently. I was working with the local people and made much progress. Along came the Ottomans and Egyptians and also the British in the area. Napoleon is very stupid. I do not know what he is doing. The man wants to go to India with his forces but is stuck here," she said. Hatathor pretended to show anger.

"I also agree with you on this. Napoleon knows nothing. I wonder what he is doing here," he lied through his teeth.

She nodded in agreement. She made two cups of coffee but forgot to ask him about it.

"Hey! Are you sure you don't want coffee? This is one of the best brews I have tried in France. You are missing out on some fine coffee," she said, tempting him. Hatathor was still making up his mind.

"I must also add that this brew is so much better than the European style version. I mean, when it comes to Arabic style—it is the best." she sipped some coffee, closing her eyes.

Hatathor shook his head. "No. I am not in the mood for it. Maybe some other time—this does sound enticing," he remarked casually.

Laura put the other cup down. She wanted some companionship, but it seemed that her guest was likely in a hurry.

Hatathor felt guilty on the couch, saying no to such splendid company. He had more pressing matters to attend, however. This was when Laura started to talk again.

"You have not answered the question still. What are you? Arab or an Egyptian? I cannot put my finger on it. Maybe some part of Africa that I do not know.

Chapter 9. In Damanhur

Even more intriguing is that you speak English better than many people in Britain," she said to herself.

God! This woman likes to talk all the time.

Hatathor had to improvise yet again. Why was he doing this in the first place? It was not like he needed her. "Well, I woke up in the middle of the sea. The boat owner was paddling it somewhere in a felucca. I was sleeping for a long time. But when I woke up again, I was in the sea, but the boat owner was not there this time. I was alone on it," he explained to her. Laura's eyes opened wide. This was so interesting.

"Keep going. What happened then? The story is very exciting," she said, taking the couch immediately.

Hatathor seemed pleased with his on-the-go storytelling.

"I spent many lonely days on the boat. I had to eat raw fish and drank the river water, which was inside the water-skin I had," he said dismissively. Laura nodded and motioned him to go on.

"After that, I saw some fire and torches and houses nearby. My spirits were never like this before. I cried in joy and shouted at the people fishing there," he said. "And just like that, you were rescued? Voila! I am excited to hear that," she completed the story for him.

He nodded his head and carried on.

"I paddled the boat towards the town until I reached the shore. But things were difficult for me," he said darkly. Laura sat up straight.

"What do you mean by that?" she asked suspiciously.

"The people thought I had escaped from somewhere," Hatathor said.

"But I reached Alexandria and worked minor jobs to keep myself alive," he said. Laura nodded.

This was an interesting story. Hatathor had a lot more to tell than he let on.

"You should thank your stars for all that," she said, finishing her coffee.

He nodded.

"I guess I need a fortune teller today. Never felt so excited ever since I arrived here," she looked into her coffee cup and said to herself. Hatathor stood looking at her, mystified by how much she would lose herself in a sea of her thoughts. He cleared his throat just to see the reaction from her. She snapped out of her thoughts and looked at him.

"Well, as far as I think, your friend is headed to Al Qahirah. I wish I knew what the future held for me," she longingly said. She turned to him. Hatathor had been silent all this time.

"Can you say the name again? Pardon me, but you spoke in a low tone," he said cautiously. She nodded. "That is perfectly fine, Hatathor. I can say the name again. Your friend has probably gone towards Al Qahirah," she said in her high-pitched voice. "Al Qahirah?" he asked again.

She nodded.

I should record this stupid word before I forget it.

Chapter 9. In Damanhur

He stood up and looked at his sleeve device. Now how to record without arousing her suspicions? That was another challenge for Hatathor. God! This mission presented more and more challenges. There were few moments of respite for Hatathor. This moment seemed like a good escape from his troubling reality.

"Record Al Qahirah," he barked into his sleeve device.

Laura turned around to look at him, bewildered.

The thing seemed dead. It was not working.

"I said to record Al Qahirah," he shouted a bit loudly this time.

The device was still dead. *God damn it. It is not fully charged yet.* For now, he would need to remember the name of the place in his memory. He looked up to see a bewildered Laura staring at him in amusement and shock.

"What the hell are you doing? Was that a ghost or djinn you were talking to?" she asked, laughing.

Hatathor smiled at that. Humanity on this planet was light years behind him. It seemed ridiculous to think that she would know what he was doing. Laura laughed louder as Hatathor was slapping his sleeve device quite hard. She hadn't noticed the sleeve device under his jalabiya.

The stupid thing needs charging!

He was thinking of another model that ran on an ion battery. This was the next best thing after this sleeve device. Unfortunately, the turn of events shaped them in a bad way, compelling him to leave Lyra. He felt slightly bad that he had left his home planet for such a sour planet—all for this boy. Laura stared at him to see if he was actually serious.

"You must be messing with me, right? why would you need to talk to your body? Are you mad?" she asked incredulously.

Laura crossed her arms to let this sink in.

"Have a seat. I want to talk. Your friend in Al Qahirah can wait, I guess. Something tells me you are not serious about finding him," she said curiously. Hatathor smiled again, slapping his wrist.

"Stop hitting yourself, mister. You are one queer man," she said in irritation.

Hatathor was fuming inside. The sleeve device was still a few hours away from a full charge.

"You are a strange man, mister," she said again. Hatathor stopped slapping his wrist. It could wait later.

Hatathor stared outside the window, thinking of a way to make up with Laura. She could prove to be a valuable asset to him. But asset aside, he also needed a good friend by his side.

"Come to think of it—I have decided to translate some of the ancient artifacts you have. Bring them on. I want to see what the previous civilizations left behind." he changed the topic. "Oh really!" she smiled at the proposal and disappeared downstairs.

Hatathor looked around to see the environs of her house. He could go out, but Laura seemed like a nice lady and she helped him, so he must reward her in

Chapter 9. In Damanhur

some manner. He felt softer after a long time.

After a few moments that felt like an eternity to Hatathor, Laura returned with some relics in her hands. She put them on the table in the room. Hatathor and Laura sat at couches on different sides of the table. Hatathor looked at the relics with some interest while Laura set them so they could set to work.

"These are few ancient Egyptian relics but nobody knows what is written on them. I heard there are some people in Egypt who know how to read hieroglyphs, but I haven't come across any of them yet," Laura said.

Hatathor started inspecting the small figurines and plates.

"We will need a paper and ink. Actually, many papers and ink for that matter," she smiled and disappeared again.

Hatathor stared at the relics. A few elements felt familiar, while others looked kind of strange to him.

Laura came running, seemingly hurried. There was no time to waste. Hatathor may change his mind and leave at any moment. She looked up suddenly. "Oh. Just so you know, there is no direct route from Alexandria to Al-Qahirah. You will need to start your journey from Damanhur. It is a city in south and then it is easy from there," she finished.

Hatathor nodded. She smiled at that.

"I will guide the way. I may not accompany you there, but I hope that you reach there with ease," she said in a low tone. Hatathor thought about her for a while. God! She was caring. He raised his hand for her to stop.

"It is okay. I am in no hurry. I want to translate these relics and catch some breath while I am at it," he explained his plans. But Laura was not deterred that easily.

"But if the thing leaves the port, what then? You can never find it afterward. Some buyer will take it and it is as good as gone. Maybe if you are lucky, someone will sell it inside Egypt, but then you will have to look for it all over the country," she explained worriedly. "But before you leave, the first thing that I need to translate is an inscription on this silly little black statue. Can you help?," she said sweetly. She turned the statue. Oddly enough, something was on it.

"This thing looks beautiful. I wonder who crafted this thing," he lied.

He was surprised to see ancient Lyrian writing on the thing. But he could understand it—although it would be a pain to make out the eroded text over the centuries. "Here we go. This is going to sound a bit weird, but bear with me, okay?" he said, getting ready. Hatathor first taught Laura some basic alphabetical writings to her and then started to translate. Bit by bit, they worked together. Laura was impressed by the extent of his knowledge of the language. At first glance, she did not make much of him overall. But maybe he was right—the man was full of surprises. She stole a few glances at him to see him work.

CHAPTER 9. IN DAMANHUR

Hatathor had not mentioned it, but some interesting things had come to light. Of course, Laura did not need to know that. Laura meticulously made notes, double-checking it with him as well. She was overwhelmed by these translations. They were opening a new world for her, but more so for him. As they came to the last line, Laura had a desperate expression on her face. She wanted him to stay for longer, but Hatathor was in a hurry.

Hatathor did not show it, but he wished to stay here just the same. But it could compromise his mission. "And we have come to the end of the line. I should better get going before that friend gets away. I am not confident about finding him. But I will drop by on my way back," he said firmly.

He was speaking the truth.

"I will miss you, Hatathor. Am I getting your name, right?" she asked, shrugging. She almost has tears in her eyes by now.

"Oh. Come here you," she cried.

She ran to hug him tightly. Hatathor thought she was light. Now he saw Keb in a different light than he did before. Something was oddly peculiar here.

He walked out of her house with a heavy heart, thinking about Laura and the fun they had here. He would remember this for a long time.

Laura could see him go. She wiped a tear rolling down her eye. God! The local man was a sweetheart in his own way but peculiar, though.

I am not going to hold that against him.

"Hey. Do come back if you can. I am posted here for a few more years until I am not," she said from behind. Hatathor looked back and nodded. He could not handle the flurry of emotions and turned to look forward. *Remember the mission!*

Laura's house was fading into the distance as he marched forward with a sinking heart. *I may not come back, Laura, I wish you best in your planet.* He turned into a street corner and entered an alley.

A strange sound alerted him. It felt like an animal or something. He poised himself for the worst! A crow flew over his head —he jumped in one swift motion and caught the crow by the throat. Hatathor was slightly disappointed by the size of the bird. It was a small, black bird and completely harmless at that. The thought of Ehsis and Queen Hathor came to his mind. The anger rose in his blood, and he smashed the bird against the wall. The poor thing fell dead at the point of impact.

I will smash Ehsis's head when I get my hands on her, he thought madly.

A child looked at him and ran away, fearing he was an insane. Hatathor looked at the child go and recalled the incidents of the previous night. He was running away from brothel to avoid identification.

God! Egypt was presenting challenges to him time and again.

He silently walked through the streets of the city, keeping his head low. Some farmers were idling around, stealing a glance at him. Hatathor was taller than peo-

Chapter 9. In Damanhur

ple of this area. Hatathor had a physique and height that you could not forget at once.

He looked at them and felt a tinge of pity. These men had wrinkles on their foreheads and worn-out faces. Poor souls were toiling all day in the fields, it seemed. Oddly enough, he found some sense of peace and tranquility on their face. This was comforting to look at. The farmers gave him a glance and went back to work as if the show was over. The animals roamed around the field. It felt like another day in this part of the city, a little outside the city.

Hatathor walked for another hour until the green fields disappeared into the distance. The climate became more intense here as the afternoon wore on. I wish I was back on Lyra. He regretted the turn of events that went against him.

The terrain changed into marshy land. Walking here felt squishy—he stared at his feet to see them covered in damp mud. It hampered his pace a bit. He slapped his sleeve device to find out more about the terrain of the area, but the device was dead as a doornail.

Ouch! His foot hit a rock, and he stumbled face-first onto the damp mud. He fell with a big splash, sending mud everywhere.

Wait, a minute! Why am I sinking here? Hatathor looked around. He had never seen this kind of sand back home. There was no ground beneath his feet. In a frenzy, he realized that he could simply drown in the sand. He tried to swim frantically, but he sunk more and more with each passing moment.

"Help," he shouted. But some birds flew away from him. There was no one in sight around here.

God! What am I going to do? He tried to activate his sleeve device to create a shockwave and help get out of this mess.

Damn it. Stupid device—the thing was still dead like before. The shockwave would often throw his enemies far away from him. This often helped him to counter the numbers game when up against enemies.

His body had sunk into the quicksand by now. His face still above ground, he desperately looked around for something. The stench of the quicksand was getting to him, making him sick. Some tree branches were dangling into the distance.

I will hang on to them in some way, he thought. Little by little, he moved to get closer to the tree branches. With no ground to support his feet, he moved towards the tree branches and roots. With one lunge, he caught the tree branch firmly.

He breathed a sigh of relief and managed to pull himself out. After a few moments, he sat to catch his breath.

What the hell was that, he thought. As he sat panting, he wondered about the weird nature of the planet and its people. It was no surprise that people did not live here. He gave the place a look around to see if anyone lived here.

Mud covered his entire body. God! I need a change of clothes and also a bath. The sun was burning a

Chapter 9. In Damanhur

hole in his body. But the mud dried off and fall off bit by bit. By the looks of it, he was like a walking mummy soldering through the marshes. He regretted not taking the woman's advice of heading to Damanhur instead. "I am never walking through the marshes again," he retorted.

Instead of moving ahead, he traced his steps back to the farmers. After an hour of walking, he reached the farmers who were still working in the fields. They lazily looked at him, but a look of fright crossed their face. "Run. Run. Run" they said and fled at full speed.

He looked at them stupidly. Why are they afraid of me? I need to reach Damanhur. He chased them and caught one running farmer and threw him on the ground. He knelt above him, blocking the sunlight.

"Stop running from me. I have a question to ask. Where the hell is Damanhur? Tell me right now or I will break your neck here," he thundered. The man was trembling, barely able to mumble a word.

He stood up, deciding to move ahead—enough of this nonsense.

"Where is Damanhur?" he shouted.

The man was staring in his eyes, still fearful.

He slapped him angrily. What the hell was wrong with this chap here?

"I will ask again. Where the hell is Damanhur?" he shouted again.

Dead silence. He could hear the animals in the backdrop.

This was not working. He had to try something new here.

"Okay. Can you point the direction I should go towards Damanhur?" he asked softly this time.

The man mustered some courage and pointed towards the south.

Right! They were making progress. Some of the other farmers were secretly looking from a distance.

"How much time will it take for me to reach there?" he asked the farmer.

This time the farmer spoke.

"A few weeks on foot—but you can take this donkey cart. It will take a few days then. We use this for reaching other cities. But please, don't kill me," the man said pleadingly.

Hatathor looked at the donkey cart for a moment, and his heart sank. God! These people were behind the times.

He let go of the man and untied the rope. The donkey was staring at Hatathor blankly. *God! I am going to regret this.* He sat on the donkey cart, but the donkey was not walking. What the hell is wrong with this animal?

"You have to use the rope and pat the donkey with it. That is the signal to start walking," the farmer explained.

Hatathor nodded and followed his advice. Amazingly, the donkey started moving. Off he went towards Damanhur. He thanked the farmer behind, who waved back. The rest of the farmers had come out now that

Chapter 9. In Damanhur

he was moving away from them.

"Who was that?" asked the farmers.

He shrugged because he was not sure. Was he an ancient mummy that had rose from the dead? Maybe he was just a tall man who came back from the marshlands. "I don't know," he replied. "I am glad he is gone. By the looks of it, he could have killed you. But he was looking for something. Glad we are safe. But we should tell the others about this strange, tall man," the other farmer said.

They agreed and went about their business.

Hatathor felt hungry, but his alien superfood kept him going. He would stop the donkey for some rest by the river so he could catch some sleep. The next day he woke up and sat up, staring at the sky. *I wish I was back on Lyra. Life was so easy, and I sat back there.* He turned around to look at himself and nearly shouted. Who the hell is that?

He was staring at his reflection in the river. The donkey was fast asleep. He was covered in mud from head to toe.

As he was moving towards the city, he came across a pond. The bottom of the pond was muddy, murky, and green. But its surface was transparent, and it reflected the light from the sun above in a delightful manner. He sat down at the edge of the pond with his feet dipped in and rested for a while. The water rose to his knees, he relaxed and then went further into water, letting it rise further, submerging him waist-deep in the water. The sensation was relaxing after the stress. He closed his eyes and took a deep breath, letting out a sigh as he sank deeper into the water. When he came out, he heard nothing but the sound of crickets and a bird calling in the distance. He wasnt sure if it was just a sound of a distant city or if it was a bird in the Nile Delta.

He closed his eyes and let his body submerge into the water. He could see the children swimming with their heads above water. He swam for a bit more and moved ahead. An eerie silence filled the air as he stepped out from the river. Hatathor felt lonesome and upset. It had been a long time since he had left Lyra. No one from his planet knew where he is. Then he recalled that a fugitive on the run was off-limits for citizens of Lyra.

Is Ehsis still in power? He was not sure. His spirits sank at the thought, but he had to move forward. The fact remained that Queen Hathor and Ehsis were dishonest to their people. *What exactly made him a criminal?*

As he walked towards his donkey, he could hear some birds and crickets chirping in the air. He could reckon that the city was near because a faint sound of city life was apparent in some distance. He felt hopeful and, with fresh vigor, moved ahead.

The terrain changed as he moved from a desert to a more arable region. He could see several water reserves along the way and grasslands. Up ahead, the city was visible in plain sight.

On the evening of the next day, he neared the city

Chapter 9. In Damanhur

and felt glad that his journey would come to an end. The sleeve-device was fully charged by solar energy. He entered the city, hoping to see a center of thriving activity and commerce. However, this felt like a smaller city and less active.

There were many people here. He could hear several languages spoken here. The skin color of the people was radically varying, which amused him. This was a place where he could blend in with ease. The people went along their way. It seemed like they were in a hurry here. He stared at his device—it was rapidly translating a bunch of languages in his ears. He could understand what they were saying easily. Some talks were about family disputes, marriage and love issues, while others were trading-related talks.

His device could translate 450,000 languages spoken across the galaxies.

"I need to solve the battery issue, first things first. This is the worst battery technology I have seen. And also think of a backup as well," he said to himself. He felt something more was missing. His device should also be able to racially profile people and state their characteristics. This would further help him in mixing well with the crowd. The device certainly needed an update, but his relations with Lyra were not the best at the moment.

But he could not blame himself for this state of affairs. Until last month, he could not fathom he would stand on a new planet—this was not on the cards. This is how politics unfolded on Lyra. Those who stood against Ehsis and Queen Hathor were reprimanded, and Hatathor was just one of another casualties. He laughed at the pettiness. He refocused himself on the mission. The city was bustling with activity as people hurriedly moved, cursing and shouting at each other.

Hatathor found that funny. It was a novel way of lifestyle for him. He was himself on an animal while the others moved on horses. God! These people were behind. But somehow and someway, he had warmed up to these people.

He thought of Al-Khidr. *I should get him as fast as I could!*

Hatathor was looking around the new city. This seemed like a good place, albeit different from the last town.

His gaze landed on four men who were staring at him with great interest. Who were these men? Was he followed? But how was that possible? He had made sure that no one was on his tail. The farmers were afraid of him, hiding in the bushes the last time he saw them. He could recall them standing in fright, wondering what he was capable of. But it was time to lie low and stay out of public sight for a while. It would be the mission protocol until he would find the human and the sphere.

The men were chatting frantically, passing a couple of gazes at him. This was strange because he was still a foreigner to them. Why the sudden interest? He stared at his sleeve device. Voila! It was fully charged after all those days of traveling. "I am glad

Chapter 9. In Damanhur

it is working at least. Now I need to get closer to these men and find out what they are talking about," Hatathor said to himself. He activated the sleeve device, created a blinding flash that did not faze him in the least. But the people looked around shell-shocked, wondering how did the blinding flash happen?

Time froze as people looked at each other for answers. This was his chance.

Hatathor kept his head down and tried to get closer to talking humans. This was problematic for him because the thriving metropolis was bustling with activity and commerce. He could hear the translation of several people around him, which was annoying him.

"How much for the vegetable?" one man asked. "I am not selling my cows at this price," another farmer said furiously.

Hatathor ignored the voices and moved through the crowd swiftly. Maybe he could know who they were and ask them a few questions. Somehow, when he arrived at the spot, the men were nowhere to be seen. His height allowed him to tower over his gaze and look around. The men seemed to have disappeared into the crowd. "Dammit. I lost them," he growled.

He stood staring at the people passing by.

Lyras technology needs drastic improvements! He had to fix it further to find the one he needed. "I think this software needs an update. How can anyone work with this archaic equipment? I cannot find two men for the life of me," he said through his gritted teeth.

It drizzled a little. Hatathor realized he had to make a run for it and hide under a shelter or something. He was feeling in this sweltering heat, but the rain energized him a bit.

No! not again, he thought.

He sped towards the city to find some shelter. People were dancing, and children were singing songs in the rain. *Interesting, but I have no time*, he thought himself.

Hatathor hated rain. It was an abnormality in the climate of this Keb. Back on Lyra, it had not rained for millenniums. For the people on Keb, it seemed like a godsend gift. They would dance and bathe rain to their heart's delight. While walking, he had overheard the region had suffered from famine for a year. The rain would help grow crops and stir economic activity. So, the rainy season had arrived in Cairo and the rest of the cities in Egypt.

After running around, he found an empty shed and sat under it. He took out his superfood and had a snack away from public view. While running, he had stolen a cloth to wrap his wrist and hide the sleeve device. Some kids or a pickpocket would steal it and sell it for a dirham. The rain went on for the evening. Tired and sleepy, Hatathor fell asleep under the donkey sled. It rained and thundered and rained more heavily through the night. But Hatathor was undisturbed, sleeping like a baby.

***

Chapter 9. In Damanhur

Vivant was sitting alone in his room, writing a letter. He had sat on his desk to write the letter after a lot of thinking. He saw a slightly different future ahead of him. Maybe it was for the best. He gave it a thought and ran with the idea. He believed in the greater good.

9 December 1798

Excellency,
  I can honorably inform you that many of the statuary marbles and fragments of granite have been sent to Marseille to be used in a museum on Egypt. The museum will cover all periods of Egyptian history, with most items being from the most prominent site in Egypt. The collection can be accessed by people in.
  We are anxious about the news of your engagement with British forces in Syria and the spread of the plague. We are all engaged in executing your grand plan of doing the hydrographic study of the upper Nile. Jean-Marie Dubois-Ayme is working on it. But here in Egypt the Malaria and ophthalmia are stopping us. Many of our soldiers had contracted the Malaria disease. Some of them died. I am sure his Excellency is well aware of it.
  I would like to inform his Excellency of including a Berber man into our savant circles. He is well-trusted, and his name is Al-Khidr, and his mother was initially a French-bound woman. He speaks French fluently. In fact, better than some savants even. His zeal for the alchemical arts and his Connaissance showed to me as being useful in art or in that of erudition. I will keep you updated on this matter.

Denon.

As he finished the letter, Vivant felt satisfied with his work. With just one piece of paper, he had sealed the fate of Al-Khidr with Estelle. As far as he could see, Estelle and Al-Khidr were getting closer to one another. During the following weeks, he could see them taking long walks in the garden and spending a lot of time with each other. His concerns of Al-Khidr hiding something were hardly of much concern. He saw good things in the boy and valuable addition to the French scientific community.

Effectively immediately, Al-Khidr was included in his list of savants that would board the ship back to France. Their mission in Cairo was over, but he prolonged the stay to have a change of space. Cairo was a world away from the Parisian lifestyle, but he was not complaining. The simple, carefree lifestyle had perked that Parisian living could not offer with rapid industrialization and stuff.

"My boy! You are coming with me to France. We are going to have a ball of a time there," he said smiling.

The letter would be sent this afternoon to Napoleon, who would probably sign it without reading it. Napoleon had high regard for people like Vivant and his lot. Just the name of the letter was more than enough for a mandatory signature of approval by him. The two had struck an unlikely friendship on the ship headed to Egypt. Napoleon came from a political family who had mostly seen wars and revolutions in his lifetime. For him, it was a pleasant experience to meet Vivant and exchange ideas on the intellectual front. As they reached Alexandria, the famous port of Egypt, Napoleon had decided to award Vivant some privi-

Chapter 9. In Damanhur

leges. However, Napoleon had several things going on in Egypt, making him inaccessible to everyone except the ground forces. As a result, he was sending any correspondence through his aides and military personnel. The letter could take weeks or months depending on Napoleon's excursions into the heart of the desert. "No worries till then. I will enjoy myself and explore Egypt till he returns to the capital city," he said to himself.

He stood up and called it a day. Vivant had thought long and hard about taking the boy with him. The conclusion was that the man was slightly eccentric and different from the regular guys back in France. But he would adjust to their lifestyle after a while. He and Estelle would help with a bit of stuff there. The man could speak fluent French and Arabic. This meant that he could establish an institute in France to study ancient Arabic texts and help translate them. The Muslim world had a long list of scientists who made great strides during the pre-medieval period. It would benefit the European research community just the same. Also, Vivant could see a potential suitor in Al-Khidr—a man who came from a culture where men spent entire lives with their wives and raised their children. Vivant saw the man as someone who would stand faithful to him during thick and thin.

Vivant had asked neither Al-Khidr nor Estelle about this plan he had in mind, but he was sure that all will be fine when they will return to France.

Chapter 10

The Boraqis

AL-KHIDR was walking with a wide grin on his face. He was a few steps away from finding out the events that transpired eons ago. Help came from an unlikely source in the shape of Lucas. The guy had several Arabic medical texts lying around unread. It was probably an excellent choice to translate most of the books in their scientific pursuit. Lucas would call him again.

Estelle walked along with him, lost in a world of her own. She thought about the time till now in Egypt.

Chapter 10. The Boraqis

It had been a revelation to her. She felt at home after such a long time. The Parisian lifestyle was becoming dry and mechanical and she was glad she got to experience something new.

She looked at Al-Khidr, who had not spoken a word so far. It was as if he did not wish to be disturbed. Now would be a good time to talk as they hurried back to the institute.

"Did I tell you how I met Lucas in Egypt?" she blurted.

He shook his head, still walking.

"Well, it was a funny incident. He had taken permission from the Ottomans to work here alone. He arrived here two years ago and made this garden. The ottomans liked the idea of gathering plants and gave him some Arabic manuscripts as they wanted to make drugs for the hospitals. Lucas' task was to gather plants which may help in curing not only humans but animals as well. Later I came with my father to Egypt. Lucas is unhappy by the invasion as this ruined his career plan and he lost funding from Ottomans as well. He is a lucky guy. Both Egyptians as well as French like him," she explained.

"But how do you know him?" Al-Khidr continued the conversation.

"How do I know him? Well, I was the only French girl of his age here. This means that I would need someone my age to talk to and connect. You know, the elders talk can get boring. I met him in the Cairo bazaar one day and I talked to him for a while, and he invited me into his lair. Voila! As a naturalist, I had some training earlier in France on plants identifications and I started helping him with the native plants and collecting samples—until you came along," she said cheekily. Al-Khidr smiled at that. *God! The girl is talented at warming up hearts and flirting around.* They had reached the institute and made their way to the Al-Khidr's room. The two sat down, and Al-Khidr opened the book, flipping through the pages. The book in question was titled *Kitab Al-Haywanat Al-Mahtadhara* (The Book on Dying Animals).

"Look at the book-binding skills of the ancient Arabs. It is an art that they take great pride in and do for generations. Come over here and touch it," he said. She came over and touched the leather-felt cover. Her eyes opened in surprise. It was unlike anything she had experienced.

"See? This is a fine-bound spine with exquisite detail—this kind of detail is common in Arabia and Ottoman Empire. You should take some book back to Europe and see how you guys fare," he said earnestly. Estelle was disinterested in the conversation but smiled anyhow. It was amusing to see his excitement at looking at leather covered books.

"Yeah! I have to agree with that. This is something right here. I will take some books as souvenirs," she said, smiling back.

He nodded and started looking at the book with excitement.

"Can you open the window? We need light here,"

Chapter 10. The Boraqis

he pointed out.

Estelle nodded and went to the window. For a while, it looked like Al-Khidr was another Lucas, but more likable and rather grounded.

Walking back, she thought about Lucas.

What was Lucas up to now? Had he told Al-Khidr about the research he was doing? Having known Lucas for a while, she took the matter into her own hands.

"You should not trust Lucas just like that. The man still owes me money for the work I did for him," she said abruptly.

Al-Khidr smiled and nodded his head, and went back to reading.

"Like I was telling you, tread carefully with Lucas, okay?" she explained.

He raised his hand to maintain silence. He flipped the book cover and started reading the title and side notes along the main text.

"This book is in the ancient Arabic language. Can you understand the text," she asked.

He looked at Estelle and said: "I read old books now and then. This book right here was penned by someone in the 8th or 9th century. The writing style is very much from the scribes of those days. I am amazed to read it and get some much-needed answers here as well," he made up a story since he didn't reveal to Estelle about his travel to planet Lyra.

She nodded, still admiring his skills.

For a while Al-Khidr was lost in the book. While he read, Estelle disappeared into the lobby, where she met Vivant. They struck a conversation about Al-Khidr. He filled her in about his plans of returning to France with her and the boy. She listened to him, hiding her surprise from him.

I have time till I break his bubble, she reasoned.

After the talk, she returned to the room, where Al-Khidr had his nose in the book. She talked about exotic plants with immense passion. Though Al-Khidr listened intently, he did not take his nose out of the book. It seemed he was onto something here.

"What does the book say? Find anything useful here? Say thanks to me for the lead," she asked.

She was interrupted since he went on about the book yet again.

"Here, look. The book begins, as they always do, with praises for God. Then it lists down the known prophets in the Middle East to date. So, you know that the cures are from the God. After few pages the discussion on the illnesses and diseases in the region started. This is an exciting read and tells me a bit about trends of health conditions here. Thankfully, alchemists like me have been active. See here. They have a list of cures for the ailments. I can recognize some common plants famous for medicines. And this section right here talks about the diseases specific to a region. How perfect is that? This chapter actually I read long time back; It remained in memory but I forgot the details, but now as I have read it again, I recalled it," he said excitedly.

Estelle was listening to all this intently. He was in

Chapter 10. The Boraqis

his zone right now. She walked over to see the listing of diseases. Maybe some may overlap. But before she bent to look, he flipped the pages.

"And this right here is a complete explanation of the plants found in the regions. So, I can see how people would cure illnesses in their regions and buy from other places. It is a complete guide to diseases and cures," he said excitedly.

She leaned closer to see the plants and their cures when Al-Khidr closed the book again.

"What is wrong with you? I am looking at the plants here," she protested, snatching the book from him.

He laughed at her impatience—Estelle and Al-Khidr were poles apart. One was patient and liked to wait. The other wants it right now.

While Estelle flipped the pages and looked for common diseases, Al-Khidr thought he would find the right plants in the region or take the wrong ones by mistake. This was a worrying thought for him. But thankfully, Estelle broke his chain of thoughts.

"All of this is interesting. But I have something to say here. You seem to have become good friends with Lucas. But I will repeat my self. He still owes me some money. He promised to return in a two months. But he didn't. Take the money first and then work for him. He roams around Alexandria and Cairo looking for ancient manuscripts," she said in disgust.

But then again, Al-Khidr had that distant look. It was as if he was not listening at all.

"Hey, are you alright? What is wrong? Did you find the cure, or is it difficult to create?" she asked.

He nodded, smiling this time.

"I have found the cure. It was right here in the book," he said more brightly.

She felt happy. *Well, his mission here was over then. Would the boy return to his home in southern Egypt now?* "Here. Let me show you what I am saying," he said.

"I will translate this Arabic so you can understand the gist of the matter here," he said.

She nodded. Al-Khidr started translating: "It was the year when Allah Almighty granted the Caliph Al-Saffah the seat of the caliphate when a mysterious epidemic struck the land of the pure. The disease hit the regional animals with a vengeance. One by one, the animals died after large spots formed on their bodies and their bodies dried up," he said. Estelle was listening to him intently.

A long time ago, an epidemic had wiped off a significant part of the population. It was just like the Black Death that had plagued Europe a few centuries ago, Estelle thought.

The bubonic plague was a bane on the lives of the Europeans, changing their lifestyle completely. It nearly wiped half of the European population and then some in North Africa. Those were scary times as people and recorded history told. Some of my ancestors said the story in vivid detail and horrifying ways they survived to live another day, Estelle thought.

Chapter 10. The Boraqis

"Hello. Are you listening to me?" Al-Khidr shook her arm. She snapped back to reality.

"Oh, I'm sorry. It was just that a plague much worse had hit Europe, killing the human population like flies. This seems something similar but hit the animals instead. You can find more about if you were to join us in France for a bit," she explained.

He nodded his head.

"As I was saying, the animals in Iraq were dying left, right and center. The Caliph took notice of this situation and called for action. The animals would die within a few hours as the disease raged through village after village. The farmers and people became panicky, trying to stay away from the animals as much as possible—some feared the epidemic would attack the human populations. Other religious saints and scholars thought it was a bad omen. They reasoned bad times were upon us. But the Caliph rubbished those claims and set up a task force to tackle the issue. But glory is to Allah, who Seeth all, he bestowed the cure of all diseases to humans. Sages were summoned, and Caliph Al-Saffah ordered the search for a cure as soon as possible. Things moved along slowly as the alchemists and sages put their heads together in order to find a cure. Nothing worked! A bunch of solutions were thrown. Most of the livestock was almost gone. The farmers complained that they prayed to Allah for divine intervention. The animals would dehydrate and collapse because of weakness. This was when a Babylonian Jewish sage found out about the epidemic and came with a cure. By then, the population of the livestock was buried deep in the sand to prevent another epidemic. He reached out to the Caliph and requested him to find a plant family near the city of Qena. He was heading towards Jerusalem, so he could not take them to the plantation himself. The Caliph, desperate for answers, decided to give it a shot and wrote a letter to the Egyptian Governor, telling him about the cure. The Governor immediately took to the farmers and ordered them to assemble near Fustat. This was the first major development in a month. The farmers flooded to the desired area in search of the herbs. Soon enough, good news spread. Some Egyptian sages also confirmed that the herbs for the cure. The local population benefited from the herbs, while the Caliph sent his caravans to take the herbs. The herbs were taken to Yemen, Khorasan, and other regions in the Middle East area. Some animals on the deathbed were brought back to life. Though it was a little too late since the pandemic hit the epicenter of the villages in Egypt and other countries. The herbs were collected by caravans and shifted to Baghdad. From the seat of the Caliph, the herbs were distributed evenly. These herbs were called Boraqis, which grew near the banks of the River Nile in Qena region. Thus, began a wave of cures all over the Middle East and Africa. However, farmers were still unhappy since they had lost a fair share of their livestock. The Caliph donated some animals to others to avoid discontent. The said Caliph was very pleased by the Babylonian Jewish sage and

Chapter 10. The Boraqis

rewarded him handsomely. Finally, the entire land was back on its way to recovery, with trade slowly booming, and markets populated again after the epidemic slowly was on its way out," he said, looking at Estelle.

Estelle clapped in excitement. *Al-Khidr was almost successful. He would be on his way back to his village soon,* she thought. She was still not sure of Vivant's plan for the two of them. Though Estelle thought it was doubtful for him to join them. She said nothing and smiled at him.

"I am so glad that you can return after taking this plant herb. Are you sure they are still there? Centuries have passed since then, right?" she said cautiously. The brightness on Al-Khidr's face vanished. She was right. It could well be possible that the plant had mutated or its family became extinct somehow. He opened the book again to show her the picture. She stared at the plant with no expression on her face.

"What is it? Do you recognize these plants?" he asked worriedly.

She put her finger on the plant and asked.

"Is this the plant? Are you sure?" she said plainly.

He nodded.

Her lips curled into a smile.

"Come with me downstairs. I have to show you something here," she said excitedly.

Al-Khidr followed her. She was onto something here.

They rushed through the lobby down towards the massive hall—he could see bookshelves on his left and his right. Large paperbacks greeted him through the hall as they went. They came to a special part of the hall. Over here, books were neatly placed behind glass shelves to prevent outside contamination. "This is beautiful. All these books behind glass cases; I like them," he said.

She did not respond to that. He had seen nothing yet.

"Wait till I show you what I have," she said, smiling.

Al-Khidr walked behind her, raging with excitement. This was possibly his biggest accomplishment. He could cure an entire population, putting him in high regard for the people. Nefertiti would be there by his side. He could see himself giving a speech to a packed audience.

"Hey. Are you with me?" she said, looking at Al-Khidr. He was lost in a world of his own.

"Lucas and I have been doing some digging this past year. We came here some time ago, so we collected in our journals an extensive list of plants and herbs of this region. Lucas took me to mountains and valleys for sightseeing and herb collection," she explained.

She took out one book from the glass case and opened it up. Al-Khidr sneezed when she blew dust from the book cover.

She laughed at that.

"You are funny, monsieur," she remarked and busied herself with finding the plant.

Chapter 10. The Boraqis

She flipped through pages and pages, browsing through an extensive catalog of herbs and local plants in Egypt.

"I am sure it was somewhere here. Give me a moment here," she said.

Al-Khidr waited for her to get to it.

"Here we go," she said, brightening up.

In front of her was a large parchment. She ran her fingers through it. After a few moments, she moved the parchment to him.

"See this," she said.

"We named this thing differently. It is called *Anemone Arabis*. This looks familiar to the one you saw in that ancient book upstairs. Am I right?" she said.

Al-Khidr stared at the plant—the resemblance was uncanny, for sure. The plant had some strikingly similar physical features.

"You are right here. This is just the one I saw in the book upstairs. I am halfway done," he said, cheering.

"We have the famous Boraqis. Congratulations. No need to worry about its existence. It is there. We saw it some time ago near upper Egypt," she explained.

She closed the book and put it back inside the glass case. She locked the case and placed the key in her front pocket.

"This is my favorite bookcase. These books are treasures and historical artifacts, as many savants compiled these pieces of information. A glass door protects the contents behind it," she said.

He nodded, thinking about the possibilities.

Estelle looked at him for a moment. Should I tell him about Vivant's plans, or was it too early?

"I am a naturalist who draws plants and herbs. I was not messing with you. That is Boraqis," she said, chuckling.

Al-Khidr had that look again. He was thinking about something.

"Come. Follow me. I also drew pictures of this plant in my journal. I will show you," she said, grabbing his hand.

Al-Khidr did not move right away.

"Should we just grab this tome and compare?" he asked solemnly.

Estelle looked heartbroken and she walked away, leaving Al-Khidr in the shadows behind. He knew it was a mess up. He immediately ran to console her.

"Hey! It is all right. I was messing with you. Of course, we are going to your room to see the sketches. Why not? I am looking forward to it," he whispered.

She cheered up slightly on that and punched him on his shoulder.

"I knew you were messing with me. Please do not do this ever again. I am a sensitive person," she said.

He nodded, thinking about the near-disaster he was about to face.

"Yes. Never again," he said, thanking the lord his lie had worked.

They walked silently to her room this time. Al-Khidr wished he was out in the fields looking for that

175

Chapter 10. The Boraqis

silly plant and was off. But something told him that Estelle was sitting on something.

They arrived at the door. Estelle unlocked it and entered. It was a beautiful room and unlike something he had seen before or since. He could see the paintings of unknown women and Napoleon, of course.

"These are all paintings which I had made. Someday, someone will paint my picture, if I would become a famous person," she said and giggled. "Impressive!" Al-Khidr said.

She went to a drawer and pulled out a prominent, thick journal.

"Hey! Come to my bed. Be comfortable. This will take a while," she said, opening the journal.

He rushed to her bed. Sitting on her bed, he felt very comfortable. This was exceptionally good.

Estelle stared at him and laughed.

"You like this bed, right? It is all over your face. Tell you what; you can sleep on it for today. I will take the floor. No worries," she remarked.

He nodded dumbly.

"Thanks a lot. I would like to sleep on it," he casually said.

She raised an eyebrow as if it was decided. He smiled sheepishly at that.

Flipping through the pages nonstop, she finally came to the page of her choice. Al-Khidr also looked at the sketches. They differed from the other sketches in the journal. The plants were of different, each as different as the next.

"They are beautiful. I wish I could draw like this," he said.

Estelle was not even listening. She was brimming with excitement, as it was.

"This is my beloved compendium of all the flowers and herbs that I came across. They are so adorable. I drew the ones I think are memorable and unique in their own way. The locals uttered some local names, so I named them that. I would sometimes find the same word for the same plan in a European language like Italian and French. This journal has information about nearly all the flowers and herbs I think are interesting. I gave to some Latin and French names. Lucas wrote their Arabic names alongside the sketches in his journal. Look at them. Some plants are amazing, and people use them in cooking. Others are common in dyes and medicines. This is amazing stuff. You can also copy these notes and see how they help you. I have cataloged them extensively in here," she explained.

Al-Khidr liked this session with Estelle a lot. This was probably the first time he was enjoying his time on Keb since he had returned. Lyra and Nefertiti were not on his mind right now. Estelle was becoming a useful ally in his mission to take the herb and bolt Keb. However, as things were developing, he was in no apparent hurry. Better yet, he could chill out for a little while. It was the finest day of his life since he set foot on Keb to help the diseased population on Lyra.

There was silence between the two. Both of them were thinking of what to do and say to each other.

Chapter 10. The Boraqis

Al-Khidr let do the talking. She was hurt just a few moments before, thanks to his slip of the tongue.

"What will you give me if I help you find the herb of your dreams?" she asked coyly.

"I have nothing to give. I am a poor man who will return when his quest is over. Sorry. I wish there was more," he said dejectedly.

It seemed Estelle was closing in. He had to throw her off his trail. Things were becoming severe.

"You are incredibly sweet. I will always remember you. I will be indebted to your kindness forever," he said meekly. She smiled at that. It was good enough.

"My life's ambition will be complete then," he said as an afterthought.

She nodded, as if understanding his point. It was good that she could help him in his quest.

"Very well then! We need to head south to get these plants. I saw them before the revolt in Egypt. It will be nice to accompany you and have some fresh air for a while. I am so tired of living between these walls. After the revolt, Vivant and others are cautious when I go out," she said.

He nodded. That make sense. *The hostilities between the two nations could spell danger for the young woman.* "So, when will we go?" she asked him.

"So, when will we go?" she asked him. "As soon as possible," he said. "Where are we going in southern Egypt?" she asked him. "Qena, of course," she answered.

A look of worry crossed her face.

"I think Vivant may find the trip for me problematic. The reason is that it is not too difficult to fathom. He will lock me in the room if I tell him I am off with you to find those herbs. Egypt is under French control, and hostilities are still here and there. Chances are someone will attack us, probably the insurgents. The locals are also infuriated by the fall of Egypt. The French soldiers are tired and need rest. But General Desaix has strict orders to be vigilant. No time off for the soldiers, fresh after the attack, which makes them annoyed," she explained the political situation.

He nodded again dumbly. He had heard all this before in the bazaar. Well, Al-Khidr had been eavesdropping on some of the French soldiers who filled him in on the country's current affairs.

"True. They are right," he said weakly.

Estelle thought for a while.

"What are you thinking?" Al-Khidr asked her.

She raised her hand.

"Don't talk. I cannot think," she said.

He laughed at that. Boy! She had a sense of humor.

"I may go somehow. We need to walk around the problem and add Vivant to the fold. Otherwise, you may have to find it yourself, and that would be very difficult," she said coyly.

He nodded. He would have a hard time finding the famed herb without Estelle's help. "We will have to take Vivant with us. I will throw in an extra trip to the ancient ruins or a lost temple somewhere near the

Chapter 10. The Boraqis

river. If we cannot find anything, I will say maybe the map is outdated. Anyhow, I will tag along and enjoy the walk outside for a bit," she said, clapping her hands. She thought for a while.

"It all made sense somehow. Vivant was a sucker for ancient artifacts and ruins. He would not miss this for the world. But you will have to tell this story. He will see through the ruse if I lay it out for him. That is a tough sell. We will find the herbs in the Qena region and return," she said and widened her arms. It meant how does the plan looks like so far.

"That is good. I like the idea. Let's ask him first thing tomorrow morning. He would be fresh and energetic," he said after a while. She bit her lip for a bit.

"By the way, why you are so keen to find these plants? Who is suffering from disease which you wanted to cure? Any loved ones?" she asked the question. That was her strategy; throw the question when he was least expecting it.

He scratched his head.

"Well, my uncle's animals in southern Sudan died quickly. He is worried about the cure, so I searched for him," he managed quickly. *Boy! She is clever.* The one thing he was not expecting from her was that. By this token, she could weasel her way in through difficult situations. She clapped her hands as if the plan was all ready. He would have to agree with that.

***

He left Estelle smiling and went back to his room. The plan was all ready to execute. The manuscript which he took from Lucas were on his bed. He looked at the page again and indeed the drawings of Boraqis were similar to Anemone Arabis. He took the manuscripts and placed them on the writing desk.

He crashed into the bed, feeling somewhat energetic. His mind was baffled with possibilities ahead of him. God! This was amazing.

Al-Khidr was toying with a few novel ideas now that Vivant was part of the plan. He turned on his back and thought more for a while. *What more can I say to entice Vivant that will make him come crawling? Maybe I should talk about all about the alien entry on Keb and stuff like that? That will certainly pique his interest. Should I do that?* He thought to himself.

As interesting as it was, it would also open his original plan to some scrutiny.

"I know the French savants will have a bunch of questions when I tell them all about Lyra and stuff. They will head south in search of it," he tested the idea. He thought of the discussions on Lyra and memories of Ehsis. Queen Hathor and Nefertiti came to his mind. He was missing them already.

Vivant would soon realize the reason Al-Khidr was being secretive all along. It is what it is. Estelle would be shell-shocked since Al-Khidr was dropping a cannon ball on her somewhat.

The idea was shaky to test. It may not work anyway. Vivant and Estelle would think he had drunk

Chapter 10. The Boraqis

or taken some other drug. Also, questions would raise more questions. It would take some time to bring them on board regarding his history with Lyra.

Okay. I will move ahead with the decision. Maybe it can lead to interesting areas just the same, he thought. He had a lot of options here. From the obelisks, the pyramids, to the Sphinx, the options were there. But then he realized it was nothing they had not seen before. They were touring Egypt, searching the length and breadth of the country. Chances were more that they would take him to new places instead. He closed his eyes and started thinking about Lyra — about Nefertiti. Thinking about her, only God knows when he went asleep. He saw he was moving in the cosmic tunnel with leaves of Boraqis in his hands. The tunnel was spiraling up towards Lyra. All the stars were also spiraling. His vision changed. He saw the stars came closer and formed constellations, then constellations took the shapes of snake, dog, lion, eagle, and many more, and they all started rotating. Then all these images fell on Earth, one by one, and he went closer to look at them. The images landed on the stone and were engraved on the stone. A rotating zodiac appeared, which was carved on the stone. He woke up. Did I sleep? I just took a power nap? He recalled his dream. His eyes lit up.

That's it. I will tell savants about the map of the stars. It was something they would have hardly seen or heard of before. Now where do I find the map of stars, he thought. The ideas and possibilities kept coming to him until his thoughts were interrupted.

There was a knock on the door. He stood up and went to open it. This is weird. Who in his right mind would visit him? It was Estelle, and she smiled brightly. She raised her hand as if he was expecting her somehow. He was not, though. He felt very shy seeing at her this hour. Al-Khidr's face said it all. She came into the room with no invitation, pushing him aside. He nearly lost his footing. "Hey. Easy there. I am also a human. Should I push you?" he asked in annoyance. She looked at him and smiled. "I am bored to death. Can we go outside for a bit? I will take permission from Vivant, of course. Anytime I go outside, I tell him. Either that or I am with him. I am sure he will send some guards to accompany us. It is a safety net, so I guess that is fine by me. The guards will walk along the Nile bank. We will admire the sunset. God! I love the Nile sunsets. I do this whenever I am bored and not in a mood to read. What do you say?" she asked longingly. He thought for a while. But that was not what he was thinking. Al-Khidr felt lazy. "It is late, and the sunset is within one and a half hours. So, I suggest some other time," Al-Khidr suggested. She smirked at that excuse. "Oh. Come on. I will wait for you in the lobby. Come quickly. We have no time to waste. I am running this by Vivant," she said and disappeared. Al-Khidr felt stupid sitting there. What the hell was that? She just left without even waiting for him in her room. She was a fun thing to be with—he had to admit that. He lazily stood

Chapter 10. The Boraqis

up. Man! I wanted to sleep, and the gal was taking him places uselessly. He wished he had not met Estelle. The gal was a firecracker. He came down into the lobby wearing his usual attire. Estelle looked at him and nearly hugged him. She was getting excited for no reason. The thrill of an adventure excited her to no end.

"Okay. We are all set. After you," Estelle said jokingly, trying to hide her laugh.

Vivant also broke into laughter.

Al-Khidr did not get that joke. He stood looking at the two. She motioned him toward the door.

"Stay safe. Guards! You, you, and you escort them," he said sternly. Three guards followed them. Al-Khidr was annoyed at this security detail. He liked some alone time with Estelle. Maybe they would share some intimate moments. As they stepped outside, Estelle sprang in action.

"Take ten steps back. I am not in the mood to shout today. All right? Step back. All of you," she roared.

It was a different Estelle. Al-Khidr felt low-key proud of this new size of her.

As she spoke, some guards stepped back, far from the earshot. Estelle and Al-Khidr felt this was enough. He raised his hand for the guards to stop. They had enough distance.

Estelle shivered slightly. The Egyptian nights were breezy.

"I forgot my coat inside. Can you fetch it for me,

please?" she asked.

"Here, take mine. It will keep you warm. I suppose you were getting ahead of yourself. I made this myself. It is perfect for this region. Also, I am in no mood to go upstairs again," he said proudly.

The broad smile irked Estelle slightly.

"There is that look again. When you feel you have the upper hand over me," she said in irritation.

She slipped into the sweater, still annoyed by his primal instincts. They were worlds apart, so that was true.

He had to agree with that. He felt pride flowing through him when it was the case.

He took her hand in his hand and began walking towards the Nile. It would be a while before they would reach the famed river. They walked in silence for a while. When she spoke, she sounded hurt.

"When my dad was sick, he immediately wrote a request to Napoleon. The application said to send him and me back to France. I was optimistic about it since they were friends. We would be out of here in less than a week. He had that clout. However, he passed away in Egypt and that made matters worse for me. I am stuck here until Napoleon sees the application again. He is tied up in something down south. And then you came here, so I am confused—sort of. You are a nice guy, and I feel there is some connection between us. I wish I could stay here forever. Do you feel the same between us?" she asked softly.

Al-Khidr was in a predicament here. He could not

Chapter 10. The Boraqis

tell about his true feelings and stuff like that. She sounded sad and hurt today.

"Of course, I would like you to be here. I connect with you so well. It is like magic," he opined.

Estelle disagreed with that.

"That is not the point. The thing is that permission to leave Egypt can arrive any time. I have been talking to people. When it comes, I need to leave then. I cannot reverse the order," she said softly.

As an afterthought, she put another question.

"Who is your fianc? She must be a lucky gal. I am sure of that. After spending time with you, I can vouch for that," she said, brimming with a smile. Al-Khidr felt a lump pass through his throat. He could not tell much about her. It would arouse suspicions.

"Yes. My fianc is one of the kindest persons I have met so far. She would like to meet you as well. Honestly, if you had left Egypt, I would be very bored here at the Institute. I connect with everyone here, but there is something special about you and me. You are a genuine friend. That I can say for sure. Vivant is okay, but he is no Estelle," he said without looking at her.

Estelle felt her heart melt at that. These were genuine words for him. She was about to hug when the guards behind her influenced her decision to keep walking. He continued talking. He was thinking about Nefertiti: "That is true, and I am lucky to have her in my life, as truly Estelle is something else. Though my respect for you has increased the more we talk," he said further. Estelle was red in the face.

They came to the corner of the riverbank. It was turning in another direction. Estelle motioned him to sit down by the bushes. She took her slippers off and dipped her feet in the water.

"Ah. The water feels amazing. Feel the water chilling your insides," Estelle said, laughing.

Al-Khidr followed her lead. He sat down beside her, holding her hand. They looked ahead—the light of settling sun was shining everything. It was beautiful. "Can you bring her to France with me? That would be great. I hate writing letters, as they make me sad and teary-eyed. So when I return to France, I will give you my address. You can write letters, and maybe I may send one," Estelle said.

She took her hand away from him, taking him by surprise. Al-Khidr saw her descend into deep thinking—her head was in her hands. The gal looked more depressed than before, and maybe that is how she felt when alone in her room.

She looked at his hand, and something struck her. What the hell was that? Al-Khidr was staring ahead. Without a moment's notice, she grabbed his hand again. "What is that on your hand? I have never seen such a thing before. These are holes. How did you get these holes? Do they hurt?" she asked him. The sun was setting far ahead. The situation was getting worse with every passing minute. Al-Khidr sat up straight.

He looked at his hand. The Ar-t Heru Seal had

Chapter 10. The Boraqis

become visible in the settling sunlight. The sudden discovery from Estelle freaked him out. He pulled his hand, but it was probably too late. Estelle stood up; her hands were on the mouth. He was hiding something from her all this time.

"This mark is familiar to me, and I saw it in the ruined temple of the Egyptians back last year. Why the hell do you have this thing on your hand. Explain it to me, mister," she said, leaning closer to him.

It was strange. The seal was invisible to humans. But it became visible during the sunset. Someone should have told him that. He was annoyed momentarily. She nudged him.

"Hey. I asked you something. What is wrong with you?" Estelle asked again.

He was lost in a world of his own somehow. "Who made this on you? Be honest with me, man. You have taken an eternity to answer," she said a bit sternly. Al-Khidr was still recovering from the shock of life. The first shock was probably heading to Lyra in a strange sphere, and the second was this—the care and compassion in her voice was history.

Al-Khidr felt the sweat dripping from his temple. He was still thinking about what to say to her. He had a lot of explaining to do—something he was not planning to do right out of the gate. Estelle could see the nervousness of the man sitting there, looking ahead. He seemed visibly confused. Maybe he did not know the meaning himself. In that case, he could say that. However, he was not very forthcoming.

She changed her mind. "Do not worry. If you wanted to share, you would have done that by now. But it seems you are not ready yet. I guess everyone is different. I expected more from you," she said, sitting again.

He felt terrible for this sudden turn of events. They sat silently, staring ahead into the developing darkness. Estelle would feel differently about him, and it was fair game as far as he was concerned.

"Well, it is something that I had since my childhood, and I do not know what it does or where it came from, okay? I wish I knew about it myself. Somehow my parents also passed away early on, leaving me to figure out this mystery for myself. If I knew about this, I would have just told everyone," he said, trembling. He was a nervous wreck. Estelle could see that as well, and she did not answer that right away. Vivant said something about him in passing, and Estelle thought he was a bit more suspicious than usual. He had a way of seeing things.

"Sure. Suppose that is what you believe. I am not asking what that thing is. Maybe we need time to establish this. Who knows," Estelle said dejectedly. Again, a strained silence followed.

***

They were back at Institute. Al-Khidr was in his room, and Estelle was holding his left hand. She was looking at the dorsal side of his hand again, using the most oversized lens she got from the Institute, focusing

Chapter 10. The Boraqis

on the three holes. A surgical box and a pot of hot boiling water were also nearby Estelle, and she put the scalpel in the hot boiling water.

As a naturalist, she had experience in cutting plants, insects, animal bodies. Al-Khidr wanted to learn a lot from her, and he knew that an upgrade to his knowledge was definitely required after ten centuries.

"I can see some markings. They are shinny like a small mécanisme (mechanism) inside you; Amazing!" Estelle said. "This is all shinny inside. I had never seen such a thing." her utterances were making Al-Khidr more nervous, and he felt the urge to get rid of the thing inside as soon as possible.

"Are you ready?" She asked.

"Aaaa... Yes. Go ahead." Al-Khidr said.

Estelle took a long needle in her hand, and she inserted it in one of the holes in Al-Khidr's hand. "You feel anything?"

"No," Al-Khidr said.

"Okay, hold on. I'm going to proceed further down." Estelle said.

Al-Khidr was now thinking to remove whatever he had in his hand. It was good that Estelle discovered it, and he himself could not do the minor surgery. Estelle pressed the needle further down. Al-Khidr felt a tingling sensation on his hands, like a mild static shock. An electric surge issued, and both Estelle and Al-Khidr felt the bolt. They were jolted, and they were looking at each other. Their bodies were shaking, and only "Aaaaaaa" was coming out of their mouths. The electric shock ceased their mind, and within seconds they were unconscious of everything.

***

"Ah, my hand!" Al-Khidr said, waking up from his unconsciousness. It was almost time for dinner. Taking turns holding his hand, Al-Khidr stared at the three reddish holes on his wrist. "What had happened," he recalled.

Then he realized he was on the floor, and he received the bolt. *A seizure, Ah, I cannot describe it — a shock.* "That made me unconscious," he realized.

"But... where is Estelle?" He saw Estelle lying on the bed, and she was not moving. He slowly stood up using nearby furniture and, after a few minutes, he finally got on his feet. The surgery kit, needle, and lens were lying near Estelle. "Oh, she is unconscious too," "No... no. That's too bad."

He lurked towards the bed and flipped Estelle to look at her face, and she was indeed unconscious.

Al-Khidr took the water jug in the room and threw the water on Estelle's face. Woosh! Estelle woke up. "What... what happened. Ah, my head!" she came back to consciousness. They sat in the room for a while. Al-Khidr was quiet and felt terrible about whatever happened.

"Estelle. I couldn't help but feel sorry for this, and I did not want to endanger your life. It is my mistake that I should have told you all from the very

Chapter 10. The Boraqis

beginning, and I was afraid that you would not believe me," Al-Khidr said.

Estelle looked at him and said: "You don't need to hide anything. Just tell me."

"I am sorry that I was not that forthcoming with you. If I had told you before, maybe we did not have to go through this. I cannot help but feel sorry about all this. Imagine Vivant's pain if he had found you dead. I am still a stranger to him." he said, thinking about the repercussions.

Estelle looked at him, waiting for more.

Al-Khidr started his tale from the time he entered the pyramid—967 years ago. Estelle was listening with utter bewilderment. "I should have told you from the very beginning. My story will surprise you. However, you will understand why I was so secretive and dodging people on Earth. Those plants that I was looking for are special for a reason and key to healing people on another planet." he said.

When Al-Khidr finished his story, Estelle was silent. Al-Khidr was too nervous, as he did not want to lose her friendship. It was the moment Al-Khidr was most afraid of; He knew that this was all new information for an eighteen-century girl that no one from this era knew of.

"Wait. Did you go to another planet? But how is this even possible?" she said, raising her eyebrow.

"I am a man not from this era, Estelle," Al-Khidr said and paused.

"What are you saying?" Estelle looked confused.

"I am indeed an alchemist, but I am from ten centuries earlier. It was the time when I entered the pyramids, exploring them, looking for the long-lost or hidden books of alchemy — but my destiny was different," Al-Khidr said and went to his bag and took out the sphere from the bag.

"I found this inside the pyramid, and it sent me in the sky, through the tunnel — a cosmic tunnel, and I arrived at a new planet, ruled by a queen and people there were struggling with a disease. They suffered from an unknown epidemic that affected their males. However, women were able to avoid the epidemic for some reason. The virus affected men for the most part. I give them the promise that I will bring the cure from planet Earth."

"Is it true? Are you joking?" she lurked and took the sphere from Al-Khidr's hands.

"*Magnifique! pièce de métal exquise* (magnificent, exquisite piece of metal)," she uttered.

While Estelle was still mesmerized to see the metallic sphere, Al-Khidr continued: "I came back to earth to get the plant leaves, which may cure Mutmut!" he said.

"Mutmut!" Estelle uttered.

"Yes, Mutmut is the disease which alien contracted from earth-based plants," Al-Khidr said.

"Ah, now I understand. It makes sense," Estelle said as her eyes brightened.

"The aliens or that other planet...."

"Planet Lyra," Al-Khidr informed her.

Chapter 10. The Boraqis

"Yes, the people of Lyra did not have the cure for it from any of the plants they have. Right?"

"Exactly!"

"This is possible. Certain plants from Earth can cause disease or death," Estelle said.

Estelle looked at Al-Khidr and said: "If I hadn't experienced the strange surge which had jolted my whole body, I might think that you are joking, but the experience, the sphere and the marking inside your hand, made me realize you are truthful in your account."

It was a moment of great relief, as Al-Khidr was most afraid that she might consider him a lunatic, but thanks to God, she didn't believe him a lunatic or a liar. Now that she knew the secret of the Lyrian seal, Al-Khidr was much relieved.

Chapter 11

The Encounter

THE lightning was blinding for anyone who stared directly at it, and the thunder was deafening. Beneath the many swelling and churning clouds, Hatathor was sleeping on a donkey cart, which he had parked outside of a house in the city of Damanhur. His short reddish-brown hair and strong jawline, along with his tall and upright physique, gave him a sturdy look. The sleeve weapon was covered by cloth. The house was

Chapter 11. The Encounter

deserted, and there was no other house nearby, making it a perfect spot for him to sleep, as he was feeling extremely drowsy. But, before he slept, he pressed a button on his sleeve weapon and a compartment holding the small bottle opened, containing the superfood. He took a portion of the paste to survive. After consuming the superfood, he felt satiated and was even sleepier than before. He lay on the donkey cart and fell asleep quickly. His loud snoring could be heard from twenty meters away. Even the donkey tied to the nearby pole was disturbed by his snoring. Despite the donkey's high braying, Hatathor saw Lyra in his dreams.

Suddenly, the ominous sound of thunder brought him back to reality and he woke up with a harsh jerk. He yawned deeply, but was thoroughly energized by the quick nap. He looked around, but there were no street lights like the Lyra. It was all dark — pitch-black dark — and the heavy clouds and rain made it difficult for him to see. Even he himself was nearly camouflaged in the darkness because of his black cloak. Within a few minutes, the water flooded everywhere, and the extended roof of the house started leaking.

Hatathor started looking for a dry place and found that the roof was not leaking in one particular spot. However, he noticed that underneath the spot lay a large stock of logs. He climbed over and sat there to see the heavy rain. While he was sitting on the stock of logs and planning his next move, he saw four men approaching the house at a distance of roughly five hundred Supris. They were the same men who had been watching him in the city before. Two of the men were Arab and donned floor-length, milky white robes that were woven from pure cotton. On their heads lay white headdresses, along with heelless slippers made of pure leather. The other two were Europeans who were wearing hand-knitted light-red cloaks and long white socks that covered their legs completely, along with fine pairs of heavy brown leather boots.

The Arab men were equipped with Arabian Swords with curved edges, while the Europeans owned long powdered guns similar to the ones used by Napoleon Bonaparte's army, and one of them carried a large black sack. The men were talking in slow whispers. It was strange that they were still outside together at that hour of the night, especially when it was raining so heavily.

Are they really thieves? he thought, staring at the men with utmost suspicion, along with a tinge of inquisitiveness. Luckily, the sleeve device was charged, and Hatathor activated it and switched it to the language translation mode, also activating the distant-hearing module. After he applied the noise filter to remove the roaring sound of the rain and thunder, he could easily understand what the men were talking about, even though the sound was lower than 10 decibels.

He learned that their names were Lorenzo, Francesco, Ahmar, and Saleem. Two of them were from a place called Italy, whereas the other two were the inhabi-

CHAPTER 11. THE ENCOUNTER

tants of a place called Misr (Egypt in Arabic).

Misr, I think I have heard this name before, but where? Hatathor thought intensively, trying to recall the place and time where he heard the name of the unknown place. According to what Hatathor was hearing, the men worked for some dealer named Florence Belzoni.

"Ahmar and Saleem, Master Belzoni wanted two mummies this time. He said he would give two thousand dirhams for each," said one of the men. He was clean-shaven, nearly seven feet tall, and heavily built, along with possessing pale white skin and striking light blue eyes. "Francesco, I told you I have searched for a second mummy, but I haven't found it yet. I have only one at home, and it is precious! A hell lot of a lot of black stuff comes out of it," Ahmar told the others in a highly enthusiastic tone.

"The tall man you asked me to follow, he was sleeping here. Saleem and I checked that. If we missed him, then we would miss two thousand dirhams. Remember, he looked like an ancient Egyptian, but he could be a local farmer. These are all the villagers who work in the fields and could have many friends around," the man named Ahmar added, who was of medium height and slim built. He sported a long black beard and possessed an aquiline nose and dark brown eyes. "Yes! Ahmar is absolutely right!" agreed the other Arab man by the name of Saleem, who was nearly six feet four inches tall with muscular arms. He sported a chinstrap beard with a slim and small nose, and his complexion was reddish.

One of the two men who possessed emerald green eyes and golden-blond hair, along with a beefy and towering figure, spoke to the other with a mixture of relish and greed: "We have to hit precisely on his head to make him unconscious. And we need to be extremely careful that we do not fracture his skull. Otherwise, the price will be decimated. Master Belzoni already warned me about it. He wanted a pristine mummy — a delicious one," said the man named Lorenzo, who was wearing a hand-knitted, light-red cloak and long white socks that covered his legs completely, along with a fine pair of heavy brown leather boots. "Yes, he will first order the mummy to be ground, then the dead mummy will be served and consumed. In Europe, such mummies are a delicacy, and therefore are sold at a much higher price than in Asia or Africa. Some nobilities would even be ready to give five thousand British pounds for one mummy," The Arab men's and the other Italian man's eyes widened in shock and amazement.

"But I have never really understood," Ahmar inquired while scratching his head, genuine confusion spread across his pale face. "Why is a mummified body such a beloved delicacy among the Europeans?"

"That is because," Francesco began casually, staring into the air and rain as though expecting something to appear out of nowhere. "Dead mummies offer an instant, as well as a miraculous cure for various deadly diseases like gout, pneumococcal disease, and

Chapter 11. The Encounter

a lot more." "How do you know so much about all of the diseases and this cure?" Ahmar asked in a surprised tone, with a tinge of admiration at the amount of knowledge he possessed.

"I got these things from various elite customers who were buying antiques from me. They were continuously asking me for mummies. I thought they would use them to surprise their guests at European parties, but then I learned they would eat them. The filthy rich people wanted to try anything that could cure them, so I came to Egypt to hunt the mummies. This is the business now."

One of the Italian men nodded and then whispered to the other enthusiastically, "Yes, and also we must keep in mind that Egypt is indeed a land of wonders and marvelously priceless treasures. It is especially famous for its golden idol statues, and if we are fortunate enough to gain even one of those precious statues and sell it in either the Prussian market, it will provide us with endless wealth. To such a tremendous extent that each of our next ten generations will bathe in gold and wealth. They would never even have to work like us!"

Hatathor still had no clue what these men were talking about. *Were they following me? Nay, they are not searching for me; they are looking for the mummy. What is a mummy, by the way?* He thought intensively, with an extremely confused look on his face. "Maybe I should ask one of them." "The last time I saw, the guy was sleeping on his donkey cart and was snoring badly," Saleem informed the others.

It is definitely not me! Hatathor was pretty sure now that they were not talking about him but about somebody else. *I never snored in my entire life.* Well, that's what he thought at least. The donkey probably had a different opinion. Hatathor was ready to face the men, so he jumped down from the logs and began walking towards them as the heavy rain turned into a drizzle. The men saw the dark silhouette approaching towards them. Completely baffled, they started whispering to one another. Hatathor said: "Do you guys know the way to Al-Qahirah?"

"Signor, we have also lost our way due to rain," one of the Italian men said and put his hand in the large black sack. "Why do you wish to travel to Al-Qahirah, by the way?" inquired one of the Arab men casually, who initially believed that he was a local farmer. His eyes were glinting with greed and thrill.

"Well, I have some really crucial work to do there. I am looking for someone in Al-Qahirah, and it's a matter of great importance and necessity that I find that person as soon as possible. Otherwise, something really disastrous will happen to my people, which I can't even think of or imagine," he explained solemnly, thoroughly hoping that those men, whom he believed to be gentle travelers, would guide him — or at least tell him a way through which he could reach Cairo and find the damned human, Al-Khidr.

"Well, what is your name, brother?" asked Ahmar slowly. "And where are you from? You don't really seem to be someone who is from around these lands.

CHAPTER 11. THE ENCOUNTER

Are you from the Middle East?" Ahmar asked with curiosity, staring at his reddish-brown hair and matching skin tone in amazement. *Perhaps he is of mixed race*, thought Ahmar.

Hatathor gave a smile at his question. He had no idea what place he was referring to, and neither could he reveal to them that he was not an inhabitant of the earth, but a superior life-form from the planet Lyra. He ignored the question about his place of origin and introduced himself solely through his name. "My name is Hatathor," he replied, offering his hand to Ahmar and the others, who shook it excitedly. He didn't bother asking their names, as he had already heard them while using the distant hearing module.

"Well, Signor Hatathor," Lorenzo began as a wicked smile spread widely across his sharp jawline. "The four of us are perfume sellers and were traveling and lost our way in the rain. Would you like to smell our new best-selling perfume?"

Lorenzo started looking into his bag while the rest of them smirked at him stupidly. Lorenzo took out a small bottle and before Hatathor could say no, he brought the bottle close to him. The bottle was filled with a mysterious green-colored liquid. Hatathor stepped back with caution, "No, no." Lorenzo brought the bottle back towards his chest. "Oh Signor, smell it. It's very nice."

"I do not want to smell any perfume. I just wanted to know the way to Al-Qahirah."

Hatathor was waiting for the guidance for direc-

202

tions to Al-Qahirah from the men as Lorenzo smiled and suddenly removed the bottle cork and threw the green-colored liquid on Hatathor's face. The fumes erupted, causing his nostrils to feel a horrible burning sensation. His eyes began watering terribly and his nose started dripping. Hatathor knelt on the ground, sneezed three or four times, and then he fell. He was sneezing ferociously. The four men watched him with utter surprise. They were not expecting that sort of reaction.

"Everything you have in that sack of yours is a substandard thing. Even the anesthesia is of low-grade quality. Why in the name of God didn't he become unconscious?" "I swear on my Lord, I do not know why the most potent anesthesia didn't work on him. It has never happened before that no human could resist my chemical's power and not fall on the ground unconscious immediately. This man might either be some powerful alchemist himself who drank a potion to give him resistance or, he might not be a human at all." "Are you out of your mind, Lorenzo?" Francesco rebuked, considering both the theories to be absurd, not plausible.

"That is the stupidest thing I have heard all day. Just admit it, your chemicals are utterly useless!" Saleem shouted.

"Why did you throw liquid on me, cursed human?" Hatathor shouted at them in agony as his eyes began watering profusely and burning furiously.

Hatathor realized that the four men hadn't lost the

Chapter 11. The Encounter

way, but were looking for him and wanted to make him unconscious. "This cursed planet is filled with liars, killers, and God knows what else," he said to himself with anger as he rubbed his eyes desperately trying to get rid of the chemicals. "What shall we do now?" the four men shouted to each other.

"Kill him!" the Arabs shouted.

"No! Not now." Francesco replied.

Hatathor first sat on his knees with his head held down and began to stand. He immediately took more of the green military-grade superfood to give himself extra immunity and gain a major power boost.

The four men ran in different directions. Francesco dashed at lightning-speed towards the same house underneath whose shades Hatathor had been sleeping. Since the house's roof wasn't very high, he could grab the thatched roof and quickly climbed the top. He began panting heavily and sat on the house's roof, staring at his comrades being chased by Hatathor. The adrenaline rush that had taken over him was beginning to lower, but his face was paler than ever. "Just get away from there, Lorenzo," he kept chanting to himself under his breath like a mantra.

In the interim, one of the Arab men, Ahmar, ran in the opposite direction to Francesco and was being chased by Hatathor, who was like a raging bull on a red flag. He didn't leave the man's tail.

"Come here, you cursed human!" he abused, darting towards him with bloody eyes that were still watering profusely. "You piece of human shit, come here!"

Ahmar's mind was blank and his heartbeat was racing terrifically as Francesco's did. He didn't realize where he was heading. He continued running until he fell down. Hatathor reached him and an evil smile spread across his sharp jawline. A trickle of sweat dripped across Ahmar's forehead and his face turned as pale as a white sheet. In that state of terror and desperation, he took out his sword and began attacking Hatathor but missed him, as the mighty Lyrian had swerved to avoid his attack. He sliced the sword again at Hatathor, but this time, Hatathor bent down and with an impressive sliding kick, he caused the Arab man to fall onto the ground. The sword slipped out of his hands, and finally, it lay under the feet of Hatathor.

Hatathor grabbed Ahmar by his hair and pulled the horrified Arab towards him. With a howl of fury, he flung him like a spear. The man went flying and landed on the grassy area near a date palm tree.

Ahmar immediately rose onto his feet and began climbing the tree as quickly as possible; he was quite an expert at climbing a date palm trees. He made it to the top in less than thirty seconds and clenched the tree with full grip. His heart was thumping in his chest like a rock, and he was sweating as though a bucket of water had been thrown all over him.

Hatathor thought of climbing the tree but then decided not to do it, as the trees on Keb could inflict diseases. He began kicking the base of the date palm tree in rage to make the Arab man fall; however, he failed in that attempt.

Chapter 11. The Encounter

"You bloody pile of shit, I will bring you down, you see!" he yelled on top of his voice. His watery reddish eyes were making his vision blurry, and because of the pungent chemical, his head was shaking.

As he made another attempt to bring Ahmar down, his eyes fell on Saleem, who stood a few yards away. Saleem was rooted to the spot out of fear and was simultaneously staring at Ahmar, who lay on top of the tree, and Hatathor, who stood below like an angry tiger waiting for his prey. With the roar of a raging bull, Hatathor took a step back and sprinted at his next victim.

"Goddammit Saleem, run!" shouted Ahmar from the tree-top, while waving his hands desperately for his fellow Arab comrade to save his life from the enraged Hatathor. It took Saleem a few seconds to get out of his dilemma-filled trance, and he shook the profound fear that had frozen his feet and, stumbling slightly, he took a run for his life.

"Help me! Help me! This man wants to kill me," Saleem screamed like a little child in distress. He continued sprinting as fast as his skinny legs could take him. He turned towards a corner and stumbled a bit, nearly losing his balance. However, he ran towards the house where Hatathor had been. His heart was pumping blood at a tremendous speed, and his legs felt so numb that he couldn't even feel them. He was approximately one hundred meters away from the house and his face had shown some relief when something extremely unfortunate happened. His luck gave in as he fell into a large ditch. Saleem went rolling below and hurt his knee, which started to bleed. He yelped in pain and clutched it with both hands. Hatathor decelerated and came to a halt near the ditch.

"Finally, one pathetic and cowardly vermin in my clutches," he uttered in a booming voice. "You're going to pay for what you and your bastard friends tried to do to me. Unfortunately for you, they have left you, and you will bear their portion of my wrath. I will break every bone in your feeble and pathetic shell!" he said as he began advancing towards the ditch. He was about to descend upon Saleem when a loud voice bearing an Italian accent sounded from behind. Lorenzo fired twice through his gun-powered-based gun, and although he missed the aim, he did enough to infuriate the Lyrian warrior. Lorenzo's face turned even whiter with fear; however, he maintained his calm and courage. Hatathor continued to march like a ferocious lion towards him. In a state of desperation, Lorenzo started looking for the gun powder, but he had lost it during the run.

Lorenzo provoked him and took out a red cloth and started waving it towards Hatathor. Before he could blink, Hatathor rubbed his eyes thoroughly and darted towards Lorenzo in a fit of rage. Immediately, Lorenzo made a run for it as well.

"Cursed human, I will make your soul leave your shell!" he howled like a werewolf and chased the Italian mummy hunter furiously. Hatathor charged towards him and wanted to give him a painful death,

Chapter 11. The Encounter

as Lorenzo was the one who had thrown the chemical liquid at him. Lorenzo noticed a horse carriage that stood abandoned on the side of a deserted street.

"I should climb over the carriage," he muttered under his breath as he climbed the horse carriage.

In the interim, Hatathor dashed towards him, and he jumped and landed on the carriage.

Damn, this bloody beast of a man won't leave us alone! Is he even human? Lorenzo thought bitterly with frustration. His legs hurt as his long white socks were torn and soaked with blood from the slash on his knee. Setting aside all the pains and aches he experienced, with an effort, the cunning Italian mummy hunter jumped and ran again, although his speed had been drastically reduced now. This time, Hatathor was fully determined to make the man pay for his outrageous act. While sprinting away from Hatathor, Lorenzo slipped horribly and went flying to the ground. He squealed in pain as the gash on his leg widened and burned excruciatingly. While on the ground, he turned his head fearfully to perceive approaching Hatathor, who was moving towards him like a ravenous tiger who hadn't eaten for weeks. In that intense moment of desperation, Lorenzo took out another bottle of the anesthetic liquid.

Hatathor pulled Lorenzo towards him, with his hands on the neck of Lorenzo. Lorenzo removed the cork and held his breath. He threw the contents of the bottle at Hatathor's face again.

Hatathor dropped Lorenzo as he began experiencing a sense of intense dizziness. He began swaying uncontrollably. His head began getting heavy, and his body felt numb as well. After a bit more swaying, he then collapsed on the ground into a state of unconsciousness. The men took a sigh of relief. Ahmar thanked God and supported Saleem, who was badly injured as his feet were bleeding. Francesco helped Lorenzo to get onto his feet, and he placed Lorenzo's arm around his neck.

"Are you alright?" he inquired in a worried tone.

"I am okay, Francesco. Just a little shocked. Was this man even a human?" Lorenzo inquired as he nodded in agreement.

"Don't be ridiculous, both of you," snapped Ahmar, looking at the Italians as though they were crazy.

"Yeah, Ahmar. I mean, just think about his endless stamina. He could chase all of us at the same time without breaking a sweat. The anesthetic drug had little effect on him at first. I am really curious to know about his background and his true identity. I mean, an ordinary farmer can never possess such capabilities," said Saleem with the utmost curiosity and admiration.

The four of them, including Ahmar, nodded slowly and began taking deep breaths.

"Now, before he gives us another shock and regains consciousness, we must quickly take him," announced Ahmar anxiously.

"Yes, I know where!" attested Lorenzo wittily. With a smirk forming across his sharp face, they all

Chapter 11. The Encounter

burst into fits of laughter.

Chapter 12

The Embalming

Slowly, Hatathor opened his eyes. He was feeling nauseous and felt like he was about to puke. The unbearable smell of the pungent chemical which the human had thrown at him continued to irritate his nostrils terribly. His head felt heavy, and his vision was blurred as he saw some floaters in his sight. He couldn't realize where he was and took some time to focus on his surroundings. The first thing he perceived was a fluttering black cloth over him; it seemed like he

CHAPTER 12. THE EMBALMING

was in some sort of black tent. He realized he was indeed inside a tent's compartment, alone. He looked to his left and right and saw no humans around. He then slowly lifted his head, and the feeling of chillness hit him as he found that he was naked. In the light of the lanterns coming in, he saw his shimmering body. Oil had been smeared over his body. He lifted his head a little. However, he could neither see his clothes nor the sleeve weapon.

He discovered that the tent had two compartments. The room was dimly lit by a light coming from the other compartment of the tent where some humans were present and talking.

Is it the same night, or have I slept for a few hours? He wasn't sure.

He turned his head to the left with a little moaning sound and focused on the ambiance. The first thing he saw was that his left hand was tied with a rope around it. He tried to move his right hand and found that it was tightly fastened with a thick rope, as well. His hands were at his head's level, and apparently, his hands and feet were fastened to the legs of the table on which he was lying.

They put me on triage! Damn humans on a cursed planet! He was furious, and he had to do fast.

He heard some sounds. People were talking outside the tent, but he could only understand four distinct men's voices. The men were talking to each other as they entered another compartment of the tent. Their voices were not very audible. Besides that, he could not understand what they were talking about, and that made him more nervous. He had absolutely no clue what he was doing in this tent or the four men's purpose behind bringing him there. *Certainly, their intentions are not friendly,* he thought.

He continued looking around and saw several wooden boxes on the floor. He also noticed a metallic tub in the tent, large enough to fit a tall person. Near the tub were many bottles with different liquids. There were some jute bags also, and one bag had fallen on the ground. He tried to examine the contents and found that it looked like some sort of salt-like substance. Also, he saw an enormous pile of linen strips near the table.

"These men made me unconscious, and by doing so, they have dug their own graves!" Hatathor said firmly under his breath.

"This planet is undoubtedly a cursed place full of thieves, robbers, and highly deceptive bastards!" he muttered in a fit of intense rage and revulsion. "What do these deceptive thieves want from me?"

He tried to focus intensely on their conversation, but since he had no sleeve, he couldn't understand what they said.

Meanwhile, in the other compartment, the men were discussing their plan.

"That strange man is still sleeping. So, before he wakes up, we must begin the process of mummification!" Lorenzo exclaimed as he gulped down a glass of beer and wiped his mouth.

Chapter 12. The Embalming

"Yes! We do not know how long we will control him if he regains consciousness, so we must act now." Ahmar agreed with Lorenzo.

"So, what do we do first?" Saleem asked Francesco, who was enjoying a glass of beer too.

He gulped down the last sip and replied, "First, we must rupture his skull by running a small metallic rod through his nostrils. After that, I'll pour a drug, and his brain will become a paste. Then, we need to use a reed straw to suck out his brain and spit it out quickly."

"Ah! That horrible. Saleem can do it," Ahmar said. Saleem rolled his eyes and replied, "No, no, no. I have no experience with such."

"Sucking out the brain needs to be done cautiously, and I can do this job," Francesco proclaimed.

At his words, Lorenzo let out a loud and unpleasant burp, and Francesco scoffed at him disgustedly.

"I am the best at this job. I shall do the brain-sucking part, fellas. Leave it to me!" Lorenzo told them, but they continued to argue loudly and made a lot of noise. Hatathor had already realized that these men were mummy hunters, and as they hadn't found the one for their dealer, they were planning to kill and mummify him instead. He had to carry out a plan fast to teach these ruffians one last lesson before releasing their souls from their bodily shackles.

He gathered all his energy along with his strength and pulled his hands towards him, which were tied to the pillars of the table on which he was lying. He soon realized that probably wasn't an excellent idea; if the pillar broke, he would be in a much more difficult position to do anything. He knew that his sleeve weapon was fully charged, and if he shouted with full force through the depth of his throat, he could activate the sleeve weapon if it was nearby.

The sleeve weapon should be nearby as most likely the mummy hunter had taken off my clothes and weapon in this tent, he thought.

He cleared his throat and issued a deep guttural noise from his throat, more like fluttering in human ululation. Ululation was a Lyrian way to communicate danger or pleasure to someone, and this sound differed completely from the humans. His high-pitched ululation made the glass bottle shake; some went down in the sand, and some shattered and exploded. The sound of the ululation alerted the mummy hunters, and they realized that the subject was up to something.

Immediately, the four of them stood up and ran towards the room where he was placed. But just before they entered the room in which he was lying, he commanded his sleeve weapon in Lyrian.

"Bekhkh Khakab!" (*Enemy around. Create Shockwave!*)

"Affirmative," the device sounded, and a loud boom was heard.

The tent rose into the air as the shockwave not only flipped the table on which Hatathor was lying, but also blew the tent away and unclamped it from

Chapter 12. The Embalming

the ground. The camels and donkey outside fell to the ground and rolled over. The burning cloth of the tent soared high into the air. Hatathor realized he was in a desert, and it was nighttime. The shockwave caused the burning of the jute ropes, and he was able to release himself. The tent came landing back onto the ground and the wind made it fall back on to the mummy hunters. Their bottles were horribly shattered because of the shockwave, and the liquids seeped into the sand. The animals were agitated and erupted into all kinds of sounds. Meanwhile, the humans were struggling to come out of the fallen burning tent and started rolling in the sand to stop their clothes from burning.

Hatathor had gotten onto his feet and was ready to teach the bastards a lesson. Lanterns were flameless, and the sky was dark. He immediately looked for his sleeve weapon and identified it with the blinking light. The humans took time to get a sense of their surroundings, as they were confused. They rubbed the sands off their faces and half-burned clothes and spit out the sand that had entered into their mouths and nostrils.

"What the hell just happened? What was that sound?" cried Lorenzo with an irritated expression.

"Your chemicals reacted, and bottles exploded — mother fucker!" Ahmar shouted.

"Check that guy. He could run away," Lorenzo shouted back at the baffled Arabs.

They ran up to the broken table, but there was no

one there. Feelings of terror and shock spread across their faces, and suddenly they heard a voice. "Say your last prayers!" the voice boomed. The angry and confused expressions of the four mummy hunters instantly turned into that of colossal fear, distress, and agitation.

"How... how... on Earth did you untie yourself?" stammered Saleem. His eyes widened with trepidation like they would pop out of their sockets. Hatathor's lips moved and took the form of one of the most vicious smirks they had ever seen. His eyes were blazing with rage and bloodlust for revenge. He clenched his fists tightly and breathed deeply with fury. Hatathor started moving around the men like a shadowy beast.

He pressed some buttons on the sleeve device that he was wearing now and announced, "I am the Hatahor, bloody humans! I can do things you pathetic and cheap scums could never think of inside your tiny brains."

"Look... O Hatathor.... we are gentle folks; we had no intention of doing anything bad to you. In fact..." Saleem's stuttering halted as Francesco raised his hand to silence him.

"Oh, come on, fellas. We are mummy hunters and we are not intimidated by any human on this planet. And besides, what are our guns and swords for if we get scared of this piece of shit? Take him down," ordered Francesco.

At Francesco's word, Hatathor let out a massively loud and mirthlessly cold laugh of spiteful mockery,

Chapter 12. The Embalming

which nearly made the mummy hunters tremble from head to toe. "I am not like you, you pitiful humans. I am someone you would never meet again on this planet. I am from planet Lyra," saying that, he moved his clenched fists up and got ready to fight the cunning and deceitful mummy hunters. "Give me your best shot, humans."

The moment he finished his sentence, Francesco and Lorenzo took out their guns while Ahmar unsheathed his sword and aimed it at Hatathor.

Saleem stopped, "Wait, guys. Let us resolve the dispute. You are free to go Hatathor."

"Shut up! I give orders here,"Francesco growled at Saleem. "Master Belzoni will be furious if I go empty-handed!" But before Saleem could say anything, Lorenzo raised the gun and fired at Hatathor.

Francesco also shot bullets at him, but Hatathor swerved and dodged. He immediately pressed the button on his sleeve weapon, which created a protective force field around him. He started moving towards the humans. They fired again, but the bullets dropped on the sand as soon as they touched the shield. The guns eventually ran out of gun powder.

Ahmar moved towards Hatathor. He struck him with all the force and strength he could muster. Ahmar aimed the sword right at Hatathor's chest. Meanwhile, Hatathor activated the energy shield. The man looked at it and said, "Cheap magician! He is showing his tricks!" "Teach him a lesson!" Francesco said to Ahmar.

Ahmar smiled and leaped forward, and he pushed the sword into the energy shield. The powerful jolt of electricity made him cry for help, and his clothes started burning. The smell of burned flesh started erupting from his body.

Hatathor withdrew the force field around him.

Saleem put both of his hands on his face and dropped on the sand, and he started crying, "Spare me, please!" Ahmar was moaning in pain, and Saleem was in a state of anxiety.

The Italians were filling up their guns with gun powder.

"I will teach you a lesson with my hands!" Hatathor said.

He did a backflip and kicked them both in their faces. With the mighty force of Hatathor's powerful kick, the Italians were thrown backward and went soaring through the air; they then fell to the ground. Their bodies began aching terribly, as though they had just been hit by a steel bar, and they lay on the ground moaning in extreme pain with their noses bleeding profusely.

They finally stood up and made a desperate sprint at Hatathor, empty-handedly attempting to punch his face, but the indestructible Lyrian clamped their punches with both his hands, effortlessly and expressionlessly, and held them tightly between his palms. The mummy hunters stared at him in utmost horror, their faces as pale as a white sheet with the shadow of death lurking in their eyes. Within a fraction of a second,

Chapter 12. The Embalming

Hatathor moved his palms and crushed their fists. A terribly ear-bursting roar of agony broke away from their mouths as their knuckles crushed. The men kept howling and screaming for mercy, but the ruthless Lyrian didn't grant it to them. After hearing the gut-wrenching cracking of bones in their knuckles, he released their hands, and they collapsed on the ground once again in unbearable agony.

In the interim, Ahmar had gotten onto his feet and yelled.

"You scoundrel! You piece of shit, you burned me! I'll rip you apart limb from limb! You should have thanked God and accepted that painless death of a mummy. But alas, your fate wants to give you the most ghastly and spine-chilling death!" he growled. With intense rage building up inside his slim body, he picked up the sword again and darted towards the empty-handed, indestructible juggernaut.

Ahmar's height of desperation caused him to wave his swords furiously at Hatathor, who avoided his attacks with enormous ease like he was playing with a little Lyrian kid who held a plastic toy sword. Ahmar bent down and swished the sword aiming at his legs, but he bounced in the air instantly and aimed another kick at Ahmar, which hit him squarely on the side where a human's heart was located. He rushed backward and rolled on the ground. The force of the kick felt like that of a boulder to Ahmar, who yelped in pain and clutched his chest.

Hatathor gave Ahmar time. The Italians and Saleem

were watching all in horror.

"How dare you hit me!" Ahmar growled like an aghast lion as he swished his sword with a firm intention to slice away Hatathor's head. Hatathor made a swinging movement with his arms, and before Ahmar knew it, he clamped the sword's blade skillfully between his palms, which blocked the attack. In a gigantic state of desperation and frustration, Ahmar struggled to free his sword by yanking at its handle while roaring and yelling, but in complete vain, as the Lyrian's grip was too firm for the sword to be released.

Ahmar moved his palms apart, and he was able to free his sword. He nearly lost his balance due to the humongous force of his own yanking to set the sword's blade free. Hatathor ran towards Ahmar and began delivering light punches to his chest and belly, who could do absolutely nothing but bear his wrath. After delivering three high-speed punches, Hatathor turned around and struck the side of his slim face with his elbow. Hatathor's colossal force caused Ahmar to vomit blood, and he fell to the ground.

Slowly, Hatathor towered above the pathetically injured body of the mummy hunter. Ahmar lay in a pool of blood on the sand, gasping for breath and ready to give up. He could barely speak and was on the verge of embracing death when they muttered something that sounded like "have mercy" as his mouth filled with fresh blood. The ruthless Lyrian could hear him, and he asserted proudly, "I, Hatathor, the unbeatable warrior of the great planet, don't show mercy to my

Chapter 12. The Embalming

enemies at any cost. For the crime of trying to deceive me and to mummify my body, you all must pay and be sentenced to nothing but an unavoidably gruesome death." He ended the sentence and, placing his hands around his throat, lifted Ahmar into the air. The mummy hunter had barely any air left inside his lungs and no strength to raise his head. With a final look of pure evil and a smile that made his teeth glint, Hatathor applied one more bit of his strength and crushed Ahmar's windpipes and thus, granted him a cold-blooded death. He slackened his grip, and Ahmar's body slid through his palms like paper and lay like a dog on the ground. "Ahmar!" Saleem screamed in hellish agony and fell onto his knees. With a river of tears gushing out of his puffy eyes, he painfully mourned the death of his dead friend.

Saleem mourned over the dead body of Ahmar. It seemed like the world had ended for him, and he felt like his heart had been ripped out of his chest. The pain of Ahmar's lifeless body lying in the sand afflicted him unendurably. He felt as though his soul had been taken away, too, along with his best comrade. Meanwhile, Lorenzo and Francesco had recuperated and risen, although their knuckle bones were broken. "What do we do now, Lorenzo? He is way too powerful, brother, and unlike any man we have ever fought before," affirmed Francesco. "He is not human. Maybe he is a djinn of the desert! I heard from local Arabs about them."

Lorenzo and Francesco started running into the

desert while Saleem was in a state of shock, crying.

Hatathor looked at the Italians and made a few jumps, reaching the men who were filled with dread. Francesco died on the sand, and still, on the ground, he flipped himself while facing the enemy. He was pushing himself away from approaching Hatathor by ferociously moving sand with his feet. He saw Lorenzo still running into the desert.

"Jesus, help me!"

Hatathor pulled him up by his hair and spit on him, and then threw him like a ball on Lorenzo. They both fell and Hatathor reached them, twisting their heads one after another to make them meet their Lord.

Hatathor came back towards Saleem, who lay knelt on the ground, crying about the death of his friend. "Spare me please," Saleem said while he wept painfully, without moving his eyes away from Ahmar. Hatathor did not want to waste his time anymore, so he pulled the man by his hair and dragged him like a donkey. He brought him back to the campsite and then he asked the Arab man to search for his clothes, which he did. Hatathor then put on the clothes and demanded loudly in the Lyrian language, "Where is Al-Qahirah, you filthy human? Tell me, or die a cold-blooded death like your comrades-in-arms."

"I do not understand your language," Saleem uttered.

Hatathor activated the Arabic mode on his sleeve weapon translator and repeated his question.

A broken and defeated Saleem moved his feeble

Chapter 12. The Embalming

fingers slowly and pointed towards the east.

"Spare my life!"

Saleem had no strength left in his body or in his willpower to either threaten or fight any further with Hatathor. Unbearable sorrow had overcome him at the death of his brother-like friend.

"Very well, human, I shall spare your life for guiding me in the right direction. Consider this mercy from the great Hatathor, and wish that you never get to face me or my wrath ever again!"

Hatathor left Saleem alive and started moving over the sand dunes towards his destination — in search of another human whom he desperately wanted to stop.

Chapter 13

The Lure of Zodiaque

T HE next day, Al-Khidr woke up early at the break of dawn. After completing prayer, he went down towards the lobby. He discovered that most of the French savants were still sleeping, and few servants were cleaning every nook and corner meticulously. He went out and looked at the Institut d'Egypte building. After so many days, he felt as if he could breathe freely. The Ottoman's base used the building as the residence, and it was one of its kind luxurious buildings in the entire

Chapter 13. The Lure of Zodiaque

city of Cairo. The design was exquisite and modern. Perhaps that's the reason the French liked that building so much, he thought admirably.

He went into the garden. The morning dew was refreshing all his senses, and he took a deep breath and enjoyed the freshness of the smooth morning breeze.

I should go to the Nile and stroll there. It's been a while that I did some exercise! He thought. Ah! Those were the days when I played with my friends. The poignant memories took over, then he came back to his senses and shrugged them all off.

Al-Khidr was glad to get out of this cage. There were no soldiers around, and he found the perfect opportunity to have a respite.

He started strolling through the city, heading towards the Nile. It was a pleasant morning and the wind from the Nile was quite refreshing.

Some local Arabs were turning their heads to look at him, as he was an Arab and wearing a French dress, which people found both interesting and odd at the same time. While he was strolling on the road, he heard some French guards talking to each other as they walked ahead of him.

One soldier exclaimed while looking above at the clear light-blue skies.

"How delightful the weather is today. However, it is still not as good as the lovely weather that we find in France," the soldier paused. Becoming nostalgic, he took a deep sigh.

He continued, "Ah, I missed the lovely frimaire,

brumaire, and the nivôse(frost, mist, and snow) so much!"

The second soldier nodded serenely in agreement and added, "You know, I have heard somewhere that the total number of French men who have died because of heatstroke in Egypt is way more than those killed in the recent revolt."

"Holy Jesus!" The first soldier exclaimed, placing his fist on his mouth in shock. "Dammit! I despise the brutal sun along with those feral dogs, insects, those bloodsucking devils, mosquitoes, fleas, as well as those tiny gnats. They are the most annoying creatures in this world and attack us ruthlessly like Ottomans," the first one replied in a bitter tone while clenching his fists tightly.

"Sunlight in Egypt feels like a heavy punch, like massive distress on the face. The atrocious bugs attack and bite mercilessly, and all I can do is try my best not to scream," he laughed coldly with bitterness in his voice.

Al Khidr found the soldiers' conversation amusing and quite interesting. The soldiers took a turn, and he continued his walk. The sound of birds chirping increased, and he saw the river right in front of him. There was a jetty and many ships were around. Suddenly, he had the feeling that he should run away from all this mess.He felt like he had been stuck in this building for eternity. *Savants liked me, but what was the reason?* He thought, but he had no clue.

Are they monitoring me?He brooded, his mind rac-

CHAPTER 13. THE LURE OF ZODIAQUE

ing thoroughly to look for a quick way out of that place.

Do they feel I am a spy or something? He did not know. "Perhaps they simply like educated people," Al-Khidr said to himself.

He had many blunt questions that he wished that someone could answer; however, he simply couldn't ask those questions directly. He just needed to wait and see. Estelle was the sole reason he felt hopeful while staying there. She was an extremely encouraging soul and helped him with everything.

I hope she has no harsh feelings towards me as I sometimes say things which I cannot explain to her. He thought nervously while strolling on the river bank. The sun was too bright, and the ships loaded with the local people were arriving at the jetty. People were looking at him in a way that made him nervous; he had been made an alien on his planet by Hatathor. The memory of Hatathor filled his insides with extreme anger and fear at the same time. Suddenly, a loud call from the ships embarking made him realize he needed to go back.

***

When he returned to the institute, he discovered some unfamiliar faces dressed in frock coats, waistcoats, and breeches, along with silk stockings and cotton shirts with decorated cuffs. Some wore spectacles. Some were young and some were old.

They were all scholars or scientists or university professors, Al-Khidr pondered. Vivant introduced him to some of the men. Al-Khidr greeted them mechanically as they smiled at him with mundane formality.

The entire atmosphere of the mansion had completely transformed and was quite similar to the one he had experienced at House of Wisdom in Baghdad. One by one, all the savants were arriving, and they started chattering continuously about their respective duties and responsibilities. Some of them were showing their sketches of the temples while others were displaying the drawings of animals, plants, and insects, while the others spoke vainly of their expertise in measurements. However, each of the scholars were engulfed in one unifying endeavor, which to decipher the fascinating mysteries of ancient Egypt.

Al-Khidr came across a multitude of ideas on different topics in a single day. One of the Frenchmen by the name of Algernon had a book in his hands, and he was enthusiastically showing the passages to his fellow scholar.

"Aristotle says that the River Nile has magical properties, and its water boils in half the time compared to other water bodies in the entire world. Quite an amazing piece of information, don't we?" he exclaimed, his eyes glinting sharply with the knowledge he had just received from the book. "And this is precisely the reason twin births occur in Egypt frequently."

"Marvelous piece of information, Algernon Pascal!"

Chapter 13. The Lure of Zodiaque

Conté sarcastically replied.

Some scholars laughed hilariously and mockingly said, "In that case, Algernon, I will drink the holy water of the Nile every day to produce more army men!" Laughter broke out instantly among the scholars at this amusing statement.

While they were all absorbed deeply in the intense discussion about pyramids, temples, and writings, Al-Khidr began thinking of Lyra and started looking into the array of beautiful paintings hung on the massive walls. As an alchemist and originally a Berber dyemaker, he was interested in plant-based colors, especially blue. They always fascinated him. The French had brought a great amount of artistic equipment from their homeland, like pencils, colors, brushes, and measuring instruments. While he busied himself in deep observation and admiration of the art, a voice called to him suddenly, and he turned.

"Al-Khidr, I would you to meet my dear friend Gaspard Monge, a geometer and an enthusiastic lover of writing Arabic scripts," Conté introduced excitedly. "Pleasure to meet you, Monsieur Monge," Al-Khidr expressed genuinely as he shook his hands.

"We need more scientists among Egyptians, but unfortunately, the local population is not that interested in what we are doing here." "These Ottoman Egyptians are stupid or lack curiosity. We are here to ignite new learning," Monge expressed serenely, revealing his disappointment at Ottomans and rebellious Arabs. He smiled as he said further, "I am surprised to meet you, young man!"

"Where were you? I mean, a few months ago, during the time of the revolt."

Al-Khidr felt nervous and looked at Vivant to explain everything. Al-Khidr again narrated the same story to the scholars about his mother being French, how she married an Arab man, and that their relationship was why he could understand both the languages well and converse in them fluently. *The French savants were not like the military or spy-catchers — they were merely scientists and engineers who were keen to share their abundant knowledge in their respective fields of science and technology.*   Politely excusing himself from the French scholar, Al-Khidr continued his exploration and started looking at new things the savants had brought as free giveaway tokens. He noticed a box full of wood sticks with some black stones protruding out of it that lay in a corner.

"You can have some. These are called Crayons in French; I invented them four years ago," Nicolas said to Al-Khidr enthusiastically, with a strong sense of pride for his invention that was noticeable to Al-Khidr.

Al-Khidr slowly placed his hands inside the box, and retrieved four fascinating pieces.

First, he tried them out by writing with them on a piece of paper that was present on a table nearby, and then he furiously tried to analyze where the ink was coming from. He then smiled and placed one Crayon inside his large pocket.

Chapter 13. The Lure of Zodiaque

Nicolas laughed and said, "Have some more. We have a lot of these."

Utterly impressed by the tool, he placed some more into his pocket. He found it very interesting that those Crayons could write without ink. Suddenly, the smell of rich coffee filled the air, and the gravitating aroma hypnotized the French.

"Time to grab some coffee!" one savant announced keenly, and everyone rushed to the table.

They grabbed their tiny, sizzling ceramic cups of Arabic coffee, and the deep discussion started again.

"We have counted and you would be pleasantly surprised to realize that there are nearly one thousand three hundred and fifty coffee houses in Cairo alone," informed a man by the name of Lebron Bellamy. "It is really enjoyable to spend an evening outside these cafs. Most of the time, aspiring poets go there and ecstatically recite their latest poems and compositions. If you know Arabic, then that is a feast, as their skills are marvelous. The poetry is composed of improvised verses regarding the activities on the streets," a savant mentioned the pleasures of Arabic coffee houses delightfully.

"I have been posted in Saint-Domingue. Let me tell you, friends, the slaves who work there for us produce the best sugar and coffee in all of Egypt. About four hundred and fifty thousand slaves work day and night on plantations and export sugar and coffee to France," another savant proclaimed haughtily.

Al-Khidr learned from Estelle that her country had

abolished slavery, but she had also felt that eventually, it would be reinstated, as the elite French people couldn't imagine life without them.

Al-Khidr was attentively listening to the savants' discussions on different topics. They expressed their ideas and theories openly and with amusing elaboration. Al-Khidr continued to listen to their discussions and tried to make sense of every piece of information he considered interesting. Being a student of one of the greatest scholars in Baghdad, his listening skills had been sharpened over time, and now, thanks to the Lyrian technology, his brain could decipher the multitude of languages spoken across the various galaxies. He was lost in his amusement, thinking back about Lyra, when suddenly a voice loud enough to pierce the ears of an insect brought him back to Earth. The man called tienne Geoffroy Saint-Hilaire was blasting his theories with full force.

"Nearly every organism has a similar design, no matter what they are, a plant, an insect, or a human. God created one form of being, and it gradually developed into multiple beings," he proclaimed.

One savant laughed loudly at this statement and commented, "Stop it, tienne, you would turn me into an insect." He laughed incessantly.

Al-Khidr smiled as he saw Vivant coming towards him with a man he hadn't noticed before. He introduced him to the man called Berthollet. "Hello Monsieur Al-Khidr, how are you? I am Claude Louis Berthollet, a chemist like you. Vivant has told me a

Chapter 13. The Lure of Zodiaque

great deal about you." He greeted him, shaking his hand with utmost enthusiasm. "We share a common goal, to learn from the unique elements like the past of our ancestors," Berthollet continued.

"By the grace of God, I am all fine," Al-Khidr expressed, with a genuine smile that showed his sparkling white teeth.

"Great that you liked us!" he said.

"You know, Mr. Al-Khidr, I believe in the human spirit, its freedom and free-thinking. God is like a far-fetched idea for some of us," Berthollet added composedly, and he pointed towards the savants.

Al-Khidr smiled. "Yes, Mr. Berthollet, I can sense that. But I would like to politely disagree here," began Al-Khidr slowly and carefully, trying hard not to sound too contradictory or harsh. "Believing in God doesn't stop one from thinking, right? I mean, we may think whatever we may like, isn't that true?" The idea of blatant atheism was new to Al-Khidr.

"Indeed, you can. However, the strictly one-sided and stiff belief that an unknown and unseen power created this universe and ran it, frankly, prevents us from exercising our free will, and this prevents us from testing our limits," Berthollet rebutted.

"And how does it prevent us from testing our limits?" Al-Khidr counter-questioned politely, trying to comprehend the point.

"For example, it is claimed in the Bible that God created the first-ever man in his full-grown form. Some people believe that as the 'word of God' and are not ready to believe or even ready to speculate on other theories. For example, the theory put forward recently by our French Biologist Lamarck, who concluded that microscopic organisms appear spontaneously from inanimate materials and then transmute, or evolve, gradually and progressively into more complex forms through a constant striving for perfection." He gave a detailed explanation without a pause while holding his unending smile, which left Al-Khidr quite confused yet mesmerized by the information that Berthollet provided.

Al-Khidr asked, "So, according to you and the eminent scholar you spoke of, this universe and everything compiled in it so brilliantly just appeared out of nowhere?"

The narrative reminded Al-Khidr of some thoughts and views that he had read about in the books of Greek philosophers. Al-Khidr expected that the Frenchman would be annoyed or irritated with his question. To his surprise, the French scholar continued to smile.

"Now, that is a very good contradictory question, Mr. Al-Khidr," he commented cheerfully. "I am even more impressed by you now that you are an open-minded person, despite being so religious. To answer your question, I would say that the world is held together by some force field or energy that we haven't yet discovered. Still, I am pretty sure that our progressive scientists will unravel the mystery of the universe's existence. But I can guarantee you this: there is no unseen force like God that controls the business of this universe. It has developed through some energy which

Chapter 13. The Lure of Zodiaque

will be specified in the coming years by our brilliant scientists. Mark my words, I have a feeling you will be among the first to know about it. Until then, have a lovely day, Monsieur. Al-Khidr." With another handshake and a smile, Berthollet exited the conversation and moved over to the others.

Besides that, he heard few savants talking about God and praying to Jesus, while a few others were indulged in mundane politics, which was of no interest to him. Al-Khidr held the view that some savants had no convincing argument to deny the existence of God, and that is exactly why Monsieur Berthollet had waved the conversation aside with a well-timed compliment to him. Al-Khidr was astonished to realize that nearly all the savants had their theories on the origin of civilization. Quite a substantial number of them did not believe in the existence of a higher power that controlled the affairs of this world. The ones who did were even looking for the place where Moses crossed the Red Sea to escape the Pharaoh's army and free the Israelites, as he heard one of the savant ranting about it restlessly.

"It will be a tremendous achievement, perhaps even more valuable than the discovery of fire was for the people of the Stone Age, that we find the exact spot where Moses used his staff to strike the Red Sea which set aside its water and allowed him to escape the Pharaoh!"

"Indeed!" exclaimed another Frenchman, who was bald and stood near him. Al-Khidr was fairly inquisitive, so he joined the conversation. "Hello everyone, it is a marvelous pleasure to meet you all. I am Al-Khidr," he introduced himself and shook their hands lightly. "I apologize thoroughly for eavesdropping on your conversation, but I just couldn't resist. Gentlemen, I am extremely curious to know how you people are going to go about finding the exact spot where Moses crossed the Red Sea." The savants burst into speech with excitement and explained simultaneously, "First, we want to go to India, but our ships are in the Mediterranean Sea. We need a path now to cross over the Red Sea to enter Arabia to get to our ships somehow."

"However, there is a big problem," the bald man said in a disappointed tone. "The local Arabs are restricting our march towards the south. In the east, the bloody British are stopping us." *The political landscape of the Middle East had changed,* Al-Khidr realized. Since he had nothing more to imbibe from those savants, he excused himself politely and left the conversation.

Completely engrossed in a whirlwind of thoughts, Al-Khidr looked outside the large window and became engulfed in his thoughts, bounded to a promise to return to the stars.

Amidst those thoughts of the promises he made to Nefertiti, Al-Khidr suddenly realized that Estelle was not there.

Where is she? It's late already. He thought in a state of anxiety. Perhaps she slept too late.

Abruptly, he was detached from his thoughts when

Chapter 13. The Lure of Zodiaque

a servant arrived and informed him that Madam Estelle was still sleeping.

In the meantime, the lunch got ready. Al-Khidr joined the savants in the humongous dining hall.

First, the national anthem, the Marseillaise, was sung to commemorate the day.

"In the memory of our late friend Dominique Testevuide who was assassinated during the October 21, 1798 Revolt..." Monge mentioned a few words to honor him, and everyone held their heads low during his speech.

When it ended, they all sat down on their respective chairs and dug into their plates. The enormous table was laden with the most scrumptiously mouth-watering French food. He heard the name 'croissant' for an oval-shaped cheese puff, which was a French starter. Al-Khidr bit into it and experienced the appetizing cheesy delight with the utmost pleasure. He had never tasted something like that previously, and he relished every bite. After munching on the starters, he feasted delightfully on a non-vegetarian dish named boeuf bourguignon, which was a tangy beef stew. This was a traditional French delicacy that all of the upper-class French people loved. The dish tantalized his taste buds and he was intensely reminded of his home-cooked beef dishes, which his mother used to cook, and he nearly became emotional. He was so overcome with nostalgia that he had to clench his teeth tightly to prevent himself from succumbing to tears.

"This is delicious," he commented weakly to one

savant sitting beside him, who nodded approvingly while holding a mouthful of beef in his mouth. "Fellow friends and colleagues, today we drink the water of the great Nile!" Vivant announced grandly while raising his glass in the air as the rest of the savants copied him while cheering loudly.

"Let me quote Diodorus Siculus!" he exclaimed and cleared his throat. "The Nile surpasses all rivers of the inhabited world in its benefactions to humanity." There was a round of applause at the great quotation, and one savant added, "Seneca the younger wrote about the Nile that all other waters wereVulgaris aerae, which suggests that all the water bodies were nothing compared to the water of the River Nile."

Meanwhile, the servants poured more of the Nile water into their cups.

Monge gulped down some brandy quickly, a bottle which he eagerly clenched in his hand, and began chattering away on some unknown topic with a fellow savant who was sitting beside him.

"We hold meetings like these every two months and share the knowledge that we acquired in those two months," one savant informed Al-Khidr proudly, who raised his eyebrows with admiration.

"I wish we had discovered some passages into other pyramids," said one savant, who was seated opposite to Al-Khidr.

"Oh, I made one passage once using acids," Al-Khidr blurted out without thinking. An instant surge of regret flowed across his mind.

Chapter 13. The Lure of Zodiaque

All the savants looked at him in utter bewilderment, and there was an awkward silence for a few seconds. Then one savant piped in, "Which pyramid was it?" "It was a small one somewhere in Sudan," Al-Khidr lied instantly. With some quick thinking, he twisted his narrative to prevent his previous story about his parental background from collapsing. "So, Al-Khidr, do you believe the pyramids were tombs of pharaohs, or did they comprise something else? And do you think the pyramids are four thousand years old?" Monge asked him with overflowing curiosity.

"I think they are much older, perhaps over eighty thousand years old. Our local sages informed they were built when the star called Vega was close to the North Pole." While Al-Khidr was saying this, the words of Ehsis were resounding in his mind about the pyramids and the casing stones which he had seen earlier. The paintings over them flashed across his eyes.

"That's very ancient!" exclaimed Monge, his pupils widening with every word that Al-Khidr spoke.

"I have seen no Zodiac or any star maps yet in the temples."

Al-Khidr recalled the Lyrain star map which Ehsis mentioned, as he wanted to go to Qena to get the herbs. He realized that the moment was right to cast his spell and lure the savants into the star map. This would provide him with a golden opportunity to move out of that place and escape.

So he said, "I can share some ancient secrets with you, Monsieur Monge, which have been passed down from generations among my people."

As soon as he said this, every scientist on the table pointed his eyes at Al-Khidr. They were locked in to what Al-Khidr was about to reveal to them.

"Somewhere in Egypt, there is a map of stars, which is much older than humanity itself."

This astonishing piece of information created a cacophony of contending voices among the French. Soon, everyone began coming up with their own theories. Counter-arguments were moving like waves, one over another over another.

Monge became irritated and yelled at them on top of his lunges, "Keep quiet, everyone! Let him finish first!"

"Please continue, Monsieur Al-Khidr," he requested politely, eagerly waiting for him to start speaking once again.

"My friends told me that there could be one in the south near Qena. We just need to look for it, and it may give us more clues. I can help you," Al-Khidr added hopefully.

"We were planning to visit the pyramids tomorrow, and now I think I should extend my journey and pass by the Qena as well. So, my dear friend Al-Khidr, I would like to invite you to come with us too," Vivant requested courteously, eyeing him with admiration.

"Thank you, Monsieur Vivant. I'll be glad to come," Al-Khidr said triumphantly, as the first phase of his escape plan succeeded.

Vivant smiled and said, "Estelle also held an in-

CHAPTER 13.   THE LURE OF ZODIAQUE

tense desire to visit the pyramids before she goes back to France, so she will accompany us as well. I am wondering where she is now?"

Al-Khidr was brimming with joy at hearing the news, and he wanted to leave the table as soon as possible to go to Estelle's room. "Good idea. Devilliers and Dubois-Aym have also visited the pyramid, and trust me, they found it completely enchanting," one savant informed Vivant, who beamed with glee.

"We will travel by boat to Qena, as the land is infested with ruffians and attackers," Vivant informed, with a feeling of disgust, as though the ruffians were repulsive insects.

Al-Khidr was overjoyed with this idea, as the open space would provide him with a better chance of getting rid of the French engineers and soldiers. When he was about to leave for Estelle's room, Berthollet stopped him in his tracks.

"Wait, Monsieur Al-Khidr!" he exclaimed hurriedly as a servant brought a fat book laden on a golden tray. Berthollet gestured to the servant curtly to present it to Al-Khidr. The book's title was in Arabic, and it read 'The Rights of Man' by an author namedThomas Paine. Al-Khidr held the heavy book in his hands, flipped a few pages, and thanked him politely for the gift.

"The pleasure is all ours, Monsieur Al-Khidr," he said, with a deep bow of respect. "By the way, it has been translated on the orders of Sultan Napoleon," Berthollet notified him with his trademark smile.

"Oh, okay. I will give it a read as soon as I can," Al-Khidr affirmed, and with a deep bow, he stood up and left for his chamber.

Chapter 14

The Martyr

NEARLY an hour had passed since Hatathor murdered the four mummy hunters and left the campsite. However, it was still pitch-black outside. The fierce wind of the desert continued to stroke his face viciously as it flew in the opposite direction. The wind was strong enough to push any ordinary being backward easily; however, Hatathor wasn't affected by it much and moved forward with ease. The darkness of the night continued to envelop Hatathor and everything

Chapter 14. The Martyr

else that surrounded him like a blanket. He moved like an intimidating juggernaut over the sand dunes. His mind bulging with pure hatred for the accursed human, Al-Khidr, as well as the rest of humanity on the planet Earth.

By hook or by crook, I need to find that human dirt Al-Khidr in Al-Qahirah and stop him. He thought furiously as he trampled the dense sand beneath his feet. As he reached the peak of the dune, his eyes widened with astonishment. His jaw dropped as he perceived the gigantic dark structures and he moved his head up to view the topmost peak that appeared like lifeless giants to him. Hatathor had seen no pyramid on Earth before. The sight of the giant structures took him down memory lane, and his stony heart softened a little as he recalled the pyramids back on Lyra. The pyramids made him feel like he was back on his home planet.

"I cannot believe my eyes," he said to himself as he continued to gawk at the marvelous structures with his mouth wide open. "The presence of pyramids on this darned planet is a miracle!"

They were the three pyramids of Giza that Hatathor was viewing. A cold realization hit him at that point that the mummy hunters were performing the embalming procedure on him in the desert, so that his cries of pain couldn't be heard, as there was no human population nearby. The sand was striking his face intensely, and some of it went inside his eyes and nose, thus, making his eyes watery and irritating his nostrils.

The majesty of pyramids made him fall on his knees on the desert sand. He looked on the ground, and tears gushed from the corners of his eyes as he cried, "This was the HSS team landing site, where dad used to work."

Hatathor became overcome with emotion and wept.

Abruptly, he gained control and wiped away the tears. He got back onto his feet and traversed the area around and discovered that the three pyramid structures comprised a square base and four smooth triangular sides that rose to a towering point in the sky. He activated his sleeve device and measured the monuments, and the device gave the readings. Out of the three massive pyramids, two were four point two five (one hundred and forty meters) and three hundred and ninety-two Supris in Lyrian unit of distance, while the shortest pyramid that lay on the right rose merely to a height of nearly one point eight two Supris (one hundred and sixty meters). He began walking around the three pyramids and found an enormous statue. That one statue grabbed his attention in particular, as it possessed the shape of a dog-like body with a face of a human. Hatathor gazed at it in utter amazement as it appeared to him as a creature from planet Kebirum, Anpu (Anubis), sitting.

It is a Lyrian monument defaced by humans, he thought to himself, continuing to stare at it with admiration.

He knew these monuments were extremely ancient and built by the HSS team who were stationed in the

Chapter 14. The Martyr

Keb. Suddenly, extreme rage built up inside Hatathor, and his heart was pounding heavily. His eyes were bloodshot, and his nostrils expanded as he breathed deep with anger. He raised his index finger in the air and looked at the sky — looking and pointing it towards the Lyra. He burst out in a fury.

"Ehsis! You treacherous old hag! You will pay for your sins! I, Hatathor, I'll find you, no matter which hell hole you are in!" He shouted these words, and his loud cursing blended with the whooshing sound of the wind.

As he was moving across the sand, his sleeve weapon started beeping loudly. Hatathor was instantly alarmed and peeked into the panel. He pressed a few buttons, and the display showed the alert: "Lyrian metal detected!"

Hatathor was astonished, and he pressed a few more buttons. He then brought the device close to the ground and placed one of his knees on the sand as the beeping intensified.

He was surprised.

He activated the scanning mode and moved over the area marked by the device as the likely location of the Lyrian artifact. The device scanned the ground, and a large holographic image formed in front of his eyes, showing the spot where the Lyrian artifact was present.

A Lyrian relic was buried underneath his feet; however, it was too deep in the sand to grab, roughly thirty Supris (one kilometer) deep.

He activated the sleeve weapon and checked the power. He estimated that if he could generate multiple shocks at one spot, he could reach the exact spot where the relic was present. But if he did that, the tracking would be lost for two days until the device was charged again with low-intensity radiation from the sun.

Maybe it's another jump-sphere. He thought, as a swarm of theories floated inside his mind.

It took him a few minutes to adjust the intensity of the shockwaves and optimize the drilling process. He stood over the relic location and turned around while throwing multiple shock waves. A hole began forming on the ground. Loud booms were generated, and tremors on the ground were shaking his body. Within thirty minutes, he created a small crater around him, and the relic was now accessible. He jumped into the crater and started removing the sand with his bare hands; suddenly, he touched something.

"Finally, I got it!" he exclaimed with enthusiasm as he pulled the object out of the sand.

It was an alien bone. Its size and length were more likely characteristic of a Lyrian creature.

"It must be of a Lyrian!" he blurted out loudly as a strange bubble of anxiety popped inside his stomach.

He removed the sand as fast as he could, and to his amazement, he found below it a Lyrian man's skeleton that was slightly shorter than him. This was the first thought that came to his mind, but then he realized that there was a badge inside the rib cage. He picked it up and cleaned it by rubbing it thoroughly using the

Chapter 14. The Martyr

edge of his clothes. Eventually, the writings started becoming visible. There was a Lyrian name engraved on it, which he read intently. The badge dropped from his hands in horror.

The ground beneath his feet vanished; jolts of electric current flowed through his veins. His mind seemed to stop functioning for a few minutes. As reality struck him like a lightning bolt, he knelt on the ground. His body turned cold, and goosebumps covered him as he lay there, expressionless, as if his soul had been sucked out by an unknown force. Like an empty shell, he couldn't get over the intensity of the shock that he had received.

The badge read Seth. The skeleton was of none other than his own father's.

High above in the sky across the Milky Way, the celestial Iteru was smiling at them. As the hours went by, he lay there on the ground along with his dead father's skeleton, talking to him as though he could listen.

Hatathor, holding his father's bones in his arms he began talking to him, "Look, father. I am back. I am back!" His voice quivered as he shook the skeleton slowly and looked at it with the innocent eyes of a child. "There is no need for you to worry about anything now... I have grown up into the mighty warrior of the Lyra! No one can lay a finger on you now, let alone hurt you now. Let's go back to Lyra now together! You do not know how delighted mom would be to have you back!" A flood of tears erupted out of his eyes as he blurted those words, "All of your books have been kept the same way as they were when you had left. I have cleaned your room myself."

Hatathor was in a state of shock at the sight of his father's remains as his stony heart had melted by the gush of uncontrollable emotion that he had imprisoned inside himself for decades.

He became silent and closed his eyes as he began recalling the events from his past when he was an eight-year-old child.

Since early childhood, he had been traumatized by the loss of his father. It was the loss of his father that had deprived him of a normal childhood.

He experienced an extreme mental breakdown and a mild panic attack when it happened. He remembered sitting at the dining table with a napkin wrapped around his neck as his mother cooked his favorite dish for dinner.

"Mom!" he yelled, his stomach making horrible noises out of extreme hunger. "How much longer? I am hungry!"

"The lunch is coming in three minutes, dear!" she replied in a sing-song manner. Her mood seemed to be jolly that day, as Hatathor's father was finally going to come back home after accomplishing his prolonged mission.

Young Hatathor kept sulking and making disgusting faces until his mom swayed across the room holding the frying pan and slid his favorite snack into a small platter. "Here you go, sugar pie," she said, pulling his

Chapter 14. The Martyr

cheeks affectionately and whisking away back into the kitchen. "Your favorite snack. Enjoy!" Within a fraction of a second, he grabbed his fork and spoon and attacked the scrumptious dish ravenously. After having a mouthful, he realized that his mother was still working in the kitchen.

"Mom, aren't you going to eat with me?" he asked loudly.

"No, sugar pie. I am going to wait until your dad comes home and will have dinner with him," she responded sweetly. Her face seemed to glow with glee at simply the thought of seeing her husband after months of being away from him. Hatathor suddenly felt that he should also wait so that they should all have dinner together, so he left his half-eaten snack and rushed inside the kitchen to assist his mother.

"What happened? Why aren't you eating? Is it not good?" she asked him serenely.

"No, mom, it is the best as ever!" he yelled with enthusiasm, causing his mother to playfully covers her ears with her hands. "But I also want to have dinner with dad and you, so I will help you with the cooking."

His mother gave him the widest smile she had ever given him and kissed him on his chubby cheek.

"My little angel has become a big now, eh," she expressed as she caressed his cheek lovingly. "But you don't worry, mommy will handle the kitchen works. You clean up your dad's room. When he comes home and sees the room spick and span, he will jump with joy!"

"Yes, I will clean up his room!" screamed Hatathor as he darted out of the kitchen to clean his father's room.

Hatathor's eyes opened, and he returned from that happy memory. That was just one memory from his childhood when he and his mother used to wait for his father to return from his prolonged missions, which would often last for months. Yet, he would always come back, and they would rejoice and have lovely family time together. However, death had embraced his father on his final mission to Earth, and their family was torn apart. Hatathor had already murdered Queen Hathor for killing his father, and now, he wanted to end the life of Ehsis as well for not stopping her.

Seth's skeleton was still in his arms, and his tears had fallen onto the skull. Somehow, after seeing his father's skeleton, the fear of death seemed to evaporate from Hatathor's mind, as he imagined the horrible death his father likely faced. Thinking about that unthinkably painful death, he felt that any other type of death was trivial and painless in comparison.

Thinking of death, he was reminded of another agonizing memory of his life, and his eyes closed again. He recollected the time during his teenage years when he had returned home after a long day of intensive training.

He entered the moment, and what he perceived made his heartburn agonizingly. His mother was sitting on the floor with her legs folded, staring at the

Chapter 14. The Martyr

framed photo of her dead husband. She was young, but her hair had turned grey. Hatathor was rooted to the spot near the entrance, and he clutched his fists tightly to prevent the tears from gushing from his eyes. His body was quivering with the lava of distress bubbling inside him. His heart was torn into bits seeing that aging lady lying on the ground, who was once a hearty and jolly woman whose smile could make anyone's day better. Hatathor moved towards her and knelt on the floor beside her. "Mom," he called, placing his rough palm on her soft ones.

"You know, son," she began, without moving her eyes away from the photo frame, which showed Seth standing in the corner of their house with a warm smile on his face. "Your father always wanted to explore the universe. He had this desire to unravel every secret that this mysterious universe held." Her eyes were dry and lined with dark circles, which resulted from the various sleepless nights that she would spend in his remembrance. However, there was an inexplicable glow on her face when she spoke about her beloved late husband: "I would sometimes quarrel with him about his unending missions to various planets and how he would leave me in solitude for months. To which he would smile and say, 'The joy of reconciliation with your loved one is greater than any other joy in the world. And the short-term separation strengthens bonds and makes you value your loved ones.'" She paused and caressed the photo frame gently, as though expecting her husband to come out of it. "Before he would leave for any mission, I would make him promise that he would return to me, and he always did. I had no complaints with him, except for one," she claimed, and Hatathor looked at her with curiosity.

"And what is that, mom?" he asked her with mild keenness.

"That he didn't fulfill his last promise. He did not return to me." She paused and rested her head against the wall with her eyes wide open. Hatathor didn't know what to say, and he simply continued to stare at his beloved father's photo frame beside her. The smile on his face made Hatathor's stony heart melt like a candle. "Mom, dad died a martyr's death. He gave up his life for his people and his planet. Let's not hurt his soul by being sad and forlorn for any longer," he explained anxiously, without moving his eyes away from the photo frame. "Dad does not want us to be just thinking about him all the time."

However, his mom did not respond and remained quiet; she was just silent.

"Mom.... mom," he called her, but she didn't reply.

He looked at her instantly and found her eyes opened wide, but she didn't blink at all. He called out to her three times while shaking her shoulder rigorously, but there was no response.

"She is no more on Lyra!"

The reality pierced his heart like a bolt of lightning, which ripped him. His mother's soul had departed Lyra and moved up to join her husband's. Hatathor

Chapter 14. The Martyr

placed his head on her lap and wept bitterly.

"You can't leave me, mom... You just can't," he kept muttering under his breath, as sorrow had overtaken him completely.

The young man suddenly jerked his head up and staring at the ceiling, he let out a thundering roar of agony and called out to his mother. He felt like tearing his flesh and banging his head against the wall as the anguish of losing the only woman who he loved more than the entire universe. His heart burst into a billion pieces. He wished he had rather been set ablaze with fire than witnessing his mother's death, and too at such a tender age in his life.

There were a million things he had wanted to do for his mother and a million things that he wished he had said to her earlier. He felt like the loneliest man on Lyra, as life had orphaned him at such a young age.

The massive distress and trauma caused by Seth's death had slowly eroded her soul; she had continued to exist, but like an empty shell, having no emotions, desires, or any purpose. Her life was taken away from her when she first heard about her husband's death.

Hatathor's eyes opened, and the memory of that sorrowful day of his mother's death brought more tears into his eyes.

"Dad," he said, wiping the tears from his face. "Mom left this world; she left this world because she could not bear the separation from you. It slowly eroded her soul, and she died right here in my arms."

Saying that, he gently placed his father's skeleton

where it was in the crater and started putting the sand back over it. He wanted to do it with his bare hands in order to feel the satisfaction of fulfilling his duties as a son — out of respect for his father.

Hatathor realized he was becoming too emotional, and this would jeopardize his mission. Therefore, he moved from there as soon as he could. He stood up instantly and gave a last glance at the place where he had buried his father's skeleton and then searched for the badge which he had thrown. Unfortunately, he could not locate it anymore and his sleeve's battery was dead. As he walked away from the crater, his foot got entangled in some rod. He dug it out and was amazed to see that he had discovered a bident — a Lyrian bident buried in the sand. He examined the bident with curiosity and clutched it firmly.

The sound of the gushing Nile could be heard. He walked towards it and dipping the bident inside the water, he washed it thoroughly. It had kept its shine and luster despite being buried underneath the sand for ages, as it was made from the Lyra's finest non-rusting metals. He opened the power unit of the bident and noticed that it was empty. He was missing Amris badly. Hatathor let out a roar of frustration and was about to throw it far away when his eyes fell on a blitz occurring in some distant clouds — the clouds were coming towards him. The thunderous roar of the storm shook the sky. Hatathor's eyes sparkled with the dazzling light of the clouds as he fixed his eyes up above.

Chapter 14. The Martyr

Suddenly, an idea flashed into his mind. I can use the electricity to jump-start the bident power unit! The sheath of the batteries is covered with radiation scales that absorb radiation. The batteries of a Lyrian bident were made of cold fusion technique, which required their secondary cells to be charged with the help of solar radiation. The batteries, though small, were powerful enough to energize a city block for two days. Those were the same powerhouses of Hatathor's formidable and versatile sleeve weapon. The batteries would glow with a blue light when the weapon was activated. He needed to act as quickly as he could, so he began sprinting towards the largest pyramid of Giza and started climbing. He sweated profusely as he mounted the colossal pyramid as fast as he could. Within a few minutes, he reached the apex, and without wasting a single moment, he clamped the bident on the topmost stones and began descending the pyramid briskly. He came down and started looking at the approaching clouds while howling in Lyrian, "Strike, strike." Few seconds passed, and nothing happened. His mind began hoping desperately, "Come on, come on, come on," he chanted rigorously. "It's now or never!"

Still, nothing happened. Filled with disappointment and extreme frustration, Hatathor turned around to walk away, when suddenly, there was a crashing sound, and the blitz inside the clouds zoomed down and struck the sharpened prongs of the bident. As a powerful electromagnetic surge occurred in the sky, he turned immediately and let out a smile of victory.

"Praise the Lord!" he shouted as he punched the air in triumph.

However, since he was too close to the pyramid, a tremendous bolt of lightning surged through the sky again and struck him as well. The Lyrian warrior was thrown backward, and he landed several hundred meters away with a gut-wrenching thud on the sand. He was knocked out cold.

***

Hatathor's eyelids fluttered open as the distant calls of the *Adhan* from Cairo brought him back to his senses. "Ah, my body!" he moaned intensely as his ribs throbbed and a terrific pain shot through his muscles like they had been crushed with a stone. He looked at his half-burned clothes and felt repulsed; however, he was pretty happy that he was not dead and that he was still in one piece. "Thank God!" he said gratefully, placing his hand on his chest in relief. He listened to the soothing sound of the Adhan closely and exclaimed with a mixture of amazement and tranquility, "What is this strange call that I am hearing? Are the humans announcing something?" He was utterly perplexed by the call to prayer.

Whatever it is, it is very soothing! He thought as the *Adhan* pacified him thoroughly. He fell back on the sand again and fell asleep, as he felt weak.

When he regained consciousness, he noticed the sun setting gracefully across the peaceful horizon, and

Chapter 14. The Martyr

his body was covered in the sand. Slowly, he sat himself up and looked at his sleeve. His sleeve weapon was not fully charged as his arm had been under his torso while he was unconscious, and so the sunlight hadn't reached it. He had been lying there unconsciously for an entire day. He placed his palm on his leg and flinched loudly, as the place where the lightning bolt had struck him still hurt horribly.

"I need more energy!" he muttered, and opening the sleeve, he took out the military-grade superfood. Within a few minutes, he regained his full strength, and rising to his feet, he began looking for the bident.

He discovered the bident laying on one rock of the pyramid. Gathering all the strength left in his body, he began mounting the pyramid again. Upon reaching the bident, he picked it up and was extremely glad to discover that the lightning had jump-started the batteries of the bident.

He connected the it with the sleeve and charged his sleeve device as well. Hatathor was fully equipped now with another potent weapon in his arsenal. Unfortunately for Hatathor, though, the tracking unit was not functional, as that battery was completely drained.

"Prisoner, I am coming! And this time, you cannot escape my wrath!" he affirmed loudly, as though the prisoner could hear him. With a last glance at the great pyramids, he resumed his journey towards Al-Qahirah.

Chapter 15

The Antique Collectors

Cairo Egypt, 8 January 1799

NEFERTITI and Al-Khidr were standing in front of the most magnificent museum that could have ever existed. A massive display of the classiest artifacts, especially the relics of war, were present. From an array of enchanting ancient pots and solid statues to the indestructible chain mail armors, everything appeared like a feast for the eyes of Al-Khidr, who was simply

Chapter 15. The Antique Collectors

spellbound by the precious collection of the Lyrian civilization. As Nefertiti walked across the museum, she felt as though they had gone back in time. With each step she took, she felt as though an era walked past them — like a movie playing in front of her eyes. However, Al-Khidr felt like he had been sent back to the Abbasid Caliphate era. He experienced a strange feeling of pleasure and happiness. Suddenly, Nefertiti's eyes fell on a large drum.

"These are the war drums, Al-Khidr. They were used during the ancient era in Lyra," Nefertiti was pointing towards some ancient instruments. The Lyrians called the museum that they were visiting The House of Relics. "We have gathered all the finest ancient pieces here that we have collected over the years under this one roof. They serve as a reminder of what our ancestors did on the Lyra millions of years ago," Nefertiti said proudly.

Al-Khidr was looking at the various artifacts in utter fascination and amazement, as they were not very different from those present in Abbasid, Iraq. He had already seen most of them in Iraq and Egypt, which Nefertiti claimed to be of Lyrian heritage. He was extremely baffled because the artifacts closely resembled the ones present in the world he came from.

Could it be true that there is some sort of close connection between the Lyra and my world? A connection that nobody is aware of today? How is it possible that these artifacts so unequivocally resemble the ones back in Egypt and Iraq? These thoughts rushed through

Al-Khidr's mind as he scrutinized every piece of each relic. "Look at this drum," said Nefertiti, pointing at a massive barrel-sized instrument. "Even my grandparents used these drums." She started beating the drums like a little girl announcing an army. Hearing the drum, Al-Khidr's mind took a tremendous turn, and powerful images of war appeared in his head. The thunderous drumming made him visualize the amount of violence that war brings, how it destroys homes and makes people homeless, along with orphaned children and widowed young wives. The horrible images continued to emerge briskly inside his head, and his vision turned slightly blurry as he fell dizzy. A second later, he turned towards Nefertiti. To his utmost astonishment, he noticed that her clothes were changed, and she was wearing the Abbasid helmet and armor while carrying a sword.

"Bang, bang."

Al-Khidr was amazed to perceive so many Earthen cultures mixing, and they were all from the Lyra? There were tons of questions that he desperately wanted to ask her, but Nefertiti had closed her eyes, and she was banging the drums harder than ever, as though possessed by some warrior's spirit.

"It's too loud, Nefertiti!" Al-Khidr exclaimed, but Nefertiti was not listening; she was pounding the drum continuously.

"Stop it!" Al-Khidr yelled at Nefertiti, who did not seem to listen at all.

Al-Khidr's eyelids flashed open, and he rose with a

Chapter 15. The Antique Collectors

jerk, as though someone had thrown a bucket of cold water on his face. His heart was beating faster than ever, and he was draped in sweat from head to toe. Someone was banging on his door.

"Hey, wake up, Al-Khidr! We have been waiting for you," Estelle shouted as she continued to bang the door in the same way as Nefertiti had done in his dream. *Ah, that was a dream!* He thought as he rubbed his eyes roughly.

"Oh, I am sorry, Estelle! I am awake now. I am coming down soon," Al-Khidr apologized sleepily. Wiping the sweat off his face, he got up instantly to get ready. He realized he had overslept for nearly an hour, and Vivant and Estelle had been waiting too long for him.

He quickly took the most valuable possession out of the trunk in his room: the Sphere.

He looked at the Sphere and serenely whispered in Arabic, "It's time for work, Sphere!"

He packed a pair of clothes and the Crayons, which Nicolas gifted him. He retrieved a piece of parchment from his trunk and tried writing with the Crayon on it, and found that it was quite easy to use. He had drawn a picture of Boraqis herbs on a single parchment, as carrying a book in his luggage was not a practical idea. Besides that, he packed some dry fruits like almonds, pine nuts, and dried dates in a pouch. He changed into a fresh pair of French attire: a yellow brocade waistcoat with a floral design and a pair of white stockings, which seemed a bit tight to him.

"Just a few more hours, Al-Khidr, then you will get out of his ridiculously suffocating attire," he told himself irritatingly.

He put on a pair of black boots and was ready to go; he put on his sack himself.

As soon as he reached the stairs, Estelle demanded loudly, with her stunning light green eyes fixed on him, "You slept like a log. Did you drink last night?" Al-Khidr looked quite baffled at that statement and shook his head in disagreement.

"Of course not!" Estelle said as she threw back her head and laughed while flipping her hair onto the side flirtatiously.

Estelle offered her hand to Al-Khidr as a French custom of greeting, and he kissed the top of it. As he kissed it, she threw him a glowing look.

He is one heck of a desirable man, isn't he? She thought affectionately, unable to take her eyes off him. Estelle was wearing the blue sack-back gown, and she had woven her lovely brown curly hair into a chic braid and coiled it into a bun, which made her look even more stunning. "Let's get the hell down as quickly as possible!" she said, and they both descended the long stairway together. Vivant was waiting for them patiently. He was dressed in his trademark red coat which he put over a long waistcoat and his usual white stockings.

***

Institut d'gypte was not very far from the Nile

Chapter 15. The Antique Collectors

jetty. The jetty was a small, wooden landing stage with a movable wooden staircase connecting it to the ground. From there, you can walk towards it and embark on the Felucca, which is a traditional wooden sailing boat used all across the eastern Mediterranean countries. Al-Khidr noticed poor Arab men, women, and children walking on the sides of the jetty. The men were wearing ragged jelebiyahs, while the women were dressed in dusty black abayas (black floor-length robes worn by Muslim women).

A horse carriage dropped Vivant, Estelle, and Al-Khidr at the jetty. The large Felucca was ready to carry them first to Giza and then to the southern cities, one after another. In normal circumstances, the French would use the confiscated boats for traveling; however, Vivant wanted to show Al-Khidr that the French could travel with locals. Because of this, he ordered that they travel all in the Felucca with the local Egyptians who were also going towards southern cities. A man was shouting out the names of cities where the boat would go in Arabic.

Estelle had a small suitcase while Vivant was carrying a leather bag, and Al-Khidr had a jute bag with the strap hanging on his shoulder. One of the French guards who accompanied them took the luggage out of the horse carriage and Al-Khidr assisted the man in placing the luggage in the Felucca. Vivant was watching them, and suddenly he noticed that Al-Khidr's left hand had three dots on the dorsal side.

He became curious, but he said nothing. Monge's

words were echoing in his mind, "Beware of the man who knows mathematics and astronomy well!"

Does Al-Khidr possess some deep secrets? Is he using Estelle for some of his ulterior motives? Vivant was engulfed in his suspicions when Estelle called out to him loudly, and he came out of his intense thoughts. "What are you waiting for? We are about to embark," she said.

Vivant embarked on the boat, and they started sailing.

"Monsieur Vivant, may I help you with anything? You look troubled today," Al-Khidr asked courteously.

"Ah, nothing. It's simply nervousness, I presume." Vivant lied fervently, without thinking.

The man who had crossed the Mediterranean Sea cannot be afraid of this simple boat travel, Al-Khidr thought doubtfully, suspicions rising inside his head. *Vivant is not in a mood to reveal what he is thinking. Did he figure it out that Estelle and I are running away?* Al-Khidr thought further. The boat was crossing the Nile, and the mighty pyramids were right in front of them.

***

The boat first traveled to Giza on the orders of Vivant as he wished to see the Sphinx. The local Arab people had to wait in the Felucca until they returned. Some of the Arab people became irritated and cursed the French in their peculiar Egyptian manner. Al-Khidr understood their anger and frustration, but he

Chapter 15. The Antique Collectors

couldn't do anything at that point to help the poor civilians.

The three of them marched towards the Sphinx accompanied by a stern-looking French guard. The camels were ready to pick them up; the guards waiting for their arrival at Giza had not seen Al-Khidr before, and they considered him a slave and ignored him completely. But when they saw the importance given to him by Estelle and Vivant, they realized he was their accomplice.

"Josephus mentioned in his *Antiquities* that the Israelites built the pyramids, and Herodotus said that the pyramids were built by an unknown shepherd race," Vivant narrated serenely.

Al-Khidr laughed coldly, which caused Vivant to suspect him even more.

"I don't think so. We, the Arabs, consider them much more ancient, and they were constructed even before the great flood," Al-Khidr enlightened them proudly. "So, you mean the pyramids are not forty centuries old?"

"Definitely not so new. They are a lot more ancient than you think, monsieur," Al-Khidr informed him.

After hearing his words, Vivant rethought and reevaluated his knowledge on the subject.

"From the heights of these pyramids, forty centuries look down on us. Where the hell did he get this information from? He probably made it up," Vivant uttered in a whisper.

"Who said what?" Estelle asked.

"Never mind," Vivant shrugged off his thoughts.

Al-Khidr had seen the pyramids with the casing stones, but obviously, he could not tell that to Vivant.

"I have read in the Arabic history books that the pyramids had the casing stones, and they had images over them," he informed Vivant and Estelle.

"Who gave the name Sphinx to this statue?" Estelle asked inquisitively, looking at Al-Khidr with admiration because of the amount of knowledge he possessed about the ancient wonders.

"I heard that workers or slaves were brought here from Greece, and their ignorant populace called it Sphinx — a character from Greek mythology," Vivant explained vainly as he got a little jealous of Al-Khidr.

"In their mythology, Sphinx was a female monster with the body of a lion, and it even had breasts like a woman yet was eventually killed by the hero Oedipus," Vivant illuminated further.

"What did the Arabs call it?" Estelle asked Al-Khidr keenly ignoring Vivant completely.

"Bahwah, meaning check-post," Al-Khidr told her.

"I have never heard it," Vivant snapped at him subtly.

"Yes, the usage is now obsolete. Now mostly here the people refer to it as Abul-Houl — the father of dread," Al-Khidr said.

"But this is neither a terrifying face nor a lion!" Estelle exclaimed.

After some time, they approached the Sphinx, whose head and neck were protruding out of the sand. A

Chapter 15. The Antique Collectors

French man was leaning over his journal and drawing the Sphinx. The man stood up instantly at the sight of them and shook their hands politely.

Being an artist himself, Vivant noticed his sketch and offered him a few tips to improve his drawing.

There was a wooden staircase ready for their climb. Al-Khidr climbed the stairs first and entered the opening in the head of the Sphinx; he stood inside as he called out Estelle's name. She was surprised to see that Al-Khidr had gone all the way in so quickly, and she couldn't even see him anymore. Then he came out, followed by Estelle and Vivant, who entered the head.

"I wonder why they made a hole in the head of the Sphinx," she inquired curiously, as her beautiful green eyes surveyed the entire area with fascination. "It's the Anubis facing east! The purpose is to observe the zodiacal alignments," Al-Khidr explained to them.

Both of them were quite astonished and impressed to hear that.

"You have surprised me with this information. I never thought this way," Estelle said, as she had admired Al-Khidr even more.

***

An hour later, they were back in the Felucca, and it started sailing again, to the relief of the poor Arabs who sat there sweating horribly in the scorching sun. The Egyptians looked as though they were about to quarrel with the French, and Al-Khidr clearly understood their emotions. Estelle seemed to have the time of her life, and she relished the wind grazing her hair. The Nile's water was flowing gracefully, with no harsh waves in sight. "Look at those birds!" exclaimed Estelle, eyeing them with utmost exhilaration as she pointed. "They are so beautiful! I have never seen birds with such plumage." Estelle was thoroughly enjoying looking at the two birds who were perched on the bough of a tree. The bird's feathers were glistening in the sunlight like lilies and their eyes alight with joy as they picked at the green foliage with their beaks. The birds were large but poised, as though they were born to fly, with wingspans comparable to eagles. Then they flew away.

"Sometimes you also see the crocodiles hunting the birds," she mentioned, fear overtaking her tone suddenly.

"You must have enjoyed all this while growing up in Egypt, Monsieur Al-Khidr," Vivant asked thoughtfully.

"I did, Monsieur Vivant," Al-Khidr replied with a smile, as Vivant let out a sigh of disappointment for himself.

"We are enjoying the Nile only since we arrived here in Cairo. Ever since I arrived in Egypt, I have felt like I am in one huge sanctuary of the sciences and arts," he said admiringly. "Everything is so meticulously here — the pyramids, the obelisks, the Nile, the hieroglyphs, the coffee shops, and the warm nights. Everything is so fascinating!" Vivant exclaimed, beaming widely.

Chapter 15. The Antique Collectors

"We, the savants, wish we transfer the pyramids to France. Emperor Napoleon wanted to make a magnificent museum in Egypt," Vivant said further. "Have you told him about Point de Lendemain?" Estelle naughtily asked Vivant.

"Haha. No, I forgot," Vivant laughed hilariously.

"What's that?" Al-Khidr asked curiously, with his left eyebrow raised.

"A very interesting novel," Estelle added with a loud giggle, and Vivant glanced at her reproachfully, as he didn't want to talk about it at the moment. "Before the French revolution, we had a completely different mindset. We enjoyed being Epicurean. We enjoyed the music, the literature, the wine, the sex, the food — almost everything. We cared only about our entertainment and nothing more." He paused, staring deeply at the Nile water. He coughed loudly, cleared his throat, and continued.

"It was here, in Egypt, that we realized that there should be a goal in life. Something that our descendants could be proud of when they would take our names. We learned that our lives should not be to simply enjoy and have a carefree attitude, but to leave a lasting impact on humanity." His speech ended, and Estelle clapped slowly, eyeing him seriously.

"Well said, Vivant," she praised him loudly.

Al-Khidr was staring at him reproachfully and was mocking Vivant's words inside his head.

Yeah right! Talk about having an impact on humanity by looting the Egyptian people! He wished to mock the French army loudly; however, he controlled his emotions. "I'm not sure how long the French will like this monarchy, and I have a feeling that they will revert to older times soon. Napoleon is just a phenomenon, and I suppose he will reinstate slavery as well," Estelle claimed.

As soon as Estelle uttered Napoleon's name and slavery, almost everyone in the boat began staring at her. Most of the passengers were local Arab Coptic Christians and Muslims who started remembering their new Bey, the Napoleon, with some added adjectives, which only Al-Khidr understood. He didn't share those with his host, Vivant. The two guards who had joined the trip were also whispering to each other.

On their way, they observed that the villages near the bank of the Nile were demolished and the crops were burned.

"Both us and Mamelukes do this. They punish the innocent who want to return to their normal life, and we do it if we suspect they are rebels," Vivant said. The boat reached the nearest city along the Nile. It stopped there for a few minutes, and the passengers quickly went into the nearby bushes to relieve themselves.

"Excuse me, gentlemen," Vivant said as he also rushed there.

In the interim, some new passengers embarked on the boat. Al-Khidr noted that two more Europeans were on the jetty, ready to embark on the boat. One of them had appeared to be a young man in his twenties,

Chapter 15. The Antique Collectors

while the other seemed middle-aged, as he sported a thick white and black beard.

"They are the Antike Kunst Sammler (antique collectors)," Estelle whispered in Al-Khidr's ears.

"What in the Lord's name is an antique collection now?" Al-Khidr demanded, scratching his head in the utmost confusion.

Estelle giggled loudly, looking at his confused face.

"My dear friend," she began, biting her lips sensually at him. "Antique collection is an array of ancient objects and instruments." Al-Khidr's mouth turned into the shape of an 'O' at the realization.

Meanwhile, Al-Khidr had to focus on the European men's words to recall from the languages database.

"Do you know them?" Al-Khidr asked Estelle with mild curiosity.

"Yes, I suppose; I saw them a year ago in Alexandria. They were inside an antique shop. But we never spoke. They are not French, but from Eastern Europe, I guess," Estelle informed him while contemplating their origins.

"I had gone to the shop to get my broken watch repaired when I saw them there. They were quite keen to talk to me, but I was not interested," Estelle narrated. In the meantime, Vivant returned to the Felucca. At the same time, the two Europeans sat down near them.

The middle-aged man turned towards the group and introduced himself as Anton Boyko Miltenov.

"Gentlemen, our nations may be at war in Europe, but hopefully, we can be friends here in Egypt, right?" Anton said with a beam. Vivant mouthed an 'of course' and, smiling awkwardly, shook his hand gently. The man was about the same age as Vivant.

"Meet my friend, Mr. Kusturica," Anton pointed at the young man.

"Hello, I am Radovan Kusturica. A pleasure to meet you, Mr. Denon," the young man greeted him cheerfully.

Both men kissed Estelle's hand, who looked kind of awkward.

Al-Khidr and Vivant shook their hands, and he offered them space to sit on the plank on which they were sitting.

Suddenly, a speeding wave moved towards the boat, and the Sphere rolled out of the Al-Khidr's bag. It dropped on the wooden floor of the boat with a thump. The sound of the metallic ball hitting the wooden floor caught everyone's attention, and they immediately turned towards it.

Anton was the first to notice the jump Sphere. It rolled over towards him, and Al-Khidr jumped to pick it up; but Radovan was quicker, and he handed it to Anton. Vivant had seen the jump Sphere for the very first time, and he was also puzzled to notice the Sphere coming out of Al-Khidr's bag. Estelle stood up and went to Anton.

"Hey, this belongs to me. My father bought it for me," she explained sweetly, with a pretentious smile.

Anton looked at the Sphere and hesitantly returned it to Estelle.

Chapter 15. The Antique Collectors

Vivant had neither seen the Sphere in the hands of Estelle before, nor was it ever mentioned by her late father. He remained quiet but noted to inquire about it from Estelle later.

"It appears to be an exquisite piece of art. I like Spheres as well," Anton told Estelle after tilting his head towards it. Finally, after observing it for a few seconds, he returned it to her.

"I saw something like hieroglyphs on it," Radovan added excitedly. Estelle gave the Sphere back to Al-Khidr. As soon as the Sphere touched his palm, he felt extremely relieved, as though a heavy burden had been lifted from his heart. *Estelle is a lifesaver!* He thought. Although she was so smooth in her move, Vivant will surely inquire about it. Al-Khidr thought worriedly, glancing at the Nile.

***

The Felucca owner was a local Egyptian, and he was very enthusiastic about describing every city and place on the way.

"My fellow friends! I would like to welcome you all to Minya!" he announced as they approached the divine place. "Minya is a famous hub forcreating molassesand has Egypt's largest cornice. The governorate has several important ancient mosques from several ages, such as the Egyptian Mosque and Al Foley Mosque," the boat owner pointed at the city with ecstasy.

The sailor was working as a tour guide, too, even in the time of French occupation. Vivant was amazed by every city they passed. His thoughts forced him to realize that the European world had hardly known Egypt, as so much of it was left undiscovered. As they traveled further south, every gem of Egypt seemed to unravel. Each city had something different to entice the minds of the people who were on the Felucca. The boat owner informed them that the city called Sohag was renowned for its Islamic monuments, which dated back to the Fatimid era. The salient of which was the Al-Etiq Mosque, also known as the Al-Farshuti Mosque or the old mosque.

An intense desire rose inside Al-Khidr to visit the city; however, he somehow suppressed a strong urge to ask the boat's owner to halt the Felucca at the city. The announcer seemed to enjoy every second of the rowing and proudly continued to enlighten them about every other city and town they came across further in the south. "But this is not all, ma'am! We are going to see one ultimate treasure on the way!" he yelled and kept rowing faster. Estelle was attentively listening to the owner's explanation and enjoyed it thoroughly.

"It's simply amazing!" she shrieked and grabbed Al-Khidr's arm, who felt a little awkward, and so she released it immediately, blushing uncontrollably. *It is quite astonishing that the owner has so much knowledge about his country. He seems to be a magical lamp of the information provider,* Al-Khidr thought impressively as he continued to enjoy listening to the detailed information he provided. Meanwhile, Estelle tilted herself and dipped her soft hands in the moving cur-

Chapter 15. The Antique Collectors

rent of the river. She splashed some of it on Al-Khidr, who looked a little annoyed at her act.

"Egypt is like a hidden jewel in the massive desert of this world. In Europe, people only recognize Egypt for the pyramids, mummies, and sand. But there is a lot more to look forward to here. Look at the wildlife! The birds, the crystal-clear water, and this glorious Nile!" Estelle said to Vivant while she was viewing the water splashing on her hand.

"I am stunned by the monuments and breathtaking scenery of this magnificent land. Egypt is like a gift of God to humanity, yet it has not been completely discovered. I promise that I will go to every city when I visit it again someday soon!" she declared joyfully. Meanwhile, Anton was gazing at Al-Khidr as though he had just realized that the Arab man was present on the boat. "So, tell me Mr. Al-Khidr. You grew up in this region, right? Have you noticed any major changes?" Anton asked Al-Khidr inquisitively. Anton's initially mild interest in Al-Khidr had enhanced drastically since the jump-sphere had fallen from his bag.

Al-Khidr's mind, however, had two different views regarding the place. One of ninth-century Egypt, and the other of eighteenth-century Egypt. He could easily write an entire book on the observable changes in the social life of Egyptians, but he narrowed down his response within a few lines. "I have observed a lot of changes," he affirmed, staring at the Nile in contemplation. "The Nile's flow has been reduced. Besides that, it has changed its course. Previously, it was flowing much closer to the pyramids," Al-Khidr asserted casually.

"Really?" Radovan uttered astonishingly. Al-Khidr realized he should not have said it, but it was too late.

"It takes rivers hundreds of years to change their courses," Anton informed, with a puzzled expression on his face.

Estelle realized that Al-Khidr was becoming a suspect, and so she immediately intervened and inquired sweetly while batting her eyelashes to divert their attention, "Monsieur Miltenov, what is your business here in Egypt? How long have you been here? Is it safe for you to travel?" Miltenov's attention was indeed diverted towards Estelle, and he gave her a flirtatious smile, which made Estelle cringe horribly inside her head. "Madame Estelle, we are here on a very important mission to find some artifacts which we can sell to Frederick, the King of Prussia. We work for an antique collection company in Prussia. So, we visit Egypt every two years and stay here for six to nine months," Anton informed her while gazing at her hungrily, like a dog. Indeed, Estelle could charm anyone with her looks.

"This time, we are utterly amazed, as no one in Europe expected Napoleon to attack Egypt in this way," Radovan claimed while looking at Vivant, who simply smiled. Abruptly, the discussion turned its course towards European politics. Al-Khidr did not know which countries were fighting and which ones were al-

Chapter 15. The Antique Collectors

lies, but Vivant had become very excited about the discussion regarding Prussians.

It was a prolonged discussion that bored everyone on the Felucca, including the owner, and Estelle. Since they couldn't leave a sailing boat and go for a stroll, they simply sat in the Felucca's corner and enjoyed the mind-boggling scenery and atmosphere of the Great River Nile.

Chapter 16

The Mayhem

Hatathor was standing at the jetty in Giza and was looking for a way to travel to Al-Qahirah. He could see the minarets of the mosques, which he initially thought of as obelisks. Suddenly, he saw a Felucca tied to the jetty across the river. The boat owner was putting some things in it. He waved his hand for help, and the boat owner paddled the boat towards him.

Hatathor approached the boat owner and asked him to take him across the river to Al-Qahirah. The boat owner looked hither and thither, and after realizing that there was no other person who wanted

Chapter 16. The Mayhem

to embark on the boat, he cursed himself and then let Hatathor hop inside the boat, and started sailing. Hatathor was now standing in the Felucca's corner, holding the bident tightly, the top of which he had covered with reed-straws. He was watching the approaching bazaar area of western Cairo near the Nile. Hatathor stared intensely at the River Nile while the felucca driver was cursing either himself or the French. There were human settlements and reeds near the rivers. He could see the hustle and bustle of the human population.

His mind was racing endlessly with the thoughts about the prisoner.

Let me get my hands upon that filthy human prisoner, and I will get the sphere from him. I have landed here because of him. Within minutes, the boat reached the jetty across the river. A wicked smile spread across his jaw as he was near the place where the human prisoner was supposed to be. The boat's owner stopped the Felucca at the jetty, and wasting no time, Hatathor disembarked the boat. *Finally, I am at Al-Qahirah!* He thought victoriously.

"Ya Habibi," the boat owner called Hatathor loudly, who ignored him as he stepped onto the jetty and began walking away. "You haven't paid me yet?" Hatathor turned towards him and gazed deeply into his eyes. He threatened him silently by banging the bident base vertically on the ground. The Felucca's owner was terrorized, and he instantaneously turned his boat around and began sailing away as fast as he could. As Hatathor started walking towards Cairo city, he pressed a button on his sleeve weapon. He howled softly in irritation as his tracking device was not functional—the tracking unit's battery was dead. Luckily, he had locked the prisoner's last location, so he took a glance at the site and began marching towards the country's capital. The city was much bigger than Alexandria, and there were more buildings in Cairo than in Alexandria. The city was extremely crowded and so walking was not very easy for Hatathor. And that was because the bazaar was brimming with repulsive odors, such as the unbearable stench of sweat and animals. Besides that, the waves of fragrances erupting from the perfume sellers, the smoke coming from grilled food, and the peculiar smell of sand and dust had blended into the air. All those smells played a role in creating a unique atmosphere.

Suddenly, the sky turned a deep red, and the people began shouting in Arabic, French, and African dialects as they all watched the impending wrath of sand. And the shopkeepers started closing their stores immediately while the women began calling their children to come back home. And the animal sellers started moving their cattle to a secure place.

Hatathor had never experienced such type of sandstorm on his planet. He was intrigued by the sight and size of the approaching storm, which was ready to engulf the buildings and everything else around. Hatathor started getting irritated as the sand and dust

Chapter 16. The Mayhem

particles smashed across his face and went into his eyes, mouth, and nose. He felt uneasy while breathing. He needed to find a spot quickly where he could prevent the sand from going into his lungs. The nearest place to run was a bookstore, and he noticed the bookseller was about to close it. So, he sprinted towards the store through the running crowd and pushing the bookseller aside, and he slid inside his shop through the half-closed door. The seller held his balance and saved himself from falling. He said in Arabic: "Hey, don't be afraid. It's just a sandstorm."

Hatathor nodded his head, and without facing the man, he made the language mode Arabic in his sleeve device; then, he turned and looked at the bookseller, who was an old man. He was a venerable and wise-looking elderly man with a long white beard and deep mystical eyes that seemed to make his wrinkled face glow. "Muazra! (Apologies!)" Hatathor apologized sincerely in Arabic. "Blessings of God on you, no worries. I didn't expect that a formidable man like you would be afraid of a sandstorm," the bookseller chuckled slowly. Hatathor gave him an awkward smile and returned his greeting.

"Blessings of Eternal God on you too."

"I am Hamad. What is your name?" the bookseller asked politely as he offered his hand to be shaken. "Hatathor!" he exclaimed and shook his hand tightly. "Sounds like an ancient Egyptian name," Hamad said.

"I know little about it," Hatathor said.

"Hahaha, maybe your parents wanted to give a

unique name. Where are you from?" Hamad asked with a hearty laugh.

"I am a visitor here. Just looking for new places," Hatathor lied fervently and quickly, without thinking.

"Oh, but you don't look like a visitor. Where are you from?" Hamad inquired curiously, but he got distracted by a thundering sound. Abruptly, the bookshop walls started shaking, and the wind passing through the alleyway started creating howling sounds. The shop was getting darker and darker as the sandstorm was right over the bazaar.

"I do not wish to ignite the lamp here, as my books could get burned. We just need to sit in the darkness and talk till the storm is over," Hamad announced. "I understand," Hatathor agreed.

"I am from a very far place, called Lyra. I lost my way and entered your land," Hatathor narrated. Suddenly, his attention was diverted towards the innumerable books inside the shop.

"Sorry to hear that," Hamad expressed and followed Hatathor's gaze as he observed the large of books. "I read all these books. I had five sons, two died at an early age, and one of them was martyred in a bloody revolt that took place a few months back. Now, I have two sons only. I can feel your pain," the old bookseller said in a sad voice. "Unfortunately, I cannot offer you tea or anything else to drink now, as the entire bazaar is closed," Hamad said in a disappointing tone. "It's fine, and I am not thirsty," Hatathor said as the roaring sandstorm continued to move across the city. "How

Chapter 16. The Mayhem

long will this storm last for?"

"Maybe a few hours."

"So, you are from this land?" Hatathor asked him casually.

"Yes, I am, young man!"

"What about the soldiers?"

"They are ruthless colonialists, who snatched away land," the bookseller informed in a sad tone.

"The French people kill and enjoy drawing pictures of ruins and ancient Egyptian temples, and that's the only thing they know. They told us they would institute a tax system different from what the Ottomans had in place. We were afraid of what this new tax system would be, but the community elders assured us after negotiations with the French that it was just an extension of what the Ottomans were taking back during their time. However, the unfortunate fact is that it is much higher," the bookseller explained sadly.

"Ah! So, the humans are fighting each other," Hatathor said to himself.

Finding Al-Khidr while the humans are fighting each other will be a more complex task, he thought.

"By the way, who carries the name Al-Khidr around here? The locals or the occupiers?" Hatathor inquired serenely, hoping to get another clue that would take him closer to finding the human.

"Al-Khidr is a local name. An Arabic name," the bookseller replied. His curiosity was increasing with every second. "Why do you ask?" "Nothing!"

"You don't know the Arabic names, but you speak

Arabic fluently. You cannot be Coptic either, as some of them have this name. You don't look like a European or an Indian or a Chinese. Hmm, where is your place, Lyra located?" he commented further and asked inquisitively.

"It's in the stars!" Hatathor blurted out without thinking.

The older man stopped talking and gazed at him stupidly. He thought Hatathor had probably lost his senses because of his traumatizing experience. "O God, help him!" the old man said and started reciting prayers.

Hatathor felt relieved that he was not questioned any further. He covered his face with the cloth and remained inside, and he had to wait until the sandstorm was over.

***

A few hours passed while Hatathor waited till the sandstorm was over and the bazaar started re-opening. It was most likely less crowded because of the storm, and he could dash to the location of the human prisoner. The plan had many benefits, as giving a surprise to an opponent was always a good idea. Hatathor had learned that some locals hated French deeply, while the others supported them. Within those few days on Earth, he got the chance to synthesize the demographics and knew who was doing what. He now had an idea that the French were the rulers who had usurped the

Chapter 16. The Mayhem

power from the Ottomans. The felucca owner was persistently cursing—most likely the French. The woman in Alexandria was also unhappy. Hatathor was wondering on which side Al-Khidr would be? He needed to get the jump-sphere out of his hands as soon as possible. Al-Khidr was most probably a liar who had fooled Hathor and Ehsis. *The stupid, murderous women believed in a human,* he thought pathetically.

He reviewed his plan again on what he would do first when he encountered the human.

Shall I kill him? I tried it earlier, but probably that was a plan of Ehsis to trap me inside the energy shield. What if the contrary was true? He thought again. "What if Al-Khidr genuinely wanted to save Lyrians? If so, he is stupid. We are the most technologically advanced species in all the known galaxies, and Dr. Kityr was lazy. Had I learned the Virology and Epidemiology, I could have resolved the matter ages ago."

He then shrugged off all those thoughts and started focusing on the immediate endeavor. "Too much thinking makes a Lyrian weak, as the sages have said. It would be better that I do the job—kill the human. No human, no more new pathogens for Lyra or snatch jump-sphere from him".

Slowly, he saw the bazaar was coming back to life. He stayed in one corner and waited for the right moment. Some passerby put round metal disks in front of him, and then he realized the people thought he was a homeless man or a beggar.

"Primitive currency!"

The evening arrived quite fast, and the people were enjoying their dinners. The smell of barbeque on charcoal was delicious, but for Hatathor, it was not appetizing, as he was afraid of getting any disease. The torches were lit up by a bearded man, one by one.

The French soldiers started strolling through the bazaar, looking for the suspicious people. After an entire day of eavesdropping on the Arabs, the Coptic, and French soldiers, he learned that the man named Napoleon was the leader of the Frenchmen who waged war on the local people, and now he was busy in another war. Two French soldiers realized Hatathor had a striking resemblance to the Egyptian mummies. Their suspicions increased as he was sitting alone along the wall and neither eating, drinking, or talking to anyone. French soldiers approached Hatathor and asked his name and race. "I have come from the place of pyramids," Hatathor claimed softly.

"You mean, you are from the desert?" the soldiers inquired curiously.

Hatathor pointed towards the sky with his finger.

French soldiers said: "He is a complete lunatic!" and left him. Suddenly, one of them turned and started inspecting Hatathor's bident.

"Nice staff!"

It comprised a type of metal which the soldiers hadn't seen before. The first soldier said to the other, "We can take it and melt it to make a new baonnette." Hatathor, who was sitting on the ledge, got up imme-

Chapter 16. The Mayhem

diately and looking down at the young French soldiers, he said: "It's my father's inheritance, and I cannot give it!"

Both the soldiers looked at each other and got intimidated by his towering height, and left the staff untouched. The staff was the bident. Hatathor had covered it with the reeds which he had plucked from the bank of the Nile to conceal it.

***

It was already late at night. Hatathor looked into his tracking unit and observed the last site the tracker had located: Al-Khidr's location was blinking. "Distance six hundred and twenty-two point two Supris!"

If the battery was sufficiently charged, I could have reached the current location of the prisoner, he thought in frustration. He was just waiting for the hour when the streets would be empty. The French were patrolling the roads, and it wasn't a good idea to wait too long. He started walking towards the marked location, and this distance started reducing.

545.6 Supris, 441.6 Supris, 325.4 Supris, 204.4 Supris.

His tracking device gave the distance in Lyrian units. Finally, a massive villa-like building stood right in front of him. The signboard was hanging beside the door with the title Institut d'Egypte.

"Institute of Egypt," Hatathor translated it.

There was a garden surrounding the two-story building, highly secured by French guards stationed at all four corners and carrying their baonnette guns. Hatathor was a tall and sturdy man, so he couldn't go unnoticed walking around the building. The guard saw him and shouted, "What do you want? Go away, or I will be forced to fire!"

Hatathor said nothing. He knew that to enter the building, he had to show his nasty side. Therefore, he pressed the buttons on his sleeve device and activated the weapon. Also, he threw away the boarding cover of reed-straws from the bident and removed his cloak. The Lyrian warrior was ready to strike and stepped forward towards the building. The guard who had seen him alerted the other guards, and a few appeared on the rooftop. They warned in Arabic and French, "Go away, man. If you come any closer, your head will be blown away."

Hatathor pressed the button, and a shockwave was generated, which was so powerful that it scattered away all the guards, including those standing at the roof. The building's glass windows were shattered, and there was mayhem and a commotion inside. Hatathor commanded his sleeve weapon and created the hemispherical protective energy shield around him. He entered the courtyard, and a French guard fired at him.

The bullets fell to the ground, and Hatathor continued to walk into the courtyard. More French guards fired at him, but they simply couldn't penetrate the indestructible Lyrian shield and fell on the ground. Their efforts were futile, and they could only stand and watch in horror as Hatathor made his way towards the main entrance. Then, the guards started to

Chapter 16. The Mayhem

panic and ran away screaming in French: "A mummy has arrived!"

A soldier moved forward and pushed the knife in front of his baonnette into the energy shield. However, the blade melted, and the baonnette exploded. The French soldier fell to the ground, crying in extreme pain and agony.

Three soldiers attacked him with daggers. Instantaneously, Hatathor fired laser beams through the bident and with it, and their bodies evaporated instantly like steam from water. A few other soldiers who were on the verge of attacking Hatathor perceived that gut-wrenching sight and hid quickly out of fear. Hatathor approached the main entrance, and his protective energy shield shattered the door. The place was filled with darkness since the torches and lamps had been extinguished because of the sudden air movement as the shockwave formed.

Hatathor pressed a button on his bident, and the light emerged. The light was pale white, and it illuminated the great hall. The hall walls were ornated with paintings of birds, animals, plants, and temple ruins. There were many sculptures and samples of hieroglyphs placed on the shelves. He also perceived a statue of Anubis, which he found interesting, and he went close to it to inspect it in more detail. "The statue of a person from planet Kebirum?"

Hatathor had learned from his history book that some creatures from planet Kebirum were working for the Lyra, and some had even died on Earth. He focused on the next drawing. It was writing in some Lyrian archaic script, and the one showed by Laura, the British woman earlier. He started reading the story. It was about how Seth killed a man called Usir... Who dismembered Usir's body and then Hathor or Ehsis brought him back to life... Blah blah blah!

"What a piece of crap!"

Hatathor realized the humans were worshiping the Lyrains as gods.

"Alas, they lost the true God!" Hatathor uttered and turned.

A crowd of some aged humans was gazing at him, and they were all gathered on the stairs. Some fell on the stairs as he approached them. Hatathor shouted: "Where is Al-Khidr?" Savants were speechless and breathless.

Hatathor moved forward and started ascending the stairs. The savants were shaking in fear, and some even closed their eyes. Hatathor ignored them all, and he continued moving up to the second story. He searched every room, but he couldn't find a trace of the prisoner. He came down and saw that the rest of the French savants and their guards were gathered in one corner of the Institute. They were whispering to each other, and Hatathor could hear them. But he chose not to respond. Instead, he turned around and shouted: "Tell me where the prisoner is, or I will take your hearts out of your chests?"

"Spare us, please!... Al-Khidr left for Qena yesterday."

Chapter 16. The Mayhem

"Where is Qena?" He shouted.

"In... in ... the South."

"Curse him," Hatathor said and came out of the building. He marched towards the stable of horses and selected one amongst them. Then, jumping over the horse's saddle, the angry Lyrian rode off towards the south. The moon was shining on the path he was treading.

***

Savants were in a baffled state. They didn't know what had happened.

Who was this ancient Egyptian-looking person? Why was he looking for Al-Khidr?

"Have you noticed? He looked like a mummy?"

"Yes," it was a unanimous utterance.

"Some Ottoman or Arab must have performed an occult magic to raise back to life the Egyptian army to encounter us," one of the French soldiers said. "That could have been done by the British as well," another French soldier suggested.

"Whatever, but he looked like the pharaoh," one savant said.

"How do we stop him now?" another inquired.

"One of the ancient legends I heard tells that if we were to remove the noses of the statues, then the energy of the statue would be dispersed, and it could not enter the body of the dead mummy. For this energy to enter and animate a statue, an aperture similar to a nose is required. If this opening is not present, then there will be no way for this energy to enter," one of the Frenchman informed the other.

"If you learned from some Greek historian book, then do not take it seriously. The ancient Greeks, who were the first storytellers in recorded history, cannot always be relied upon. They told tales of deities and heroes and their exploits against odds that we moderns can scarcely imagine," a savant made his point. "I'm not sure who he was. But whatever he was, he was a formidable enemy. Even our entire army cannot defeat him. We need to dispatch an informant to both Vivant as soon as possible, as that bloody Berber confused him and allured him into this journey," one savant said.

"Vivant didn't go because of the Zodiac, He went there because he promised Estelle's father that he would go where Estelle would go," another one mentioned. "Whatever, that bloody Berber was suspicious from the very beginning. How and where he gathered all his knowledge?"

"We must inform Vivant, and I am now writing directly to Excellency Napolean. He is a senior, and since the plague has struck Syria, his excellency might not be here soon. Write to General Desaix. He is stationed in the south."

***

Hatathor was galloping on the beast—the Arabian horse, heading out of Cairo. He knew that Al-Khidr had already left for the south. *The previous beast I rode*

Chapter 16. The Mayhem

was too slow. As I rode it, it could not catch up with the others, he thought to himself. He was surprised to note the speed the horse had attained.

His mind was preoccupied with the thoughts of humans. Finding one particular human had become an overwhelming task just because of the wrong battery choice. He just needed to wait till dawn's early light, and then he could recharge his sleeve device again.

***

When he woke up, he was looking into his sleeve weapon and the tracking unit. He was sitting in the cornfields and could hear the French soldiers who were shouting at each other. It seemed they had discovered the horse which Hatathor had taken from the Institute the previous night. The horse was grazing in the field while Hatathor was sleeping.

Now he was fully awake and ready to handle any threat that could come his way.

He pressed a few buttons on his sleeve device and activated the language detection and translation mode.

He could now easily understand what the French soldiers were saying to each other. They had to stop the farmers from entering the fields as they looked for a man who resembled ancient Egyptians.

"Look into the bushes and cornfields!"

"Bring the hounds!"

Hatathor heard the barking animals as he was looking through the leaves. The French soldiers were holding the leashes of nearly fifteen hounds. "Benign beasts!" Hatathor said to himself.

One French soldier was simply inspecting the footprints on the ground. He had followed Hatathor's footsteps meticulously, one by one. Slowly, he was moving towards him. "Pierre, did you find something?" a soldier shouted.

"Yes," and he pointed towards the cornfields in which Hatathor was hiding.

"He could be inside it!"

"Unleash!" the soldier shouted.

The hounds were unleashed, and they were furiously running towards cornfields.

Hatathor pressed a button on his sleeve weapon. "Activate energy shield," the hemispherical energy shield formed around him. The furious hounds let out a chorus of barks as they encircled the Hatathor. They were still at a safe distance. The pack of hungry hounds circled, growling and barking with thunderous roars as they tried to find the best way to attack.

Hatathor was sitting in a kneeling position and looking at the hounds.

Some hounds moved forward and attacked Hatathor. The hounds jumped, and as soon as their mouths came in contact with the energy shield, their bodies started burning. They fell to the ground and started crying in pain. Within minutes, their bodies turned into ash and tar. The air was filled with the stench of burning skin, and more than that, the scent of burning flesh, like a campfire in a dense forest—a sickening smell of

Chapter 16. The Mayhem

blood and burnt meat.

The rest of the hounds got scared and ran away. As the French soldiers moved towards the spot where the hounds had gone, they saw some hounds were running back towards them. They were surprised and looked at each other. The hounds passed them, moaning, and disappeared into the cornfields. Some soldiers who had been running earlier had now started moving cautiously towards the spot. The smell of burned hair and flesh hanging in the air was unavoidable. Slowly, they reached the spot and were horrified to see the burned carcasses of the hounds. The bodies were lying close to a circle of burned leaves. They had seen nothing like it before. The dog's bodies were strewn across the bushes, some were missing arms and legs, and others' heads were twisted around where their necks used to be. The smell of burning flesh, smoldering meat, consumed by flames, was in the air.

They gathered around the circle and were baffled by the phenomena. Then they looked at each other and said, "Run!"

The soldiers were running across the cornfields, the shrieks of soldiers were issuing intermittently from the cornfields.

The farmers who were denied entry to the fields looked at each other with utter fear, and they were sweating profusely.

Hatathor triumphantly came out of the cornfields. As soon as the farmers saw him, they ran off in horror. He was drenched in human blood and was carrying the French military uniform of the search team leader in one hand and his bident in another hand. "They wasted my time!" he said to himself.

He walked into the river and washed his body. Then he came out and wore the uniform of the dead French soldier. He activated his tracking unit. "Given the location of the prisoner!"

"Prisoner location identified. Direction South. Distance eleven thousand seven hundred and eighty-one point eight nine Supris, eleven thousand seven hundred and eighty-three point four three Supris, eleven thousand seven hundred and eighty-four point seven six Supris...."

"He is moving through the south, either on a beast or...."Hatathor said to himself, and a felucca passed near him.

"I need to move fast. Stop!" He shouted at the boat driver, who stopped the boat. "Where do you want to go?"

Hatathor said nothing and climbed over the boat.

"Not with you." he pushed the owner into the river.

He sat at the end of the boat and put his bident inside the boat, and pressed the button. The bident started moving like a propeller, and the vessel sped up. The boat owner was saying swear words.

Chapter 17

The Mirage

The Qena, Egypt, 9 January 1799

THE boat was approaching Qena, a city in southern Egypt, the probable location of the herbs Boraqis. Vivant was busy in an unending discussion of politics with the two Europeans. Estelle and Al-Khidr were sitting some distance apart now as most of the passengers had disembarked, and now there was plenty of space in the boat to walk and stretch. Suddenly, Vivant stood up and addressed to Al-Khidr and Estelle: "We will meet our best engineers soon. They

Chapter 17. The Mirage

were assigned to analyze Egypt's lower water depth, and they had to assess every possible agricultural site. Their task was to measure the flow rate of the Nile river at various sites between Cairo and Aswan," Vivant informed Estelle and Al-Khidr.

Al-Khidr was worried as he was thinking about what would happen when Vivant would not find the star map. Estelle smiled at him and whispered: "Don't worry, we will handle the situation. Vivant would be suspicious, but not for long. After all, he had planned to meet the engineers working in south...."

"So, it's like he is doing something extra in his official work?" Al-Khidr asked again.

"Yes, exactly," she confirmed again.

Gradually, the boat was approaching the jetty. Finally, the boat docked at the jetty, and they noticed around fifteen French soldiers standing upright with an assertive posture, with their arms fixed at the side. The soldiers were dressed in their peculiar, which included a tricorn hat, long-skirted coat, waistcoat, and breeches. And one distinct feature of the uniform was the long canvas gaiters, which rose to mid-thigh and had multiple buttons. As they stepped on the jetty, the soldiers saluted in a professional military way.

One officer by the name of Edouard Devilliers had a linen strip wrapped around his eyes. At first sight, Al-Khidr thought that he was blind. But then the officer informed Vivant about it. "I got this nasty bout of ophthalmia and reached till here only because of the help of Dubois-Ayme," Edouard Devilliers said.

"Oh, Edouard, just take care of yourself, boy," Vivant advised, and Edouard Devilliers nodded his head like a child. Vivant inquired: "What is the status of the attacks here?"

"The Mamelukes and us had to stop our work and camp in Asyut for two months. We bivouacked briefly with Desaix; then he marched further south. The region is quite unstable at the moment. Murad Bey led Desaix and his men higher up the Nile. He does that frequently, and it is his favorite military tactic. In this way, our army is most often veered off into the desert. Many of our soldiers had died because of hunger and thirst," Jollois informed. "I guess it's better for you that from today onward, you go by land instead of using the boat. As we have heard some stories of attacks on the boats," Dubois-Ayme advised them.

"Qena is safe at the moment, and we have neutralized all the enemy threats in the nearby settlements," Devilliers added.

"Monsieur Vivant, what is the reason for your arrival here at such an urgent notice. We received the news yesterday that you were going to arrive soon," Jollois asked.

"We are looking for the map of stars drawn by ancient Egyptians," Vivant said, and looked at AL-Khidr.

"Meet Monsieur Al-Khidr. He is a new inclusion in our savant circles." Devilliers shook hands with Al-Khidr.

"Monsieur Al-Khidr informed us about it in Cairo,

Chapter 17. The Mirage

and I immediately felt urged to see the marvelous piece of art myself," Vivant said.

"I have seen one zodiac in the temple nearby," Devilliers informed.

"Oh really?" Vivant was glad to hear that and glanced at Al-Khidr and Estelle. They, too, found the news exciting.

"I guess God heard your prayers," Estelle whispered to Al-Khidr, who beamed widely.

"You guys must be tired of the journey, so I would say that you visit it tomorrow," Jollois suggested.

"It is truly incredible, Mr. Al-Khidr! Are you from Egypt?" Jollois appreciated Al-Khidr with a genuine smile.

"My father was a Berber from North Africa, but my mother was a slave, and she was French. My father bought her, freed her, and married her. I grew up in Egypt," Al-Khidr repeated his concocted story he told to Vivant earlier.

"Pleasure to know you," Devilliers said with a beam, gawking at him as though he had discovered fire.

"Monsieur Al-Khidr, you are an interesting man," he added, while Vivant looked at Al-Khidr with pride in his eyes.

The engineers moved their eyes off Al-Khidr and noticed the two new Europeans and Estelle. Then they moved forward and kissed Estelle's hand.

"Meet two of our new acquittances, Monsieur Anton Boyko Miltenov and Monsieur Radovan Kusturica," Vivant introduced them to his staff. The men greeted each other. Vivant turned to an antique collector. "Monsieur Miltenov and Monsieur Kusturica, my men advise you should not go further south. You should take a boat and go back to where you came from," Vivant said to both gentlemen.

Anton and Radovan wanted to go to the temple across the river, called the Dendera temple.

Vivant turned to Al-Khidr and Estelle and said: "We need to take this advice seriously. We are short of men, and we don't have the right spy network in this region. Al-Khidr, can you help us move from here? You're well aware of this region. Aren't you?"

Al-Khidr had a negative feeling that those two new guys were after his sphere, as they were constantly observing every move of Al-Khidr and keeping a close eye on his sack. Estelle also found the men suspicious. They reached a large Arabian Tent, which was used by the French military. The tents were all placed next to each other, and several big rooms were formed. Around twenty to thirty French military guards were stationed all around the camp. There was sometimes a gust of sand. The dry, gritty sand particles in the air felt hot against their skin, and they were so dry that air was occasionally difficult to breathe. Several huge canons stood across the camp, with innumerable cannon balls placed nearby each of them. Most of the French soldiers were equipped with Baïonnettes. The French soldiers could be seen training intensively across the vast camp. Some of them practiced shooting while few others marched across the camp.

Chapter 17. The Mirage

The leather flaps of the enormous tents were beautifully made and the hand-woven mats in front of each flap added to the rich smell that filled it. The flap was made of heavy canvas, divided by thick leather cords to keep the rain out. From its smell, the tent had been treated, oiled, and properly cared for. The fabric of the tent was slowly being pulled by the wind, making a subtle swishing sound.

They sat for a while in the tent to recover from the tiredness of the journey. A sentry arrived and served them a quick meal, comprising freshwater, dates, olive oil, and bread only. The dates were very hard to chew, along with being dry and tasting terrible. The bread had gone stale, and only the olive oil was edible. They ate whatever luck had thrown in their way.

They chatted for an hour and relaxed until it was close to sunset, and then Anton and Radovan departed and went for another tent. Vivant and Estelle stayed in one compartment of a large tent, while Al-Khidr was alone in another compartment. Unlike the Institute in Cairo, they were sleeping on the jute sheets with an animal hide overlaid over it. The tiredness was still not over yet, and soon they all drifted into a deep sleep.

***

The day dawned crisp and clear. The rising sun cast a rosy hue across the morning sky, making the atmosphere thoroughly enchanting and dazzling. During breakfast, Vivant announced that he had planned to visit the temple's ruins across the Nile. He asked Al-Khidr and Estelle to join them. "The ruins across the Nile must be interesting," he claimed as he sipped on a hot cup of coffee across the table near one tent where he was having breakfast with Al-Khidr and Estelle. "I learned that some Coptic Christian families used to live in those ruins. It used to be a church sometime time ago," Vivant told Al-Khidr. "That will be interesting! We should go there," Al-Khidr exclaimed excitedly as he gulped down a glass of cold milk. He wanted to visit the place, too, as that would provide him with a golden opportunity to walk along the road and search for the herbs. Estelle also liked the idea, and they decided to make the trip.

After breakfast, they packed their stuff and went to the jetty, but all their joy vanished when they found that the antique collectors were also waiting for the boat. "What are they doing here?" Estelle whispered to Vivant and Al-Khidr, who simply shrugged in disappointment. "Perhaps they too want to see the map of stars," uttered Estelle, rolling her eyes.

Vivant was there with his large journal and crayons. "Today, I will do some drawings," Vivant expressed.

"It means we can easily spend five to six hours inside the temple," Estelle teased Vivant and laughed loudly.

"We will see," Vivant chuckled loudly.

The felucca arrived, and they all embarked on the boat. It was a quick ride, but they had to take it. The felucca brought them across the river and started

Chapter 17. The Mirage

walking towards the site of the ruins, and they had to walk. After walking for a short while, they were in front of a giant temple complex. "It looked deceptively small from its outlook, but it enormous," Anton said.

"I hope we get something for the European market," Radovan added.

"We can take only if Monsieur Vivant allows us," Anton said and looked at Vivant, who was casually moving towards the complex. The temple exterior was elegant. Six perfectly sculpted columns with Hathor-shaped heads decorated the entrance as they went inside. There were intricate details in the bas-relief that illuminated the shadowy interior of this temple.

"It is very ancient. Some say that it's been renovated several times, and some say that the Greek made it," Vivant informed the others. A local Egyptian guide was there to help them out.

"Hello, I'm Yusuf," he introduced himself coldly, thus making it clear that he wasn't there willingly. "I grew up in this region and have seen this temple many times. You can ask any questions about it. Last night, few soldiers picked me up from my home in the village without my consent and brought me here; I don't know why. But in the morning, the soldiers told me I would be guiding you around this temple," the young and tall Egyptian man in white linen Jalabiya said. He sported a long jet black beard with a dusky complexion and large forehead. His puffy eyes contained deep dark circles, which suggested that he hadn't slept in days. "We are looking for a map of stars," Vivant told him.

"I do not know about any star map here, and however, there is a hidden area underneath this temple. Maybe you find something there. If you like, I can take you there," he informed.

"Yes, sure!" Vivant said excitedly.

"Very well, follow me," Yusuf gestured them to follow his lead.

They all followed him, and he pointed towards a stainless passage on the floor.

After walking inside the complex, they reached a room where a small opening was made in the ground. It had no stairs and was designed in this manner to deny the public from accessing it.

"I never been to this place before," Yusuf informed further.

"Do we simply drop ourselves into it?" Anton asked nervously.

Yusuf nodded his head in affirmation.

One by one, they all descended into the underground chamber. It was a narrow crept, and there was no light except the one coming from the few windows made ages ago. Vivant ordered his soldiers to bring some flaming torches.

As they moved through the passages, the cobwebs were burning. Some were also sneezing because of the dust on the floor. Moving inside, they stumbled over several mummified corpses in the dark. The crept was sometimes used as a burial place for executed criminals, as the hangman's noose was still attached to some of the necks.

Chapter 17. The Mirage

It took a few turns and descended on some straightly deformed stairs until they reached a narrow tunnel with no opening. The use of going inside deep into the tunnel and he stopped.

Then he asked all to look above the ceiling, and lo-and-behold, there was indeed a star map right over their heads. "Amazing," they all uttered in amazement and started looking towards the ceiling.

The Star map was an elaborately sculpted wheel beside a sculpted nude Hathor image, with her arms raised towards skyward. The two antique collectors, who were standing beside Al-Khidr, also smiling.

The place was too narrow, and they need to stand close to each other. "You were right Monsieur Al-Khidr. There is indeed and star map here," Vivant said.

Al-Khidr was surprised, as whatever he had said was just a hoax. He didn't know where the Lyrian-made star-map was hidden in Egypt, and he simply wanted to go to Qena to search for the herbs. "It's all God's plan. He gave Vivant what he was looking for, and he will give me what I am looking for!" He said to himself.

"It's the zodiac," he said.

"It's not only zodiac; It's more than that. A star map is a frozen image of the sky with both northern and southern hemispheres at one particular time. It is roughly 85,000 years old," Al-Khidr said.

"We need more discussion on this," Vivant said while looking at the ceiling.

Estelle was looking at Al-Khidr and said to Vivant: "This place is too narrow. I need some fresh air. Maybe I go out and look around for the plants I can use for the perfume making," Estelle said to Vivant, who was mesmerized by the star map. The antique collectors were also looking at the ceiling. "Sure, you can go out, take your time," Vivant said to Estelle and took out his journal and crayons. He wanted to draw the star map. "Mesurer et dessiner (measure and draw)," Vivant said to himself. While going out, Estelle pressed Al-Khidr's hand, signaling him to follow her.

Anton and Radovan smiled and said bye to them.

Al-Khidr and Estelle came out in fresh air; they shouted in joy and ran towards the Nile.

The French soldier stationed outside at the entrance was surprised, and one called Estelle: "Mademoiselle!"

But Estelle was running fast, holding Al-Khidr's hand, she didn't look back

***

Estelle and Al-Khidr were searching for the herbs. "You know, I became a naturalist because I wanted to learn the art of making perfumes. When I was in France, I once smelled Oud wood perfume, and it was amazing. Perhaps the smells dragged me to Egypt," she laughingly said.

"I know the extraction process, and I learned it from my master," Al-Khidr said.

Chapter 17. The Mirage

"We can make a perfume-making factory in France if you come with me," Estelle said, then she stopped talking and turned towards Al-Khidr. Her eyes were sobbing. "I don't know why, but since morning I had a bad feeling. I feel like I will miss you too much," she said.

"I am sorry, Estelle. You are such a wonderful girl. But you know I have a mission, and I need to go back," Al-Khidr said.

Estelle was looking into bushes and weeds grown along and the Nile, as they walk along the bank. After a short walk, they reached a stranded water pond that had formed near the bank. Many flowers were floating over the water. The flowers had their petals with a luscious dark shade of blue or purple from the top. They were opening up like a jewel. The air around the lotus was tinged with a fragrance. It was a scent that was both earthy and floral, like a bouquet of spring flowers. "Lotus bleu d'*É*gypte!" Estelle said and pointed towards the flowers.

"Bashneen Al-Azraque," Al-Khidr said in Arabic.

"It is so enchanting. I can stay here for ages!" Estelle said.

"True," Al-Khidr said.

The scent of the blue lotus was intoxicating. Estelle sat near the pond and pulled Al-Khidr's hand towards her.

"Relax! Sit down." "We missed that as we were behind the mound," Al-Khidr said.

"I can take some flowers and show them to Vivant,"

she laughingly said.

"If you are serious about perfume making, I can help you with the extraction process," Al-Khidr offered his services. "You know, French people like perfumes a lot," she informed.

"Blue Lotus is carved in many places in temples too," Al-Khidr said. Estelle moved towards the pond, which was not deep, to grab some flowers. "Stop! Do not enter the pond. The water may cause fever. I come across many patients who suffered from parasitic flatworms from such ponds," Al-Khidr warned Estelle. She looked back and said: "Merci! Merci!"

They went close to the pond and started plucking the flowers without wetting the feet. Suddenly, Estelle saw something at a distance, and she exclaimed: "If I'm not wrong, that is Boraqis!"

She pointed towards some herbs which were growing at some distance away.

They ran and set around the precious plants.

"Is itBoraqis?" Al-Khidr asked.

"Yes, yes," Estelle said, and she sat on her knees, looking closely at the plants.

"I kept a drawing of it. Let me take it out," Al-Khidr said and looked into his sack. He lifted his head and said: "Where is the sphere?"

***

Anton and Radovan were laughing and were running in the south. They left Vivant in the underground

Chapter 17. The Mirage

chamber of the temple, misled him by saying that they went to relieve themselves.

Vivant was engaged in the drawing and had lost the sense of time. The map of several rounds of the great year was in front of him. Radovan said to Anton: "You were right about Al-Khidr. He is an enthusiastic guy, and he was so passionately describing to the French about the Zodiac that he even had not noticed that I put my hand in his sack and took out the metallic ball."

"Good job, boy. You will get a handsome reward. I promise you," Anton said to his younger apprentice.

Radovan threw the sphere towards Anton and said: "What is your estimate? How much would it be? Prussians will be ready to give a lot of money for this small piece. It looks impressive, with a collage of different metals and an incomplete hole drilled in the middle and the ancient Hieroglaphs like writings over it," They were running in a vast desert over the dunes. "I suppose there is a settlement after this," Anton said. "French will take ages to understand what had happened," Radovan replied.

They laughed, and as it reached the top of the dune, they were panting and gasping for air as they both held their knees. Anton said: "Give me the water-skin!" Radovan threw the water-skin towards Anton and looked towards the horizon.

He saw water... "Nay, it's a mirage!" he said to himself.

Anton also started looking towards the horizon.

Their faces changed. An army appeared on the horizon, holding scimitars and javelins and running towards them. Anton and Radovan looked at each other and started running back towards the temple.

They were shouting: "Arabs coming!"

***

"What?" Estelle said. Al-Khidr stood up. He was sweating and moving his hand in his hair.

"O God, where did I lose the jump-sphere!?"

"Are you sure you dropped it somewhere?" Estelle inquired anxiously.

"Yes. Yes," He moved his hand towards his face and pressing his face hard. "It's not there!" he gritted his teeth in frustration.

"We need to go back and look inside the temple. Maybe you dropped it somewhere over there".

"No, I think they took it out!" Al-Khidr exclaimed, punching his fist in the air.

"Who?" Estelle inquired.

"Those bloody antique collectors!" he claimed angrily.

"It was with me when we went inside the temple. But I think they took it out when we were busy staring at the ceiling in the basement," "Bloody thieves!" Estelle was turning red with fury.

"We cannot takeBoraqis now, as the leaves will wither. We need to come back here again with the sphere. Let's run back and find out where they are

Chapter 17. The Mirage

before they escape. If I lose the sphere, it will be catastrophic!"

Without wasting a single second, Al-Khidr and Estelle ran back inside the temple. The soldiers looked at them astonishingly and asked, "Mademoiselle, is everything all right?"

"Have you seen the antique collectors anywhere?"

"Yes, they went together to relieve themselves!" the guard informed Estelle.

"In which direction did they go?" Al-Khidr demanded loudly, with exasperation. The soldier pointed towards the south.

"Dammit! They both ran towards the south,"

"Mademoiselle. Monsieur Vivant ordered us...." Before the soldier could complete his sentence, Al-Khidr and Estelle dashed towards the south at lightning speed. The soldier felt extremely nervous and confused, and so he ran to the basement to inform Vivant about the incident.

***

"Monsieur Vivant, Mademoiselle Estelle has gone towards south with the Egyptian man!" the soldier apprised Vivant in a trembling voice. "What?" Vivant said in a confused tone. "But why?"

"They ran after the two European antique collectors!"

Vivant was left completely baffled by this piece of information.

"What's going on?"

"I'm not sure, sir,"

"But there must be some urgency. Oh, Estelle, you can turn out to be such a nuisance sometimes," Vivant muttered, and leaving everything, he came out on the ground. There was no sign of Estelle and Al-Khidr there.

"They went towards the south," the soldier informed.

"Bring the horses immediately," Vivant commanded annoyingly, and the soldier ran towards the camp.

***

"Arab army!" roared Anton and Radovan as they were running towards Al-Khidr and Estelle. "Thieves!" Estelle shouted. Suddenly, the ground beneath began shaking as though an earthquake was going to occur, and they heard a series of shouts and slogans from far ahead. Al-Khidr turned towards Estelle and exclaimed: "We have been attacked! We need to run!"

Luckily, Vivant arrived on the scene with a few horses.

"Jump on the horses, all of you!" he commanded loudly, and they all mounted the horses quickly and galloped towards the jetty, where the boat was ready for them. Intense fear had struck their hearts as the French soldiers lined up as quickly as possible to tackle the advancing Arab army.

They all quickly embarked on the boat, and the boat started sailing. They were crossing the Nile and heading towards the French settlement.

Chapter 17. The Mirage

Few arrows passed by them, and they all had to quickly duck inside the boat to avoid them while some of them hit the boat. The French soldiers, lined up near the temple, fired bullets using their Baïonnettes towards the Arabs, but they missed. Unfortunately, though, the attackers outnumbered them and crossed their thin line. And when they did so, spine-chilling screams filled the sky as there was a swishing of swords and blood splashed all over the sand.

After firing a few more shots, the French soldiers ran out of gun powder and could do nothing more but face death. The savage Arabs galloped at lightning speed and slaughtered the French in cold blood. Few Arabs even lifted the heads of the French soldiers whom they had decapitated and cheered victoriously. And some soldiers tried to flee, but they were trampled under the feet of the Arab army's horses and died a gruesome death.

The French soldiers across the river quickly gathered near the riverbank and brought a cannon with them. Instantly, they fired across the river at the attacking force, which effectively blasted some Arab attackers. However, some of the cannonballs landed near the temple. Few more shots were fired, but they still couldn't completely restrict the movement of the advancing Arab army, which was simply too large for the French soldiers to handle.

Meanwhile, Vivant, Estelle, Al-Khidr, and the two Europeans managed to reach the French encampment and ran inside it to protect themselves from the spears and arrows.

The French soldier contained their barrage of fire, and within half an hour, the war was over. The sky had turned dark as the sun had concealed itself behind the clouds. A gigantic pool of blood had formed on the sandy ground as the butchered bodies of Arabs and French soldiers lay on the ground, horrendously. The brutality of the battle between the Arabs and the French shook the horizon and turned inexplicably bloody.

Vivant, Estelle, Al-Khidr, and the two Europeans were safely escorted to a safe area in the interim. An intense rage was bubbling inside Vivant like never before, and he glowered at Anton and Radovan.

"I need a clear explanation from both of you; otherwise, I will order the forces to put you two in prison!" he yelled at them and ordered the soldiers: "Bring them in; I am starting the inquiry," Anton and Radovan turned as pale as a sheet with fear and looked at each other. They were lost for words and shivered profusely.

Chapter 18

The Twist of Fate

It as midday, and the sun's scorching heat pierced through the sizable Arabian tent's entrance. It seemed as though the sun too was furious with Al-Khidr, Estelle, as well as the two European men, Anton and Radon, who were facing Monsieur Vivant's wrath. Vivant was burning with intense rage at the two new Europeans and yelling at them on top of his voice. Even the soldiers stationed outside the tent could hear his shouts, and they shivered with extreme nervousness.

Vivant was sitting on this desk, and all four were sitting opposite to him.

Chapter 18. The Twist of Fate

"I told you: you all have to follow the protocols. Everyone moved out of the temple and went somewhere without informing me!"

"We were out near the Nile when we found that these two thieves took the artifact given to me by Papa," Estelle said and looked at the antique collectors.

"We ran after them, and apparently, they couldn't vanish as they had found the militants approaching, and they retreated," Al-Khidr explained resentfully. Vivant looked at Anton and Radovan.

"Monsieur Vivant. You guys are saved today only because of us. Had we not been strolling in the desert, we couldn't have noticed the attackers," Anton uttered hurriedly, without thinking.

"Shut up!" Vivant snapped at him, trying his best to prevent his fury from being out of control.

"You two were not strolling; you were running away. I will have you both sent to the deepest and darkest prison here in Egypt for life! And I will make sure that both of you never get to return to Europe again," Vivant threatened them ominously as he glowered intensely into their eyes. Anton and Radon could have never imagined that the cheerful and jovial guy they had met on the felucca could also have a furious side.

"Ask them why they took my sphere," Estelle demanded angrily, trying her best not to succumb to fury. Al-Khidr gawked at Anton and Radovan like a hawk, and if Vivant wasn't there, he would have thrown himself over the Europeans and beaten them up ruthlessly.

Meanwhile, a soldier asked Vivant's permission to enter the tent, and he allowed him to enter with a curt nod. The soldier came forward and placed the jump-sphere at the center of the table. Then, turning around, he marched out of the tent.

"Why on earth did you both lay your hands on it? You stole the artifact to sell it to the Prussian king, didn't you both?" Vivant demanded as he bent his torso towards them and banged the table.

"No, Monsieur, we didn't..." They tried to defend themselves but were cut in by Vivant.

"Silence!" Vivant bellowed again like a raging tiger.

Estelle seemed to get a little nervous; she had never seen Vivant so enraged before. She was boiling with fury too at the European men's outrageous act, and if given a chance, she could have smacked their faces.

"Vivant, I knew these men had their filthy eyes on the sphere since the day we met them at the felucca. When the sphere fell on the boat's floor, these two simply couldn't take their greedy eyes off it. When I had asked them to return it to me, this man," she pointed her finger at Radovan. "Didn't hand it over to me immediately and kept ogling it lustily. I recognized their bad intentions instantly back then," Estelle finished, and Vivant looked at the two repulsively while biting his lips in immense anger.

"You both disgust me," he expressed. "We treated you both as friends; we respected you. But alas, you both lost our respect," saying that he called one soldier

Chapter 18. The Twist of Fate

guarding the entrance.

But before the French soldier could enter the tent and take the European man away, Radovan tilted to his left like he was scratching his foot. Shockingly, he unsheathed the sharpened dagger he had concealed in his boot. He moved swiftly and placed it against Estelle's throat.

"Radovan!" Anton shouted as he hadn't expected that.

Then he used his free hand to place the sphere in his pocket, and he buttoned it to stop the orb from falling out.

The soldiers moved forward with their bayonets, but Vivant halted them with a wave of his hand.

"Stop it, Radovan. Leave the girl," Al-Khidr warned serenely.

"Let me go then!" Radovan growled.

"Look, Radovan, you are making a big mistake," warned Vivant. His tone had turned calmer and more cautious now. "Leave the girl, and we can discuss this matter like gentlemen." Radovan began laughing coldly and pressed the dagger closer to Estelle's neck.

"Make a move, and I will slit this gibberish talking doll's throat," Radovan spat on the ground and continued to hold Estelle. "Listen, Radovan," Al-Khidr began, but he cut him in sharply.

"No, you both listen to me carefully! I will leave this stupid girl. But first, I need a boat to get the hell out of there quickly. Otherwise, I will cut open this ill-mannered girl's soft neck," he threatened with an evil relish in his voice and pressed the dagger slowly against her skin, which bled. "You can keep this old man; he is of no use to me," Radovan made a disgusted face and pointed towards Anton, who buried his face between his hands with utter disappointment and shame in his eyes for having considered Radovan as his friend.

Estelle shrieked in pain as a bit of a scratch appeared on her neck. Al-Khidr and Vivant roared at Radovan, who ignored their shouts and kept the blade against her skin. Radovan pushed Estelle and moved out of the tent while keeping the dagger against her throat. Briskly, he stepped backward while glancing continuously inside the tent. The French soldiers were helplessly watching the sudden change in the situation, and some of them surrounded the thief as he moved Estelle out of the military camp.

"Clear the way!" Radovan growled at the soldiers . He took Estelle as a hostage and moved towards the jetty at the Nile River. Few feluccas were already there. He pushed Estelle inside the boat and then seated himself in the felucca. Some of the soldiers pointed their baïonnettes at the man, but Vivant ordered them against shooting. Eventually, the boat started sailing towards the north along with the currents of the Nile. Estelle was standing in the boat and looking at them helplessly with tears in her eyes. "Dammit," Vivant exclaimed, punching his fist in the air and feeling extremely nervous and helpless. He was unsure what to order, and he feared that the shooting would jeopardize the life of Estelle. Al-Khidr was

Chapter 18. The Twist of Fate

bursting with fury. He couldn't let the man escape like that. He looked around to find something that could help him get to Estelle. Suddenly, he noticed that the French army had formed a pile of spears of dead Arab attackers at one corner of the river bank, and they wanted to burn them all. Al-Khidr's Berber spirit flared up, and he ran and grabbed one of the javelins and noted that the river was taking a turn at the point where the flow rate was low, and the boat would slow down. He ran along the riverbank, aimed it perfectly, and threw the spear at Radovan. The spear hit Radovan's shoulder, and he fell into the boat. Estelle grabbed the paddle, but she was not good at driving the boat.The hit made Radovan dropped his dagger on the boat.

"God is great!" cheered Al-Khidr, punching the air victoriously, and he started sprinting and dived into the river.

Meanwhile, Radovan stood up in the boat, holding his arm. He pushed Estelle to the side. Then, grabbing the paddle again, he turned the course of the boat away from the shore. Estelle let out a squeal as she hit her head on the boat. She rose to her feet and attempted to snatch the paddle away from Radovan by scratching him, but he pushed her again. This time, she held her balance, and moving towards him, she bit his shoulder. The European man let out a howl of pain and smacked her face very hard.

"You bloody French bitch. I will teach you a lesson that you'd never forget!" he yelled. And in a fit of fury, he took out his dagger again. "I wasn't going to kill you, but you have made me furious now, so be prepared to die a horrible death," and he was about to stab her when Al-Khidr reached the boat and climbed and kicked the dagger, which spun rapidly and soaring through the air, it fell into the river with a splash. Al-Khidr caught Radovan's shoulder and kneed him in the stomach hard. Then, carrying him on his shoulder, he threw him on the boat's floor. Radovan lifted his leg and delivered a kick onto Al-Khidr's chest, and he tumbled backward. He jumped to his feet acrobatically and turned to face Al-Khidr. They dashed forward and clenched each other's fists. Each was struggling to bend the other's fist, but both were evenly matched. Instantly, Al-Khidr hopped in the air and kicked the thief's chest with both legs, and he tumbled backward. Then moving towards him, he lifted the thief with his collar, but Radovan broke free and punched him in the gut, which knocked the wind out of Al-Khidr.

Al-Khidr fell on the boat's floor and moaned loudly. Meanwhile, Radovan went towards Estelle, and snatching the paddle away, he smacked her furiously on her face, which caused the side of her lip to bleed, and she fell to the ground again.

Roaring with a beastly rage, Al-Khidr caught hold of Radovan and delivered two consecutive punches on his face, and threw him on the side. And Radovan fell with a backflip.

"Estelle, are you alright!" Al-Khidr demanded wor-

Chapter 18. The Twist of Fate

riedly and was moving towards her when Radovan caught the back of his feet and tripped him on the ground. Lying on the floor, Al-Khidr aimed a gut-wrenching kick at Radovan's face, which sent him sliding towards the corner, and his mouth started bleeding heavily. The European man rose to his feet quickly, and as he let out a roar of fury, he bolted like an enraged bull towards Al-Khidr. The force of the tackle caused both Al-Khidr and Radovan to fall into the river. Estelle freaked out at Al-Khidr's fall into the river. Radovan and Al-Khidr began wrestling with each other inside the water. Radovan grabbed Al-Khidr's collar and pushed him deep inside the water to drown him. A large volume of water entered his lungs and suffocated him. His vision became blurry, and his body became numb because of the massive pressure of the water. He was unable to think clearly and felt as though he was taking his last breath. Then suddenly, the thought of Estelle struck his mind, and he mustered all his strength. And with a tremendous effort, he jerked up and finally reached the surface of the water. Then, using the back of his head, he smashed against Radovan's chin, and he howled in pain. Al-Khidr kept sending heavy punches at him, which he somehow blocked, and they continued to wrestle.

"Die, stupid Berber!" Radovan yelled as he resorted to dirty fighting, and he sank his teeth into Al-Khidr's shoulder. Al-Khidr bellowed as a horrible pain shot through his shoulder, and it bled. He then grabbed Radovan by the hair, smashed his head against him, and fell backward into the water. Abruptly, a massive wave sped through the river and washed all over them and carried them deep below in the water. Silence fell across the Nile as Radovan and Al-Khidr had disappeared into the water. Estelle became extremely exasperated and starting calling out Al-Khdir's name loudly in a state of desperation. But there was neither any response nor any movement in the water.

A couple of minutes passed, and there was no motion or any sound from the water. Tears formed on the corner of Estelle's eyes, and she fell onto her knees and began to sob heavily, thinking that Al-Khidr had drowned. She was filled with intense sorrow and agony at the thought of him. Somehow, she picked herself up with substantial courage and taking the paddle she was about to move the boat when suddenly there was a huge splash of water in the Nile... And Al-Khidr emerged, along with the unconscious body of Radovan.

Al-Khidr swam, and Estelle beamed with joy and rushed towards him to help him climb the boat. Estelle pulled Radovan back into the boat, who was unconscious. She then gave a tight hug to Al-Khidr that nearly hurt his ribs.

"I... I thought you... you drowned!" she stammered with anxiety, the tears still fresh on her face. Al-Khidr freed himself from her hug and told her not to worry. Then he grabbed the paddle and took the boat back to the shore.

"Oh, thank the Almighty Lord that you are okay,

Chapter 18. The Twist of Fate

Estelle!" exclaimed Vivant as he sprinted towards her and hugged her. "If anything would have happened to you, I would have never been able to forgive myself. I promised your father, Jacquous, that I would always take care of you," Estelle was not angry at all. Rather, she was pleased to get back to him.

"I understand, Vivant. No worries at all," she said to Vivant as he gave her an affectionate peck on the forehead. He then turned towards Al-Khidr. "Al-Khidr, my dearest friend. How can I possibly thank you for placing your life in danger and saving Estelle?" he thanked him gratefully and gave him a one-armed hug. "It was nothing but my duty, Vivant; there is no need to thank me. I would go to any lengths to protect my friends and save them from any sort of peril," he claimed. Vivant now understood that Al-Khidr either deeply loved or respected Estelle. Anton and Radovan were both declared thieves, and Anton was ordered to be sent to Cairo for deportation. On the other hand, Radovan was sent to castle Rumayla for the charges of theft and an attempt to murder.

Al-Khidr felt a surge of pain in his left hand where the Lyrians had installed the tracking unit. *Is the tracking unit causing me pain because I went inside water?* He thought frantically and was not sure about it.

***

Later in the evening, they had dinner together. Unfortunately for Estelle and Al-Khidr, the dinner turned out to be a distasteful affair, as Vivant had ordered a roasted vulture for the feast. Al-Khidr and Estelle didn't like to eat the exotic entre and resorted to eating mashed potatoes. "I enjoy doing experiments," Vivant declared ravenously as he took the piece of vulture and started munching on it. "Hmm, I won't say that it's delicious, but it doesn't taste horrible either," he proclaimed, making a disgusted face.

He chewed it for a few seconds, but then his Parisian palate protested, and he spat it on the side of the table and started cleaning his face with a serviette. "I told you. It won't be an easy bite," Estelle teased him and started giggling uncontrollably. Al-Khidr smiled humorously but said nothing as Vivant was serious. "What is that sphere, Estelle? Jacquous never mentioned it to me," Vivant asked inquisitively.

The question nearly caused Estelle to choke on the mashed potatoes, and she coughed intensely. Immediately, Al-Khidr offered her a glass of cold water, which she drank and felt better. Her eyes were watery because of coughing, and she cleared her throat. The question had caused her mind to go blank for a while, and she kept looking down at her plate and didn't even raise her eyes to look at Vivant.

"Are you okay, Estelle?" he asked, slightly worried.

"I am fine now," she said and kept looking down. She felt slightly relieved that her unexpected cough had made him drop the subject of the sphere. However, a brilliant idea flashed across her mind at that point, and she brought up the issue again.

"What were you asking again, Vivant?" She asked,

CHAPTER 18. THE TWIST OF FATE

pretending to have forgotten the question, and before he could remind her, she burst into speech. "Oh yeah, the sphere. Papa had bought it for me from some antique shop in Cairo before the revolt. He thought I would be interested in having a souvenir," she lied fervently, giving Al-Khidr a subtle wink, whose heart seemed to race faster than ever at the subject being brought up again. "But now, I would like to gift it to Al-Khidr as a small token of gratitude for saving my life," Estelle affirmed as she looked at Al-Khidr with a genuine smile. *Estelle, you are simply brilliant!* Al-Khidr thought and gazed at her with immense admiration and appreciation.

"Monsieur Al-Khidr, you have amazed me on various occasions. First, you conveyed some bewildering information about the Sphinx, then I was blown away by learning about the ancient Zodiac. Last, you proved to be a highly intelligent, courageous, and loyal man by saving Estelle's life. I must say that you are a master of all arts, and you spend your time in great learning."

Al-Khidr chuckled modestly and thanked him for showing appreciation. Abruptly, a soldier rushed into the dining area of the tent.

"Monsieur Denon, we have just received the news that a tall strange man attacked the Institute and stole one of our horses. Our men pursued him, but he escaped, killing many soldiers and dogs on his way out. Nobody knows where he went. Not only that, he was looking for Monsieur Al-Khidr..." the soldier paused and stared at Al-Khidr fearfully. "Perhaps with evil intentions."

"That must be some stupid Arab or Turk. A few days ago, some officers were killed at a beach near Alexandria," Vivant conveyed to them and took the matter quite lightly.

Who wants to kill me? I don't have any enemies here. Neither have I been a part of any major conflict in Cairo, Al-Khidr thought, feeling utterly confused and a little anxious as well. "The frequency of the attacks has increased," Estelle piped in, as she became frantic quickly when the soldier said that the strange man was looking for Al-Khidr. "Indeed, it has," Vivant sighed despairingly. "More Arabs and Turks have been attacking the French and slaughtering them mercilessly." "Oh, I wonder why," Al-Khidr muttered in a dangerously sarcastic tone.

"What?" Vivant asked casually "Nothing. I have meant to ask you for a long time, Vivant, that why did Emperor Napoleon attack Egypt in the first place when his main intent was to rule Europe only? And how did he manage to conquer this entire country?" Vivant looked at Al-Khidr serenely and replied in a very serious tone.

"In early 1798, his excellency Napoleon Bonaparte proposed a military expedition to seize Egypt. In a letter to the Directory, he suggested this move would protect French trade interests, attack British commerce, and undermine Britain's access to India and the East Indies since Egypt was well-placed on the trade routes

Chapter 18. The Twist of Fate

to these places," Vivant paused and gulping down a glass of water he continued his explanation.

"However, the reality of our Egyptian Campaign is less glorious. Thirty-seven thousand troops, including Estelle's father, had marched across the desert from Alexandria to Cairo. It was indeed appalling mismanagement, as many died of thirst, discomfort, disease, and death," Vivant illuminated. "The military campaign was a failure," Estelle paused and continued, "Lord Nelson in the sea destroyed our French Fleet Arme d'Orient (Army of the Orient). The shivers still go down my spine as I sometimes think about it. How my father and I ran and jumped into the boat which dropped into the sea while the cannonballs were hitting our huge vessel. We were indeed lost."

Estelle sighed in disappointment and made a sad face.

"What is the matter, Estelle?" inquired Al-Khidr.

"Our army wanted to go to India to help ruler-Tipu Sultanagainst Britain... but we are all stuck in Egypt as we lost most of our ships at Alexandria. One-third of le Arme d'Orient is dead because of sickness, malaria, and diarrhea. The survivors are now killed in wars with Britain and the bubonic plague in Greater Syria. We achieved nothing here. I lost my father, too," Estelle conveyed to him in a sad tone.

Vivant said nothing as he seemed troubled by that horrifying memory, too. They all finished their dinner quietly.

***

It was a starry night, as usual in Qena, and Al-Khidr was sleeping deeply. Suddenly, someone woke him with a rough pat on his head.

"Wake up Al-Khidr, wake up. We are tracking you. We have put a tracker in your hand." A woman in the shadows said in an electric voice. "Who are you? And what do you want?" Al-Khidr asked fearfully. His heart began to thump loudly against his chest.

The woman in the shadow said, "We want to restore the balance! We are the last hope for this planet!" Neither her figure nor her shadow was visible as it was pitch-black dark. Al-Khidr tried to rise to his feet, but his movement was restricted by an unknown force that seemed to surround him at that point.

"What can I do to save this planet?" Al-Khidr asked keenly as he was still considering their offer. Abruptly, the force that had restricted him was removed, and they sat him down and showed him he could change the world, which was under complete chaos then. Furthermore, they offered him the perfect way to save himself and their planet.

Al-Khidr, being a little reluctant, allowed them to trace his hand with a long needle and give him medication to numb his hand. The drug possessed a powerful narcotic effect that made his head spin thoroughly and blurred his vision. In addition to that, it made him completely forget what happened when he was under the influence of the drug. Al-Khidr woke up with ex-

Chapter 18. The Twist of Fate

cruciating pain in his hand.

"What on earth was that?" he uttered while gritting his teeth because of the unbearable pain in his hand.

"Another nerve-wracking nightmare, I guess," he said to himself and shook his head in irritation. "Who is tracking me here on Earth?" He was still confused about why he was experiencing the excruciating pain in his hand from time to time. "I will get rid of this pain as soon as I go back to Lyra," he said to himself firmly. He was in the large tent, and Vivant was snoring, and Estelle was also in a deep sleep.

Al-Khidr felt a little under the weather, and he felt like the air inside the tent was too humid. So, he decided to go outside to get some fresh air. He stepped outside the tent and started looking at the sky. Two soldiers stationed outside the tent, and they were in a deep discussion about the war. There was a checkpost at the tower as well. It all looked very safe, but Al-Khidr still felt in his heart that some disaster was going to come sooner or later. He had a very strong gut feeling that something would go wrong.

Al-Khidr went back inside the tent and laid down. Suddenly, a loud commotion was heard. The soldiers were shouting at each other for some unknown reason. The noise woke up everyone inside the tent.

"What the hell on earth are they ranting about!" yelled Vivant, as he yawned profoundly and put on his slippers. Estelle, too, was annoyed by the chaotic noise coming from outside, and she rubbed her eyes and got up instantly. They all rushed outside to know the cause of the mayhem.

"Silence!" shouted Vivant, and the soldiers immediately got into a position of attention. "You!" he pointed at one of the three soldiers who were at loggerheads with each other. "Tell me what this ruckus is all about?"

Vivant looked at them as a ferocious tiger, and the soldier burst into speech. "A group of jackals attacked and wounded a soldier!" The soldier exclaimed exasperatedly.

Chapter 19

The Opening

H‍ATATHOR initially sped up the boat as fast as he could. He did not want to waste any more time. Hatathor wanted to get to the prisoner as quickly as possible before he had the chance to move away from his current location again.

I won't let you escape again, human. This time for sure, you will be in my clutches, and the sphere will be mine, he thought intensely when suddenly he heard some noise from below. He looked down, and to his horror, he noticed that the nails of the boat were coming out as the boat could not handle the structural

Chapter 19. The Opening

stresses that were generated because of the high speed. Abruptly, one plank of the boat came out, andwater started filling inside it as the felucca was falling apart.

"Damn this earthly vehicle!" he cursed loudly while gritting his teeth in irritation. He was only a few miles away from the shore; therefore, he took the risk and did not reduce his speed. Finally, he reached the jetty while the boat shattered into pieces and was taken away by the speeding currents of the Nile River.

He was back on the ground, and changed his plan, decided to get the beast again. Immediately, he opened his tracking unit and began locating the prisoner. The tracker showed Al-Khidr's location a bit farther away, and Hatathor's lips curled into an evil smile.

Finally, I will get my hands on the jump-sphere, he thought victoriously and began moving towards the city.

Apparently, there was no settlement nearby. Therefore, he sat on the side of the river and took his green super-food to energize himself.

To his horror, the bottle was only half-filled. It was a matter of great concern for the mighty Lyrian, as he had no idea what could be the alternate source of food for him on Earth. Last time, the earthen plant had killed the Lyrians and had resulted in an outbreak of the deadliest disease possible across the Lyra called Mutmut. As horrifying thoughts filled his head, Hatathor felt like the earth was shaking.

His sleeve device beeped: "Tremor noticed."

He went inside the bushes to see what was happening.

A large infantry of French soldiers was moving towards the south. The infantry of French soldiers were marching parallel, and the soldiers were carrying bayonets on their shoulders. The infantry was being led by a commander who was riding a horse. Due to their tremendous marching, the ground began shaking so heavily and felt like an earthquake was on the way.

Is there a war going on? he thought.

After the infantry passed away, Hatathor moved out of the bushes and started looking at them.

"If they are looking for me, then a human army cannot take a Lyrian warrior as a prisoner," he whispered to himself.

Suddenly, someone shook his hand. He looked to the side and found a poor Arab boy.

He was a small boy wearing tattered clothes with a dirty face, and his hair was extremely messy with spikes. His skin was rough, with a few small scars and minor cuts. His eyes were dark brown, and his lips were dried as though he hadn't drunk water for weeks. His eyes were bloodshot, and there were dark circles underneath them. A pungent odor seemed to erupt out of his body, which also conveyed that he hadn't bathed in days as well.

Hatathor converted the language mode to Arabic and asked him: "What do you want, boy?"

"I want some money. I am hungry," the poor boy said in a sad tone.

"Where is your father?" Hatathor inquired softly

Chapter 19. The Opening

in a tone of concern.

"The ruthless French took him. They tied him with his arms stretched out and fired at him with rifles and executed him. They thought he was one of the rebels," the poor boy narrated his heartbreaking tale with soulless eyes. Hatathor took the young boy by the hand and led him to the water's edge. Then, using his trusted bident, he caught a few fish and gave them to the boy. The innocent child gave him the widest smile anyone had ever given Hatathor and said "thank you" in return. "Hey, do you know where I can get the beast?"

The boy didn't understand what Hatathor was referring to. So, the Lyrian created a holographic image of the horse using his sleeve. The child's eyes lit up at the sight of the sleeve device, and he clamped his mouth with his hands in extreme awe.

"What is this thing?" he asked with immense curiosity and exhilaration. However, Hatathor ignored his innocent question and pointed at the image of the horse. "This is a horse," the boy taught him with a delightful laugh. Then his tone turned forlorn again.

"All the horses and camels we had were confiscated by the French army, as they feared that the local Egyptians might use them to fight the French army. They took our cows, sheep, oxen as their army needed food. Sometimes they slaughter the horses and feast on them instead of giving them back to the locals— They starve us to death," he expressed as his innocent eyes started brimming with tears. Hatathor felt a tremendous surge of pity for the young boy, and he was able to empathize with him to a great extent since he was an orphan too. He wiped the boy's years with his palm and asked him, "Where did they take the horses exactly, do you know?"

"They took them all to the citadel, Al-Rumayla, which is near Cairo," the boy informed him.

Hatathor realized that the best he could do was to somehow get the beasts from the French army. He needed to move as fast as he could. And he missed his spaceship badly. "Where is the closest French garrison?" he asked him casually, and the little boy pointed towards the southwest.

***

The General was looking through the window. His look was rugged, and the clothes were not of the finest quality. There was a table inside the room, made of mahogany wood, polished and lustrous. It had a deep brown color with a slight sheen to it that looked both solid and expensive. The table was large enough for five people to have a discussion. The wood had a rich, dark grain, smooth and of the most excellent quality. "General, aMubashir(informant) wants to see you," an officer entered and announced.

"Send him in!"

One of the local Egyptian farmers arrived in the General's office. He was a middle-aged man with a thick greying beard, who wore a ragged silver-colored Jelebiyah and a white headscarf around his bald head.

Chapter 19. The Opening

His complexion was dusky. Looking at the general gravely with his brown eyes, he said: "O Just Sultan, how are you. I have come here to give you some bad news. Our group of farmers has reported the gruesome murders of some French soldiers at the hands of an unknown person. He also killed their dogs."

"Where exactly did the murders take place, Kosma?" the General demanded sharply.

General's manners were impeccable, and his demeanor was that of a polished French gentleman of the highest stature.

"Somewhere between Cairo and Qena. A boat owner informed us that someone snatched the boat from him. The man is described as being tall and sturdy. But he is not like the Arabs or the Coptics. He is a brutal killer, monsieur. He wouldn't leave anything or anyone alive in his path who would try to stop him. Such that, this evil and a ruthless person even burned the dogs mercilessly. It means that this 'mystery ruffian' is on some unknown mission and possesses some incredibly lethal supernatural powers which make him a colossal danger not only for the French forces but also to the Coptics and Arabs." Kosma Boqtor conveyed to the General in a fearful tone.

Desaix gestured Kosma to leave, and the poor farmer gave a deep bow and left his office.

Louis Charles Antoine Desaix was a passionate general around thirty years of age with a saber scar across his right cheek. He had long hair, which enhanced his gravitating personality. His carriage resembled that of a trained fighter filled with ambition and leadership, which sometimes defied morality. Desaix was a year older than Napoleon and was stationed near Qena. He had already received the news about the arrival of Vivant in Qena. General Desaix summoned a soldier. The soldier arrived quickly.

"Send the team to Cairo and give me a full report within a day," Desaix ordered the French soldier.

A fifteen-year-old black girl approached the General. She wrapped her arms around him and gave him a passionate kiss.

"Why do I see that my General is a bit anxious today?" she asked in a sing-song manner.

"My lovely madcap, Abyssinian. You know war is like a snake, twisting, turning, and shaking off its skin to become something new. I see that our war here in Egypt is shedding off its skin. Now, either we have a new war, or we retreat,"

Sarah gave him a sensual smile and said: "Would mighty Desaix take me to France?"

"Yes, my dear girl, I will! I have already promised you that, haven't I?"

General gazed at the fifteen-year-old dark-skinned teenager lustily. She was quite an attractive girl with big plump lips and large brown eyes that lay perfectly above a small, cute nose. Her curvy figure made her look even more beautiful and gravitating to any man who would lay his eyes on her. She wore a lengthy white gown that smelled of a lotus perfume that teased

Chapter 19. The Opening

General Desaix's senses and made his mouth water.

"Yes, you have," she said flirtatiously, moving her fingers across his neck.

"General Desaix, you are the strongest and the most handsome man in the world, you know," she flirted, staring deeply into his icy blue eyes. "That's why I am going to take you back to France with me, my gorgeous girl. And make you bloom there too," he expressed, and his thoughts started burning with lust. Then abruptly, his mind returned to the problem Kosma had conveyed, and he slowly let go of Sarah. She giggled girlishly and went out towards the Desaix's Seraglio to inform Astiza, Mara, Fatima, and the other slave consorts of the General's firm decision to take her to France.

Desaix felt very nervous, and he didn't feel like having entertainment with the girls of his harem. He was disappointed that he might have to retreat and go back to France. However, his heart was in Egypt as he had fallen in love with the dazzling country.

At that moment, an emissary entered the tent. He was a French soldier who had come from Cairo on a swift horse. Upon reaching General Desaix, he gave him two sealed letters.

The emissary's voice was low and muffled, far from the voice that Desaix was habituated to hearing. The man's sweat carried the smell of fear - an intensely spine-chilling fear.

Desaix quickly opened the first letter. It was from the savants in Cairo. It was all about the fear and apprehension they had experienced the night they had been attacked by an ancient Egyptian-looking man who possessed magical capabilities.

"It's a pile of utter rubbish!" Desaix uttered and threw the letter to the ground.

He opened the second letter, which stated: "General Desaix, we have bad news for you. A man attacked the Institute of Egypt and caused great mayhem there. And when we started searching for him, he slaughtered both our men and our hounds. We sincerely advise you to exercise great caution."

Besides the warning, there was a postscript (P.S.) in the letter which read: "We have learned that Surur ibn Musa'id, the prince or Emir of Mecca, has persuaded the Muslims to cross the Red Sea and enter the Qena area to fight for Islam. There are nearly six to seven thousand people who will leave for the Upper region of Egypt. But it has also come to our knowledge that the local Arab Egyptian peasants, whose land and horses we had confiscated, and some of those Coptic Christians are ready to join their rank as the Coptics feared we would persecute them based on their faith. General, soon they all will join the ranks of Murad Bey forces—the Ghuza. And the worst part is they are heavily equipped with guns and swords which the British army had supplied to them."

Desaix immediately set the letter aside and ordered his men to be alert as the southern area of Egypt was bubbling heavily with a fresh wave of mysterious attackers.

Chapter 19. The Opening

***

Al-Khidr woke up late and got out of his bed instantly. He looked around and perceived that he was left in solitude inside the tent. Even Estelle was not there. Slightly worried, he came out of the tent; the sun was shining glamorously across the horizon as it always did in Egypt. It struck its intensely pleasant rays on Al-Khidr's face, and he closed his eyes to bask in its glory. Then he opened his eyes and began looking around for Estelle and Vivant. However, he felt like he was all alone in the colossal encampment.

Then, he moved forward and found Vivant, who ordered the soldiers to take him across the river, and they were expecting more troops to arrive. A sentry was passed to General Desaix to send some more soldiers.

Estelle was right by his side. She was wearing a brand new dress, and she looked exceptionally gorgeous in it as her cheeks appeared even rosier than usual, and the wind was grazing her silky long curly hair.

Damn. She looks like an angel! he thought, unable to take his eyes off her. And a tiny bubble of attraction formed in his heart, but he popped it immediately, thinking of his true love, Nefertiti, and shook his head to get him out of it.

Her eyes fell on Al-Khidr, and she gave him a glorious smile, like the promise of spring in winter, and moved towards him. "Good morning, dear friend," she exclaimed and looked at him strikingly through her beautiful light green eyes. "What's going on, Estelle? Why is Vivant ordering more soldiers to come?" inquired Al-Khidr with a puzzled expression on his reddish face. Estelle sighed in disappointment and conveyed to him, "There has been a revolt by the local Arabs and Coptic Christians," "What? When did this happen?" he inquired worriedly.

"Vivant received the news about it from General Desaix just before dawn," she informed him.

Al-Khidr didn't seem shocked at the news; however, he didn't want to cross the river again.

"But don't you worry, we don't need to cross the river. I have found the Boraqis plant right here in the camp!" she exclaimed excitedly, as though she had read his mind. "Let's quickly go and get them!" she chanted blissfully, and grabbing his hand, they went near the river bank.

They discovered a variety of plants of different sizes and shapes in that area. And Al-Khidr started plucking the new leaves from the Boraqis plant. He took five to six leaves and rolled them up quickly. Then he took out the sphere and realized that he had forgotten the needle.

"Oh damn! I forgot to keep a needle."

"Don't you worry it, Al-Khidr, I have a needle with me," Estelle assured him with a graceful smile.

"You are just brilliant, Estelle!" he praised her in a thrilled tone, which made her blush slightly, and she muttered, 'It's okay". She took out a needle that con-

Chapter 19. The Opening

tained a thread inside the purse in her leather bag. She swiftly removed the thread from the needle and handed it over to him. "There you go!" she said enthusiastically, unable to contain her excitement at getting to know the contents of the mysterious sphere. Al-Khidr gazed at the needle intensely, which was quite sharp and thin enough to be inserted into the sphere.

"In the name of Allah, the most gracious, most merciful!" he recited calmly and inserted the needle slowly and carefully inside the sphere. The needle went inside and pressed something. Nothing happened for a few seconds. Then, abruptly, the sphere let out a clicking sound. And following that noise, the top of the sphere moved instantaneously and then got opened from the top like a scarab beetle's wing. However, the two portions were still connected and gave access to a tiny chamber inside.

Al-Khidr moved the covers, and they opened further, giving him access to the internal compartment. Eventually, concealed deep inside the compartment, lay a shard of Amris right at the center, as Ehsis had told him before he left Lyra.

Al-Khidr's heart seemed to beat faster than lightning at the sight of the Amris. His eyes glowed brightly when they fell on it, as he couldn't believe his eyes that the answer to all his problems lays right in front of his eyes now.

This is it, Al-Khidr. You have finally unlocked the key, which will help you accomplish your mission.... And also, you will finally be able to go back to the

Lyra again, he thought, as a massive bubble of joy and excitement formed in his heart.

Al-Khidr took the shard out and proudly showed it to Estelle.

"This is Amris—a powerful fuel from the planet Lyra. Without it, the sphere will not work," Al-Khidr explained to her, holding the shard as carefully as any average person would hold a lump of gold.

The compartment had enough space to accommodate the leaves. Strangely, that side of the sphere was freezing internally. Therefore, Al-Khidr placed the curled-up leaves inside it and closed the covers. Finally, the sphere took its original shape.

Estelle was looking at Amris in utter amazement. Her eyelids widened, and her pupils expanded, along with her mouth, which was left open in utmost bewilderment. There was nothing in the world that she had seen which came any close to the Amris.

"Can I hold it please?" she requested Al-Khidr, who thought for a second and then handed it to her. The moment the shard of Amris came in contact with her skin, a horrifying sound erupted from nearby as a running soldier called out to them. "Run! We are under attack!"

The moment he said that, a hissing arrow passed right across them, and they had to duck instantly to avoid it. They realized that the Mamelukes' forces had attacked, and this time they were arriving in boats and on horses. The swarm of arrows hissed across the grass behind them like venomous snakes. Some ar-

Chapter 19. The Opening

rows missed their targets. However, they left a trail of smoke in the air around it, and one of the soldiers collapsed on the ground. The burning arrows smelled of sulfur and burned as though they pierced their throat.

Estelle and Al-Khidr rolled across the grass and weeds and then darted towards the camp as fast as their legs could take them. In the interim, the soldiers were being led in formation over the sand, which was white and blazing furiously under the scorching ball of sun. They were extremely nervous and lay cautiously on the edge. The soldiers were wearing caps decorated with a cockade in red, white, and blue colors.

Monsieur Vivant had a grim expression on his face as though he was disappointed by the alertness of the forces. However, he was internally afraid of losing the battle against the Mamelukes. His heart was banging heavily against his chest as though he would suffer from a heart attack at any moment. His insides trembled continuously, and his mind had turned nearly numb. He stood there rooted to the spot in fear and exasperation as the Mamelukes continued to attack the French army. Al-Khidr and Estelle ran towards the French forces, who were just waiting for them to provide the soldiers with a clear sight to fire at the Mamelukes. In the interim, the Mamelukes forces shot another swarm of arrows, which hit the French soldiers, and they fell to their death instantly. The soldiers kept falling one by one, but none of them opened fire till the two of them had safely reached them. The howls and cries of the French soldiers freaked out Estelle, who tripped on a stone and fell onto the sandy ground. Instantaneously, an arrow was shot right in her direction.

"Estelle!" Al-Khidr roared while turning around and sprinted like a cheetah towards her. Estelle sat up and froze in immense terror as the arrow was heading towards her. But before the arrow could pierce through her heart, Al-Khidr screamed and, diving into the air, he caught her, and they both rolled over, and the arrow missed its target.

"Are you alright!?" he demanded as she lay over him.

"I am alright," she muttered, staring at him tenderly as he had saved her life again. Then, without wasting a single second, Estelle and Al-Khidr darted as fast as they could towards the military camp and went behind the lined-up soldiers. As soon as they reached the camp safely, there was a shout of "Open Fire" from the army commander, and the French forces finally began firing at the attackers.

Estelle continued to gaze at him with immense affection in her heart. And amidst the chaos spread around, love bloomed within the French maiden's heart for the Arab man. "This is the second time you saved my life, Al-Khidr," she whispered slowly to him. "I owe two lives to you, dear," "It was nothing at all, Estelle. Like I said before, I would always protect my family and friends, even if that required me to put my life at stake," he said mechanically. Al-Khidr was able to sense clearly that Estelle had fallen head over heels

Chapter 19. The Opening

in love with him, but he had to set her mind straight, as he was already someone else's. And he did not wish to fill her heart with false hopes. Then he recalled the famous saying and understood that they were indeed true: "Love can happen anywhere, anytime."

Al-Khidr tried to be platonic with her in that situation and avoided any sort of eye contact. Estelle continued to gaze at him with the sparkle of love in her eyes. All the horrible noises and the surrounding mayhem seemed to quieten as all her senses were fixed on Al-Khidr, the man whom she loved. However, the glint of love vanished from her eyes as a bitter realization hit her hard like a brick.

"Oh, my dear Lord! I don't have it! I have lost it!" Estelle screamed exasperatedly, clutching her hair and glancing at Al-Khidr.

"What? What is it?" Al-Khidr asked in a state of anxiety. But Estelle didn't reply; rather, she continued to lament desperately in shock.

"How could I lose it? It was right there in my hands! How could I be so damn careless?!" she continued to lament and curse herself for her carelessness.

"What happened, Estelle? What is the name of Lord did you lose?" he demanded again hurriedly.

"The... The glass... I have lost the Amris piece!" Estelle stammered and slapped her forehead in agony.

Chapter 20

In the South

A̲ʟ-Kʜɪᴅʀ's mouth was dry, and he felt like it was on the verge of cracking. His heart was thundering in his chest, and his eyes were tearing up from the overwhelming surge of emotions that he felt. It seemed like everything he had done till this point had gone. He felt like he had lost the way back to the Lyra. He was looking at the sphere with eyes full of emptiness. He was furious at his own mistake. He should have kept the Amris shard in his hands. He was lost in thoughts when another hissing arrow passed nearby him and brought him back to his senses. The attack was still

Chapter 20. In the South

ongoing near the river bank. The smoke of baïonnettes had filled up the atmosphere. "It's from fate," he said to himself.

He had to accept whatever God was doing, and he just needed to do whatever was in his hands. He also did not want Estelle's life to be endangered in his mission. "I am very sorry, Al-Khidr," Estelle apologized in a nervous voice.

"There is no need for you to apologize, Estelle," Al-Khidr said with a tiny smile. "Whatever happens, happens by the will of the Almighty Lord, so we should place our trust in him and his plans, no matter what,"

Al-Khidr's words had a soothing effect on Estelle, and she nodded innocently like a little girl. However, she was adamant that she would find it for sure. "But just let me go, Al-Khidr. I will search for it," Estelle said, and she began to move towards the river. However, Al-Khidr lurked behind and holding her hand, he said: "Don't do that!"

"I am going. I will look for it," she nervously said incoherently.

"No. Don't go! You are more precious than Amris, and I do not want to endanger your life," Al-Khidr exclaimed in a state of desperation. Estelle became quiet, and then she burst into tears. Al-Khidr hugged her and caressed her head slowly.

***

The sky was bright as Hatathor stood in front of the French army settlement. A vast, open space lay in front of it. It was a large garrison-like area and had roughly a hundred French soldiers. He just needed one horse, and he didn't want to use his precious time in killing humans, but it seemed like he had no other option. He moved towards the entrance. A soldier came forward and asked him his rank and other questions as he was dressed in a French uniform. They immediately realized that Hatathor was not a real French soldier as he didn't look like a European breed. They ordered him to stop, but he continued walking. "I want a beast!" Hatathor said.

"You are not allowed in this area."

He kept quiet and continued walking.

"Stop, or we will fire!"

The soldiers took out their guns and pointed towards him.

But before they could pull their triggers, he jumped high into the air. The French soldiers were baffled as they looked up. Hatathor, while still in the air, pointed his bident towards the soldiers. A blinding flash and the sting of fire were seen, and then a loud boom echoed through the air as the soldiers collapsed on the ground. The birds flapped their wings in the nearby reeds at the river Nile when the explosions rocked the area. And the soldiers' bodies evaporated like steam. Hatathor ran towards the stable, and there was chaos and commotion everywhere inside. The soldiers were assembling to encounter the new enemy. All eyes were on Hatathor, who boldly walked towards the horse stable and reached it unharmed.

Chapter 20. In the South

The air was heavy and pungent with the stench of the soldiers' uniforms, and horse manure. Many of the horses were unharnessed, and the stable reeked of its inhabitants. Horses were shrieking and agitating, but the soldiers remained motionless. They were simply curious to see what Hatathor was doing. The confusion struck the soldiers, as they could not decide what to do with the lone attacker.

"Murderous thief! You cannot go out from here!" a French officer shouted. "This is your last chance; either surrender or die!" Hatathor, on the other hand, sat on the saddle of a horse and held its reins tightly. Hatathor could feel its skin, its coat, and its muscles between his arms and legs. Eventually, the horse felt the hard ground beneath his hooves and started galloping. And the pounding of its hooves against the ground reverberated loudly in its ears.

"Open fire!" shouted another French soldier, and bullets sprayed across the air and soared towards Hatathor.

Before the bullets could reach him, Hatathor pointed the bident at the soldiers, and in a fraction of a second, more lifeless bodies lay pathetically on the ground. The smoke of started rising from their bodies. The Lyrian came out of the stable and experienced the cries, smoke, and a blazing fire spreading across the settlement. But he was least bothered by it, and he continued to gallop fast towards the South.

***

"Although the attack on the French encampment

was repelled, the frequency of attacks on Qena has increased," Vivant informed General Desaix, who reached the encampment. The soldiers saluted him as he took off his Bicorne, held it between his chest and arm, and moved towards the tent. "Good morning, general!" Vivant greeting in a cheerful manner.

General Desaix, on the other hand, returned the greeting in a nonchalant way that conspicuously displayed his arrogance and prejudice towards the people below him in rank or stature.

Firstly, he shook hands with Vivant then kissed Estelle's hand as Vivant introduced her to him. He kept gazing at her and kept her hand into his palm, longer than needed, which made her quite uncomfortable. He shook hands with Al-Khidr and looked into his eyes. Then, he entered the tent leaving everyone outside, and sat on the desk with the main chair. The rest of them followed him and entered. General Desaix, being an extremely cocky and conceited man, showed that he was the boss there and not the savants.

A table was placed especially for his arrival. As everyone seated themselves on the chairs, Desaix waved his hand and asked Al-Khidr to sit right in front of him across the table. He surveyed every person that was seated in front of him with his icy blue eyes. His gaze traveled from Vivant, then Estelle, and finally, it rested on Al-Khidr.

"I would like to know more about you, monsieur. Where are you from? And what is your tribe?" General interrogated him while piercing him with his bril-

Chapter 20. In the South

liant blue eyes. "I am a Berber from one of the tribes of the North African Amazigh people, but I grew up in Egypt as my father settled here and married a French girl," Al-Khidr narrated the same tale he had fed Vivant and the others. "Monsieur Al-Khidr is now considered as one of our savants-" Vivant began, but the General cut him in.

"Did I ask you to explain, Monsieur Denon?" General said grudgingly in a bitter tone. And Monsieur Vivant remained silent.

"So, Monsieur Al-Khidr, ever since you arrived here in Qena, why have there been so many attacks on us?" General Desaix demanded sharply as he continued to survey him with his piercing stare.

Al-Khidr remained silent while Estelle made an unexpected intervention. "Pardon me General Desaix, but Monsieur Al-Khidr is a gentleman. He saved my life!" Estelle proclaimed sharply and questioned the attitude of General Desaix. Suddenly, Desaix's demeanor changed entirely at the French girl's intervention.

"Mademoiselle, let me do my work, please," he requested with a smile, but clearly, he was not very impressed with her interruption. Desaix continued, "What exactly do you do for a living? Who is in your family? And do you have any friends?" "I am an alchemist, General. As for my family, I am an orphan. I had few friends a long time ago, but I have met no one after the revolt," Al-Khidr responded confidently.

"Where exactly were you at the time of the revolt?"

"I was in Meroe, Nubia, on a trading mission, selling spices to merchants."

"But you said you are an alchemist, then why were you involved in the business of spices?" General asked him a pertinent question.

"I started making medicines, but my business didn't flourish, so I started selling spices as I have knowledge of the herbs and plants,"

"Interesting," Desaix commented in a mocking tone. There was a brief pause, and then Desaix spoke again.

"I need a moment of aloofness with Monsieur Denon," General Desaix announced and looked at Estelle and Al-Khidr.

He clearly wanted them to go out as he wished to discuss something confidential with Vivant alone.

Once Al-Khidr and Estelle had gone out, Desaix looked at Vivant and said, "Monsieur Vivant, you are an artist and a novelist, but I am a general. I see things differently,"

Vivant looked quite perplexed and asked: "What happened, general?"

"The attacks in this area have increased ever since you arrived with this Berber guy!"

"It is true, General Desaix. However, I disagree with the notion that he is the reason behind all these attacks," Vivant stated explicitly. "The man is not a threat to us, and as a matter of fact, he saved Estelle's life on two different occasions," Vivant asserted further.

"Despite all that, I strongly suggest that you send

Chapter 20. In the South

him back to Cairo along with Mademoiselle Estelle," Desaix advised sharply, which sounded more like an order. "I know you like temples, monsieur, and you spend hours drawing impressive sketches of them. But you are not aware of your purpose here, monsieur," Desaix affirmed while standing up.

Vivant was furious, but he was helpless in front of him. He had to follow the General's orders. In case something bad happened, he could complain about him to Napolean. Vivant had no idea what to do.

"I can grant you only a few days to do this," he proclaimed and left the encampment.

***

General Desaix was back in his office. He summoned an officer and advised him to bring the informants from the tribes of Abibda that resided in the upper region of Egypt. Abibda was one of the local Bedouin tribes that had changed its allegiance from Murad Bey to the French army. They had secretly started supporting the French army and were giving them information about Murad Bey's forces. They were also providing them with logistic support in the South of Egypt and Nubia. Abibda tribe's elders believed that French forces would surrender to British forces as they didn't have the ships to escape to Europe. The British forces had given them a tough time both across the sea and in Syria, and now God had thrown the plague over them. The French were dying every day due to war, thirst, and plague, and their numbers had dwindled. And to every sane Egyptian, it was quite clear that the occupation of Egypt by the French would not last longer than two years. The Arab tribal elders were acting as intermediaries between the opposing armies.

After a few hours, there was a knock on General Desaix's door. The local Egyptian Bedouin politely asked the reason for summoning him. "Ali, I have a task for you. You know that in the last few days, Murad Bey's men had attacked this region several times," General Desaix said serenely. "Yes, I have heard about it. And now they are coming through boats," Ali said.

"You know your villagers well. This is your region. I would like to get rid of the informants and spies who could work for Murad. There is a man called Al-Khidr recently discovered by our savants. He claimed he is from north Africa and he is a Berber. I want your people to kidnap him and send him to the South. I do not want to kill him. How merciful I am," he laughed and continued: "I just want to extradite him. But you be careful because I do not want to infuriate some of my French friends." Desaix laid out his plan.

"Very well, general. You should not worry about this. Where is that man staying?" Ali asked. "At Qena, in our encampment," Desaix informed Ali.

"I will inform the soldiers stationed at the camp, and they would help in the execution of this task," Desaix said further.

***

Chapter 20. In the South

It was close to sunset, and Al-Khidr and Estelle were frantically searching for the Amris shard near the Nile. Vivant was worried as he strolled near the Nile. Suddenly, his eyes fell on Al-Khidr and Estelle, who were nearby and were anxiously searching for something. "What are you both looking for? Did you lose the sphere again?" Vivant inquired.

"No, I lost my necklace," Estelle lied quickly without thinking.

"I can order few soldiers to help you out," Vivant suggested helpfully.

"Thank you, Vivant, but I will handle it. Don't worry, Al-Khidr is already helping me," Estelle asserted with a genuine smile. "Let's join for dinner later?" she asked politely. "Estelle, I feel extremely haggard and exhausted. I don't think I will be able to join you two for dinner tonight," Vivant lied as he turned away. He was purposely trying to avoid them as he didn't wish to break the General's order so quickly, especially at night.

"Alright, then have a goodnight," she wished him with a fake cheerful smile, and they continued their search. Vivant returned her wish casually and went back to the camp. The soldiers were also busy with their work, so he avoided them too. He was feeling forlorn at General Desaix's order to send Estelle and Al-Khidr back to Cairo. When Vivant returned to the camp, four men with their faces covered with black scarves emerged from the bushes suddenly. The men were Arab Bedouins who approached the duo with a scimitar. Estelle and Al-Khidr had no weapons.

"What in the name of God do you want?" Al-Khidr shouted sharply in Arabic, but they remained silent and approached them like a pack of wolves advancing towards their prey. In a state of desperation, he called out to the soldiers for help. He was loud enough, but no soldier came to their rescue. Some French soldiers were watching them from a distance.

Estelle grabbed Al-Khidr's arm out of terror and whispered to him, "Who could these people be?"

"I think they are a bunch of local thugs who want to kidnap us and ask for a ransom," he assumed, holding her close to him.

A few seconds passed, and two other bedouins brought a boat and gestured them to embark on it quickly.

"We have no other option," Al-Khidr told Estelle in a nervous tone, and she nodded helplessly.

"What the hell on earth are those darned soldiers doing? Are they blind or dead or drunk?" Estelle grumbled softly, but Al-Khidr placed a finger on his lips as a gesture for her to remain quiet. They seated themselves in a corner, and the Bedouins sailed the boat.

The boat sailed. From a distance, they could see that some French soldiers had arrived on the bank of the Nile. They realized that the French soldiers were talking to each other while Estelle and Al-Khidr were being taken away, and they were not doing anything about it. Al-Khidr and Estelle knew that something fishy was going on. Estelle was furious and had turned

Chapter 20. In the South

red with anger.

***

Vivant woke up in the morning, and he came out of the tent. He washed his face and looked for Estelle but couldn't find her. He then asked for Al-Khidr, and he was also not at the camp.

Vivant then called the soldiers and asked them to search for every nook and corner.

"Where has that girl gone? She never tells what she is up to?" Vivant was too mad.

"Al-Khidr too has become too frivolous. He should have followed the protocols."

A soldier arrived after 30 minutes.

"Monsieur Denon, we found no traces of Estelle and Al-Khidr," he said.

"Damn! Bring me a horse. I need to inform general Desaix!" Vivant shouted.

The soldier went out of the tent, and Vivant followed him. He took off his Bicorne, which was made of horsehide. The leather had been soaked in a vat of linseed oil and got its aroma from it. The sun was shining over his head, and he was sweltering profusely.

"I am going to see general Desaix. I will request him to court-martial all of you in case Estelle is not found before sunset," he warned and started galloping his horse.

Vivant reached the Desaix office, and he entered it without even permission. His mouth was already dry, and with the weight of the hot, heavy sun above, his world felt enormous. He was speaking incoherently. Desaix ordered a soldier to bring water.

"General, please help. My late friend Lieutenant-colonel Jacquous Molire's daughterMademoiselle Estelle Molire is lost, along with Monsieur Al-Khidr. I looked for them in every place that I knew. Your soldiers were also searching for them. My worry is they are lost in the desert or fell in some hole in the temple or were raped or killed by Bedouins."

Vivant burst into crying.

"Hold yourself, Monsieur! I am sure that soldiers would search them out." Desaix gave more water to Vivant.

"You don't need to worry. You go now, and I will search by myself." Once Vivant left. Desaix was furious. He summoned theMubashir from the Abibda tribe and shouted. "I asked you to kidnap the Berber man, not the French girl. Return the girl immediately," Desaix shouted. The man left with a poignant face.

***

Estelle and Al-Khidr were on the boat. Luckily, Al-Khidr had brought a sack with him which contained the sphere. The sky above them was full of stars.

"Where are you taking us?" Al-Khidr shouted in Arabic.

The men with covered faces answered nothing. Two of the men were paddling the boat, and the splashing of the water was heard intermittently. The moon-

Chapter 20. In the South

light softly shimmered over the unchanging river water, which glistened and shone in different shades of blue, black, and silver. Sometimes it looked as if it were shimmering with a pure sky-blue glow, or sometimes like a dark void that held stars at its heart. The air was rich with the scent of fresh water, moist and clean and sweet. What a refreshing scene to behold as the water sprayed into the air, chilling in the night air. "I'm sorry, Estelle," Al-Khidr said.

Estelle said nothing. She was sad and in a somber mode. She couldn't comprehend why the soldiers had not fired at these ruffians. "I'm sure Vivant will do something for us," Al-Khidr said to Estelle. She was speechless and confused.

After several hours in a boat like this, the boat finally stopped in the middle of a desert. The man asked them to get out of the boat first, and then they disembarked the boat. They were standing in front of the desert. The man behind them pushed them and ordered them to move forward. They continued their walking straight into the desert for an hour, and finally, they reached the village, which was mostly composed of mud bricks. There were 10 to 15 houses there. Al-Khidr and Estelle were asked to enter one house. The door was comprised of metal and wood. They stepped inside, and it was pitch dark. The men who were pushing them also entered this room. Then on one side of the wall, a man pushed the heavy black curtain made up of straw and black cloth and asked them to enter that room.

Inside the dimly lit room, there were few lamps whose light was apparently not going out, and it was not perceptible that the room was carrying ten to twenty-five people inside. In fact, it was a large hall, and there were carpets on the floor. On the sidewalls, there were cushions the men were sitting on both sides. Right in front was a bearded man with the turban over his head. He was wearing a black cloak, and he was looking right at them, half-reclining on a bank of pillows. His scimitar was lying nearby him. The room air was filled with incense smoke, and apparently, it was much colder inside. A man came forward and gave Estelle a piece of cloth to cover herself. Al-Khidr nodded his head as if requesting her she should take it. Estelle wore the peplum. A man came forward and snatched Al-Khidr's bag from him. "Welcome to Abu Simbel!" The turban man said. "Blessings of God be on you," he said to them.

"Blessings on you too," Al-Khidr replied, "why have I been kidnapped along with my friend?" Their chief ignored the question and said in a stern tone: "Seated on my left and my right is the Ikhwan (friends) from the tribes of Bili, Al-Huwaytat, Al-Sawaliha, Al-Habayba, Al-Hannadi, Al-Khabiri and others. To which tribe do you belong? ... Where are you from? You speak in an ancient dialect of Arabic?" The turban man inquired. "I'm from the Amazigh tribe of North Africa."

"Amazigh! Amazigh?" The men inside the hall were surprised.

Chapter 20. In the South

"What were you doing with the French?" The turban man posed another question.

The conversation was turning critical. Al-Khidr looked at Estelle, who looked frightened and was the only woman inside the tent. Al-Khidr said: "I am an alchemist — a Tabeeb (doctor). A few months ago, I had an apothecary in Cairo. I constantly need herbs and plants for making new medicines. When the French attacked Cairo, I was in Akhmim searching for some herbs. I realized Cairo would be an unstable place, so before the revolt, I closed my apothecary and left Cairo; I moved to Qena. Recently some French soldiers came to know about my skills, and they wanted treatment for the snakebite. One of their soldiers had been bitten by a snake. This lady was helping me in finding the right herbs, as she is an expert in herbs. But your men kidnapped us." "We have a different story about you," the turbaned man said.

"We were told that you're a spy of Murad Bey," Al-Khidr was shocked to hear that.

"I never met him in my life," he said to the turbaned man. The man laughed and said: "I know you're not lying. But I'm surprised why they have sent you to me?" "May I know your name," Al-Khidr asked. "I am Murad Bey," the turbaned man said.

Estelle and Al-Khidr looked at each other.

They were still in front of Murad Bey. The man who took the bag earlier came forward and presented the sphere to Murad Bey.

"I found this in his bag!"

"Interesting metal piece. We can melt it and convert it into spears of arrows," Murad said and looked at Al-Khidr as if he wanted to evaluate his reaction.

"No. Don't do this," Al-Khidr said. He was sweating.

"Are you an alchemist or collecting the treasures of the ancient pharaohs?"

For a moment, Al-Khidr felt speechless. But he gathered all his thoughts and said: "This is the gift of my father. It's a family relic. It's close to my heart."

"All the people in Egypt are giving tribute to this holy war. You should give it to us as your contribution. The price of a rate (500 gm) of gunpowder rose to half of the price of silver and that of bullets ninety dirhams."

He said and threw the sphere at Al-Khidr, which he caught easily.

"It's already too late. We'll talk tomorrow," Murad then nodded at his men to take them out of the big room.

They were back under the starry sky. A man came forward and asked Estelle to come with him. Al-Khidr moved forwards, but he lifted his hand and singled him to stop. "Where are you taking her?" Al-Khidr asked.

"Don't worry. You are Muslim, and you know you cannot stay with a woman alone," a man said.

"Yes. I am aware, but you should respect her that is also the teaching of Islam, isn't it?" Al-Khidr said in a bitter tone.

"Don't teach me. You are curing the wounds of infidels," the man shouted back.

Chapter 20. In the South

Al-Khidr was taken by another man in another direction. He was furious and couldn't control himself. He said: "I save a life no matter whether he or she, whether friend or enemy. God has said: whoever saves one human, he indeed saved whole humanity!" Al-Khidr was determined to convince the brute man.

"We are at war," the other man said.

"What kind of war? French handed me over to you. You took me without my consent. It is a war for sufferers, but eventually, you expect you will be the ruler again. Isn't it? A fighter will die to glorify your commander," Al-Khidr replied in a bitter tone. "We are warriors, and you are a Tabeeb(doctor)—I guess we think differently," the man said and pushed Al-Khidr into a dimly lit room. Al-Khidr and Estelle were in separate rooms. Estelle was with Arab Bedouin women, and Al-Khidr was given a separate room. The room he had been assigned to was anything but luxurious. It was a worn-down room with a dilapidated bed stuffed with husk and straw. He tried to sleep, but he could not. Only God knows when he had fallen asleep.

***

An informant came to General Desaix and said: "General, Murad Bey is not releasing the French girl. He gave an ultimatum. Within a month, you give the compensation to him for killing his men and release the Bedouins men; otherwise, he will make the girl his concubine."

Desaix smashed his fist on the table and shouted in rage.

"All this is the mistake of your tribe's men... Get lost. I will deal with him in my way!"

Desaix was sweating. He removed his cap and sat on the table. He started writing a letter to Napoleon:

> From General Desaix, south Egypt
>
> As his Excellence has shown his confidence by posting me in solving the delicate situation of the South of Egypt, I would like to update you on the mercurial South. It is getting more complicated. The rebels have increased their attacks, and recently they have kidnapped a French girl who has been doing research on the herbs. I am now trying my best to recover the girl and teach rebels a lesson. I am moving further south with 1000 men along with cannons.
>
> *Desaix.*

When he finished his letter, he sealed it and summoned a sentry.

"Dispatch it with the fastest emissary to His Excellence."

Colonel Blaise entered the General Desaix office and said: "Our camp near Asyut had been destroyed single-handedly by one lone, strange man. He is equipped with strange fiery weapons, and he is heading towards the South.

Actually, he passed nearby us on a horse, and several spies had seen him too. It is probably the same man who attacked at Institute in Cairo and later killed the search team members and hounds."

"Mobilize the military, Colonel Blaise. Prepare

Chapter 20. In the South

thousand men and move with cannons towards Abu Simbel," General Desaix said while looking outside.

Chapter 21

The Pyramid

Hatathor, who was dressed as a French military commander, stopped for a while. He had been following the human, but the human was constantly moving towards the south.

He allowed the horse to eat the plants and drink water on the Nile.

"I should check the prisoner!" he said to himself.

"Prisoner found: 534.56 Supris," the tracking unit announced.

Chapter 21. The Pyramid

"Prisoner is going towards the south further down!" he said to himself anxiously.

"Perhaps he is running away," he brooded.

After a few meters' walk, he saw an Arab village. There were Bedouin soldiers in every corner, and torches were burning. "Where are you, human!" Hatathor exclaimed exasperatedly.

Hatathor was far away from the city, in a desert with no trees and no structures nearby for him to hide. The only option left for him was to move forward and enter the Bedouin village. He started moving boldly towards the village. The Bedouin village was composed of walled, mud-floored homes built of mud bricks. There was a small well right at the center of the village, which was the only source of water for drinking and bathing purposes for the Arab villagers. The Bedouins wore white cotton jalabiya with scarves around their heads. They stared at him curiously as he marched towards the village. Some even ran inside their homes as they believed him to be a French soldier.

Besides that, there were many armed Bedouins on the rooftops who gazed at him distastefully. Some of them shouted at him. "Stop, French man, or you will die! If you value your life, then get the hell out of here. Or else, we will kill you. Stop or dig your grave right here in the village!"

Hatathor ignored these threats and shouts and continued to march forward. Some men on the roofs started firing bullets and arrows at him. The Bedouins kept firing the shots for several minutes and then reloaded their Turkish and British donated rifles with gunpowder. They realized they were running out of time. The rifles were a new weapon for them. It hadn't even been three months since they received the new ammunition from the British forces to defeat the French in Egypt. They had to continue firing. Otherwise, they believed the enemy would take them over.

Apparently they all missed the direct aim. There was tremendous chaos everywhere, as the firing resulted in a mass panic among the common Bedouins. The firing and arrow hissing sounds made the cattle nervous, and it triggered a horrible stampede. Many camels ran towards Hatathor. When Hatathor saw the camels running towards him, he got alarmed, and he rolled onto the side to avoid the large animals from trampling him to death.

However, as he rolled onto the side, one of the speeding camels hit his sleeve weapon, and sleeve came out of his hand. As the impact of the camel's padded feet was on his sleeve weapon, it didn't crush his arm; however, it sent an excruciating pain down his arm. The padded feet of the camels were trampling the sleeve weapon, and it was moving away from him as the animals were running. Hatathor turned in the opposite direction and bolted towards the nearest building to avoid being crushed by the stampede. Hatathor was climbing the building when a bullet fired by a local Bedouin hit his arm, and he was wounded. Hatathor flinched slightly as his arm ached horribly because of

Chapter 21. The Pyramid

the shot.

He gripped the bident tightly in his hands. Hatathor climbed onto the roof of the brick building and started looking for his sleeve weapon from the top. He was amid several houses which were constructed using stones and bricks and were separate from each other.

While he was still on the roof, he looked towards the North and saw the approaching army, and he felt that the earth was trembling underneath his feet. To his astonishment, he noticed the colossal French army approaching. They were heavily equipped with cannons and a vast number of human fighters. The soldiers carried bayonets. They were led by a commander who was riding a black stallion. The massive infantry of French soldiers were dressed in a long-skirted coat, waistcoat, and breeches along with tricorn hats on their heads and the long canvas gaiters which came up to mid-thigh and had multiple buttons.

***

Al-Khidr was locked in the room, and he heard the constant firing. "The war has begun!" he declared loudly, his heart beating faster than it ever had before. His door was locked, and he could only see through the window. The firing was constant, and he had to hide to prevent himself from getting shot from time to time. He quickly jumped to the side and checked the contents of his sack. The sphere was inside. He strapped the sack across his shoulder to make sure that it did not fall off while running.

He was anxious about Estelle. He knew she was present in one of the nearby houses, but he didn't know which one exactly. That was a puzzle that he had to solve before anything terrible happened to her. Luckily, a cannonball landed on the roof of the room he was in and created a breach. Using the mud-bricked broken wall as a staircase, he quickly climbed to the ceiling and pushed himself up out of it. Reaching the top of the roof, he discovered dead bodies lying around on the blood-stained sand. Then, he went to every corner and tried to find the house in which the women could be.

He saw some ladies' clothes hanging from the window of a house at the far end, so he guessed it might be the place where Estelle would be, along with the other women of the tribes. He kept jumping from one roof to another as the houses were close to each other, and so not that difficult for him. "Hey, you!" shouted one of the Bedouin men from below. "Where the hell do you think you are going? Get down immediately, or we will come up and kill you!" But, since they were engaged in fighting the French forces, they could not stop him. Al-Khidr reached the end of a house and, with a run and jump in the air, grabbed the house's ledge. He dived inside the house through the window. As soon as he entered the house, the women shrieked. He looked around. The children were crying, and all the women were gathered in one corner of the house. And fortunately, Estelle was also among them.

The woman shouted in Arabic: "Leave immedi-

Chapter 21. The Pyramid

ately; you're not supposed to come here."

"I just want to check on my friend." He informed slowly.

The women were already in a state of confusion, and they were afraid. They simply pushed Estelle towards Al-Khidr.

"Al-Khidr!" she exclaimed and fell into his arms. They embraced warmly for a few seconds and then broke away.

"Estelle, you won't believe me, but the French were the ones who attacked. We don't know who is playing the double game," Al-Khidr conveyed to her. "I don't believe it," she uttered in disbelief and shock.

"Never mind that. We must help the women and children," Al-Khidr affirmed.

"But what can we possibly do to help them?" Estelle demanded hopelessly.

Al-Khidr went out through the same window that he dived in and looked around for a few minutes. Then he came up with a workable plan.

"This area is a total war zone. They need to be taken out somewhere far from here. I go to the ground and check first. In the meantime, you gather all the children and women on the ground floor." Al-Khidr instructed her, and she nodded in agreement.

But before he could move, she held his hand and said, "Be careful...." Her gorgeous eyes were glinting with concern and love for him.

"Don't worry about me," he assured her with a smile, and she left his hand.

He stepped out of the house through the main door and started looking for a safe spot where the women and children could be sent. Finally, he figured out a meandering path that could lead them out of the war zone. He came back to the house and explained all in Arabic to the ladies. "No! That is dangerous; we cannot do that," one of the middle-aged ladies said.

"This is your only chance, sister," Al-Khidr persuaded desperately. "It's now or never. Don't do it for yourself, just do it for the children..." There was a brief pause as the ladies were arguing with each other. The old lady consulted one of her acquaintances among the women, and finally, she gave the nod. "Excellent!" cried Al-Khidr, and the women, children, and Estelle were ready to move out.

"Cover the young children's eyes and run!" he instructed firmly as he guided them out through the back-door of the house. They saw a gruesome sight. The mutilated bodies of the Bedouin men were scattered on the ground. And the entire area was filled with smoke and dust, shrouding death that seemed to lurk everywhere.

They began scampering as cautiously as they could; trying their best to avoid being out of sight. Suddenly, they came to a halt and concealed behind a house. Fortunately, the children had stopped, so they could move without making any noise. Slowly, Al-Khidr watched from the edge of the wall to see if the ground was clear and when it was, he gestured them to follow him, and they began walking carefully. And eventually, they

Chapter 21. The Pyramid

came far into the desert, where there was no sign of an army. The women and children had tears in their eyes, and they thanked Al-Khidr and Estelle earnestly.

As they were about to run away, an elderly Arab woman approached them with tears in her eyes.

"May the almighty Lord bless you both, and you live a long and healthy life," she blessed while grazing her hands on their heads. "Take care both of you".

"Ma'am," began Al-Khidr as she kissed Estelle on the forehead. "Can you tell us a place where we can stay low for a while," he asked hopefully. The elderly lady gave them a broad smile and nodded.

"Go to the southwest. There, you will find a small pyramid in the desert. You can hide there for a while till this bloody war is over. May God help us all!" Al-Khidr and Estelle thanked her and left. They darted in the direction which the woman informed them about — towards the small pyramid in the southwest.

***

Murad Bey's forces held the view that Hatathor was a new commander in the French troops. However, for Hatathor, all the humans, be it Bedouin or the French, were his enemies.

Hatathor was surrounded by two different levels of forces. He was getting ready to battle them when suddenly, his eyes fell on the person he was going through all that trouble for— Al-Khidr. He couldn't believe his eyes.

Are my eyes deceiving me, or is it truly the prisoner that I perceive right now? he said to himself.

After weeks of roaming hither and thither, fighting and killing filthy thieves, battling hostile human forces, and finally, I find you—just like that? He thought in utter disbelief. His lips curled into the first genuine smile in weeks, and his mind seemed to relax.

It is the moment that I have been waiting for weeks, he thought.

"Finally, I have reached my destination," he muttered. "I will finally be able to get my hands on the jump sphere and get the hell out of this hideous planet full of thieves, murderers, back-stabbers, and ruthless tyrants who torture innocent women and children for satisfying their greed," he gritted his teeth in disgust. "I have to get to him now, but first, I need to grab my sleeve weapon."

Lady luck smiled at him, and his eyes fell on the sleeve weapon lying near the corner of a house that was burning. The roof of the house was about to collapse, so he sprinted like a lightning bolt and, with an impressive dive, he caught his precious device and rolled away from the falling roof.

He got to his feet instantly, and turning around, he looked again for Al-Khidr and viewed him running away with a female.

The sight of Al-Khidr running away drove him crazy.

No! You cannot escape me, human. Not this time! he thought aggressively and went on a horrible onslaught.

Chapter 21. The Pyramid

He didn't even bother using the two-pronged weapon to vaporize them. Instead, he sprinted like a cheetah across the Arab Bedouins and the French forces and, swishing the bident like a spinning wheel; he slaughtered nearly all the attackers instantly. His ruthless killing spree didn't even spare the innocent youngsters and elderly men, as he considered all humans to be his enemies. The time was running out. After butchering anyone coming in his path in the Bedouin village, Hatathor put his sleeve back on and calmly started walking towards Al-Khidr, who was only a few hundred meters away.

Meanwhile, a few French soldiers and Bedouins, who had been hiding behind the houses, ambushed Hatathor and started spraying him with bullets and arrows. Still, they simply could not penetrate the hemispherical energy shield which Hatathor had activated casually without looking at them. The French and the Bedouins ran out of gunpowder and arrows, and so, in a state of nervous desperation, they attacked him with daggers. However, they got blasted into smithereens the moment they came into contact with the protective shield.

While the mighty Lyrian kept moving towards Al-Khidr hurriedly, Estelle and Al-Khidr continued to move at a steady pace. Finally, the pyramid which the Arab lady was referring to came into their sight. The duo stopped pacing when they discerned the triangular-walled monument. It was a comparatively small pyramid with a sharp apex that comprised stones.

"Al-Khidr," began Estelle while panting heavily. "You sure we can hide here till the war is over? I mean, they can't possibly find us here, right?" "I don't know, Estelle. I guess we should simply trust the Arab lady's words and the almighty Lord and find refuge here. At least, till the time we are sure that it is safe to move out".

Saying that, they began walking slowly towards the pyramid. They had barely reached the entrance of the colossal monument when a booming voice calling Al-Khidr's name stopped them in their tracks.

When they turned around to look for the source of the voice, Al-Khidr's eyes widened, and his legs froze as he became rooted to the ground in immense shock. Oh, my Lord! How on earth is this possible? Am I dreaming or hallucinating?

Al-Khidr couldn't believe his eyes. Standing right in front of his eyes was none other than Hatathor, the last person he expected to encounter, both on earth and at that moment in time. Al-Khidr wished he had rather encountered a wild beast instead of this alien.

Estelle seemed confused at Al-Khidr's reaction, and she asked about him. At which, he clenched her hand and said: "He is a ruthless alien, Estelle. He can harm anyone without shedding a tear."

Estelle was bewildered beyond words; she hadn't encountered an alien before. She looked at Hatathor in bewilderment. "He looks little different from a human; nothing extraordinary," she said to Al-Khidr.

"His skin color is reddish like an Arab's, and his

Chapter 21. The Pyramid

reddish-brown hair is like that of some of the European man. I do not think he is alien," Estelle said again. "Have you seen him before on the other planet?" she asked him distractedly, as her eyes were still glued to the Lyrian. "Yes, I have. He is a major general on the Lyra." Hatathor roared at them furiously, which raised the hair on the back of Al-Khidr's neck in trepidation.

"Woman, you better get the hell out of here. I have nothing to do with you. My business is solely with this bloody prisoner!" Hatathor said to Estelle, who didn't move and clutched Al-Khidr's hand tightly. "What do you want from me, Hatathor?" Al-Khidr demanded sharply as he looked at him straight in the eye. Al-Khidr wasn't afraid of the powerful Lyrian. He was ready to battle him if he had to. However, the only thing he was concerned about was Estelle's safety, as he knew that the spiteful and merciless alien would go to any lengths to gain what he wanted, even if it required him to murder countless innocent humans.

"Give me the jump sphere, human!" Hatathor demanded. "And then perhaps, I may let you live."

"I do not have any jump sphere," Al-Khidr lied quickly and firmly.

"You are lying filthy human!" Hatathor accused him as he clenched his fists in fury, "Listen, human. You dare not test my patience. Either you hand over the sphere and continue living your pathetic life on this planet, or I kill you and get the sphere myself. The choice is yours."

Al-Khidr thought for a moment and considered giving him the sphere. And so, he peeped into his sack to look at the sphere. But he changed his mind again. "Tell me one thing, though," Al-Khidr asked him serenely as he closed his sack. "You came down all the way from your planet just to get your hands on a small sphere?"

Hatathor gazed at him distastefully, as Al-Khidr was right. However, the Lyrian was too pompous and egoistic to admit the fact outright. "Of course not, you piece of shit!" he denied.

"It is because of you and that darned old hag Ehsis, who forced me to come here. Otherwise, I would have never set foot on this accursed planet where my father was killed!" Hatathor confessed with extreme hatred and disgust in his bloodshot eyes.

Hatathor demanded the sphere again, but Al-Khidr simply remained silent, which enraged the alien even more.

"That's it now. You have left me no choice but to kill you, filthy human!"

Saying that the mighty Lyrian advanced towards them like a ferocious beast. Estelle observed the wind's direction, and an idea flashed in her mind. She leaned forwards quickly, and taking a fistful of sand; she hurled it at Hatathor's face, who started rubbing his eyes and coughing violently as some of the sand had entered his eyes and lungs.

"Ah! You bastards! You will not escape my wrath now!" While Hatathor writhed in irritation, they started

Chapter 21. The Pyramid

running towards the pyramid's entrance. Hatathor could not focus as his eyes were watery, and his vision was blurred.

They both will die!

He increased the fire level to maximum. He fired one shot with the highest intensity of laser beam, to evaporate both of them. The laser beams missed them and hit the sack instead.

Suddenly all of the laser energy vanished as if it was taken by something else.

"What!" Hatathor was perplexed. The laser energy all went in the jump-sphere, which Al-Khidr was carrying in his sack. The sphere started beeping loudly, and all the charging marking on its surface suddenly lit up, which was a clear sign it had been fully charged. Somehow, the laser helped in reactivating the jump sphere in the same way that was expected from the shard of Amris.

Al-Khidr removed the sphere out of the sack and held it in his hand.

"Praise the Lord! The sphere has been fully charged!" he exclaimed in bewilderment while fixing his eyes on it. "But it is activated; any time, it will form an energy cocoon!" he realized. He was not sure what to do, as he had to save Estelle from Hatathor. "Estelle, no option left. You have to come with me; we go to another planet," he said.

Estelle and Al-Khidr were close to the pyramid's entrance. They ran as fast as they could. "Damn, all power levels are drained!" Hatathor exclaimed.

Now he had no other option but to make one last attempt. Hatathor let out a thunderous roar and threw his bident towards Al-Khidr with full force. However, in throwing, he lost his balance and slipped in the sand, and some sand went into his mouth and lungs again. He started coughing violently.

The two-pronged weapon missed the target, and a loud shriek echoed from the pyramid's wall.

Al-Khidr's pupils widened in horror as he came to a skidding halt and turned to his side. He knelt beside Estelle and began shaking her insanely. "Estelle! Estelle!" he clamored madly as he yanked the bident out of her back and threw it aside. Blood began gushing out of her wounded back. He looked into Estelle's eyes as his tears were falling on her face. She smiled and said:

"Ne pleure pas. C'tait destin ainsi. Puisse Dieu toujours t'aider. Je sais que, o que tu puisses aller, tu ne m'oublieras jamais. Je ferais toujours partie de tes souvenirs desormais!"

("Don't cry... It was destined like this... May God help you always... I know, wherever you go, you will never forget me... I will always be in your memories now.")

Estelle's mouth filled with blood, and she breathed her last.

Al-Khidr let out a thunderous roar of agony as every inch of his skin seemed to be pierced with needles. Pulling her into his arms, he began screaming, "No, please no! Please wake up!"

Chapter 21. The Pyramid

But she didn't move. She is gone, he realized and said: "Indeed, we belong to the Lord."

Hatathor pulled himself together, and he removed the sand from his face.

"What! The prisoner is not dead!"

Al-Khidr saw Hatathor. He stood up and screamed at the alien: "By God, if I had not given the promise to your Queen, I would prefer to die today in killing you!"

"Death to all humanity!" Hatathor shouted back. The blue particles started blurring the vision of both which were now issuing from the exotic matter boiling inside the sphere. He glanced at Estelle for the last time, and with a sprint, he entered the pyramid in case Hatathor tried to attack him again. The particles started forming an aura of blue energy cocoon around the pyramid.

The enormous buildup of energy around the pyramid produced the electric sparks which started interacting with the pyramid's walls. Hatathor ran and jumped several feet in the sky and landed on the outer casing stones of the pyramid before the energy cocoon engulfed the entire pyramid.

Without wasting a second, he pressed a button on his sleeve and created an aperture in the pyramid wall, and slid into it. The humongous cocoon of energy engulfed the entire pyramid. Whatever the energy cocoon touched, it was melted, and the pyramid was uprooted as the cocoon cut the floor from the ground. The cocoon was now carrying the whole pyramid, and it started to ascend.

Al-Khidr was inside it and crying about losing his last earthly friend.

The lifeless body of Estelle lay on the ground. Her soulless eyes were reflecting the sparkling light of the energy cocoon that was shooting up towards the sky—towards the planet Lyra.

About the Author

Nassim Odin holds PhD degree in Aerospace Engineering and he teaches engineering. He likes to read about the pyramids and ancient civilizations.
https://www.nassimodin.com

The Cure for Stars

— book blurb —

One man. Two worlds. A million reasons to say no but at what cost?

Al-Khidr was inside the Hall of Stars, and now he was moving inside a wormhole– a cosmic tunnel that opened up right above the Hall of Stars was spiraling down through galaxies like a coiled serpent from planet Lyra towards Earth. He was unaware of the alien major General Hatathor who was also sucked into the wormhole due to his own act of charging sequence disruption. Where the wormhole was leading? None of them knew. But the one thing sure to the aliens was that the jump was going to happen both in time and space.

The Sphere Trilogy

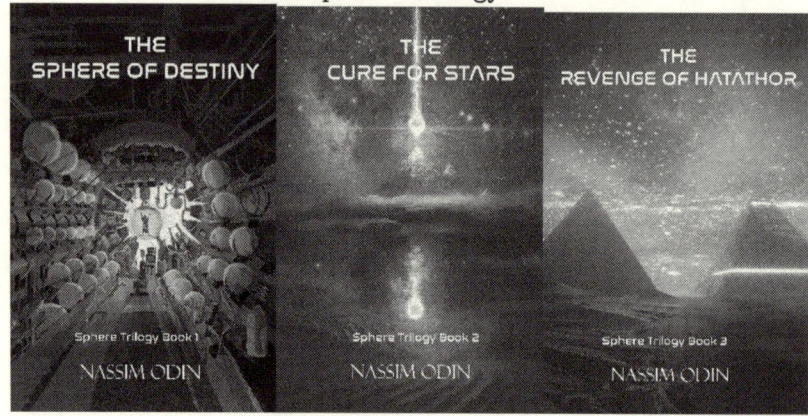

THE SPHERE OF DESTINY
Sphere Trilogy Book 1
NASSIM ODIN

THE CURE FOR STARS
Sphere Trilogy Book 2
NASSIM ODIN

THE REVENGE OF HATATHOR
Sphere Trilogy Book 3
NASSIM ODIN

Following QR code will lead you to the Sphere Trilogy page at Amazon store.

Made in the USA
Columbia, SC
24 July 2025

14297605-2ae3-463e-bf3e-78ce74e24720R01